THE SKY IS STARLESS

M. R. PRITCHARD

Midnight Ledger
Publishing
14391 Spring Hill Dr. Suite 203
Spring Hill, FL 34609
MidnightLedger.com

First Edition: May 2025
ISBNs: 9781957709666 (ebook), 9781957709673 (paperback),
9781957709680 (hardcover)

Printed in the United States of America

About "The Sky is Starless"

This novel marks the next generation of *Veil of Shadows*, following Rue as she carves out her own path in a world steeped in supernatural secrets, battles between good and evil, forgotten memories, morally gray characters, and a destiny that refuses to be ignored. While Rue's story stands on its own, it is deeply rooted in the trials and tribulations of those who came before her.

For those left wanting more—seeking the origins of the sacrifices that shaped Rue's very existence—be sure to explore the Veil of Shadows series.

In those pages, you will find the tale of Rue's parents, Meg and Sparrow, as they fought against impossible odds to live and love, facing off against omens, curses, and the forces of Heaven and Hell. You will witness the paths of warriors, humans, angels, and demons alike, each bound by fate and blood.

Now, the next chapter begins. New dangers stir, old

legends resurface, and Rue must confront not only the enemies in the dark but also the memories buried deep within her own soul.

———

Her memories were stolen.
Her nightmares won't let her forget.
And now, the shadows are coming for her.

Caught between worlds, Rue fights to unravel the truth of her past while resisting the dark pull of Dacre, the one man she shouldn't trust—but can't stay away from. Love was never meant to be easy, but for Rue, it could be deadly.

You can't outrun your bloodline... or the shadows it casts.

Rue is determined to live a normal life, far from the dark legacy of her family. College is supposed to be her fresh start—a chance to blend in, bury her secrets, and maybe even discover who she truly is. But when shadowy figures begin stalking her and nightmares plague her nights, normalcy slips further out of reach.

Her parents' solution? A bodyguard.

Nothing could be more infuriating than Dacre; the mysterious, maddeningly handsome man assigned to shadow her every move. Rue's stubborn streak refuses to make it easy for him—until she notices her nightmares quiet when he's near, and when shadow demons attack, Dacre sends them back to the darkness with startling ease.

Rue's missing memories hold the answers she needs, but everyone—including Dacre—seems determined to keep her in the dark.

Dark secrets.
　　Forbidden love.
　　A battle for her soul.

The Sky is Starless is a spellbinding dark fantasy romance perfect for fans of supernatural intrigue, steamy tension, and heroines fighting for their destiny.

He was a monster.
He couldn't keep her.
A pretty little thing like
Rue deserved better.

THE SKY IS
STARLESS
M. R. PRITCHARD

ONE

Early morning light was creeping through the blinds like unwelcome fingers. Rue watched the coffee maker brew, steam rising from the dark liquid as it streamed into a Hedwig mug. It made her think of smoke and dark magic, of fire and brimstone. Her vision blurred. Rue blinked a few times but it was too late, her mind was going elsewhere... drifting. The stream of coffee turned to thick blood. It dripped in slow, deliberate rivulets, each drop echoing in the small kitchen. *Drip. Drip. Drip.* Rue's throat felt dry. Sweat beaded her forehead as last night's nightmares resurfaced. She was drowning, gurgling on blood but so *so* thirsty. Rue gripped the edge of the counter, willing the memory to pass.

"It's not real," she whispered, her voice soft, her heart thumping against her ribs. Rue squeezed her eyes shut and shook her head, trying to erase the phantom sensations; the taste of iron and the warmth spreading down her throat, filling her stomach until it no longer ached. It was all so real and it felt *too* good.

Rue rubbed her eyes until she saw stars. When she opened them again, the coffee maker had stopped and the mug sat innocently on the counter. The owl stared back at her, unmarred. The counter was dry and there was no blood in sight. The mug was filled with dark brown liquid, not red. Rue licked her lips and her stomach growled in protest.

Her hands trembled as she reached for the mug, but she paused. She couldn't shake the feeling of being watched. A shadow passed the edge of her vision. Turning slowly, Rue scanned the empty kitchen, her heart racing.

Nothing.

She blew out a nervous breath and muttered to herself, "There is nothing here. No Demons. No Angels. Just you, Rue. Nothing else. No blood. No monsters."

She took milk from the fridge and a spoon from the drawer. She sat with the coffee mug near the window, opened the blinds, and watched the sun continue to rise. Rue's leather messenger bag was in the chair next to her. She opened it and took out her planner. She had class in a few hours, midterms later in the week. She turned the page as she sipped the coffee and glanced out the window again, watching the oak tree drop orange leaves.

She shivered, although she wasn't cold. It was the understanding that she'd have to leave this world soon and visit home for the winter break. She just wondered if it would be Heaven or Hell and if the dreams would follow her.

Two

Shower steam fogged the tiny bathroom of Rue's apartment. She stepped out, wrapped herself in a towel and reached for the door to let the steam out. Something written on the mirror caught her eye.

A message: *Meet me at the Coffee Connection at two.*

Rue swiped her finger over the message and got ready. She chose jeans, sneakers, and a chunky black cable knit sweater. She loosely braided her hair to keep it under control from the wind.

Rue slung her leather bag over her shoulder and locked the door to her apartment. She lived in a little brick Tudor style house that had been converted into two apartments, one above and one below. Her parents had bought the house for Rue to live in, but when Rue argued that it was too much space for just her and the kitten, it was magically renovated. Rue took the upstairs apartment since she liked the view of the trees and surrounding Loyola campus. The downstairs apartment was rented quite possibly to a ghost because she never saw the person, only heard the occasional creaks and door squeals. She never saw anyone coming or going, never saw packages get delivered, never heard a vacuum running. She had hoped the person living down there wasn't a complete pig. But, she figured she'd smell something if they were.

Rue jogged down the stairs and past her car, opting to walk to class since the weather was nice.

———

RUE SLID into her usual seat near the back of the lecture hall. The room was already buzzing with conversation and students flipping through notebooks and idly tapping on laptops.

Professor Camden, a wiry man with round glasses and patches sewn over the edges of his brown suitcoat strode into the room. He clapped his hands together, voice booming with too much energy for the hour. "Good morning, everyone! Today, we're diving into the mysteries of the Zapotec civilization!"

Rue opened her notebook and clicked her pen, but the tip hovered over the page. Professor Camden's voice became a distant drone as her mind wandered. She felt like she was being pulled under water.

A soft tap on her arm dragged her back. She turned to see Evelyn, her perpetually cheerful classmate, grinning like she had a secret.

"Hey, Rue. We're all going to Justin's party tonight. You should come." She swiped at blonde fringe before pressing a Chapstick to her lips.

Rue hesitated, grip tightening on her pen. "I don't know." She hated parties, she found it too hard to relax and have fun. She blamed it on the way she was raised, which was not on the Earthen plane.

Parties meant a performance to appear wholly human... parties also meant relaxing, loosening up. She'd been to one of Justin's parties years ago. There was always alcohol and probably drugs. She thought for a moment about young men playing stupid games and getting injured. That first party she'd gone to, someone fell off the balcony and broke their arm. There was blood... so much blood. It was all Rue could do to get away from it before she made a mistake.

Rue touched her lips, thankfully she'd gone her whole life keeping the blood thirst under wraps. She'd buried it so deep that–

"Oh, come on!" Evelyn pouted. "You never come to these things. Just for a little while, okay? It'll be fun."

Rue forced a small smile. "I'll think about it."

"No," Evelyn pressed. "You will come. It's the last Halloween party of the season. You haven't seen any of my costumes this year."

Rue's cheeks flushed. She needed to be a better friend. "But... I don't have a costume."

"Good. I'll bring one for you." Evelyn winked. "I've got the perfect one. See you at six."

Rue grabbed Evelyn's sleeve and looked her dead in the eyes.

"What?" Evelyn asked.

"It better not be... slutty," Rue warned.

Evelyn smiled widely. "No promises."

Rue slipped out of class as soon as it ended, her bag slung over her shoulder. The campus buzzed with the energy of students heading to lunch. Rue felt like she was moving through a different world, one she didn't belong in. The feeling was what held her back from campus parties and dates and fully putting herself out in the world. The thing was, she didn't belong in this world. She didn't even belong in this realm. She watched people walk by her, and none of them had any clue that they were so close to a princess of another realm. Rue shuddered at the thought. She had stopped thinking of herself as a princess a long time ago. Now she was simply Rue.

Rue the runaway. Rue the atypical who chose a life in the Earthen plane amongst the normies. She fidgeted with her dark braid and raised her face to the cool breeze. Even if she didn't belong here, it did feel like home.

The Coffee Connection was a typical college town coffee shop with alternative music playing low on the sound system and a sagging couch in the back corner that no one in their right mind should ever sit on.

A bell hanging over the door jingled as Rue stepped inside and was greeted by the smell of roasted coffee beans.

"Welcome to the Coffee Connection," a barista called from behind the counter.

Rue waved and smiled before scanning the shop.

There she was. Short-cropped black hair and bright blue eyes hidden behind big sunglasses, and legs twice as long as Rue's. One thing Rue didn't inherit from the woman was height.

Meg, her mother, waved and motioned for Rue to come to the small table she'd chosen near the window. Rue went and Meg stood, pulling her in for a hug.

"Rue, I've missed you," she whispered like it was a secret.

"We met here last week," Rue reminded her.

Meg sat, crossed her long legs, and took off her leather jacket. She was wearing a wide necked T-shirt, scars and tattoos marring her arms and shoulders.

A man walked by and did a double take, spilling hot coffee on his hand.

Meg received looks and stares a lot and Rue was unsure how she ignored it all.

She slid a mug toward Rue. "I got you the pumpkin spice latte. I hope that's okay?"

"It's perfect. Thank you," Rue said as she sat and scooted closer. The woman was slightly overbearing at times, but she was Rue's mother. It was easy to see that Meg was struggling with letting Rue carry on with her own life but that was normal. That was family.

Rue sipped at her coffee and remembered why she'd limited the meetings and moved away from home. They were too close, and she needed distance. Rue needed to get out and find her own place in the world. She had to stop living in the shadow of her parents. She had to get away from the secrets and lies.

"Have you been drinking the bagged blood?" Meg whispered and touched Rue's face. "You look pale."

"I don't need it. I'm fine." Rue plucked the menu off the table and considered a pecan muffin.

"I thought I was fine when I was your age too." Meg frowned. "Your father is worried. He wants you to come home."

"And you?" Rue asked.

"I want you safe. Hidden. But... happy." She stared at Rue. "Would you tell me if something was wrong?"

"Sure." Rue rubbed her arm and pushed away the thoughts of her nightmares that had interrupted every moment of peace.

"You seem distracted."

"I have exams this week." Rue sipped at the coffee. "It's just stress. I promise."

"Did you pick a major?" She asked.

"A long time ago." Rue chuckled. "Archaeology."

"Oh, you did say that. I forgot. Sorry." Meg nodded. "Just don't... do anything dangerous. I'm glad you didn't choose criminal justice or healthcare." She shook her head. "I don't want you in more danger."

"Mother." Rue rolled her eyes. "I can handle myself. I'm fine. Nothing has happened for years and years and years. I'm not in any danger."

There was a pregnant pause. She didn't bring up Angels or

Demons because it would be wrong to discuss them in a coffee shop amongst normal humans. But, it wasn't that long ago when her mother sent Rue away to live with her Aunt Shay and Uncle Jed while she saved the world as they knew it. No one here would know anything about that though.

The man was still staring. He'd sat at the table behind them, his eyes focused on Meg's back and the two vertical scars that marred her shoulder blades. Rue's mother once had wings but they'd been cut off.

Meg touched Rue's long, braided hair. "I know you can take care of yourself. Remm wants to see you."

"I'll be back for holiday break," Rue reminded her.

"Maybe call him?" she suggested. "I think he likes talking to you. Maybe you could convince him to find a girlfriend."

"I have called him. He never answers." Rue sipped at her coffee. "Why does he bother having a phone if he never answers? Plus, he could come visit me."

"He's been busy…" Meg bit her lip and looked away. "I'll tell you more about it when you come home to visit. This isn't the place to discuss such things."

"Sure." Rue checked her phone: nope not one reply from her brother to any of the text messages she'd sent him last week. She showed Meg, then lowered her voice before asking, "Where are we having the holidays this year? Heaven or Hell?"

Meg smiled wide. "Hell, of course. You know those fucking Angels will ruin every peaceful moment with some shit-fuckery."

Rue laughed, seeing her mother's sharpness reveal itself. She always tried to hide it but every now and then it escaped when everyone least expected it. Her dry humor and lots of swearing always made Rue laugh.

"What?" Meg scoffed innocently. "You know they will. How is Lucipurr?"

Lucipurr was Rue's cat. A little black kitten with green

eyes that her brother had found and brought her when they were kids. The kitten never seemed to grow much, but was smart and friendly and everything Rue needed in a companion.

Rue was still nodding in agreement at the shit-fuckery comment when she replied, "He still acts like a kitten, hiding and escaping." Rue glared at the man behind her mother's shoulder and when he noticed, his eyes went wide before he looked away.

Too late. Meg noticed. She leaned back and sipped at her coffee before saying, "You know, this city isn't what it used to be. People used to have respect." She shifted in her seat, turning to face the man and smiled, flashing sharp teeth.

He startled, spilling his coffee. Dark liquid spread across the table and into his lap. "Jesus Christ," he muttered, looking around.

"Meg?" a barista shouted from behind the counter.

She stood and walked toward the counter. The barista passed her a bag.

"Thank you. My husband really loves these," Meg said.

"You tell us every week." The barista was smiling wide, smitten with her. She must've left a big tip.

Rue smiled as she sipped at the pumpkin spice latte and watched the orange and yellow leaves tumble across the sidewalk. Her gaze drifted across the street. The shadows moved just a little too deliberately. She squinted her eyes as it lingered just long enough to send a shiver down her spine.

THREE

Rue's apartment was small but cozy with mismatched furniture and stacks of books threatening to topple. She was perched on the edge of the thrifted couch, flipping through the assigned pages on Zapotec civilization. A sharp knock on the door startled her.

Before she could get up, the door swung open and Evelyn bounded in, a garment bag slug over one arm and an enormous grin on her face.

"Why isn't your door locked?" She kicked the door closed and locked it. "I come bearing gifts," she sang, not giving Rue time to answer.

Rue raised an eyebrow, setting her book aside. "I knew you were coming so I left it unlocked."

"Where's Lucipurr?" Evelyn asked. "I demand a greeting from the dark void."

"Probably sleeping in the linen closet," Rue replied.

Evelyn tossed the garment bag on the couch. "Now, don't argue. You're wearing this tonight." Evelyn spun. "Do you like my costume? Oh, one sec. I forgot my mask." Evelyn pulled a sparkling vampire mask out of her bag. It completed the Elvira costume she was decked out in, complete with high hip slit in the dress and cleavage out for all to see.

Rue hesitated, eyeing the garment bag like it might contain something alive. "Do I even want to know? I mean, you look spectacular, but..."

"Oh, come on, girl." Evelyn unzipped the garment bag with a dramatic flourish, revealing a glittering, pale green pixie costume with tiny wings. The fabric shimmered in the light and Rue reached out to inspect the skirt that was a cascade of gauzy layers.

"You're joking," Rue said flatly.

"It's not even short," Evelyn said. "You said, *not slutty*," she used air quotes and rolled her eyes, "so I improvised." Evelyn grinned holding the outfit up to Rue. "You're small and delicate. This is perfect for you. Like, come on. Tinkerbell vibes, but make it spooky."

Rue snorted. "I don't think I have the personality for Tinkerbell." Rue was internally panicking at the thought of wearing this getup to a party.

"You don't need personality, you just need the look." Evelyn smirked, giving her a once-over. Then, with a teasing lilt, she added, "Honestly, Rue, did you just stop growing when you were fifteen?"

Rue stiffened for a half second before forcing a laugh. "Yeah, pretty much." She tried to sound casual. "Guess I missed the growth spurt memo."

Evelyn didn't notice the awkward edge to her tone. She just laughed, shaking her head. "Maybe you should have drunk more milk. This is going to be spectacular. Now, come on, try it on!"

The costume fit too perfectly for Rue's liking. The snug bodice and fluttery wings made her feel like a princess from another realm. She erased that feeling as soon as it crossed her mind. She felt like a fairy from a fairytale book. There, that was better.

Evelyn's enthusiasm was hard to argue with. Rue stood in front of her cracked bedroom mirror, twisting slightly.

"I look ridiculous," Rue muttered.

"You look *amazing*," Evelyn countered, leaning on the doorway. "The guys at the party are going to lose their minds. Speaking of which..." she grinned mischievously. "What about that guy who lives downstairs? Have you ever talked to him?"

Rue frowned, distracted. "Who?"

"The tall, dark and brooding one," Evelyn said, wiggling her eyebrows. "I just saw him when I got here. He's... I mean, wow."

Rue's stomach twisted. She didn't know anything about the person who lived downstairs.

"Whoever lives down there is not the chatty type. I've never talked to him."

"Never?" Evelyn asked.

"He keeps to himself," Rue said quickly, brushing past her to grab a pair of strappy heels for added height.

Evelyn pouted. "Shame. I was hoping you'd have some juicy info on him. Oh well, maybe we'll run into him tonight and I can get his number."

Rue shrugged. "He's all yours."

Evelyn clicked her tongue. "You wouldn't be saying that if you laid eyes on the guy. I'm telling you... ugh."

Rue stood upright and faced Evelyn. "Okay. Tinkerbell at your service."

"Dang, chick. You'll get your pick of the party tonight."

"Doubt it." Rue dug in her closet for a small handbag. "Guys aren't interested in girls that are just five foot two-ish." She was being generous with herself.

"You're hot *and compact*." Evelyn checked the time on her phone before tucking it away. "We should head out."

FOUR

HEY. RUE. I SEE YOU.

DACRE ADJUSTED the silver mask over his face, the cool metal brushing against his skin. He tugged at the cuffs of the suit he'd hastily borrowed from a demon tailor in hiding down the street who owed him a favor, muttering to himself about the ridiculousness of this entire situation. A costume party. Humans really knew how to come up with the most asinine ways to gather in poorly lit, unsafe places.

But Rue was going, and that meant he was going too. So he would be spending his evening in the poorly lit, unsafe place.

He stood across the street, leaning against a lamppost cloaked in shadow, as Rue and her friend Evelyn emerged from the house. He froze the moment he saw Rue.

Christ almighty, she was dressed as a fairy. Or what passed for one in human circles. Glittering wings framed her back, their edges catching the light like fireflies in the dark, and her dress... if you could even call it that... left precious little to the imagination. The soft, sheer fabric clung to her curves, and her legs seemed to go on forever beneath its short hem.

Dacre clenched his jaw, his teeth grinding together.

How did she think this was remotely safe? And when exactly did she grow legs that long? It was physically impossible for her height. Must be an optical illusion. Dacre rubbed his face with a sigh.

He fell into step a careful distance behind them as they started walking, keeping to the shadows. Evelyn was dressed as some sort of vampire, mask and all. She chatted animatedly, waving her arms in grand gestures. Rue laughed, her voice soft and melodic. Dacre's chest tightened.

He rarely heard her laugh. He wanted to smile at the sound.

His mood darkened as his eyes scanned the street ahead. Groups of humans, some already drunk, loitered in alleyways or stumbled out of bars. Every shadow seemed to move, every passing stranger a potential threat. He cursed this night. Why couldn't Rue stay home and hand out candy for Halloween like she'd done the past five years?

Did she have no idea how many things in this world could harm her? He knew she didn't. That was a rhetorical question. She never had. Even as a teenager, Rue had been blissfully unaware of the dangers around her. It was a miracle she'd survived this long without more than a few scratches, but he wasn't about to leave it to chance. Not tonight.

Evelyn bumped Rue with her hip, drawing his attention.

"You're going to be the belle of the ball, Tinkerbell," Evelyn teased, grinning.

Rue rolled her eyes. "I'm not Tinkerbell. I told you, this is just 'generic fairy.'"

"Whatever you say," Evelyn replied with a wink. "All I know is half the party is going to be trying to get your number."

Dacre's fists clenched, nails biting into his palms. The thought of anyone—even mortal idiots at some silly party—trying to get close to her made his blood boil. It made him want to shift forms and cause... damage.

As they crossed the street, a car slowed, its driver leaning out the window to holler something crude. Dacre's fingers twitched, the urge to shift was now bubbling under his skin like a tidal wave.

Rue and Evelyn brushed off the driver, Rue shaking her head and laughing it off like it was nothing.

Nothing?

It wasn't nothing. It was dangerous.

They reached the party, the music thumping loud enough to vibrate the pavement beneath Dacre's feet. The house was packed with costumed humans spilling onto the front lawn, some already clutching red plastic cups and shouting over the music.

Dacre followed them inside, slipping through the crowd with ease. The silver mask and suit were apparently enough to make him blend in, though he felt absurdly out of place. His eyes never left Rue, tracking her every move as she wove through the throng of people.

She didn't look back once.

After all these years, she still didn't notice him. He couldn't blame her, her family had hired him to keep her alive not make sure she knew who he was. Or even that he was there.

A pang of something uncomfortably close to disappointment stabbed at his chest. He pushed it aside, forcing his focus to stay sharp. He rubbed at the small scar on his neck and swallowed hard, tucking away a thirst he could not quench. He hadn't been able to satiate it for years and years. The one person who could help him with it didn't even know he existed.

Rue and Evelyn found a corner near the kitchen, grabbing drinks and laughing as someone in a dinosaur costume tried—and failed—to navigate the crowded room without knocking over decorations. Dacre stayed near the doorway, leaning against the wall, his gaze flickering between her and anyone who got too close. He was glad to see her dispose of the red cup, but then she pulled a small bottle out of her purse and drank it.

Adding alcohol was never a good idea. Every instinct in him screamed to pull her out of this chaos and take her somewhere safe, somewhere quiet. But he couldn't. She didn't know he was here—didn't even know he'd been watching over her all this time.

And she couldn't know. He had been instructed not to interrupt her life until she was ready to deal with the truth. He leaned against the wall and thought maybe she needed a little push in the right direction.

She had no idea the lengths he'd gone to keep her safe, no idea the shadows he'd chased away so she could live her life without fear.

But that was fine.

FIVE

THE PARTY WAS IN FULL SWING BY THE TIME EVELYN and Rue arrived. The house throbbed with energy, music shaking the floors and walls. Strings of cheap Halloween lights glowed orange and purple, casting jagged shadows across the packed rooms. Costumed co-eds spilled onto the front lawn, their laughter cutting through the crisp night air.

"Put your mask on," Evelyn ordered. "This is a night for mystery and reveling." Her fist pumped in the air as she pulled down her Elvira mask and shimmied toward the door.

Rue pulled on the mask Evelyn had given her. It was black and sparkly. She hesitated at the threshold, her fingers tightening around the layers of skirt. Evelyn grabbed her arm, dragging her forward with a grin.

"Come on, pixie queen! Time to let loose!"

Rue couldn't help but laugh as they slipped inside, swallowed by the crowd. The warmth of the room packed with so many bodies hit her immediately, mingling with the sharp tang of alcohol and smoke. She righted her shoulders to feel taller and when the wings caught the light, Evelyn squealed with approval.

"It's perfect. Come with. I want a drink." Evelyn dragged Rue toward the sound of clinking glasses.

Rue followed.

A drink was thrust into her hand, a red Solo cup sloshing with cheap beer. She pretended to take a drink and smiled at her friend.

It didn't take much for Rue to lose herself in the rhythm of the party. The mask and costume obscured her just enough to feel like someone else, someone who belonged here. The edges of the mask blocked her periphery as she scanned the room. She set the Solo cup down on a nearby table and pulled a small bottle of cinnamon whisky from her purse and drank that because it was safe. She took a burning sip, the liquid warming her chest and cutting through her nerves.

Kids danced around her, their movements chaotic and carefree. There was a lot of grinding and touching, and plenty of skin showing between guys and girls alike. Everyone wore a mask; she couldn't identify any of her classmates.

Evelyn began dancing with a guy dressed like pyramid head, abs and all. The guy was the epitome of *"hear me out."*

It didn't take long for the whisky to take effect. The music vibrated with a beat that seemed to sync with her pulse. She let herself move with it, swaying then dancing more freely as her body loosened up.

Someone joined her, a costumed man dressed as a devil, complete with red horns and a mischievous grin. He had straight white teeth and tattoos down his arms. He held out a hand. Rue hesitated before taking it. They spun through the crush of bodies, his moves exaggerated and theatrical. Rue found herself laughing and not shying away from the devil's hand as it landed on her hip and pulled her closer.

For a moment, Rue forgot the shadows that always seemed to follow her. She forgot about the blood.

As the devil twirled her one last time, Rue stumbled back

slightly, the room spinning just enough to make her head light. She blamed the whisky since she had drained the bottle moments earlier. Rue caught herself against the edge of the table and turned to thank the devil for the dance, but he'd already melted back into the crowd. Rue rose up on her toes and saw the devil dancing with Evelyn. She smiled and took a moment to catch her breath.

But then, she felt a hand on her shoulder.

Rue froze, the warmth of the touch radiating through the thin costume.

A man moved in front of her, taller than anyone in the room, dressed in all black. A silver mask obscured his face, reflecting the Halloween lights in fractured shards. His eyes were dark and piercing as he stared down at her, unblinking.

For a moment, everything else faded; the music, the laughter, the crowd. All Rue could hear was the rushing of blood in her ears.

"May I have this dance?" he asked, his voice smooth and almost hypnotic.

Rue's breath caught in her throat. Something about him felt... familiar... but she couldn't place it. Maybe they had a class together? She searched his mask, the eyes, his shoulders, the dark hair. No, she'd remember someone with this kind of vibe. Rue's fingers twitched at her sides, unsure if she should reach for him or step away. Or maybe even run away screaming.

The room pulsed around them, the crowd moving like waves on the edge of her vision. It was as if the man in the silver mask existed in a different plane.

"I..." Rue started, her voice barely audible over the music. Her heart was pounding against her ribcage.

The man in the silver mask didn't move, his hand still outstretched, waiting.

The crowd surged and ebbed, jostling her closer to him.

She swallowed hard. Something about him was magnetic, pulling her in despite every instinct screaming at her to step away.

"I don't usually dance with strangers," Rue said, her voice quieter than she intended.

The man tilted his head, his dark eyes catching hers. "And yet, you danced with the devil just now," he said, his tone edged with amusement.

Rue opened her mouth to respond but nothing came out. He wasn't wrong. Her pulse quickened, and she hated how easily he'd unsettled her.

"Who are you?" she asked, unable to look away.

The corners of his mouth lifted just slightly. "Someone who doesn't like to be forgotten," he said cryptically.

The words sent a chill down her spine.

Before she could reply, he extended his hand further. "Just one dance, Rue."

Her stomach flipped. "How do you know my name?"

The man leaned slightly closer, his voice dropping to a murmur that only she could hear. "I know more than your name."

Her breath hitched. The room around her blurred, the noise fading to a distant hum. His presence was suddenly overwhelming, as he filled the entire space, bending it around him. She didn't trust him, but curiosity rooted her in place. She felt the beat of the music deep in her chest.

Against her better judgement, Rue placed her hand in his.

The man led her to a less crowded corner of the room with a firm grip on her wrist. He turned, then spun her, his movements fluid. He guided her in a slow, deliberate rhythm that felt out of place with the pulsing, chaotic music.

"What are you?" she asked, the question slipping out before she could stop herself.

"What do you think I am?"

Rue frowned, searching his masked face. "You don't feel... normal."

He chuckled a low, velvety sound that sent shivers down her spine. "Good. Normal is so boring, don't you think?"

"Why are you here?" she asked.

"I could ask you the same."

His cryptic responses were beginning to irritate her. She stopped moving, pulling back slightly, but he reached forward and settled a large hand on her waist.

"Let me go," Rue said.

He leaned closer, towering over her. "I'm not here to hurt you," he said softly. "Quite the opposite."

Her breath caught.

"You're afraid," he said, studying her. "But you're not afraid of me."

His voice sounded like whisky, and it oozed through her body, warm and soothing.

"How do you know what I'm afraid of?" she challenged.

His head tilted and she could tell he was smiling beneath his mask. "Because I've seen the things you're running from. And if you're not careful, they'll find you."

Rue gasped, her knees threatening to buckle. She pulled out of his grip, the skin of her waist feeling chilled without his warm hand there. She stumbled back a step. The crowd surged again as a new song started, momentarily blocking her view of him. Then, when the wave of people parted, he was gone.

Rue stood frozen, her pulse racing. She scanned the room but the man in the silver mask had disappeared.

Her eyes darted around the room. The crowd had swallowed him whole, which she could barely believe based on his size. She felt the press of bodies around her, laughter and music cascading in waves, but it was all muted.

Her skin still tingled where his hand had touched her. She replayed his words, the way he'd said her name, the cryptic warning: *I've seen the things you're running from. And if you're not careful, they'll find you.*

How could anyone know that?

"Rue!" Evelyn's voice snapped her back to reality.

She turned to see her friend weaving through the crowd, a drink in hand and a bright grin plastered across her face.

"There you are!" Evelyn said, reaching out to Rue. "You disappeared for a minute. Who was that guy you were dancing with?"

Rue opened her mouth, then closed it. "I don't know," she admitted.

"Well he was *hot*," Evelyn said with a teasing smile. "I mean, the mask was a little intense, but still. Mystery man vibes for days."

Rue forced a laugh but it came out hollow. "Yeah, sure."

Evelyn frowned, her playful demeanor dimming. "You okay? You look like you've seen a ghost. You didn't drink the spiked punch did you?" She shook her head. "I think there's some GHB in that shit. Stay away!"

"No," Rue said. "I only drank what I brought. I'm fine. Just... got a little dizzy. It's hot in here."

"Well, duh. Half the campus is crammed into this place." Evelyn glanced around before tugging at Rue's arm. "Come on. Let's grab some air. I saw this guy and, hear me out, you might–"

"Pyramid head?" Rue asked.

"Yeah." Evelyn clutched her heart. "He could dance."

"He was half naked."

"And those abs..." Evelyn licked her lips.

Evelyn led Rue through the throng of people, pushing their way toward the back porch. The cool night air hit Rue like a splash of water, and she inhaled deeply trying to steady herself.

Evelyn leaned against the railing, sipping from her Solo

cup, and chatting idly about the party. Rue barely heard her, her mind still replaying the encounter.

"*What do you think I am?*" His voice echoed in her head, smooth and teasing. And that unsettling familiarity, why did he feel like someone she'd met before?

"Earth to Rue," Evelyn said, waving a hand in front of her face.

Rue blinked, startled. "Sorry, what?"

"I said, are you sure you're okay? You're acting super weird tonight," Evelyn said, narrowing her eyes. "Is this about the guy? Did he say something creepy?"

"No," Rue said quickly, but softened her tone. "It's not that. He just... he knew my name and I don't know how."

Evelyn raised an eyebrow. "Okay, that's definitely weird. Are you sure you don't know him? Maybe he's in one of your classes?"

"I'm sure," Rue said. She stared off into the distance, her stomach clenching when the shadows shifted under the trees in the distance.

Evelyn watched her for a moment, then sighed. "Look, maybe it's just one of those things. Loyola is small, you know? Maybe he's seen you in class or something."

"Maybe," Rue murmured, though she didn't believe it for a second.

"Anyway," Evelyn said, tossing her cup into a trash bin, "we're here to have fun, remember? Mystery guy or not, let's not let him ruin the night."

Rue forced a smile, nodding. "Yeah, you're right. I was dancing with a handsome devil earlier, I could take another spin with him."

"Yeasssss, girl," Evelyn pumped her fists in the air.

As they stepped back inside, Rue couldn't shake the feeling that the man in the silver mask wasn't just a random stranger. His presence lingered like a shadow in her mind, and the warning he'd left her with felt more like a promise.

SIX

The party had thinned out by the time Rue and Evelyn left. The streets were quieter, the occasional group of costumed students laughing as they wandered off into the night. The autumn air was crisp. Rue separated a layer of skirt and pulled it up over her shoulders, shivering. Evelyn chatted about pyramid head guy and his rock hard abs, oblivious to Rue's silence.

Rue glanced up at the stars and the moon. She felt smaller than ever underneath a clear sky like this. She took a deep breath. It was calming though–watching the stars. Something she'd enjoyed doing for ages when life got too big and she needed to shrink herself down.

When they reached Rue's apartment, Evelyn gave her a quick hug before unlocking her car door.

"Can you drive?" Rue asked, worried because they'd both had drinks at the party.

"I'm sober now," Evelyn promised. "It was that cold walk, it metabolized everything."

Rue nodded absently. The whisky had left her system too

and now she was left with a morose mood. She hated the way she felt after drinking alcohol.

"Text me when you wake up, okay?" Evelyn asked. "And try not to overthink Mystery Man. He was probably just some random dude."

Rue nodded absently, waving as Evelyn backed her BMW out of the driveway and drove away.

Rue lingered on the front steps for a moment, watching the stars and the rustling of what leaves remained in the trees. She scanned the shadows that pooled along the edge of the street. Nothing moved, but she couldn't shake the feeling that someone was watching.

An uneasy feeling started to creep up her back. She turned and ran up the stairs as fast as she could, struggling with the key to unlock her door as her fingers shook. She finally got the door open as fear radiated further up her spine. She shoved the door open, then closed.

Rue locked the door behind her and leaned against it, exhaling slowly. The apartment was silent, the faint hum of the fridge the only sound until a meow came from the shadows.

"Lucipurr," Rue called as she shrugged off her fairy wings and set them on the couch. The black cat meowed a few more times before leading Rue toward the kitchen.

"Are you mad at me?" Rue asked.

Lucipurr made a blat sound that sounded like, "Yes."

"Maybe it's the late dinner that's upsetting you." Rue opened the cabinet and got out a can of paté. She opened it and scooped it into a bowl before setting it in front of the cat.

Lucipurr made soft mewing noises as he ate. Rue assumed he was scolding her for leaving him alone for the night and coming back late, making him wait for dinner.

"I'm sorry." Rue rubbed her nose against black fur. "I'll

never do it again." She sighed before making her way to the bathroom to wash the night off her skin.

Sleep didn't come easily, but when it did, it came with the nightmares.

She was running through a dense forest, the trees twisted and blackened, the branches like claws reaching for her. The air? was thick and smelled of smoke. Her feet pounded against the ground, her breath ragged as she glanced over her shoulder.

Something was chasing her. She couldn't see it, but she could feel the presence, the rumbling of a roar in the creature's throat. Rue stumbled, falling to her knees. When she looked down, the ground beneath her wasn't dirt but a slick, crimson pool. Wide eyes filled with terror stared back at her.

A shadow slid across the surface until it loomed over her. A low and familiar voice whispered, "They're coming, Rue."

Rue woke with a start, her heart hammering against her ribs. She sat up, gasping for breath, sweat clinging to her skin. Her throat was dry, so dry. She grabbed the glass of water off her nightstand and drank it down but it didn't help the dryness in her throat.

Her eyes darted to the window. For a moment, she thought she saw a figure there, which was impossible since she was on the second floor. She blinked and whatever it was disappeared, replaced by the swaying branches of the oak trees outside her window.

Shaking, Rue got up and went to the kitchen to refill her glass of water.

There would be no more sleeping.

She sat cross-legged on her small couch, a blanket draped over her shoulders and the TV on low volume. She'd put on her comfort movie, Howl's Moving Castle, but she was too anxious to watch it. Her gaze flicked to the windows. She'd double-checked the locks, pulled the curtains tight, and even wedged a chair under the door handle. But it wasn't enough to quiet the unease clawing at her chest.

Her thoughts kept returning to the man in the silver mask, the soothing sound of his voice, his words. *I know more than your name... If you're not careful, they'll find you.*

She bit her lip before reaching out to stroke Lucipurr. If the cat wasn't alarmed, everything must be fine. It was just... all in her head.

A faint noise broke the stillness.

Rue's head snapped toward the door. The sound was barely audible, like a faint scrape against the hallway outside her apartment. She held her breath, straining to listen.

Nothing. Lucipurr didn't even move.

Get a grip, Rue, she told herself before grabbing the TV remote and turning the volume up a notch.

But then it came again, louder this time. It wasn't her imagination. Someone or something was outside. Maybe it was college students playing pranks. Last year they'd toilet papered her neighbors' trees during the night.

Rue rose to her feet, moving as quietly as possible toward the door.

"Who's there?" she called out.

No response.

She reached for her phone, fingers fumbling to unlock it. She tapped Evelyn's number. Her screen flickered, the call dropping before it could connect.

"Damn it," Rue whispered, glancing back at the door.

Suddenly, a voice from the other side spoke. Low, steady, and familiar. "It's me, Rue."

Her stomach flipped as she recognized the voice. The silver masked man.

Her hand hovered over the lock, torn between fear and curiosity.

"What do you want?" she asked.

"They're close," he said.

"Who?"

"They're not from this realm," he replied, his tone grave. "Let me in, Rue. They're already too close."

Ice chilled her veins. No one spoke like that here. Whoever was on the other side of that door knew what she was and that was impossible.

"How do you know where I live?" she demanded, her voice trembling.

There was a long pause before he said, "I live downstairs."

"What?"

Something slammed against the window.

"Let me in, please. I'm not here to hurt you. But *they* will."

"Who are you talking about?" Rue asked.

"The ones who want you back. The ones you've been dreaming about."

"You're insane," she spat, but her voice wavered. She'd been telling herself for months that she was slowly going insane from the stress of finals week. It was all in her head. Nothing was watching her.

"Am I?" he asked, his tone steady. "How many times have you felt like you weren't alone? Like someone was following you? You're not imagining it, Rue."

Her breathing quickened, her mind racing. She didn't trust him, but... maybe she did.

"What do you want from me?" she whispered.

"To keep you alive," he said. "But if you don't trust me, then at least don't trust anyone else. Because they're coming for you."

Something hit the window over and over again.

"Damn it," he cursed. "Don't leave your apartment. I'll be right back."

The stairs creaked as he ran down them and it sounded

like his size changed, the bottom stair straining against his weight.

Rue paused and something familiar lingered in her mind, a de ja vu; she'd heard that sound before, just the same exact way.

THE STAIRS in the distance groaned as something big ran down them. A guttural scream ricocheted against the walls. Rue turned, ready to run down the stairs and out the door but...

SOMETHING SNARLED OUTSIDE. It sounded like branches falling and raccoons fighting.

Lucipurr raised his head before standing up, stretching his paws, and wandering over to the window. He hissed at whatever he saw.

Rue sank onto the couch, her thoughts a chaotic tangle. Whoever the man was, he wasn't just another college student. He knew too much. And worst of all, part of her believed him.

The paranoia she'd been fighting all these weeks swelled again, stronger than ever.

Rue grabbed her phone, scrolled to her mother's number. Her thumb hovered over the call button.

Evelyn's earlier joke replayed in her mind: *Did you stop growing when you were fifteen?*

Rue had always wondered why she hadn't aged like everyone else, not even like her brother. Remington was her twin, but these days he looked like he was born in a different decade. What if there was more to the story? What if her mother had been keeping secrets from her...

Her finger tapped the screen. The line rang once, twice. Then a familiar voice answered.

"Rue? It's late. Is everything okay?" Meg asked.

Rue's voice wavered. "We need to talk, mom. Some weird things are going on around here."

She could hear her father's deep voice in the background and then her mother shushing him.

"What kind of things?" her mother asked.

"I keep having these dreams and... it feels like someone has been following me. There's weirdness going on outside the house."

"Did you try drinking the blood?"

"No." Rue was annoyed, she didn't need to drink the blood. She didn't want to. She never wanted to. That wasn't her.

"The blood might help."

"That's not the problem. Someone is following me." There was a loud crashing sound.

"What was that?" her mother asked.

"I'm going to get her," Rue's father said in the background.

"No, Sparrow, sit down. Let her figure it out." There was a pause. "What else?"

"Nightmares."

"You've suffered from nightmares before," her mother reminded her.

"These seem very real."

"Sweetheart, when you decided to live on the Earthen plane, you knew strange things would happen. Our kind are not meant to stay there."

"I know." Rue's hand tore through her long hair. The sound of glass breaking echoed and a car alarm went off.

"Is someone *fighting*?" her mother asked.

"That's what I've been trying to tell you–"

"Shit. Okay. You need to get downstairs to your neighbor's apartment. He'll help you. His name is Dacre. He's a little... different. But he'll help. You might need to come home early."

"No. Mom. I can't, I have fall semester finals next week." Rue exhaled a heavy breath.

"You can retake those classes next semester."

"No. I don't want to. I want to finish this semester. There's only one week."

"You're just as stubborn as your mother," she heard her father's voice in the background. "Let her finish."

"If you stay to finish, you're going to have to let Dacre move into your apartment."

"What? No. I don't know him. He's a complete stranger."

"He knows you," Meg said. "We hired him to watch over you a long time ago."

Memories flashed through Rue's mind. She'd been here for nearly six years, and the man had always lived downstairs but she never saw him.

A fist pounded on her door.

"Let him in, Rue," Meg said. "And as soon as you're finished with finals, you come straight home."

"Okay. Fine. Goodnight."

"Hey," her father called. "You'll be just fine. We've gotten through worse. This is nothing. We can send your brother to stay with you."

"Absolutely not." Rue was quick to reply. "He is far too much trouble. I'd never get any peace with him here."

"Tell Dacre I said hello," her father said. "Goodnight, sweetheart."

"Love you, bye," her mother said before hanging up.

Rue stared at the black screen. This was crazy.

The pounding started again on her door.

Lucipurr meowed, urging her to go answer it.

Rue's hand trembled as it hovered over the lock. The sensible part of her screamed not to do it. This was the man from the party, a stranger whose cryptic words and unnerving presence had left her reeling.

Another part of her hesitated; the part that couldn't forget the way his voice had sounded when he said her name, the way he sounded when he ordered her to stay inside. And then, her parents' conversation.

Nightmares flashed through her mind; the shadows closing in, the cold, suffocating presence, and his warning: *They're already close.*

She exhaled sharply and unlocked the door, cracking it open just enough to peek out.

He stood there with the silver mask gone, but she recognized the jawline, the dark hair, and the width of his muscular shoulders. He was both striking and strangely familiar; sharp cheekbones, dark eyes that seemed to pierce right through her, and a jawline set with tension. Evelyn was right. He was hot. Insanely hot. And it appeared he liked to work out. He was breathing heavy and looked like he'd just fought twelve rounds with a heavyweight champion. His black coat hung heavy on his shoulders, giving him an imposing appearance.

"What are you doing here?" Rue demanded, voice low and sharp.

"Keeping you alive," he said, gaze steady on her face. "May I come in?"

Rue hesitated.

"Have you talked to your parents yet?" he asked.

Rue's eyes narrowed. "What's your name?"

"Dacre. Please open the door, Rue."

———

As soon as the door closed, Rue turned to face him, crossing her arms. "Start talking. Who are you and why are you following me?"

He met her gaze, a playful smirk tugging at his lips. "My name is Dacre. Your parents hired me to protect you."

"Protect me from what?"

"From the things you've been dreaming about," Dacre said. "They're not just nightmares."

"How do you know I've been having nightmares?"

His eyes widened in absurdity. "I've been living below you for–" he looked at his watch "–six years. I can hear that you've been having them–and more often now too."

"Is there a microphone up here or something?" Rue asked, annoyed.

"No." Dacre mimicked her stance, arms crossed. He was much more intimidating standing like that.

"Then how do you know I'm having nightmares?"

"Because you're loud. Which is surprising considering how small you are." He smirked.

Lucipurr meowed then began purring loudly. The cat wandered toward Dacre and began rubbing on his legs.

"Get away from him, Lucipurr," Rue demanded.

The cat meowed in defiance and Dacre reached down, picking up the cat and scratching under its chin.

Rue's stomach turned with the betrayal of her beloved cat. And then, a familiar fog started in the periphery of her brain...

A MAN in a black suit was standing on the porch, holding Rue's kitten. He stepped down and back until his feet hit dirt.

"Who are you?"

"That's no way to treat a guest." The man stroked Lucipurr's head, his firm pets stretching the kitten's eyelids back.

"Stop. You're hurting him. Give him back to me."

Something like fire and possession flashed in the man's eyes. He threw the kitten and reached forward, grabbing Rue's wrist.

The ground opened under his feet and in a split second, both the man in the suit and Rue disappeared into the ground. The only thing left in their place was a mound of dark dirt.

· · ·

SHE SHOOK her head until the nightmare left her mind.

"So you've been stalking me for years and my parents allowed it?" she asked.

"I wasn't stalking you," he said, his tone sharp. "It was protection. I kept my distance unless I had to intervene. Tonight has been one of those times, although it was much harder to do it unnoticed. Hence, I'm standing in your apartment."

"About that," Rue shook a finger at him, "my parents demanded that I let you move in."

Dacre paled. "What?"

"They threatened to send my brother."

"God, no." Dacre was shaking his head. "I can't deal with his bullshit."

"You know my brother?" Rue was shocked. How many members of her family did this guy know? And how had she been oblivious the entire time?

Rue's mind reeled. Memories of feeling watched and the paranoia that had eaten away at her for so long all snapped into focus.

"So every time I thought I was being followed... that was you?"

Dacre hesitated, setting Lucipurr down. "Most of the time, yes."

She felt her blood boil. "How dare you? How dare my parents? They had no right to spy on me like this... like I'm some helpless little girl." She scrubbed her hands across her face.

"They were trying to keep you safe," he said evenly. "And so am I. I have been for a long time now."

"Safe?" Rue's voice rose, trembling with anger. "From what?"

Dacre's jaw tightened. "The creatures that have been hunting you since you were a teenager. They want to finish what they started."

"I barely know what you're talking about. You had no right to invade my life like this," she said, her voice cold. "And my parents... they lied to me. I can't trust *anyone*, can I?"

Rue's phone rang. She turned it over and saw Evelyn's name light up across the screen. She sent the call to voicemail.

"You can trust your friend," Dacre said. "Evelyn is safe."

Rue's eyes narrowed as she glared at Dacre before sending a text to Evelyn.

Rue: Sorry, I butt dialed you.

Evelyn: No worries, Tink. Text me in the morning.

RUE SMILED to herself at the mention of Tinkerbell.

"I told you she's good," Dacre broke the silence.

Rue looked up at him. She'd left her parents' side to break out on her own and forge a new path. She needed to get out from under their shadows and their protection. Even her twin brother treated her like a child. It was all becoming too obvious that she couldn't hide from her heritage. She might have run to the Earthen plane in search of a normal life, but she could never hide the fact that her mother was the Queen of Hell and her father a King in the Seven Kingdoms of Heaven. Each year she had to travel to Montana and beg the White Horse permission to let her stay another year on the Earthen Plane to study. Evelyn knew none of this. She didn't know that Angels were real and Demons were real and Rue was so far from human.

She looked up.

Dacre's gaze darkened. "I didn't choose this, Rue. I was given an order and I followed it. But if it weren't for me, you wouldn't be standing here right now."

"Get out," Rue said, her voice shaking.

Dacre blinked, the faintest flicker of surprise crossing his face. "Rue, you don't understand–"

"No," she cut him off, "you don't understand. I don't care what you've done for me. I didn't ask for your help and I don't want it. So get out."

For a moment, he didn't move. Then with a slow measured nod, he stepped toward the door.

"I'll leave," he said, his voice low. "But this isn't over. You're in danger and I'm going to be close by whether you like it or not."

Lucipurr meowed in disappointment.

Something deflated in Rue. She didn't want to be forced to go home. She was going to finish her final exams next week.

"Wait," Rue said.

He paused in the frame to look back at her. There was something unreadable in his expression; a mixture of frustration and... something that made Rue's stomach twist. He probably was rarely told no. She doubted the guy had gotten turned away from anything he'd wanted in his entire life.

"You can stay." She pointed at him. "Don't try anything funny," she warned. "And leave my cat alone." She backed away, picking up her textbook off the couch. "There's a spare bedroom over there." She pointed to the empty room on the other side of the apartment. "There's no bed but," her eyes scanned his height, "you won't fit on the couch."

"I'll bring my bed up." He tucked his hands in his pockets and rocked back on his heels. "I'll go grab a few things now."

"I'm going to sleep," Rue said. "I have a class at noon."

Rue crossed the room and slammed her bedroom door closed. She leaned against it, her knees threatening to give out. She felt tears welling in her eyes but blinked them away.

Her world had been shattered in the span of minutes. Her parents had lied. Dacre *had* been stalking her but so was something else.

They're coming, Rue.

She sank against the door, hugging her knees to her chest. She didn't know who to trust anymore.

SEVEN

Rue woke to the unmistakable scent of freshly brewed coffee wafting through the air. For a split second she smiled, reveling in the peace of a quiet morning. Then reality crashed down on her like a landslide. She hadn't made the coffee she was currently smelling.

Dacre.

Her eyes snapped open, and the knot of dread in her stomach tightened. She groaned, staring up at the ceiling. Why had she agreed to this? Well, *agreed* was generous—her mother had ordered Dacre to move in "for her safety." Rue hated it. She'd been on her own for years, living in her little bubble of independence. Now her space had been infiltrated by a brooding bodyguard who looked like he'd stepped off the cover of a lifting magazine.

Her alarm blared, jolting her out of her thoughts. She slapped it off and forced herself out of bed, tossing on a hoodie and sweatpants before trudging to the door.

The sight that greeted her in the kitchen made her stop short. Dacre stood at her counter, dressed in a black T-shirt and jeans that somehow looked tailored despite their simplicity, pouring coffee into *her* Hedwig mug.

Her Hedwig mug!

Rue's groan of annoyance was loud enough to make him glance up.

"What?" he asked, his tone neutral but the faintest trace of amusement lingered in his eyes.

She ran a hand through tangled hair, glaring at him. "Don't touch my stuff."

His smirk deepened as he raised the mug to his lips. "Noted."

"And don't talk to me unless it's important," she added, shuffling toward the bathroom with all the energy of a sleep-deprived college student.

"Understood," Dacre replied, his voice trailing after her.

Rue shut the bathroom door harder than necessary and leaned against it, exhaling slowly. She needed to pull herself together. Finals week was looming, and she had no time for existential crises—or babysitters who came packaged as large, handsome, bodyguards.

The hot shower helped, though the irritation lingered. She replayed the events of the past few days in her mind as she got ready, the ridiculousness of it all still hard to process; shadow demons, endless nightmares, and now Dacre camping out in her apartment.

When she stepped out of the bathroom, the scent of food hit her—bacon and eggs. Rue blinked in surprise as she entered the kitchen.

"Did you cook?" she asked warily, eyeing the plate he'd set on the counter.

Dacre looked up from where he was leaning against the fridge, sipping *her* coffee. Still. "You need to eat. Finals week, right?" He opened the fridge door. "Also, you need to keep some real food in here. I brought mine up."

Rue crossed her arms, glaring at the plate as if it had personally offended her. "I can cook for myself, you know."

"Sure," Dacre said, his expression unreadable. "But you didn't."

She had no comeback. She'd planned to grab a granola bar on the way out. Muttering under her breath, she grabbed the plate and sat at the small dining table. She hated that the food smelled so good—and tasted even better.

As she ate, Dacre moved around the apartment with an ease that grated on her nerves. He wasn't loud or obtrusive, but the sheer fact that he was *there* made her space feel smaller, less her own.

"Please don't hover," she snapped as he walked past, heading toward the window.

He paused, glancing over his shoulder. "I'm not hovering. I'm observing."

"Observing what?"

"Potential threats," he said simply, as if it were the most natural thing in the world.

"The biggest threat in this apartment is you, and you're driving me insane."

Dacre's lips twitched in what might have been a suppressed smile, but he didn't reply. Instead, he turned his attention back to the window, scanning the street below like he expected a demon to pop out of the bushes.

Rue finished her breakfast and stood, carrying her plate to the sink, where she rinsed it off.

"I'm leaving for class in twenty minutes. Try not to rearrange my life while I'm gone."

"I know your schedule," Dacre said, finally turning to face her.

She caught the faint amusement in his tone and shot him a glare. He met her gaze with infuriating calm.

Rue stormed off to her room to grab her bag. As she

passed Lucipurr, who was lounging on the couch, the kitten gave a lazy stretch and flicked his tail.

"At least *you* respect my space," she muttered, scratching behind his ears.

Lucipurr purred, completely indifferent to the tension between his owner and the tall, dark, handsome intruder in their apartment.

As Rue headed to the door, she threw a final glance at Dacre. He was leaning against the counter with his arms crossed, watching her with that same unreadable expression.

"Goodbye," she said curtly.

"See you in a minute, Rue," he replied, his voice low and steady.

Her heart did a strange little flip at the way he said her name, but she shoved the feeling down and stepped out into the hallway, determined to focus on anything but the man currently occupying her apartment. Then she realized, he was going to follow her... All. Day. Long.

Eight

Dacre set the coffee mug down onto the counter with more force than he intended, the dull thud echoing in the quiet kitchen. He gripped the edge of the counter, his knuckles whitening as he stared down at the remnants of coffee swirling in the mug.

Jesus Christ, she looked adorable in the morning.

The image was seared into his brain: Rue, shuffling out of her room like a sleepy, grumpy kitten, her hair a tousled mess and her eyes half-lidded with the haze of sleep. That oversized hoodie she wore hung off one shoulder, revealing just enough skin to make his pulse spike. He'd always known she was beautiful, but seeing her in her most unguarded state, soft and vulnerable, hit him harder than he cared to admit.

He closed his eyes and tried to steady his breathing. He needed to get a grip. Moving in had seemed like the logical next step, a way to ensure her safety without constantly lurking in the shadows. But now, after just one morning, he was starting to think he'd made a colossal mistake.

Dacre ran a hand through his hair, exhaling sharply. He'd been following Rue for years, always from a distance, always careful to keep himself as detached as he could. But being in her space, surrounded by her scent, her things, her *presence*—it was different. Too different. It was too much and he was afraid of the beast lingering under his skin. There was nowhere for her to hide here from him.

Dacre rinsed out the mug and set it in the sink, the clink of ceramic on metal grounding him. He glanced around the kitchen, taking in the little details that made it uniquely Rue's —mismatched mugs, a calendar with scribbled notes and doodles in the margins, a fruit bowl with exactly one apple and a very overripe banana. He was glad he had food in his fridge to bring up or they'd both be very hungry.

He shook his head and walked to the small spare room she'd grudgingly given him. His duffel bag sat in the corner, and he pulled out a leather jacket. He didn't need much to blend in on the Earthen plane, but he still checked his reflection in the mirror. His expression was neutral, calm—though the faint tension in his jaw betrayed his lingering unease. Shadows danced across his face and he willed them to stop. Today would not be the day that he inadvertently let the monster out.

He followed her, keeping a careful distance as he always did. The morning air was crisp, and the city buzzed with life as Rue made her way to campus. Dacre blended into the crowd effortlessly, his years of experience making him practically invisible.

Ahead, Rue turned onto the path leading to her building, her steps quick and purposeful. Dacre followed, his gaze scanning the area for any signs of danger. She might not think she was walking into a war zone, but he knew better. Danger lurked in the shadows, and he'd be damned if he let it touch her.

As she disappeared into the building, Dacre leaned against a nearby tree, his posture relaxed. He ruminated on the morning's events: Rue emerging from the bathroom, her damp hair pulled back into a messy bun, him leaning against the counter and scrolling through his phone as if he hadn't just spent the past twenty minutes psyching himself up over offering her breakfast. He'd never made food for another soul in all his life. It was nerve-racking.

NINE

Rue tried to ignore Dacre's presence as she went about her day, but it wasn't easy. He followed her to campus, keeping a discreet distance, but his presence was impossible to miss. Every time she glanced over her shoulder, there he was leaning against a tree or trying to blend into the crowd and sucking at it. His leather jacket and sharp features gave him an air of unsettling authority. She wondered how she didn't notice him before. Well... she *had* felt like she was being followed. Rue assumed he was just closer now.

"Be careful," Dacre said, his voice low but firm.

Rue startled as she sifted through her bag. She turned to look at him, her expression a mix of annoyance and resignation. "I'm going to the library, not a war zone."

He was standing next to her, watching the shadows in a nearby cluster of oak tree's she'd stopped next to.

"Still," he said, meeting her gaze.

She rolled her eyes but didn't argue, muttering a half-hearted "whatever" as she started walking again.

Evelyn noticed immediately.

"Okay, why is your hot neighbor following you?" Evelyn

asked as they walked across campus after their archaeology lecture.

Rue sighed, glancing over her shoulder to see Dacre lingering near the library steps, his gaze fixed on them.

"It's... complicated," Rue said hesitantly.

Evelyn raised an eyebrow. "Complicated how? Is he a stalker? Because I'm all for calling campus security or... maybe I'll volunteer for tribute if he needs to stalk the willing."

"No," Rue said. "He's not a stalker. Well, not really. It's... my parents hired him as a bodyguard."

Evelyn's eyes widened. "A *bodyguard*? What are you, secretly royalty or something?"

Rue laughed dryly. "Ummm, can we go somewhere private and I'll explain everything?"

Evelyn nodded, leading Rue to a secluded bench under a cluster of oak trees. Once seated, Rue took a deep breath and told Evelyn that her parents were royalty, she just didn't tell her they were royalty of a different realm. She told Evelyn that someone had been following her, about the nightmares, her parents' betrayal, and Dacre's revelation that he'd been secretly guarding her for six years.

"Six years!" Evelyn exclaimed. "How on earth did we not notice?"

"No clue." Rue was shaking her head.

"Well," Evelyn began slowly, "this might be the wildest thing I've ever heard. But... I believe you."

Rue blinked. "You do?"

Evelyn nodded. "Yeah. I mean, you've always been a little... different, you know? And if hot-neighbor Dacre says you're in danger, I'm not going to brush it off."

Rue hesitated, glancing back toward the library where Dacre still stood. "I don't know."

Evelyn leaned closer, her expression serious. "Well, if he's staying, you'd better keep me in the loop. I don't want you dealing with this alone."

"Dacre said I could trust you," Rue admitted, her voice soft.

Evelyn smiled. "Whatever happens, I've got your back."

Rue smiled back at her friend and held back a worried gaze. She knew she was putting Evelyn in danger, more so now.

"I have to get your costume back to you," Rue said, changing the subject.

Evelyn waved a hand, dismissing it. "Oh you keep that and wear it again. You looked spectacular." Evelyn licked her lips. "Hey, was Dacre at the Halloween party?"

Rue nodded.

"Silver mask, dude?"

Rue nodded.

"Damn." Evelyn's expression downturned. "I saw you dancing. I'm jealous."

"There's always pyramid head," Rue reminded her.

"Shit. There sure is. I'm meeting him tomorrow for drinks." Evelyn rubbed her hands together. "Guess I can't steal all the hot boys." She knocked her shoulder against Rue's. "Although, I've never seen you with anyone."

"I just really wanted to focus on my studies," Rue said. "I went on a few dates but no one stuck. There will be time for boys later."

"Live a little, Tink," Evelyn winked. "You only live once." She looked up and saw Dacre leaning against a tree, arms crossed and heel kicking at a pinecone. "Do you think he can hear us?" Evelyn asked.

Rue shrugged.

"You should tell him to wear something that doesn't make him look like a hot piece of meat. Rawr." Evelyn scratched at the air.

Dacre looked up and smirked at her.

"That fuck has good hearing," Evelyn whispered.

"I don't think it matters what he wears," Rue said. "His body will still be the same."

"Maybe he should be shirtless then," Evelyn suggested.

They watched Dacre reach down and gently grip the hem of his shirt with two fingers. He began lifting it up, revealing a hint of skin.

Rue covered her eyes. "You are such a flirt, Evelyn." She stood. "I have to go study."

"Sure you do, Tink." Evelyn slapped Rue's butt as she walked away, heading toward the library.

TEN

IN THE CAMPUS LIBRARY, THE FAINT RUSTLE OF turning pages and the soft hum of fluorescent lights were the only sounds. Rue sat at a corner table surrounded by a fortress of open books. A half-empty bottle of water sat next to her, untouched for hours.

She tried to focus on her notes, scribbling down key points about artifact dating methods, but her mind wandered. The events of the past week pressed on her, a suffocating mix of stress, fear, and anger.

The nightmares lingered in the back of her mind like shadows at the edge of the forest. She shook her head, trying to shake off the unease. Her eyelids felt heavy. She hadn't been sleeping well, always waking when the dreams turned frightening. She rubbed her temples, telling herself she'd take a break after one more chapter. But the words blurred on the page and her pen slipped from her fingers as her head dipped forward.

———

Rue was back in the twisted forest, running as fast as her feet could take her. The air was thick, choking almost, and a familiar coppery scent was everywhere.

She tripped, falling hard onto the ground. Her hands sank into the crimson pool again, the reflection staring back at her. But this time it wasn't just her face – it was distorted, monstrous, with hollow eyes and sharp teeth.

The shadow loomed over her once more, and the voice whispered: *You can't run, Rue. It's already inside you.*

She screamed as clawed hands reached for her–

———

"Rue."

Warm breath tickled her ear followed by the press of a large hand on her shoulder. Rue jolted awake, her heart pounding as her vision swam. She jumped and looked up to find Dacre crouched beside her with a to-go cup of coffee. It smelled like pumpkin. But then Rue noticed concern creased between his brows.

"Nightmare?" he asked quietly, sliding the coffee toward her.

Rue nodded, swallowing hard. Her throat felt dry, and her palms were clammy. She wrapped her hands around the coffee cup, letting its warmth root her in reality. She shivered and wished she'd worn a heavier sweater.

"Sorry," Rue whispered before looking around to see if anyone had heard her.

Dacre stood, towering over her, and crossed his arms. "Don't apologize for something you can't control."

She sighed, rubbing her temples. "I'm fine. It's just... stress from finals week."

He frowned. "You've been studying for days. I think you'll do fine."

"No," she shook her head, "there's still notes to cover." She flipped through her notebook.

A large hand stopped her. Dacre tilted his head, his expression unreadable. "Running yourself into the ground won't help you ace the exams. Come on, I'll walk you home."

"I don't need you to–"

"Yes, you do," he said, cutting her off. "You're exhausted and it's late. I'm walking you home, Rue. And this time I'm walking beside you. The library is closing and it's nearly midnight."

Rue checked her watch and could barely believe it.

"Collect your things." Dacre stepped back and waited as she closed books and loaded her bag until it was bulging. He wondered how such a small person could constantly lug around such a heavy bag. He held out his hand and offered to carry it, but Rue walked past him with a sigh.

———

THE CAMPUS WAS EERILY quiet as they stepped outside, the air crisp and cool against Rue's flushed skin. It was strange having Dacre walk next to her instead of lurking in the shadows or watching from a distance.

Rue sipped her coffee, the warmth soothing her frayed nerves. The crunch of leaves underfoot was the only sound. There was a faint shimmer of stars visible between the wispy clouds.

"You're quieter than usual," Rue said, breaking the silence.

"Just thinking," Dacre replied.

"About what?"

"How I'm gonna survive finals week when you insist on driving yourself into the ground," he said, a faint smirk tugging at the corner of his lips.

Rue rolled her eyes. "Walking home from the library isn't dangerous, Dacre. You're paranoid."

He didn't respond, but the way his gaze shifted, scanning the shadows ahead made her uneasy. She knew the truth; she was paranoid and had been for a while now. She just didn't want to admit it. Her eyes lingered on Dacre, her bodyguard. Right now he just looked like another college student in jeans and his leather jacket. She licked her lips. He also looked quite good.

They turned onto the street where they lived, lined with barren trees swaying in the night breeze. The lampposts cast long, flickering shadows from the branches swaying underneath them. It had an eerie effect.

That's when Rue felt it–a prickling at the base of her neck, the unmistakable sensation of being watched.

She slowed her steps, glancing over her shoulder. The street behind them was empty, but the shadows between the trees seemed darker than before, as if something lurked just out of sight.

"Something has been following us since we left the library," Dacre said, his voice sharp. "Ignore it. Sometimes they go back when they're ignored."

"It's probably just a raccoon," Rue whispered.

"I don't think so." Dacre suddenly stopped, stepping in front of her. "Stay close to me," he said.

They had barely taken a few more steps when a sudden gust of wind swept through the street, carrying with it the faint scent of sulfur. Rue's stomach twisted.

"Dacre–" she started, but before she could finish, the shadows ahead of them shifted and took shape.

A figure merged, cloaked in darkness. Its form was humanoid but wrong–too tall, too thin, and glowing red eyes that pierced the night.

"Stay behind me," Dacre ordered, his voice cold and demanding.

Rue stumbled back, spilling her coffee. Her heart pounded as the creature stepped closer. It moved unnaturally, as if it didn't quite belong to this world, its limbs bending at impossible angles.

The creature hissed, its voice like scraping glass. "Sssshe belongs to usssss."

"She does not," Dacre growled.

The creature lunged faster than Rue could react. She dropped her coffee cup. Dacre moved just as quickly, intercepting the creature with a fluid motion that seemed inhuman.

The street erupted into chaos. Dacre shoved Rue behind him as he grappled with the creature. It was strong. But Dacre appeared stronger as he moved with precision, his every strike with the knife he'd pulled from his inner jacket pocket calculated.

The creature shrieked, its claws slashing through the air. Dacre turned feral, his eyes glinting with a dangerous green light that sent a shiver down Rue's spine. Something wasn't right. Dacre didn't move like a human, he moved like a panther.

She backed up, her spine pressed against the trunk of an oak tree. Rue had seen plenty of battle in her life. Heck, she'd trained with her parents' warriors as a child. It was less so now that she'd left the royal home but she'd been there. She realized that Dacre moved like he'd trained his whole life to fight demons. She swallowed hard. He didn't look like a Hellion. Maybe she should have asked her mother *what* Dacre actually was.

Dacre managed to pin the creature to the ground, his hand pressing against its neck. "You don't belong here," he snarled.

"Go back and tell your master to stay away or I will come for him next."

The creature laughed, its voice a chilling echo. "You can't protect her forever."

With a guttural growl, Dacre punched the creature in the jaw so hard its neck snapped. It disintegrated into ash and its remains scattered in the autumn wind.

Rue stood frozen, her legs trembling as Dacre turned to her. His expression was calm, but his eyes still burned with a wild intensity. The green shine disappeared.

"Are you hurt?" he asked, stepping closer.

She shook her head, her voice caught in her throat. "What–what was that?"

"A shadow demon," he said simply. "You haven't seen one before?"

"No." Her knees buckled and she gripped the tree.

Dacre hesitated, his jaw tightening. "We need to get you back to the apartment." He held out a hand. "Come with me."

Rue nodded numbly, her mind spinning.

Dacre walked closer, his hand hovering near hers, their knuckles brushing every few steps as if he were ready to catch her at any moment or as if he were afraid she'd be pulled into the nearby shadows if she got too far from him.

Rue suddenly realized this wasn't just paranoia and night-mares–this was real. And whatever was coming for her wasn't going to stop.

Eleven

As Rue climbed the stairs to her apartment it felt like she was climbing a mountain. After the nightmare at the library and the attack on the way home, she was wiped. Dacre's heavy footfalls behind her were the only thing that kept her moving. She wanted to show him that she was strong despite her small size. She could make it home.

She dug in her bag for keys then unlocked the door.

Lucipurr bounded toward them, meowing loudly in a cat-shout of anger for leaving him for so long.

Rue dropped her bag on the floor with a thud and picked him up. "I'm sorry, buddy. I was gone a long time."

Lucipurr blatted out a quick and angry double meow-meow.

Dacre closed the door and locked it.

"You should go to bed," he urged Rue before heading toward his own room.

Something was off with the guy–he was holding onto a hell of a lot of dark energy. Rue would have to have been dead not to feel it. She carried Lucipurr to the kitchen and got him fresh food and water before heading to her room.

Rue dug through her dresser and found a pair of pajama shorts and an oversized T-shirt. She had put off doing laundry all week and was down to just a few clean pieces of clothing. She changed quickly before leaving the room again to grab something to eat. Her gut hurt from drinking coffee on an empty stomach.

She searched the cupboards and fridge, settling on a microwave pizza. She sat in the dark, watching out the window as she ate.

"Jesus Christ," a dark voice whispered.

Rue turned. "What?"

"Why are you sitting in the dark?"

"I was hungry."

"With no lights?"

Rue glanced up at the ceiling. "I can't deal with the big light after everything. I just need some darkness." She glanced out the window. "And I was just watching the stars. It's calming."

A noise rumbled in Dacre's throat.

Rue pushed the half of pizza across the table and the plate scraped. "You want the rest?"

"You're not going to eat it?" he asked.

"I'm full."

"You should eat better." He crossed the room and sat opposite her.

Rue shrugged then scowled as Lucipurr sidled up to Dacre and crawled into his lap.

"Traitor," Rue muttered. "Thanks for taking care of that shadow demon."

Dacre took a bite of the pizza and nodded his head like it was just another day. She wanted to ask him why his eyes had changed and where he'd learned to fight like that, but she didn't.

TWELVE

DACRE LEANED AGAINST THE KITCHEN DOORWAY, his broad shoulders casting a shadow into the dimly lit room. The faint glow of the refrigerator illuminated Rue as she sat at the tiny table, eating pizza in her pajamas. Her legs were tucked up beneath her, her oversized T-shirt slipping off one shoulder, and those damned tiny shorts that left way too much skin exposed made it impossible to look anywhere else.

He scrubbed a hand over his face, willing himself to focus. This was harder than he'd anticipated—being so close, watching her move around like she didn't have a care in the world when he could still feel the remnants of the fight lingering in his veins. The adrenaline from earlier hadn't worn off, and his nerves were on edge.

"Damn it," he muttered under his breath, so low even she couldn't hear.

Rue took another bite of pizza, her eyes half-lidded with exhaustion, and for a moment, Dacre thought she might doze off right there at the table. She had no idea how close she'd come to disaster tonight, how bold the shadow demons were becoming. They weren't just watching her from a distance anymore—they were hunting her, and the attacks were growing more frequent.

He exhaled sharply, trying to steady his racing thoughts. Six years. Six years of keeping her safe from the shadows that wanted to devour her; of staying in the background, unseen and unacknowledged. He'd told himself it was enough and that as long as she was safe, it didn't matter if she didn't know who he was.

But tonight had rattled him. The fight had been too close, the danger too real. Watching her now, so calm and unbothered, made him want to shake her and yell that she couldn't keep walking through life like this–oblivious to the threats lurking in the dark. She just walked around assuming she was safe and there was no danger, ever.

He let out a thick breath, his hand clenching at his side. It took a hell of a lot of restraint to keep his distance, to not push her to remember.

The truth was kept from her for her own safety, yes, but also because he wasn't sure he could handle what might happen if she did remember.

"You want the rest?" Rue's voice startled him out of his thoughts. She turned to look at him, her head tilted in that way she did when she was curious, then she scraped the plate across the table.

Her casual tone nearly undid him. How could she sound so normal, so completely unaware of the danger she was in?

The shadow demons were getting braver, their attacks more coordinated. He didn't like it, didn't like the feeling of being one step behind. They were brave breaking through the veil like that.

She looked out the window to her right, her expression unreadable. Dacre glanced out and saw the stars she'd mentioned.

Rue stood, grabbing her plate and walking past him to the

sink. She didn't say anything as she rinsed it off, but he could see the tension in her shoulders, the way her movements were just a little too quick.

"Everything will be fine," she said finally, not looking at him. "It always is. I'm not going to live in fear of them."

He wanted to argue, to tell her that she didn't understand the gravity of the situation, but the exhaustion in her voice stopped him. She was tired—physically, emotionally, maybe even spiritually. Pushing her right now would only make things worse.

"Go to bed," he said quietly. "I'll take care of the rest."

She hesitated, glancing at him over her shoulder. For a moment, something unspoken passed between them, a flicker of understanding. Then she nodded and turned, heading down the hall to her room.

Dacre leaned his elbows on the table, letting out a slow breath. He'd come closer than ever to losing her tonight. If he'd been further way, they'd have taken her. He scrubbed his face with his hands.

Thirteen

As the week went on, Rue did her best to focus on her studies, burying herself in textbooks and practice exams. Dacre remained a constant, quiet presence in the background, never interfering but always watching.

On the last day of finals, Rue sat in archaeology class, tapping her pencil against a notebook as the professor droned on about what to expect next semester. All these years, she longed to attend a winter session and stack up on classes but she couldn't–she had to go home.

"Any plans for Christmas break?" Evelyn asked, glancing behind them.

"Just the usual." Rue said. "Family. Dinner. Drama. Not necessarily in that order."

"Nothing planned with that hunk?" she motioned to Dacre.

Rue laughed. "No."

Professor Camden wished the class a Happy Holidays and collected his laptop.

Rue tucked her notebook in her bag and turned to Evelyn.

"Text me, okay?" Evelyn asked.

"Of course."

"And when we come back in January, Justin is throwing a huuuge party. So bring something amazing to wear."

Rue nodded and smiled. "No costumes?"

"Yes, there will be costumes." Evelyn winked.

Rue made a face. "I'll look but I don't have a lot at my parents' house. I'll probably have to buy something."

Evelyn smirked. "Oh, say no more, Tink, I'll find something for you to wear."

Rue looked her in the eyes. "It better not be slutty."

Evelyn pursed her lips as she stood and said, "Happy Holidays. Eat some pie for me."

Rue looked up and Dacre was right behind her.

"You don't need to be so close," Rue warned.

Dacre looked down at her and said nothing.

The walk back to Rue's apartment was thick with tension. Dacre had stuck close to her side, his presence both a comfort and an annoyance. The streets glimmered with holiday lights, and the air carried the faint scent of pine and woodsmoke and snow. But Rue wasn't in the mood to enjoy the festive atmosphere. She'd been filled with unease since she woke up this morning. The nightmares had been bad but worse was the knowledge that she was going home for the holidays. It had been nearly twelve months since she'd left the Earthen plane and she wasn't looking forward to leaving it again.

When they reached her apartment door, Dacre broke the silence. "Are you packed?"

Rue paused, her hand on the doorknob. She frowned, glancing back at him. "I have to do that now."

"I assume you'll want answers from your parents," he said matter-of-factly, his expression unreadable.

The mention of her parents sent a jolt through her. Her jaw tightened as she pushed the door open and stepped inside, flicking on the lights. Dacre followed, closing the door behind him.

Rue sighed heavily, frustration bubbling just beneath the surface. "I wasn't planning on asking them much," she muttered, kicking off her boots by the door. "I figure they'd just lie to me."

"You should," Dacre said, his tone calm but firm.

She turned to glare at him, her arms crossed. "Why do you care so much? What if I don't want to deal with their cryptic nonsense and lies?"

Dacre met her gaze, his steady, dark eyes unyielding. "Avoiding them won't change what you need to know."

Rue hated that he was right. She hated even more that a small part of her did want to see her family. She missed her brother, despite everything. And as much as her relationship with her parents grated on her nerves, the questions gnawed at her—questions about who she really was, about the shadow demons chasing her, the nightmares, the missing memories.

"They've been lying to me for ages," she snapped, brushing past him toward her room.

Dacre smirked faintly, leaning against the doorframe. He said nothing but clearly knew something.

Rue rolled her eyes, stepping into her room and shutting the door behind her with more force than necessary. She leaned back against it, letting out a shaky breath.

Lucipurr meowed from her bed, stretching lazily as if to remind her she wasn't entirely alone. She crossed the room and scooped him up, pressing her face into his soft fur.

"This is a terrible idea," she mumbled to the kitten, who purred in response.

Dropping him gently onto the bed, Rue grabbed her duffel bag from the closet and began tossing in clothes haphazardly. A heavy sweater, a pair of jeans, her favorite scarf—she barely thought about what she was packing, her mind racing with everything she'd been avoiding.

What would she even say to her parents? What if they didn't give her straight answers? What if the truth was worse than the lies? She loved them and they were nice to her, gave her everything she'd ever wanted–except the truth.

A soft knock on her door interrupted her spiraling thoughts.

"What?" she called, annoyed.

"Remington is hosting a formal party," Dacre said from the other side. "If you want to bring something nice to wear."

Rue clenched her teeth, debating whether to ignore him. A party. She groaned and shoved another sweater into her bag.

"I've got it," she said curtly.

"Good," Dacre replied. She could hear the faint amusement in his voice, which only irritated her more.

When she opened her door a few hours later, bag slung over her shoulder, Dacre was waiting in the living room. He was leaning against the wall, arms crossed, his expression as unreadable as ever.

"Ready?" he asked, straightening.

"No," Rue said honestly, brushing past him toward the door. "But let's get this over with."

Dacre followed her silently, his presence looming but steady. Rue tried to ignore the way her chest tightened as she locked up the apartment. She was heading back to a place she'd been avoiding for years, with a protector she didn't fully understand.

As much as she hated to admit it, she was semi-glad Dacre would be there. Even if she'd never tell him that.

FOURTEEN

Rue had never had an escort to the portal, but it seemed lately that every day was a new first. Dacre motioned for her to go ahead of him as he looked over his shoulder. She stepped through the portal which was nothing more than a decorative arch in the overgrown gardens of the abandoned Peabody Library a few miles from her apartment.

She stepped out into Hell. It wasn't as bad as humans thought, just a dark reflection of the Earthen plane. There were cars and food and homes. It wasn't too terrible. Of course there were demons and strange supernatural creatures but they all seemed to get along.

Rue walked across the cobblestone walkway, toward the front door of the castle, where her family spent half of their time. If only Evelyn could see this, Rue smiled to herself. Her human friend would lose her mind if she found out the truth. Dacre's footsteps echoed behind her.

Before Rue could touch the door handle, Remington whipped opened the door. "Sister!" he lurched forward and grabbed Rue, squishing her in a tight hug and lifting her off her feet. "It's been so long. I've missed you." He kissed her cheek.

"Put me down, Remm." Rue tried to wiggle out of his grasp but it only made him squeeze her tighter.

"I'm still your big brother," he joked.

"In size. I was born first," Rue argued as she was finally set on her feet.

"Dacre, my man." Remington reached out and gripped Dacre's hand. "She brought you back this time?"

"You knew?" Rue asked, eyes wide.

"Everyone knew," Remington said. "Everyone *knows*. Except you. Living in your little bubble on the Earthen plane."

"Whatever." Rue went to grab her suitcase but Dacre had picked it up. He motioned for her to go inside.

Rue huffed but walked toward the living room, eager to find her parents. She searched the usual rooms of the castle but was unable to find her parents. She returned to the living room to find Remington and Dacre sitting on the couch.

"Where are they?" Rue asked.

Remington shrugged. "Probably off doing King and Queen things."

"I need to talk to them," Rue said.

"I've needed to talk to them for days." Remington stood. "Plus you leave for a year at a time and only come back for the holidays. They're not going to drop everything just because you showed up for Christmas."

"I drop everything each time mom visits me. And plenty of people go to school for six years." Rue put her hands on her hips.

"Yea, they're called doctors." Remington laughed, slapping his knee. It was a quote from an old movie their mother made them watch as teenagers.

"Well if I didn't have to skip every winter session for the

holidays, I'd be done by now." Rue noticed her suitcase and grabbed it. "You're such a punk," she spat.

Both men stood as though the mild insult were something more.

Dacre looked between the two of them. Rue noticed he had been relatively quiet and that he stood just a few inches taller than her brother. Remington must've had some kind of a growth spurt. They looked like they could be brothers or on the same rugby team–both tall and muscled and handsome. They both had the kind of presence that turned heads without even trying.

Rue decided she hated them both in that moment. They were both so... perfect. It was like her little world had been upended and now she was the outsider, the one who didn't belong. She hated this feeling, it was one of the reasons why it made leaving home so easy.

"I'm going to my room," she said.

Remington raised an eyebrow. "Do you remember where it is?" Remington teased.

"Fuck off, pretty boy." Rue picked up her suitcase and stormed away.

She found her room just fine. She set her suitcase on the dresser and considered unpacking it, then decided against it. Tomorrow. She looked through her closet for a costume to bring back after holiday break. There was nothing that didn't look childish.

She'd outgrown this room ages ago. She flopped down on the bed and glanced at the door, heart still hammering in her chest. She heard a meow from the hallway and rolled off the bed to let Lucipurr in. She almost forgot Dacre had put the kitten in his pocket when they left the apartment. Rue opened the door and Lucipurr darted past her, a blur of black fur, and hopped up onto the bed with a little mew. He curled up into a ball before purring loudly. She wished she was that at ease here.

FIFTEEN

THE CASTLE WAS QUIETER THAN USUAL IN THE LATE hours after dinner. The shadows stretched long across the hallway as the night settled in, the faint glow of candlelight flickering from the windows. Rue had excused herself to her room, and Meg and Sparrow, her parents, had disappeared for a secretive meeting with a high demon. Dacre, having finished his last patrol of the evening, was standing in front of the large fireplace in the sitting room, his mind still heavy with thoughts of Rue, the demons, and the complicated feelings swirling inside him. He'd been to the castle plenty of times, though never when Rue was there. This was the first time and he was feeling strange about it. He was unsure how she'd feel about him knowing his way around since she'd expressed her anger for people lying to her. Dacre sighed and considered a strong drink. Screw it, he was going to relax for a few hours. The whole castle was loaded with Hellions for protection. A shadow demon would have to be out of its mind to attempt to get Rue while she was here.

Dacre barely noticed Remington until he walked into the adjoining room, casually leaning against the doorframe with an amused grin plastered on his face. Dacre looked up, instantly on guard, his hand subtly resting on the hilt of the dagger he kept tucked at his waist. The last thing he wanted was to be blindsided.

"Something on your mind, Remington?" Dacre asked, his voice calm but with an underlying tension. He was always alert, always prepared for trouble—but with Remington, it seemed like trouble came in the form of teasing and half-baked questions.

"Thought I'd join you for a little chat," Remington said, pushing himself off the doorframe and walking over to the bar. He grabbed a glass, poured himself a drink, but never took his eyes off Dacre. "You've been hovering around Rue like a shadow lately. And I know the job's important, but come on... it's been how many years now? Five? Six?" He raised an eyebrow as he swirled the drink in his glass, clearly enjoying the discomfort in Dacre's posture. "Has she started to remember?"

Dacre sighed, rubbing his fingers over his eyes. He had learned to expect this from Remington—the guy had always been good at pushing people's buttons, especially when it came to Rue.

Remington sat down in a nearby club chair.

Dacre shook his head. "Nothing substantial. But the shadow demons are getting bolder. They're coming out of the woodwork on the Earthen plane. I fought one and killed it on the sidewalk."

"That can't be good," Remington replied, sitting and leaning back in his chair, the glass of whisky now pressed to his lips. "She's going to have to remember. And then we're all going to feel her wrath."

Dacre's jaw clenched, and he took a step forward. "You can't blame her."

Remington set the glass down and shrugged casually.

"We've been waiting for Rue to remember you. For her to figure it out on her own." He let the silence settle for a moment. "For years, Dacre. She's so stubborn with the blood."

Dacre's hand shot out, bracing against the back of the chair next to him. He had never dared to push past the boundaries that had been set between them.

"I haven't been waiting for anything," Dacre muttered, his voice rough. "I've been keeping her safe. That's it. I'll never push her for the blood."

Remington raised an eyebrow, unconvinced. "Really? Because it sure looks like you've been waiting for her to wake up, to realize the truth about who you are. To remember what happened in that dungeon just before the war. I saw you watching her. I'd have to be blind not to see it." Remington lowered his voice. "Everyone can see it."

Dacre was silent for a moment, his thoughts racing. The memory of Rue, that first night she had asked him to stay with her, her vulnerability in the aftermath of the attack—it haunted him. But there was always the question of timing. She wasn't ready. She wasn't ready for him. She had to remember on her own, or it wouldn't mean anything.

"I've stayed out of her way," Dacre said finally, his voice low. "I don't want her to remember me that way, Remington. I want her to have a normal life, a chance to figure out who she is without any of this... without me being a part of it. I've watched her from the shadows because that's what she needed. Even if she never remembers, I'm fine with that. She can live her life."

Remington stood up, the chair scraping against the floor as he moved to stand in front of Dacre. "And what happens when she tries to date someone? How safe would that make her? What happens when she starts putting the pieces together on her own?" He studied Dacre's face, his eyes narrowing as if he could see right through the man. "You're afraid of what will happen if she remembers too much. If she remembers *you*."

Dacre's pulse quickened. He couldn't deny it. There was a part of him that feared what might happen if Rue truly saw him, if she really remembered who he was and everything that happened. She was too young and scared. What she did... it was all an accident. It should have never happened. She didn't know better. He had always been afraid of pushing too far, of forcing her to confront a past she wasn't ready for. It was easier to stay in the background, to be the protector, to keep her safe.

But Remington wasn't wrong. Rue was starting to remember. He'd heard her mumbling during the nightmares.

"She's not ready," Dacre said quietly.

Remington nodded, his smirk gone. "Maybe not. But she will be. And when she is, you'll have to decide. Because she'll remember you. And when she does, she'll need to know if you're willing to be more than just her bodyguard." He paused, studying Dacre's face. "If you're willing to be the man she needs."

Dacre looked away, running a hand through his hair. He had always kept a wall between himself and Rue, but Remington's words felt like a crack in that wall, an ever widening divide. He had spent so long keeping his distance, not allowing himself to want more. But the truth was he *did* want more. He wanted all of her. Every bit. Every moment that she was in his presence he could barely contain the urge to drag her away from everything.

He just didn't know how to get there.

"Remington," Dacre said, his voice hoarse. "Right now, I'm focused on keeping her safe. And that's all."

Remington's gaze softened, just slightly. "You've always been good at that, Dacre. But you can't protect her forever. Sooner or later, you'll have to let her in."

Dacre didn't respond, his mind swirling with memories of her. Remington had a way of pushing him to confront his own feelings, and right now, Dacre didn't know how to answer.

"Are you inviting her to the party?" Dacre asked. "I warned her before we left."

Remington smirked. "She won't go. She never does. It's just not her vibe. Imagine, Rue dressed all proper and mingling amongst Angels and Demons." He traced a pattern across the armrest of his chair. "I wish she would embrace the lifestyle." He glanced up at Dacre. "Maybe in the future you can help her transition to accepting her future here. Maybe you can get her to come back to us."

Dacre shrugged and poured himself some whisky. "I don't know, man. I've been sitting in on these lectures and classes she goes to and... shit, she is focused." He huffed out a laugh. "There could be a bee in her ear and she'd never know. At classes, at the library, walking home on campus... she is in a different world."

Remington frowned into his glass and swirled the liquid. "I was afraid you'd say that."

Sixteen

Rue settled into the castle. The familiarity of the place was a comfort, but she couldn't shake the feeling of being an outsider. It wasn't that anyone had been unkind, not at all. They all seemed pleased to have her there—her mother was the perfect hostess; her father was the laid—back but commanding figure; and Remington was a playful brother who still managed to make her laugh even though his teasing often bordered on irritating. But there was always something underneath it, a tension that she couldn't put her finger on, like they were all hiding something from her. No. She knew they were hiding something.

Dacre's presence felt equally strange. Her family had insisted he stay in the guest wing of the castle under the guise of her still being in danger, and though he didn't seem to mind, Rue thought he seemed a bit too comfortable, like he'd spent time here before. He needed no direction anywhere on the royal grounds.

As the evening wore on, Rue found herself slipping into the rhythm of family dinner. Meg had been gracious, setting the table with an array of food that Rue had only seen in extravagant feasts in history books. The roasted meats, colorful vegetables, and crusty bread filled the air with tantalizing scents. Lucipurr had his own little stool and plate beside Rue, a tiny bowl of finely chopped chicken just for him. He mewed happily as she filled his bowl twice, bringing a smile to Rue's lips.

"Does the guest of honor enjoy the chicken?" Remington asked, staring at the kitten. He wagged his fork at the fluffball. "You know, when I found you on the beach I never thought I'd be sharing a dining room table with you."

Lucipurr replied with two quick meows, that sounded a bit like an explanation that the kitten always belonged here but could never find his way without help.

Rue scratched between his ears and whispered, "You'll always be welcome at the table."

Everyone was chatting easily, but Rue still felt the familiar weight of expectation pressing against her chest. She was the one who'd left—left the family, left everything they'd known. But now that she was here she couldn't help but feel like everything was changing, something was coming. And now, Dacre —her quiet bodyguard—sat at the table with them, awkward but polite.

"I'm glad you could join us, Dacre," Sparrow said, giving a welcoming nod to the bodyguard.

Dacre stiffened slightly, his gaze flicking to Rue. She felt his tension in the air, the discomfort of a world that he wasn't quite a part of. But he didn't flinch. He simply nodded in acknowledgment before politely saying, "Thank you for the hospitality." His voice was low but clear. "It's an honor. I haven't had a family meal like this since before my mother died."

"May she rest in peace," Meg whispered before reaching for the wine to refill her glass.

Rue noticed Dacre didn't touch his glass, keeping his

hands neatly folded on his lap. It wasn't exactly awkward, but there was a strange kind of silence that fell between them all. The clink of silverware against plates seemed louder in the moment.

Remington, sensing the tension, leaned back in his chair and broke the silence with his signature smirk.

"I think we should host a football game. Hellions versus Angels," he said, his voice tinged with playful mockery. "Like a Superbowl, right here in Hell."

Rue couldn't help the laugh that escaped her. Remington had a way of making everything feel lighter, like he was always ready to turn even the most serious situation into something humorous.

Meg rolled her eyes, a small smile tugging at the corners of her lips. "You've spent too much time watching cable television."

Sparrow grinned absently. "What's a Superbowl?"

"Are we taking bets?" Meg asked. "Because I'll be betting on my Hellions."

"Is betting legal in this realm?" Rue asked.

Remington chuckled. "We make the rules."

Dacre shifted in his seat, a faint crease in his brow as he looked at Remington then back at Rue. He didn't say anything, but his discomfort was evident.

For a moment, the room settled into a peaceful rhythm as the family began to eat. Lucipurr happily devoured his chicken, his tiny paws leaving little marks on the plate as he scooted it closer to him. Rue absentmindedly stroked his fur, her mind wandering back to the thoughts that had plagued her since arriving at the castle; the feeling of being watched, the hushed conversations between her parents when they thought she wasn't paying attention, the memories of the secret looks exchanged between them all when they thought she was too young to understand.

She didn't ask because she didn't know where to start, and she wasn't sure she was ready for the answers. But she could feel it. There was something they weren't telling her, something they weren't sharing about her place in all this, or about Dacre's presence and why the shadow demons were suddenly after her.

"So, Dacre," Remington said, breaking the silence once again. "You must be used to protecting Rue by now, huh? She does seem to get into some trouble wherever she goes."

Rue shot her brother a look, but he ignored it, a grin tugging at his lips. Dacre didn't answer immediately, his gaze meeting Rue's for the briefest of moments before he responded.

"I've gotten used to it," Dacre said, his voice calm but guarded. "She's a handful, but it's my job."

There was something in the way he said it that made Rue's chest tighten, but she didn't have the energy to analyze it. She nodded, shifting in her seat and trying to focus on the meal in front of her. The food was good—comforting, even—but the weight of being surrounded by family, by the people who had always been just out of reach, was heavy. As was learning she was a job. She should have known better than to feel anything else. Even if it was just for a fleeting moment.

The night carried on with laughter and light conversation, Lucipurr purring contentedly on Rue's lap as she picked at her steak. She was trying. She was trying to relax, to enjoy this time with her family, but the tension lingered. She was stuck on thoughts of spring semester classes and graduating. She needed to meet with the archeology chair to try and get her independent study approved. She'd like to get her books now and start reading ahead of time. Rue took a deep breath and tried to force the tightening in her chest to release.

She was going to let herself enjoy the moment for once.

She'd let herself believe in the warmth of the family around her, even if a part of her knew something was off.

She took another deep breath and smiled, raising her glass. "Here's to family," she said.

Remington raised his glass in a mock toast. "And to survival," he added with a grin.

Sparrow shrugged as he said, "It's a family issue."

"One we know well," Meg nudged Sparrow and smiled softly.

Rue felt a pang of something inside, a warmth that reminded her that despite everything, this was still her family. Her parents had gone through hell and back to be together and keep their children safe. Rue's gaze lingered on her mother's scars and tattoos, then her father's. If they could get through this life together then Rue had nothing to worry about. She could still find moments like this where the world felt right—even if only for a while.

But, deep down Rue knew things were changing. And not all of those changes were in her control.

"Are you coming to the party tonight, Rue?" Remington asked, brows raised.

Rue stopped chewing, remembering that Dacre had told her Remington was throwing a fancy party. She hadn't brought anything to wear.

"You can borrow something of mine," Meg said, reading her daughter's expression.

Rue shook her head. "I don't think I'll be going." She looked down at her plate, moving the mashed potatoes around. "I'm kinda tired."

Seventeen

A LOW, PULSING RHYTHM VIBRATED THROUGH THE walls of the estate. Rue hadn't planned on wandering this far, but the sound had drawn her. She was curious and restless after family dinner.

She said she wasn't going to go but she was bored sitting in her room. Sleep would never come with the noise pulsing through the castle.

Rue smoothed her hands over her long sweater and glanced down at her black leggings and boots. She wasn't dressed formal, had strategically left all her nice clothes at home so she wouldn't be tempted to mingle.

The grand ballroom was alive with energy when she slipped inside, pressing herself against the wall to avoid notice. Gilded chandeliers hung from high ceilings, their soft golden light casting a warm glow over the crowd. There were plenty of demons that looked like humans, but they had to be something else; half-bloods maybe, a few spirits. The scent of spiced wine and something darker–sharper–lingered in the air.

Rue scanned the crowd, her gaze landing on Remm at the

center of a throng of women. His charm was effortless, his laughter loud and infectious as he held court. Her gaze drifted further until she recognized a figure in the distance: Dacre.

He was on the far side of the room, standing near the bar, his broad frame impossible to miss. He was wearing a black suit and his hair was slicked back.

Rue froze, her pulse quickening. She had never seen him in a setting like this. The Dacre she knew was quiet, brooding, always watching. This Dacre was... different. At ease, almost. He held himself with regard, tall and confident. He looked very good.

Rue figured that must be what he's like when he's not babysitting her. She suddenly felt guilty for ruining his life.

Her stomach twisted when she realized he wasn't alone. There was a woman beside him, impossibly tall and elegant, her scarlet dress clung to her figure like molten fire. Her black hair tumbled over one shoulder and her feminine face was framed by dainty horns that curled gracefully at her temples. She rested a hand on Dacre's arm, leaning in as she spoke to him.

Rue couldn't hear what they were saying, but the woman's laughter rang out, light and melodic. Dacre didn't laugh, but his lips curved into a faint smile–it was an expression she had never seen him wear.

Rue's breath hitched, her chest tightening. She told herself it didn't matter, that Dacre was free to speak to whomever he wanted. But the sight of him with the demon woman–so poised, so beautiful, so... tall–stung in a way she couldn't explain.

She stepped further into the shadows, her fists clenching at her sides. *Why does this bother me?* she thought bitterly.

Rue was trying to reason with herself. She knew Dacre was there to support Remm with whatever endeavor he was working on. Dacre had brought up Remm before and his parties. He was probably just doing his job, but Rue's emotions didn't care for logic.

The woman leaned closer, brushing her fingers against Dacre's chest as she whispered something in his ear. Rue's stomach churned. She turned away, unable to watch any longer.

As Rue moved to leave, Remington's voice caught her attention. He was speaking to someone nearby, his tone light but laced with meaning.

"Dacre does clean up well, doesn't he?" Remm said. "I've been telling Rue she's lucky to have him around, but she doesn't appreciate company."

"Such a shame," an unfamiliar voice replied. "He's been held up for years with his current job, we'd like him back to continue paying off his family debts."

Remm made a noise. "His debts have been cleared. My father saw to it."

"A man that looks like him could help us."

"No," Remm's voice was stern. "He's not going back to that life."

"Suit yourself. There are other ways to get souls."

It felt like a hundred rocks had dropped into Rue's stomach. There was no way her parents would send an ex-skin trader to be her bodyguard. They knew how she despised the business.

Rue turned away, feeling sick. The cool air of the hallway was a relief but did little to calm the storm raging inside her. Rue leaned against the wall, closed her eyes, and tried to steady her breathing.

She glanced toward the ballroom, hearing the faint echo of music and laughter. She felt like an interloper in a world she was supposed to belong to. But she'd made her decision to move away from this world.

Pushing off the wall, Rue decided she didn't need to stay and endure this any longer. She'd leave early and return to the Earthen plane where things made sense. Tomorrow, she would find a way to disappear.

Eighteen

Dacre noticed movement near the door to the ballroom. He had been hoping Rue would change her mind and come down for the party. Remembering her at the Halloween party when he'd stolen a dance with her, he'd planned on stealing another, here. He didn't care who saw.

Kit was still whispering in his ear about what she'd seen with the shadow demons at the Black Mansion. Dacre was nodding along. The ballroom was alive with laughter and music, a stark contrast to the tension simmering beneath Dacre's skin. He wasn't here for the party. He was here for information and for Rue. She'd sworn she wouldn't attend, but he couldn't help but hope she'd change her mind.

Kit's dark eyes scanned the crowd as she murmured details about the movement of the Black Mansion. It was an enchanted manor that could move locations depending on where its current owner wanted it. Known as a key element in the skin trades, no one close to the royal families had seen it in years.

"They're moving supplies through the west," Kit said, her voice low. "Crates of something. I can't tell if it's weapons or..." she hesitated, glancing around as if afraid to say the next part aloud. "Bodies. Whatever they're preparing, it's getting bolder. You know how badly they want you back." Kit swallowed hard.

Dacre's attention snapped toward the far end of the room where a familiar shadow flickered unnaturally near the ornate doorway. He straightened, his senses sharp. The figure was gone but it was enough to set his pulse thrumming. His gaze darted toward the crowd, searching. A flash of deep emerald fabric caught his eye near the door before disappearing. Rue.

"I'll get more information," Kit continued, oblivious to the distraction. "I have to be careful–"

"Later," Dacre muttered, cutting her off. He didn't wait for her response, instead he stepped away and slipped through the partygoers on his way to the doorway.

Once in the hall, the sounds of the ballroom dulled. He closed his eyes briefly, inhaling. Lavender. Rue had been here.

Dacre's chest tightened as he followed the trail. Her footsteps were echoing, light but quick, fading into the distance. He stalked after her, his long strides silent on the polished marble floors. A sharp turn led him toward a dim corridor where he slowed his pace and listened.

Ahead, where her room was, he heard the faint creak of a door closing. He moved closer, stopping outside the door, his palm resting gently on the carved wood. For a moment, he considered knocking. But what would he say? He clenched his jaw, his hand dropping to his side.

He reminded himself that Rue felt at home in libraries and coffee shops and the wide hallways of University. He could sense how out of place she felt here. He wouldn't disturb her.

He took a step back, leaning his shoulder against the wall across from her door. He let his eyes close as he listened to the faint rustle of movement within the room.

Nineteen

The estate was cloaked in silence when Rue made her move. The grand hallways that had been bustling with servants and guests mere hours ago were empty.

Rue clutched her suitcase, packed hastily with essentials. It wasn't much, just the few changes of clothes she'd brought, and a small bottle of cinnamon whisky she was smuggling back with her. Everything else could stay behind since she didn't plan on returning any time soon.

The thought sent a pang through her chest, but she shoved it down. She couldn't stay here–she felt too out of place, too tormented by the things that had happened in her childhood; the war, the running, the demons always trying to find her. Rue itched the runes on her chest, remembering when her uncle Jed had tattooed them on her. She hid them well on the Earthen plane with high necked shirts and sweaters.

Rue eased her bedroom door closed, cringing as it clicked softly into place. She paused, listening for sounds in the hall-way. Nothing.

Dacre was likely still in the guest wing–or worse, still at the party or with that woman. She shivered, reminding herself that she didn't care what he did with his life. There was nothing personal between them. She didn't care where he was as long as he wasn't here to witness her cowardice.

She navigated the winding corridors of the estate, her heart pounding with every step, her ears straining for the faintest noise. Her parents would be so disappointed, but it wouldn't be the first time, or the last. They always seemed to forgive her.

"Running away again?"

The voice froze her in her tracks. It was calm, low, and laced with disappointment.

Rue turned slowly to find Remington leaning against the doorway, arms crossed. His brown hair was disheveled and his sharp eyes gleamed with amusement. He looked as if he'd been waiting for her, like he'd never slept after the party, like he was still a bit inebriated.

"I've never run away, Remm," Rue said.

He chuckled, pushing off the doorframe. "Oh, Rue, you know exactly what I'm talking about. Sneaking off in the middle of the night, just like you did last time. You're predictable, little princess."

"Don't call me that," she snapped. "And it's morning."

He studied her a moment, his expression softening. "You can't keep running forever. Sooner or later, you're going to have to face whatever it is you're running from. Whether it's this family or..." he paused.

"Are you keeping something from me?" Rue asked.

"No." Remm shifted, uncomfortable.

"It's just really strange. Since the war I've had this feeling that everyone was keeping a secret from me. I'm missing memories, things don't make sense." She looked up at him. "And I stopped growing."

"It's just shit genetics," Remington shrugged, refusing to meet her eyes.

"That's bullshit. Our genetics are top-tier. Our parents are descendants of Archangels. How tall are you?"

"Like.. Six foot ten."

"Fuck," Rue snarled. "Why the hell am I stuck at five foot two. Why, Remm? It doesn't make sense."

"Maybe you should drink the blood," he suggested.

"I've drank the blood. It does nothing. It only makes the nightmares worse. I don't want to drink it."

"Maybe you're drinking the wrong kind. Did you tell mom?" he looked concerned.

"Yes. No. Kinda." Rue stumbled over her words. "It doesn't matter."

"Maybe all that Earthen plane coffee has stunted your growth."

Rue rolled her eyes.

"Maybe it's about him," Remm tipped his head toward the guest wing and raised his brows.

"Who?"

"Dacre."

Rue's jaw clenched. "This isn't about him."

"Isn't it?" Remington's voice was infuriatingly casual.

"I'm not doing this with you," Rue said. "Just let me go."

He sighed, stepping aside with a dramatic flourish. "Fine. Go. But don't expect me to cover for you when Mother starts asking questions."

Rue began walking away, but then she paused and released her suitcase. She turned and ran back, jumping and wrapping her arms around her brother's neck.

"I do miss you. Every day I miss you, jerk," Rue whispered as tears beaded her eyes. "Don't tell anyone I left."

"Fine. But you're the only person I will lie for."

"Good."

Remington wrapped both of his arms around her.

"When you're all ready to tell me the truth, maybe call a

family intervention." Rue sighed as she pushed away and Remington set her on her feet.

"See you next year, sis," he said sadly.

"Come visit me."

"You know I can't. Last time we were both on the Earthen plane together, all hell broke loose."

"Fine. Be a loser." Rue walked away and grabbed the handle of her suitcase.

Remington motioned to the door. "I'll walk you to the portal. Can't have you wandering these parts alone."

———

THE COLD AIR of the Earthen plane hit her like a slap as she stepped through the portal. It was snowing and the snow was up to her knees. She should have checked the weather. Rue sighed and glanced around. She was standing in the alley near the abandoned Peabody Library, about a fifteen minute walk home. The familiar sights and sounds of the city soothed her. She exhaled a breath of relief as a weight lifted off her chest.

Rue adjusted the strap of the bag on her shoulder and made her way to the front door of her apartment. Snow had piled up in the driveway and the steps that led up the porch. She made a mental note to shovel the walkway.

She passed the door to Dacre's apartment then climbed the stairs to her door. Something ached in her chest. She released Lucipurr from her pocket and he bounded indoors.

"Home sweet home," Rue said to the kitten as it leapt onto the couch, spun in a circle, then snuggled in for a nap.

"A nap sounds good." She set her suitcase down, finally feeling at home. Rue thought of the nightmares that had woken her early that day. "Better yet, I'll make some popcorn and we can watch Howl's Moving Castle."

Lucipurr meowed softly and stretched his little legs.

TWENTY

RUE TRIED NOT TO THINK ABOUT DACRE ACTING like a man-whore at her brother's party.

"What's wrong with me?" she asked herself, slamming a coffee pod into the coffee maker. "Who cares about him? It's none of my business." Rue slammed her finger down on the largest cup setting. She watched the coffee dribble out.

But then, her vision blurred. Rue blinked a few times but it was too late: the stream of coffee turned to thick blood. Each drop echoed in the small kitchen. Rue's throat felt dry. Sweat beaded her forehead as a collection of nightmares resurfaced... she was drowning, gurgling on blood but so *so* thirsty. Not again!

The knock on the door was sharp and insistent, echoing through the quiet. It pulled Rue to the present. Her heart was already racing but it switched to a quick stuttering beat that made her stomach churn.

She already knew who it was.

When the knock came, louder this time, Rue sighed and trudged to the door.

She cracked it open, and there he was–Dacre, his dark eyes stormy beneath the harsh lighting of the hallway. His broad shoulders filled the doorway, his expression a mix of anger and something else.

"Dacre," she said flatly, her voice carefully devoid of all emotion.

"You left," he said, cold and clipped, "without telling anyone. Do you know how reckless that was?"

Rue crossed her arms and leaned against the doorframe. "I don't owe you an explanation. I don't owe anyone an explanation."

There were small snowflakes melting on his hair and shoulders. Rue wanted to brush it off.

Dacre's jaw tightened. "Do you even care how many threats are circling you right now? How many of them were waiting for a moment like this? You're lucky you made it back here alive."

She scoffed and ignored the shiver that slid down her spine. "I can handle myself."

"Clearly," he said, tone dry and gaze flicking over her, taking in the oversized sweater and dark circles under her eyes. "You look like you're thriving."

Rue bristled, but before she could snap back, Dacre pushed past her, stepping into the apartment, and closing the door behind him. He'd tracked in snow.

"Excuse me," she said, glaring.

"No," he snapped, spinning to face her. His voice was sharper now, the calm exterior he usually maintained beginning to crack. "You don't get to do this, Rue. You don't get to put yourself in danger and expect everyone else to clean up after you."

She blinked, stunned; he didn't make sense. "I didn't ask you to follow me," she shot back. "In fact, I didn't ask for any of this. You, my parents, the whole damned bodyguard act... I didn't ask for *any* of it."

"Do you think this is what I wanted? To babysit someone who goes out of her way to make things harder?"

Her chest tightened. "Then why don't you just leave?"

"Because I gave my word," he said, "to your parents. To you, even if you don't remember it."

"Then tell me!" she begged. "Why is everyone hell bent on keeping secrets from me? I can tell you're all lying about something." A sharp pain bolted through Rue's skull. She pressed the heel of her hand to it and sucked in a breath.

"What's wrong?" Dacre asked, suddenly concerned.

"Nothing." Rue went to find her coffee mug in the kitchen and poured in a little milk and a spoon of sugar.

"My job is to protect you, Rue, whether you like it or not." Dacre had followed her. "There is so much you don't know."

Rue narrowed her eyes, anger boiling over. "Oh, right. Is that what you were doing at Remm's party? Protecting me while you flirted with women? I know it's tough being saddled with me on a daily basis, I'm sure I completely ruin your game."

"You don't..." Dacre's expression hardened. "You don't understand what you saw."

"Then explain it to me." She sipped at her coffee, hoping it would soothe the throbbing in her skull.

He hesitated, his gaze dropping for a moment before locking onto hers again. "The woman you saw is a contact. Someone who feeds me information about potential threats. That's all it was. Business."

Rue laughed and it sounded bitter. "That's convenient. I don't want you talking with other women about me. Demon or otherwise, they don't need to know anything about me."

"You don't have to believe me," he said, his voice softer.

"But it's the truth. Everything I do is to keep you safe, even when you're determined to make it impossible."

She sipped her coffee before asking, "Why do you care so much?"

Dacre didn't answer right away. Instead he kicked off his boots then cleaned up the loose snow he'd tracked in. He hung his coat by the door. When he finally spoke, his voice was quieter. "You're important, Rue. More than you know."

Her throat tightened, and she hated how his words made her feel small and seen all at once. It was like standing under a star-filled night sky. The same feeling.

"I didn't ask for this," she said again, her voice trembling.

"I know. But that doesn't change what's at stake."

Rue met his gaze, searching for any hint of deception. She didn't want to trust him, didn't want to let him back in after everything.

"Are you still hell bent on staying in my guest room this semester?" she asked.

Dacre's jaw tightened as he nodded. "Yes. I'm staying close. No more running off."

Rue walked past him, headed for the couch. "Fine," she said, but the word felt hollow. "You act like I've spent a lifetime making bad decisions and all I did was come home early."

"This is a reminder that I've been following you for six years, little princess. I've seen you do plenty."

Rue wasn't sure how to respond to the way he said *little princess*, it was unlike the way anyone else said it. It made her blush.

"I'm watching a movie if you're bored with being an almighty bodyguard. There's popcorn in the cupboard."

"I'm not hungry," Dacre said as he moved toward the opposite end of the couch. "For popcorn," he added as he sat down and leaned on the arm rest. "What are you watching?" he asked.

"Howl's Moving Castle."

"Never heard of it." Lucipurr jumped up onto the couch and made his way to Dacre's lap.

"Uncultured swine." The insult was meant for both male species in the room. Rue tapped the play button and reevaluated all of her life decisions.

Twenty-One

Rue stood in front of her mirror, staring at the dress Evelyn had bullied her into wearing. It was blue, fitted, and far more revealing than anything she would have chosen for herself. She tugged at the hem, trying to convince herself it wasn't too short.

"Stop fidgeting," Evelyn said, her voice muffled as she worked on her eyeliner using a compact mirror. "You look amazing."

Rue sighed. "I look like I'm trying too hard. I said nothing slutty and this looks exactly like a slutty Cinderella costume."

"You're in your twenties, Rue, this is exactly the time to try too hard. Besides, Justin's parties are practically a campus tradition. Everyone who's anyone will be there. And you're Sleeping Beauty."

"I've just never been a real party person."

"I know, which is why this year I challenged you to get out and stop hiding in the library."

Rue smiled to herself. Evelyn had a way of making everything seem exciting. "I didn't realize it was your New Year's resolution."

A sharp knock at the door interrupted them.

Evelyn groaned. "That better not be the pizza guy again. I tipped him ten percent!"

Rue opened the door to find Dacre standing in the hallway, his arms crossed and expression unreadable. He looked her over, his dark eyes lingering on the dress for just a moment too long.

"What are you doing here?" Rue asked, her tone sharp. She'd asked him to stay downstairs while Evelyn was over; she didn't want her knowing Dacre was staying in the guest bedroom.

"I need to talk to you," he said, his gaze flicking toward Evelyn.

"If this is about the party, save it," Rue said, stepping aside to let him in. "I'm going. Evelyn is forcing me. There's nothing you can say to stop me."

"It's not safe." Dacre looked like he was grinding his teeth.

"Of course it's not safe," Rue shot back. "Nothing is safe, according to you. But I'm not going to lock myself in this apartment and hide from the world."

Evelyn raised an eyebrow, glancing between them. "Is this a private fight, or can anyone join?"

Dacre ignored her, his focus on Rue. "If you're going, I'm going with you."

Rue threw up her hands. "Fine. Do whatever you want."

"Yeassss." Evelyn clapped. "Hot-bodyguard in attendance. I can't wait."

JUSTIN'S HOUSE WAS PACKED, the music loud enough to make the floor vibrate. Rue weaved through the crowd, doing her best to avoid both Dacre and the eyes that seemed to follow her wherever she went. She was trying to lay off the paranoia, but the dress wasn't helping.

Evelyn took some attention off her, dressed as a glittering mermaid. She dragged Rue to the bar and ordered drinks.

The bartender handed her three shots. Evelyn shouted, "The man in the suit is paying."

Rue laughed and then hoped Dacre carried money with him.

Evelyn passed Rue and Dacre a shot of what looked like straight vodka.

Dacre's masquerade mask only hid half his face, and Rue noticed his jaw working as he threw back the shot then passed the bartender a handful of bills.

Rue threw back her shot, then coughed as the vodka burned its way down her throat. She wished she'd brought the cinnamon whisky she stole from her parents' house.

"Let's dance," Evelyn shouted over the music, her cheeks pink. She grabbed Rue's wrist and dragged her to a nearby room where the music was blasting. The motion jerked Rue and made her mask go crooked.

Costumed students swayed and spun to the beat of the music. For a moment, Rue let herself relax, the infectious energy of the party pulling her in. She set her mask straight and started to sway a little to the beat of the music.

A hand touched her arm, and Rue turned to find Dacre standing behind her.

"What are you doing?" she asked, narrowing her eyes.

"Keeping an eye on you," he said, motioning to the far wall where three men were pointing at her.

"I don't need a babysitter," Rue said.

He didn't respond. Instead he held out his hand. "Dance with me."

She hesitated, her pulse quickening. "Why?"

"Because I asked," he said.

There was something in his voice... it matched the feeling in her chest. She took his hand.

The music shifted to a slower tempo and Dacre pulled her closer. Rue's heart pounded as his hand rested lightly on her waist, his other hand holding hers securely.

"You're pushing your luck," she murmured.

"I know," he said, his lips quirking into a faint smile. "But it's either me or them." He glanced to the men across the room. "And if it were one of them, I'm afraid I'd have to throttle them."

"Not safe?" Rue smirked this time.

"Definitely not."

They moved together, the crowd fading into the background. Rue's initial tension melted away replaced by a strange, electric awareness of how close they were. He was bending slightly so he didn't seem so tall compared to her and she missed the warmth of his body pressed against hers. She cursed herself for not being taller or wearing taller heels.

"Why do you do this?" she asked suddenly, looking up at him. "Why act like you care?"

"Because I do," he said, his voice low and serious.

Rue's breath hitched. There was no way, he must be teasing. She wanted to argue, to push him away, but the intensity of his dark gaze held her captive.

"You're impossible," she muttered.

"Good," he said, a flicker of amusement in his eyes. "Don't you want to kiss me, dark princess?" Dacre said, releasing her hand and gripping her jaw.

"Don't you have some brothel-demon to go fuck, Dacre?" Rue surprised herself with the words.

There was a glint in his eye. The corner of his mouth kicked up in a dark grin of satisfaction. Before she could say anything else, he leaned down, his lips brushing hers in a soft, tentative kiss.

Rue found herself leaning into him, her hand tightening on his shoulder. His kiss deepened, slow and deliberate, sending a shiver of ice down her spine.

When they finally broke apart, Rue's cheeks were flushed, her heart racing, her knees weak. She felt like she was going to melt into a puddle on the dancefloor.

"You can't just do that." Her voice was unsteady.

Dacre's lips curved into a smile. "Apparently, I can."

She glared at him, the flush in her cheeks betraying her. "You're insufferable."

"And yet, you're still here." He tipped his head.

Before Rue could say anything, Evelyn appeared, her eyes wide with excitement. "There you are! I've been looking for you. You're never going to guess who I just ran into."

"Pyramid head?" Rue asked.

"Yeassss. But tonight he's dressed as Prince Erik." Evelyn giggled and spun. "Isn't it perfect? Anywho, I wanted to ask hunka hunka here if he could see you home safely." She winked.

Rue's lips still tingled from the kiss. Whatever that was could be more dangerous than the thing stalking her.

"Text me when you get home," Rue said. "Let me know you're safe."

"I will," Evelyn shouted before running off.

Rue turned to Dacre. "Please tell me that you looked into this Pyramid Head slash Prince Erik guy. Ev has been stalking him for weeks."

"He's safe," Dacre said before holding out his elbow.

Rue only hesitated a moment before she slid her small hand into the crook of his arm. He was warm and she let him walk her home.

Twenty-Two

Dacre knew she was mad at him for going to the party. Hell, he was mad at him, he shouldn't have stolen the kiss from her. But she looked so good in that dress Evelyn made her wear. He couldn't help himself, could barely keep his hands off her as he walked her home. He had been hiding in his room ever since.

Now Rue was screaming in her sleep and Dacre couldn't take it any longer. Her voice tore through the apartment, sharp and raw, slicing through the quiet of the night. Dacre couldn't listen to her screams again. The neighbors were going to hear her and call the police.

The nightmares had come back with a vengeance. And Dacre had a theory about what made them worse. She refused blood, even though her family drank it freely. It was part of who they were... but she didn't know that or blatantly tried to live without it. Dacre paced the living room, fists clenched. She didn't want his help–she'd made that clear over and over again.

But her cries weren't stopping. He knocked on her door. She didn't answer.

Lucipurr was meowing at his feet, concerned. The tiny cat pawed at the door to her room, tail flicking anxiously, as though he too could sense the turmoil inside.

Dacre groaned, running a hand through his dark hair. He knew she'd be pissed, but he couldn't just stand there and do nothing.

Dacre's patience snapped. With a sharp twist of his hand, the cheap doorknob gave way, breaking under his strength. He entered her room.

The door creaked open. Lucipurr ran under his feet to investigate. Dacre paused; Rue looked so small in the moonlight. The bed was queen sized and overstuffed with extra pillows and a fluffy white comforter. Her dark hair was fanned out over the pillow, her face twisted in pain.

"No... no..." she whimpered.

Dacre knelt beside her. "Rue, wake up." He shook her shoulder.

"No, please. No." She stretched her head to the side and Dacre focused on the throbbing of the veins in her slender neck. He licked his lips. "Please, stop!" Rue screamed, her head thrashing from side to side.

"Wake up, Rue," he said louder.

Lucipurr meowed again, insistent now, as if urging Dacre to help her.

Her thrashing only grew worse. "No, Please. Don't!" she cried, her voice cracking with desperation.

"Damn it," Dacre muttered, his patience snapping. His throat tightened, his own instincts warring within him. "Rue, wake up," he growled, shaking her again.

He finally gave in, scooping her up and cradling her against his chest.

"Rue," he murmured, his voice softer now. "It's me. You're safe."

At first she struggled, her fists weakly hitting his chest, her cries muffled against his shirt. But slowly, her body began to relax. Her hands clutched at his shirt, gripping it tightly as though he were a lifeline.

"Please..." she mumbled, her voice barely audible, "don't leave me."

"I won't," Dacre said, working hard to keep his voice steady despite the storm raging inside him. He held her closer, feeling the erratic beat of her heart begin to slow.

Her head lolled against his shoulder, and her breathing evened out until she fell into a quiet, dreamless sleep.

Dacre sighed and shifted back on the bed until his back hit the headboard. He couldn't leave her. What if the nightmares came back the moment he left her alone?

Lucipurr jumped onto the bed, curling up against his hip with a contented purr.

Dacre shifted slightly, adjusting Rue in his arms so she would be more comfortable. Her small frame felt impossibly light, fragile even, and the thought made something tighten in his chest.

"I've got you," he whispered.

———

THE FIRST RAYS of sunlight were filtering through the blinds when Rue finally stirred. She stretched against him, her movements slow and lazy, like a cat waking from a nap.

Dacre went stone still.

Her eyes fluttered open and she blinked up at him, confusion flickering across her face.

"What are you doing here?" she asked, her voice raspy from sleep.

He cleared his throat, suddenly acutely aware of how closely they were pressed together. "You were screaming in your sleep," he said. "You wouldn't wake up."

Rue's brows furrowed as she sat up, her small hands pressing into his stomach and hip. "I don't remember," she murmured, then paused, shifting her hips.

"Don't," Dacre warned. "Don't move." He groaned low, like he was in pain.

Rue's eyes went wide as she realized what she'd felt pressing against her thigh.

For a moment, neither of them spoke. The air between them felt heavy, charged with something Rue couldn't quite name. She thought of his kiss and his body pressed close to her as they'd walked home last night.

"I gotta go," Dacre said, sliding his hands under Rue and lifting her off his lap. He deposited her on the other side of the bed then quickly stood and marched out of her room.

Rue looked at Lucipurr, confused. "What did I do?"

Lucipurr simply said, "Meow."

Twenty-Three

RUE COULDN'T SHAKE THE MEMORY OF THE KISS. SHE told herself it didn't matter, that she'd been caught up in the moment, that it was the vodka and the energy of the party. But every time she caught Dacre's gaze, the intensity in his eyes made her stomach flip-flop in ways she couldn't ignore.

Rue knew how to stop it for good. She would dive so deep in her studies that she wouldn't have time to remember. She focused on her classes with a near-obsessive determination, spending hours in the library or poring over notes at the tiny kitchen table. Anything to keep her mind off him.

But Dacre was always there, quiet and watchful and infuriatingly composed. He always looked too good in jeans and a T-shirt and the worn leather jacket. He was wearing cologne that smelled like pine and bergamot and smoke, which was very distracting to Rue. He smelled just enough like home to set her frazzled nerves at ease.

The air between them felt heavy, thick with charged silence. Even without seeing him, Rue could feel Dacre's presence, like a faint static hum in the background of her thoughts. It was maddening. Every creak of the floorboards or shuffle from the spare room sent a shiver up her spine.

Evelyn, completely oblivious to the tension, was draped across the couch, her legs dangling over the armrest, a bowl of popcorn balanced precariously on her stomach.

"So," Evelyn drawled, tossing a piece of popcorn into her mouth, "are we going to talk about why you've suddenly turned into Hermione Granger with this nonstop studying?"

Rue didn't look up from her notebook, furiously scribbling notes that didn't make sense even to her. "What do you mean?"

Evelyn's laugh was light and teasing. "Oh, come on. You've been glued to that thing for hours. What's the deal? Are you trying to avoid someone?"

Rue's pen stilled. "No," she said quickly, her voice a touch too sharp.

Evelyn smirked. "Uh-huh. You're a *terrible* liar, Rue."

Rue forced herself to resume writing, though her pen trembled slightly in her grip. "I just have a lot to catch up on," she muttered.

Evelyn sat up, narrowing her eyes suspiciously. "Wait a second." She grabbed another handful of popcorn and pointed a piece at Rue like an accusing finger. "Where's your hot-bodyguard guy? What's his name—Drake? Damien? No—*Dacre*. Where is he?"

Rue froze. Her heartbeat quickened, and she couldn't stop the flush that crept up her neck.

Evelyn gasped dramatically. "Oh my God, is *he* the reason you're acting like this? Did something happen? Did you two—"

"No!" Rue blurted, cutting her off. She clutched her notebook like it was a lifeline. "Nothing happened. He's just... busy."

Evelyn cocked an eyebrow, unconvinced. "Busy doing what? Brooding in his creepy downstairs apartment?" She popped another kernel into her mouth and grinned. "You know, for a bodyguard, he's not doing much guarding if he's not around." She lifted her head. "Maybe I should go look for him."

Rue's stomach churned. Little did Evelyn know, Dacre wasn't in his apartment. He was in the spare room just a few feet away, doing his best to remain quiet.

"He's just my bodyguard," Rue muttered, her voice barely above a whisper.

Evelyn snorted. "Right. Because guys like that just *hang around* twenty-four-seven. Shouldn't he have a partner or something when he needs a break? Come on, Rue, spill it. Did he make a move? Did you make a move?" Her grin widened. "Do you want to make a move?"

Rue groaned, burying her face in her hands. "Can we not talk about this?"

Evelyn leaned forward, resting her elbows on her knees. "Why not? You clearly like him."

"I don't like him," Rue said firmly, though the heat rising to her cheeks betrayed her.

Lucipurr meowed from under the coffee table, essentially calling out her lies.

Evelyn's smirk only grew. "You're blushing. You *so* like him." She pointed under the coffee table. "I heard the dark void, he agrees with me."

Lucipurr let out two little mews and Evelyn laughed.

Rue opened her mouth to argue, but a faint creak from the hallway made her heart leap into her throat. She shot a quick glance toward the spare room door, praying Evelyn hadn't heard.

Evelyn didn't notice. She flopped back onto the couch with a dramatic sigh. "Fine. Don't tell me. But if you ask me, you should totally go for it. Hot mysterious bodyguard? That's like, every girl's dream."

Rue groaned inwardly, wishing the floor would swallow her whole. The truth was, she couldn't even begin to unpack her feelings for Dacre, let alone explain them to Evelyn.

From behind the closed door, Dacre sat on the edge of the bed, his hands clasped tightly together. He could hear every word, his enhanced senses making it impossible not to. He smirked slightly at Evelyn's teasing but quickly sobered. He hated being confined to this space.

Back in the living room, Rue exhaled slowly, trying to steady her nerves. She focused on the notes she was working on.

Evelyn tossed another kernel into her mouth, her grin softening into something more genuine. "Look, all I'm saying is, if you like him, don't overthink it. Life's too short for that."

Rue forced a smile.

———

THE APARTMENT WAS FINALLY QUIET, except for the soft rustle of Rue tidying up the mess Evelyn had left behind. Popcorn kernels were scattered across the couch and coffee table, an abandoned blanket draped over the back of a chair. Rue tucked the blanket into place and straightened the pillows, her movements quick and distracted.

Lucipurr twined around her legs, his soft purring the only sound accompanying her. She bent down to scratch behind his ears, grateful for the little cat's grounding presence.

"I heard what you said, traitor," she muttered to him with a faint smile.

The creak of a door opening made her freeze mid-motion. Slowly, Rue straightened, her heart thudding in her chest. She didn't turn around but could feel his presence—the air in the room seemed to shift; heavier, warmer.

"Evelyn gone?" Dacre's voice was quiet, rough around the edges.

Rue nodded, still not facing him as she picked up the empty popcorn bowl. "Yeah. She left a little while ago." She busied herself at the sink, rinsing the bowl even though it didn't need much cleaning.

For a moment, the silence stretched between them, thick and awkward. Rue felt his gaze on her back, and her nerves prickled under the weight of it.

Dacre moved further into the room. He stopped by the couch, glancing at the spot where Evelyn had been lounging earlier.

"She's... loud," he finally said, his tone carrying a faint trace of amusement.

Rue let out a soft laugh, relief mingling with her unease. "That's Evelyn. She has a way of filling every space she's in."

Lucipurr padded over to Dacre, rubbing against his legs. Dacre crouched down, scratching the cat under his chin. "At least someone around here likes me," he murmured, glancing up at Rue.

Rue's hands stilled on the dishrag she was holding. "It's not that I don't..." she began, her voice trailing off.

Dacre straightened, his expression unreadable. "You don't have to explain."

The tension was unbearable. Rue dried her hands and turned to face him, hugging the dishrag to her chest like a shield. He was teasing her and she knew it. She saw the tension in his mouth as he held in a smile.

"I should probably head to bed," she said, her voice quieter than she intended.

Dacre nodded, stepping aside to let her pass. As she moved toward her room, Lucipurr followed, his tail flicking lazily.

Rue paused in the doorway, her hand gripping the frame. She glanced back at Dacre, his tall figure half-shadowed in the dim light of the living room.

"Goodnight, Dacre," she said softly.

His gaze met hers, something unreadable flickering in his eyes. "Goodnight, Rue."

She lingered for a heartbeat longer, then slipped into her room, closing the door behind her. Leaning against it for a moment, she exhaled a shaky breath, her heart still racing.

She finally moved, grabbing pajamas from the dresser, and changed. Lucipurr hopped onto the bed, curling up in his usual spot. Rue crossed the room and crawled into bed beside him, stroking his fur absently.

"What are we gonna do about this mess?" she asked Lucipurr.

He replied with an innocent, "Meow," that sounded like he was trying to tell her nothing was wrong and everything was perfect and not really a mess at all, that she was just too busy neglecting her true self and that's what was making her edgy.

Despite the silence of the apartment, the air still felt charged. Rue sighed, laying down beside Lucipurr. Sleep felt a long way off especially with the knowledge that Dacre was still so close, just beyond the door. She could hear him in the kitchen. She pressed her fingers to her lips, remembering the kiss from days ago, the way he held out his elbow as they walked home, the morning she'd woken up in his arms... Then everything had turned extremely awkward and remained that way.

TWENTY-FOUR

RUE'S NIGHTMARES SHIFTED INTO VIVID DREAMS of rolling plains and snow-capped mountains and a white horse with piercing eyes that seemed to see straight through her.

Rue woke one morning with a single thought echoing in her mind: *It's time*.

After class, she packed a backpack. As Dacre noticed her preparations, he raised an eyebrow but said nothing, sipping a coffee from *her* Hedwig mug and reading a novel on the couch.

"Are you going somewhere?" he finally asked.

"Yes," Rue replied absently as she sent an email to her archeology professor requesting an excused absence from her classes, then logged onto a travel site she'd used each year to book flights.

"I don't need you to follow me. I'll only be gone about twenty-four hours," Rue said.

Dacre closed his book and stood. He walked toward her room, leaning casually against the doorway, his arms crossed. "I can't allow that."

Rue glared at him. "I mean it. I need to do this alone."

"Where are you going?"

"It's something I have to do every year."

"Are you going to Montana?"

Rue froze. "How do you know?"

"I've been following you for six years. Remember?" he smirked. "I've always gone to Montana with you. You just never noticed." He sipped from the mug.

"I have to see the white horse," Rue said. "It's been a year."

"When are you leaving?" Dacre asked. He was nodding like he knew.

Rue looked down at the computer screen. "In three hours. Would you like me to book your ticket?"

"Please." Dacre's voice dropped a few octaves and it made a shiver run up Rue's spine.

She bought first class seats, not wanting to be rubbing elbows or thighs with the man who'd made her so uneasy these past few weeks.

———

THE BIGGEST SURPRISE about traveling with Dacre at her side was that TSA never once asked to pat her down or take a second walk through the metal detectors. He woke her immediately when she had fallen asleep on the plane and descended into another nightmare. Rue realized, if he hadn't been there, the whole plane would have heard her.

The rental car's heater hummed softly as Dacre adjusted the controls, his gloved hands steady on the wheel. Snowy Montana stretched out beyond the windshield, miles of barren plains dusted white under a heavy gray sky.

Rue sat stiffly in the passenger seat of the SUV, her arms crossed. She'd wanted to drive, but Dacre had overruled her with a simple "I'm driving," in that maddingly calm voice of his.

She stared out the window, her thoughts tangled.

"So," Rue began, breaking the silence. "Do you know them?"

Dacre's eyes stayed on the road, his jaw tightening until she could see the muscles working. "Who?"

Rue rolled her eyes. "Don't play dumb. Jed and Shay."

His pause was just long enough to confirm her suspicion before he finally answered. "I've met them."

"You've met them," she repeated, her voice dripping with disbelief. "And when, exactly, were you planning on telling me that?"

Dacre's grip on the steering wheel didn't waver. "It didn't seem relevant."

Rue laughed, throwing her hands up. "Of course it didn't. Just like everything else about my life, right? You and everyone else deciding what I do and don't need to know. I'm so sick of it, Dacre."

He glanced at her briefly, his expression unreadable. "It's not like that."

"Then what is it like?" she snapped. "Because from where I'm sitting, it feels like you're all in on some big secret about me, and I'm the only one left out."

"Rue–"

"No," she cut him off, turning in her seat to face him. "You don't get to 'Rue' me right now. Do they know about the creatures stalking me?"

Dacre sighed, his shoulders slumping slightly. "Jed knows a lot more than he lets on."

Rue's stomach tightened. "What does that mean?"

Dacre hesitated and it appeared he was choosing his words carefully. "Jed has been hiding from creatures his entire life. You two might have a lot in common. Although, he never had a bodyguard or family to help him."

The vague answer only frustrated her more. Rue turned

back to the window, her reflection glaring back at her. "I just wish people would stop keeping things from me," she muttered.

"You don't understand what's at stake," Dacre said, his voice low and firm.

"No, I don't," Rue shot back, her tone sharp. "Because no one will tell me!"

Silence filled the SUV. Rue's fingers tapped restlessly on her knee as she watched the snow-covered landscape blur past.

After a long pause, Dacre spoke, his voice softer this time. "I'm trying to protect you."

"Well... maybe I don't want your protection. Maybe I just want the truth."

"Be careful what you wish for, Rue," Dacre warned.

Tension simmered in the enclosed space. Rue took out her phone and sent a quick message to Shay to let her know they were coming.

"I need to stop at the WinCo in Lame Deer," Rue said.

DACRE PARKED second spot from the left of the exit of the grocery store.

"I've never liked Lame Deer," he said as he unbuckled his seatbelt.

Rue reached for the door but Dacre grabbed her elbow.

"Don't stray. Keep close to me," he said.

"I think you're the one being paranoid now." Rue slid out of the passenger seat and tucked her hands in her coat pockets. The snow was up to her shins and the wind was wicked, chapping her face in seconds.

Dacre ran around the front of the vehicle and waved for her to follow.

The automatic doors hissed open, letting in a gust of icy

air as Rue and Dacre stepped inside the grocery store. They paused to stomp snow off their boots. The warmth inside was welcome and the faint scent of fresh bread mingled with the chemical tang of cleaning products was familiar. Rue picked up a shopping basket. Dacre grabbed a shopping cart.

Rue scanned the produce section as Dacre pushed the cart beside her, unhurried. "I'm going to grab a few things. But let's get what you need first."

Rue knew where she was going–she'd done this every year since arriving on this plane. She examined a few bunches of carrots, checking for firmness and freshness while Dacre loitered nearby, tossing an assortment of chips, beef jerky, and bottled water into his cart. He also grabbed a bag of organic Gala apples.

Rue grabbed a half-pound worth of the organic carrots that she'd inspected.

"Carrots?" Dacre asked.

"A peace offering," Rue said. "That's all I need. You eat like a teenager," she teased.

"I eat what's easy."

Rue dropped the bundle of carrots into her basket and turned to walk past him, but Dacre was faster. He snatched the basket from her hand and set it inside his cart with an air of finality.

"Hey," she protested, trying to reach for it.

"I'm paying," he said simply, steering toward the checkout area.

Rue groaned, trailing after him. "It's just carrots, Dacre. I can handle it."

He didn't break stride. "You bought my plane ticket."

"It's fine," she argued.

"It's emasculating. I'll need to pay you back."

Rue sighed. "My parents pay that credit card. So it wasn't really me who paid for your ticket. It's not that big of a deal."

"It is to me," he said, glancing over his shoulder.

By the time they reached the cashier, Rue gave up. She stood by as Dacre paid for the carrots, and along with his snacks he added a few protein bars at the last second.

"Since you're already in the habit of spending money unnecessarily, can we at least grab a coffee?" Rue asked, half-joking.

Dacre raised an eyebrow but led her toward the in-store café without a word. Moments later, she stood near the counter with a steaming latte in hand, watching him pay the barista.

"Thanks," she said.

He nodded, his expression unreadable as Rue carried the coffees and he carried the bag of groceries.

Rue braced herself for the wind as the exit door opened. Dacre ran ahead of her and opened the passenger side door for her.

"Thanks," Rue said, brushing snow from her pants.

He closed her door then rounded the SUV and got behind the wheel, taking a package of jerky out of the grocery bag before reaching into the back seat to deposit the bag.

Rue watched as he stretched, her eyes drifting to the inch of skin exposed at his waist. Heat flooded her cheeks when she noticed the dips and planes of muscle. She looked away quickly before passing him his coffee.

"What?" Dacre asked tugging his jacket down and adjusting himself in the seat before starting the vehicle. He turned the heat to high and started the windshield wipers to clear the dusting of snow that had accumulated.

"This is nice," Rue said, blowing on her latte. "Usually I do this alone. Well, I thought I was alone."

Dacre tilted his head slightly. "You don't have to do it alone anymore."

Rue's heart twisted. She glanced down at her cup, tracing

the edge of the lid with her thumb. Anymore... he said that like he'd always be here. She couldn't believe it. He had to move on with his life sometime, he couldn't be her bodyguard forever.

"I guess I'm not used to it," she murmured.

"You'll get used to it." Dacre opened the package of jerky and offered her some.

Rue shook her head but he insisted. "I've only seen you drink coffee and eat air for nearly a day. Eat something. Please."

It was the way he said please that made Rue sigh and take a piece of jerky. "I was holding out for Shay's buttermilk biscuits."

Rue no longer felt like arguing with him. Instead, she let the warmth of the coffee and the strange comfort of his presence settle over her.

Dacre shifted the vehicle into gear and drove away from WinCo, headed for Colstrip. As they passed snowy plains and pine forests, Rue found herself thinking that maybe, just maybe, having Dacre around wasn't so bad after all.

TWENTY-FIVE

It was late afternoon by the time they reached Jed and Shay's ranch. A golden haze was cast over the snow-dusted fields as Dacre pulled into the gravel driveway. The cozy farmhouse stood at the end of the lane, its weathered exterior softened by the warm glow of light spilling from the window.

Rue stepped out of the SUV and her boots crunched against the gravel. Nerves knotted her stomach as she paused for Dacre to join her. It had been a full year since she'd been here last, but she still felt like such a burden showing up and disrupting their lives. She had spent months living with them before the war, when her mother had hidden Rue and her brother to keep them safe. But then... there were faint memories with them, like a half-remembered dream.

Jed emerged from the house first, his broad figure silhouetted against the doorway. His weathered face broke into a smile as she approached, arms outstretched. "Well, look who's come back!"

Rue couldn't help but smile as she moved into his hug, the

scent of woodsmoke and leather clinging to him. "Hi, Uncle Jed."

Shay appeared behind him, her blowtorch-blue hair tucked into a loose braid. "You're back." She embraced Rue with the warmth of a mother, then stepped back, her gaze flicking to Dacre.

"And who's this?" Jed asked, his eyes narrowing.

"This is Dacre," Rue explained. "He's my... bodyguard."

Jed and Shay exchanged an uneasy glance, their smiles faltering for just a moment.

Jed extended a hand to Dacre.

"Nice to meet you," Dacre said politely as they exchanged a firm handshake.

"I know that you know him already," Rue deadpanned.

Jed started to say something but stopped.

"Come on in, both of you," Shay urged. "It's freezing out here."

The warmth of the house and the smell of freshly baked biscuits were inviting, but Rue didn't linger. She took the grocery bag from Dacre and removed the carrots.

"I'll be in the barn," she said, glancing at Dacre, Jed, and Shay. "You three can 'get to know each other.'" She added air quotes.

"I'll go with you," Dacre started to follow.

"She goes alone." Jed grabbed his arm. "She'll be fine out there."

"Nero will watch over her," Shay said.

"Nero?" Dacre asked.

"You know Nero," Shay smiled. "My horse."

Dacre glanced at Shay. Damn, they did know each other. Was everyone in Rue's life lying to her?

The tension in the room didn't escape her as she headed back outside. The crunch of snow echoed across the yard as Rue took a deep breath of cold air. The expanse of sky was massive compared to the campus in Maryland. Rue glanced up and a million stars blinked back at her.

The barn was dimly lit, the earthy smell of hay mingling with the crisp winter air as it seeped through the cracks in the walls. The white horse stood in the middle of the barn. There were no stalls. The horse's coat gleamed faintly, as if lit from within. Her intelligent eyes tracked Rue's every move as she approached, her hands clutching the bundle of carrots she'd brought.

"Hello again," Rue said softly, stepping closer.

The white horse snorted and a puff of warm breath fogged in the cold. Rue held out a carrot and she dipped her head to take it, chewing slowly as she regarded Rue.

The white horse's ear twitched, and her gaze felt unnerving. After a moment, she nodded; a small but deliberate movement that sent a wave of relief through Rue.

"Another year?" the white horse asked with a smooth, feminine voice.

"Yes, please," Rue said, exhaling a breath of relief.

"That is all you want? You could ask for two years. Or even five." She nodded toward the bundle of carrots and Rue fed her another one. "You seem to cause the least disruptions here."

"I'm due to graduate from university this year," Rue said. "I don't know where I'll go after that."

"Will you go home?" the horse asked.

"I'm not sure. I'm not sure where I'll go or what I'll do."

The white horse finished chewing before saying, "Something is wrong." She blinked. "You didn't come alone this time."

Rue stiffened but passed her another carrot. "No. I've had some trouble. Nightmares and shadows following me. My parents hired a bodyguard. He's here. He's at the house with Jed and Shay."

The white horse swallowed, her ears flicking back as though she were trying to listen to the conversation back at the ranch house. "And you trust him?"

Rue hesitated. "I... I think so. But, to tell you the truth, I'm not sure who to trust anymore. I know I'm being paranoid, but it seems like everyone is lying to me. The nightmares are bad. Really bad." Tears welled in Rue's eyes as she passed another carrot to the white horse. "I'm not sure what to think anymore."

The horse's silence stretched long enough to make Rue shift uncomfortably as she fed her three more carrots. Finally, she said, "Jed can tell you what happened. He holds some of the answers you seek."

Rue's brow furrowed. "Jed? What do you mean?"

The white horse inched closer. "Dear, you are not a creature of my realm, but you are hurting, you are lost, and there is something empty within you. I can see it. And no creature deserves to live like that."

"I can't escape the nightmares."

The white horse was gazing into her eyes. "I try not to meddle with creatures of other realms, but this must end or the darkness will never stop coming for you. You deserve peace. You're too young for this."

"I can't remember the time before the war," Rue finally admitted. "There are days missing. Everyone keeps telling me I'm wrong, but I know I'm not. One minute I was standing on the porch at my father's house then the next I was waking up on a battlefield and the war was over."

"Someone took your memories," the white horse said. "Jed was the one."

Rue's veins felt flooded with ice, her heart was racing. After all these years. "He... what?" She searched the white horse's eyes.

The horse nodded. "Ask him. The truth is not something

you can avoid. It's time to reclaim what was taken. I can no longer allow the darkness to chase you on my realm. It must end."

Rue swallowed hard, her thoughts spinning. The horse nosed her hand. Rue passed her the last carrot.

"Nero will be angry I didn't save him any carrots," the white horse said. "But he's the one who chose to take a night run in this weather."

"I'd hoped to see Nero before I went home," Rue said.

"He'll be back. He likes to run."

Rue left the barn, the chill in the air now seeming sharper with her mind buzzing with unanswered questions.

Rue had come to beg for one more year in the white horse's realm and she was given so much more.

Twenty-Six

Rue's footsteps creaked as she walked up the porch steps. She pushed open the front door, the warmth of the house wrapping around her like a blanket. It did little to ease the chill that had settled in her chest. The muffled sound of voices from the kitchen quieted as she stepped inside. Rue shrugged off her coat and hung it up. Then she stepped around the puddles from the snow and kicked off her boots. She moved to the living room where a fire crackled softly in the stone hearth.

She stood there for a moment, staring into the flames, her arms crossed tightly over her chest. Rue's mind raced as the white horse's words echoed in her mind.

"Everything okay?" Shay's voice carried softly from the archway. "Did she agree to another year?"

Rue turned to find Jed and Shay watching her, their expressions a mix of concern and caution. Dacre lingered behind them, his sharp gaze fixed on her as if sensing the storm brewing within.

There was a hint of tremor in Rue's voice when she said, "Uncle Jed, we need to talk."

Jed exchanged a quick glance with Shay before stepping closer. "What's on your mind?"

She took a breath, the words spilling out before she could second-guess herself. "The white horse told me you took my memories. That you're the reason why I can't remember those few days during the war."

Jed's face fell, guilt flickering in his eyes. "Rue–"

"Why?" she demanded, stepping forward. "Why would you do that? What gave you the right?"

Shay placed a gentle hand on Jed's arm, but he didn't look at her. His gaze stayed on Rue. "You don't understand, Rue, you were screaming all night and walking around like a ghost during the day. There was no light in your eyes. No one knew what had happened to you. You were traumatized by something. We did it to protect you."

"Protect me from what? From knowing the truth? You stole pieces of my life, Uncle Jed. Give them back!" Rue's chest tightened in disappointment.

"You were just a kid, Rue. What you went through... it was too much. Your parents thought it was the only way to protect you."

"Reverse whatever you did."

Shay touched Jed's arm again and nodded.

"It was to give you time to heal, to grow up without the weight of it all crushing you," Shay said. "It was never meant to hurt you."

Rue clenched her fists, frustration and unease bubbling to the surface. "Reverse it."

Jed was beginning to look worried. "Reversing the spell might not bring everything back. And if it does, there's no guarantee you'll be the same."

"I've been having nightmares for months," Rue said. "I feel like I'm going crazy. Nothing could be worse than this."

"Jed's right," Dacre interjected, stepping into the room.

His body was tense. "It's dangerous, Rue. You don't know what you're asking for."

She turned to him, her eyes narrowing. "Why do you care? What are you so afraid of me remembering, Dacre? Are you keeping secrets from me too?"

Dacre stiffened, but he didn't answer. His silence only fueled Rue's suspicions. Her heart was thumping against her ribcage.

Shay's voice broke the tension. "Jed, if this is what Rue wants, you need to help her. She's grown now. She can make her own decisions."

Jed hesitated, glancing between Rue and Shay before nodding reluctantly. "Fine. But don't say I didn't warn you."

Jed led Rue to the couch, instructing her to lay down while he gathered a few items from his office. Dacre paced near the doorway, his unease palpable. Rue watched him out of the corner of her eye.

Jed returned with a small bowl of sand. "This might hurt a little," he warned. "And it might take some time for everything to come back. You'll get flashes first, and then the rest will follow."

"I'm ready," Rue said calmly as she closed her eyes.

Jed rubbed his hands together before holding them on each side of her head. Blue light sparked from his fingers like small fireworks. The air felt heavy, charged. Jed closed his eyes and whispered words that sounded like the falling petals of a rose, the gentle lapping of dark lake water in the moonlight, the foggy sunrise on an autumn day. He found the empty memories that tormented Rue's mind and intensified her nightmares: the cold stone of the dungeon, the chains, Hellions, the Demons that had looked at her with hungry eyes, the taste of blood on her tongue, and... a handsome—was it a demon? Jed was no longer sure. Jed called the memories back. He wove the memories together until the void in Rue's mind was full again.

As the spell settled, Rue shifted slightly, her small hand clenching and then relaxing as Jed's magic wove gently around her mind. Rue's breathing relaxed, the creases in her face fading to a peaceful, almost angelic expression.

Jed lowered his hands, the glow around them fading. He took a step back, exhaustion settling into his features.

"It's done," he said quietly, his voice thick with the strain of the magic he'd used. The aura around him pulsed blue light.

Rue's eyes flashed open and she took a deep breath. Images flooded her mind; her heart was racing as fleeting memories rushed in, vivid and disjointed. Rue's head began to ache, a sharp pain radiating behind her eyes. She gripped her temple and whimpered.

"Something is wrong," Dacre growled, stepping closer, but Shay placed a hand on his chest to hold him back.

"She's okay," Shay said. "Give her time."

Shay glanced at Jed and he frowned.

———

LATER, after Rue's headache had dissipated to a nagging sensation, they sat around the kitchen table, the warm light contrasting sharply with the tension in the room.

Rue picked at her plate, her appetite dulled by the headache and fragmented memories swirling in her mind.

Dacre sat across from her, unusually restless. His fingers tapped lightly against the table, his gaze darting toward her and then away again.

Rue broke the silence. "You're all acting strange."

Shay smiled. "We're just concerned."

"About me or what I might remember?" Rue's tone was

sharper than she intended, but she was having a hard time caring at the moment.

Dacre's jaw tightened and he didn't respond.

Jed cleared his throat, breaking the tension. "You'll need to take it easy for a few days. Let your mind process everything. Don't push it too hard."

Rue nodded, though her gaze lingered on Dacre. She couldn't shake the feeling that he knew more than he was letting on and whatever he was hiding was something she desperately needed to uncover.

Twenty-Seven

Rue sat at her desk in the crowded library, books and notes spread out in a meticulous mess. She tapped her pen against her notebook, her mind running through every detail of her proposed independent study project. A sharp stabbing sensation reverberated through her skull. Rue hissed and pressed the heel of her hand against her temple.

Dacre was nearby, leaning against the bookshelves as he read. Rue hated that he looked so relaxed, just leisurely reading while she studied her ass off in effort to finally graduate. She sighed. He was nice to look at though.

Dacre glanced up at her, frowned, and placed the book back on the shelf. He walked quickly to her side and bent, one big hand resting next to her notebook. He smelled good.

"Is it another headache?" he asked.

"Yes," Rue said, rubbing her temple. "I think it's just from caffeine withdrawal."

He straightened. "I can go grab some coffees…"

She missed him being close. "Yes, that would be great."

He nodded before heading to the library café.

Rue's phone buzzed. She dug in her bag and checked the message.

> Professor Camden: I have thirty minutes available now if you want to meet to discuss your project.

> Rue: I'll be there in ten.

> Professor Camden: See you soon.

RUE LOOKED AROUND but didn't see Dacre. She tore a piece of notebook paper out of her notebook and left a note for Dacre on the desk, then closed her notebooks and tucked everything in her backpack. Dacre would be pissed that she left without him, but she didn't want to miss meeting Professor Camden–she'd been waiting for two days and the independent study would get her just enough credits for graduation. She wasn't going to miss this.

———

PROFESSOR CAMDEN'S office smelled like old books and eucalyptus tea. The shelves were lined with artifacts and journals. Rue stood in the doorway, her pulse quick with a mix of nerves and excitement.

"Ah, Miss Clark," Professor Camden said warmly, motioning for her to sit. "I got your email. You're interested in an independent study for your final semester."

Rue nodded, setting her proposal on his desk. "Yes. I want to focus on Fifteenth century Nephilim in the Allegany mountains and how they influenced modern mythology."

Professor Camden choked on his water. He wiped droplets from his sweater before adjusting his glasses. "Ambitious. You must know that a topic such as this is bridging on the occult. It would be a lot of work to bring it together." He raised an eyebrow as he skimmed the paper Rue had pushed across his desk. "Are you sure you have the time to commit to this while keeping up with your current course work?"

Rue straightened in her chair. "I've been planning my schedule meticulously. I'll make it work."

Professor Camden asked her more questions about her theories on the Nephilim and her interest in the subject. She didn't tell him that she knew one. But she had plenty of questions about his history because as far as she knew Uncle Jed was the only one in existence.

The conversation turned into how well she'd done the last semester and how she'd excelled in the lab.

Professor Camden leaned back in his chair, studying her. "Very well. Let's begin with weekly meetings to review your progress. And I'll expect a detailed outline by the end of next week. I might have some colleagues you could speak with as well. Let me reach out to them and see what I can do."

"Thank you, Professor. I won't let you down." Rue shook his hand and left his office clutching the proposal to her chest.

Rue glanced out the window of the quiet corridor and noticed it was dark outside. Shit. She cursed daylight savings time and checked her phone. Unease settled in her stomach as she shoved the proposal in her bag and ran down the winding stairs of the lecture hall. She wasn't anticipating so much time passing. She was sure the meeting ran over.

As she reached the front door of the lecture hall, a dark figure was pacing. Footsteps echoed on the tile floor. Dacre glanced up, his expression a mix of relief and frustration.

"You disappeared," he said, crossing his arms.

"I left a note on the desk. I was meeting with my professor. I got approval for an independent study." Rue smiled wide.

"Congratulations," Dacre replied, keeping distance between them.

"What's wrong?" Rue asked.

"You're already taking on too much," he said. "You're running yourself into the ground. Jed said that you need to rest."

"I'm fine," Rue snapped, adjusting her bag. "I don't need this. My studies are the only thing that feel normal right now."

Dacre stepped closer, taking the heavy bag off her shoulder, and slinging it over his own. "You're not invincible, Rue. Pushing yourself like this won't help."

The headache returned, sharp and stealing her breath for an instant. She needed caffeine. That seemed to be the only thing that helped.

"Hey," she realized, "where's the coffees?"

"I drank them," he said flatly.

"You drank both?"

"I had to wait for you and I didn't think you'd want cold coffee."

Rue made a face of disgust. "Definitely not."

———

THE CAMPUS WAS quiet as Rue and Dacre walked back to the apartment. He kept her bag slung over his shoulder.

The air was crisp, the faint scent of pine lingering. Dacre's hand brushed hers and warmth slid up her arm.

Rue was trying to think of something to say but then a prickling sensation crawled up the back of her neck.

She turned slowly, scanning the dimly lit sidewalk path. Shadows stretched across the pavement unnaturally, pooling together and shifting. Her breath hitched.

"Not again," she whispered.

A dark shape lunged at her.

Rue scrambled back; something grabbed her leg, twisted her ankle, and she tripped and fell. Rue's body skidded, her hands burning as they scraped across the sidewalk, then her cheek smashed against the concrete. She rolled to the side, her heart racing as the shadow demon's claws raked the air where she had been standing moments before. A blur of motion came between them.

"Get back," Dacre shouted, his voice cutting through the chaos.

Rue stumbled to her knees, grabbed her bag off the ground, and scooted away.

Dacre lunged, driving a metallic blade into the shadow's core. The creature dissolved into a wisp of black smoke, leaving the street eerily silent.

Dacre turned to her, his face pale and tight with concern. "You're hurt."

Rue looked down at her bloody hands. There was a gash on her leg and she was bleeding through her jeans. The adrenaline kept the pain at bay, but now her whole body hurt. Before she could protest, Dacre scooped her up into his arms.

"I'm fine, I can walk," she said, holding back the bile that was crawling up her throat. This was her fault.

"No," he grumbled.

The walk to the apartment wasn't more than a few blocks. Dacre held her tight against his chest. Rue was looking up at the side of his face.

"You shouldn't grind your teeth," she said.

He glanced at her, shadows dancing across his face.

Rue's eyes widened and the motion stopped.

"It was reckless," Dacre muttered, his voice sharp. "We shouldn't be walking out here at night."

"I'm sorry," Rue said. "I didn't think I'd be so late. The meeting was really important."

"You're not safe, Rue." Dacre's voice sounded pained. "They're still hunting you. When I couldn't find you in the library earlier, I nearly lost control." He blinked slowly and Rue was impressed with how quickly he walked while carrying her. He wasn't even out of breath. Of course, he was much larger and stronger. She moved her hand against his shoulder and gazed at his face while he spoke.

He looked away from her. "You're bleeding."

She held up her hand. "I have a few cuts but my coat prevented a lot."

Dacre was looking at the cut on her leg. "That fucking monster was too close." His grip tightened on her.

"You got it," she reminded him.

"But what if I don't next time?" he looked down at her, eyes dark. Something shifted in the air and Rue held her breath. She could tell he was struggling but she wasn't sure of what. So, she did the only thing that made sense. She looked up at the night sky.

"What are you looking at?" he asked.

"The stars," she sighed. "The sky is filled with them."

"You do that a lot."

"It's just a little thing that reminds me that I am... part of something bigger," she said softly. "No matter how small I feel, or how out of place... the stars are always there. Constant. Watching. Like they've been waiting for me to figure it out."

Dacre glanced down at her, her face illuminated by the faint silver glow of the night sky. "Figure out what?"

"That maybe I do belong here. Somewhere," she murmured, her voice almost lost to the stillness. "Even if I don't know where that is yet."

Dacre tightened his grip on her, his gaze flickering between her and the expanse of stars above.

"You'll find it," he said firmly.

Rue tilted her head toward him, the faintest smile tugging at her lips. "I'd like to think that maybe I already have, here on the Earthen plane."

Dacre carried Rue up the stairs to the apartment, set her on her feet just long enough for her to unlock the door, then he lifted her again and shoved open the door with his shoulder, carrying her inside and into the bathroom.

Lucipurr meowed, running after them.

"Get the blood washed off you," he said.

Rue hesitated.

"Do you need help?" he glanced down the length of her.

"No." She forced a smile and held on to the door for support. "I don't need help."

"I'll bring you some clothes."

DACRE STEPPED into Rue's room, the faint scent of lavender lingering in the air. It was tidy; her bed neatly made, books stacked on the nightstand, and a small, purring cat curled up on a pillow. Lucipurr blinked at him lazily but didn't bother moving.

"Alright," Dacre muttered to himself, stepping toward the dresser. "Clothes. Easy enough."

He pulled open the top drawer, and his movements halted as his brain short-circuited.

Underwear.

Not just underwear, but *her* underwear—delicate fabrics in a variety of colors and styles, folded neatly as though mocking him.

"What the fuck," he muttered under his breath, his face heating. Why was this such a big deal? It shouldn't have been. They were just... clothes. Practical, everyday items. Yet the sight of them made his stomach twist in ways he wasn't prepared for.

The sound of the shower turning on down the hallway jolted him back to reality. She was waiting. She was injured. She needed clothes. He closed the drawer and opened the next one, determined to avoid that particular problem.

The second drawer offered him salvation: a stack of over-sized T-shirts and a few pairs of shorts. Simple, easy, non-controversial. Grabbing a shirt and shorts, he turned back toward the door—but his feet didn't move.

He glanced at the dresser again, the thought gnawing at him. Did she need underwear? She probably did. Blood had soaked through most of her clothes; she couldn't exactly go without.

But picking *that* out for her?

"Nope," he muttered, trying to banish the thought, but his eyes betrayed him, sliding back to the drawer. *It's not that big of a deal. Just grab something and go.*

He stood frozen, staring at the neatly folded contents like they were cursed. Rue's voice echoed faintly in his head, probably calling him an idiot for being so flustered over something so mundane.

"Okay, just... pick one," he whispered to himself, reaching tentatively toward the drawer. His hand hovered over a black pair, then shifted to a plain white one. *No, too boring. Maybe the blue one? Or the—*

Lucipurr let out a low meow, startling him so badly that he jerked his hand back like he'd touched a hot stove.

"This is insane," Dacre muttered, slamming the drawer shut. "She'll deal with it."

Grabbing the shirt and shorts, he strode out of the room, determined to pretend this moment never happened.

When he reached the bathroom, he knocked on the door. "Rue? I've got clothes for you." His voice sounded wrong.

"Just leave them outside," she called back, her voice muffled by the sound of running water.

He set the folded clothes on the floor, retreating quickly before the door opened. As he walked away, his mind kept circling back to that drawer and the completely unnecessary dilemma it had created.

"Never again," he muttered under his breath.

———

RUE SAT on the edge of her bed, leg outstretched and gash exposed. Dacre knelt in front of her, wrapping a fresh bandage around her calf. His hands were steady, but his entire body was strung tight.

The room was dimly lit, the soft glow of the bedside lamp casting warm shadows on the walls. Lucipurr curled up at the foot of the bed, watching with half-lidded eyes, monitoring Dacre's every move.

"You don't have to keep changing it," Rue said softly. "It's not that bad."

"It's bleeding through too quickly," Dacre muttered, not looking at her. He tore the end of the bandage and secured it, then stood abruptly, heading for the bathroom to grab another roll.

When he returned, Rue frowned. "You've already changed it twice. Are you okay?"

Dacre avoided her gaze, focusing instead on tightening the bandage. "It's fine. Just making sure it doesn't get infected. Maybe I should get you to a doctor?"

Rue shook her head, she didn't want to get mixed up in human medicine. If the bleeding didn't stop, she'd call her mother and get a healer sent. Rue's shoulders sagged, guilt mixing with fatigue. "I didn't mean to worry you."

Dacre sighed, his expression softening. "Just... rest, Rue. Let me handle things for once."

"You must really be second guessing taking this job now, huh?" she laughed lightly.

"No. I'm not."

Rue tilted her head, studying him. There was a tension, a stiffness that belied his usual calm. His jaw clenched every time he glanced at her wound, and he seemed to hold his breath as he worked.

"It's the blood, isn't it?" she asked, her voice quiet.

Dacre froze. "Don't worry about it."

"No, seriously," Rue pressed. "Why does my blood bother you?"

He finished the bandage and leaned back on his heels, finally meeting her eyes. There was something guarded there, like a door closing just as she tried to peek through. "It's not important."

Rue narrowed her eyes. "If it's not important, why are you acting like this? Is it just my blood, or does anyone else's bother you?"

Dacre hesitated, and the silence stretched thin between them. Finally, he exhaled a heavy breath. "Just yours."

Her heart ticked up a few beaths. "Why?"

He stood abruptly, moving to the small kitchen without answering.

Rue watched him, frustration bubbling up. The freezer door opened, the microwave turned on, and soon the scent of pizza filled the air.

Moments later, he handed her the Hedwig mug filled with coffee, the steam curling up in lazy spirals. "Drink this," he said, his voice quieter now.

"Stop avoiding the question," Rue said, cradling the mug but not drinking.

Dacre ran a hand through is hair, his composure cracking.

"I don't think it's a good time to talk about why your blood affects me."

The evasiveness only fueled her frustration, but before she could press him further, a sharp pain shot through her skull. She gasped, clutching her head, the mug slipping from her hands and landing on the floor with a crash.

"Rue!" Dacre was at her side in an instant, his hands on her shoulders. He was close, searching her eyes.

"I... I'm fine," she said through gritted teeth, though the pain was blinding. Images flashed behind her eyes–fragments of memories she didn't remember.

A dark forest. Red eyes glowing in the dungeon. A voice whispering her name, low and guttural.

Her breathing quickened as more images flooded in. The taste of blood, thick and metallic. Demons surrounding her and forcing her to drink. A searing pain that made her scream.

"Rue, talk to me," Dacre's voice broke through the chaos. "What's happening?"

She blinked, her vision swimming as the headache began to subside. "Memories," she whispered. "I think... I think I'm remembering."

Dacre's grip on her shoulders tightened ever so slightly. "What do you remember?"

Rue slammed her eyes closed and took deep breaths, praying for it to pass.

"Did the coffee cup break?" Rue asked. "I think it broke."

The sound of ceramic being piled together filled the room.

"It's broken isn't it?" Rue asked. Sadness filling her voice.

"Yes."

"Damn, that was my favorite coffee cup." Tears surged to the corners of her eyes.

"I know," Dacre said softly as he cleaned up the mess. He left the room and got a towel to clean up the spilled coffee. When he was done, he crouched next to her again. "You need to rest," Dacre said firmly, guiding her to lie back against the pillows.

She let him, too drained to argue. As he adjusted the covers over her, she caught the flicker of something in his eyes: guilt, fear... maybe both.

"I don't want to sleep," she murmured, her voice weak. "What if the nightmares come back?"

"I'll be here," Dacre promised as he kneeled on the floor next to her. "I won't leave. Promise."

Rue didn't argue. She closed her eyes, letting herself drift to sleep.

TWENTY-EIGHT

RUE ADJUSTED HER NOTEBOOK ON THE DESK AND stared at the whiteboard as her professor's voice droned in the background. The lecture hall buzzed faintly with the shuffling of papers and the occasional cough. Rue's focus was on the slide topic: Ancient rituals and their modern interpretations.

"...many cultures used blood as a symbol of life, sacrifice, and power. Rituals involving blood often signified a bond between the mortal and the divine, a concept that persists in some myths even today," Professor Camden explained, gesturing toward a slide of an ancient, blood-stained altar.

The image jolted something loose in Rue's mind. Her pen slipped from her fingers and clattered to the desk. She blinked, her surroundings dimming as a memory clawed its way to the surface. A black mansion, sharp teeth, demons surrounding her, goblets of blood.

"Her soul has value. We could use her to cultivate the skin trades," the Demon offered. "We lost many willing women during the transition of power."

The voice was familiar.

"Miss Clark, are you alright?" Professor Camden's voice snapped her back to reality.

Rue jerked upright, realizing the professor was looking directly at her. Several heads turned in her direction, including Evelyn's.

"I–uh–sorry, yes. Just... a headache," Rue stammered, forcing a weak smile.

The professor nodded and continued, but Rue felt her pulse pounding in her ears. She hastily gathered her notebook and pen, determined to escape when the lecture ended.

———

"ARE YOU OKAY?" Evelyn grabbed her arm.

"I'm fine. Just a headache." Rue adjusted her bag.

"You've been having a lot of headaches," Evelyn said as she led Rue out of the lecture hall, concern creasing her face.

"Rue?"

She froze mid-step at the sound of his voice. Dacre was leaning casually against a pillar in the hallway, his dark eyes scanning her like he already knew something was wrong.

Evelyn led Rue to him.

"She said she has a headache," Evelyn announced to Dacre. "She drifted off in class."

"Tattle-tale," Rue muttered under her breath, shooting Evelyn a look. "I'm fine."

"I don't think you are." Evelyn was watching her closely. "You're pale. Like, extra pale today."

Rue scowled. "It's called lighting, Ev. It's fluorescent and it hates me."

"What happened?" Dacre asked, his focus never wavering from Rue.

"I gotta run to my next class," Evelyn said before Rue

could answer. "Will you take her home, hot-bodyguard? Maybe get her some soup or something?"

"Lord," Rue rolled her eyes. "I'm fine."

Evelyn was already walking away, throwing a quick wave over her shoulder. "Take care of her!"

Rue turned to Dacre, narrowing her eyes. "You're not getting me soup."

"I wasn't planning on it," he said dryly. He took a step closer, his towering presence both comforting and maddening. "But I am walking you home."

"I don't need to go home," Rue snapped, trying to side-step him. "I have to get to my English class."

Dacre caught her arm with surprising gentleness, tucking it under his. "You're pale. You're shaking. And you're deflecting like your life depends on it. Was it a memory?"

Rue's lips pressed into a thin line. "It doesn't matter."

"It matters." His tone was firm. "Talk to me."

Rue pulled her arm free, clutching her bag tightly against her chest like it could shield her from his questions. "You're not my therapist, Dacre. I don't need to talk, I just need space to process what I saw."

Dacre exhaled slowly, clearly frustrated. "Fine. But I'm taking you home."

THE APARTMENT WAS SILENT, except for the low volume of the television. Rue curled up on the couch with a textbook, trying to catch up on what she'd missed after leaving campus early. She tried to push away the nagging feeling of unease that had lingered since her earlier headache. Her stomach was aching and she wondered if maybe she just needed to eat something since all she'd had was coffee on an empty stomach.

Dacre had gone downstairs to shower and grab a change of

clothes. She told herself she'd be fine for the ten minutes he'd be gone.

The shadows in the corners of the room seemed darker tonight, deeper somehow. Pitch-black. Rue shifted uncomfortably and glanced at the windows. She'd already double checked the locks. She reached for her phone, thinking about texting her mother.

The lamp on the table beside her flickered once. Lucipurr meowed, concerned. His ears flattened and his brow furrowed. The lamp flickered again, then went out.

Rue's breath caught. The temperature dropped. The shadows twisted unnaturally, pulling together into a mass that oozed malice.

A shape began to form; long, clawed arms and a head too misshapen to belong to anything mortal. The demon's eyes glowed like embers as it crawled toward her, the air thick with sulfur and decay.

Rue bolted to her feet, her heart hammering against her ribs. "Not again," she whispered, grabbing Lucipurr off the couch and backing away.

The kitten hissed.

The demon lunged, its claws scraping against the floor as it backed her into a corner. Rue grabbed the lamp and hurled it. The lamp shattered against its chest and did nothing to slow its approach.

Rue stumbled, her back hitting the wall. The demon loomed closer, its claws inches from her face.

"Dacre!" she screamed, her voice cracking with panic.

The door burst open, splinters flying, and Dacre was there. In a blur of movement he tackled the demon away from her. They rolled across the floor, a tangle of limbs and shadows. Dacre had a blade, the metal flashing as he struck out. The demon was fast, its claws slashing at his side.

"Bastard!" Dacre barked, his voice edged with pain.

Rue pressed herself against the wall, her knees trembling.

Dacre's movements were precise as he fought... desperate. The demon let out an ear-piercing screech, slamming Dacre into the coffee table.

"Dacre!" Rue cried out, grabbing a heavy textbook off the shelf near her and throwing it at the demon.

The distraction gave Dacre the opening he needed. With a roar, he drove his blade into the demon's chest. Shadows exploded outward, dissipating like smoke as the demon let out a final shriek and dissolved.

Dacre's ragged breathing echoed in the apartment. He collapsed to his knees, clutching his side where blood was seeping through his shirt.

A small meow came from the kitchen counter where Lucipurr sat like a potato, having watched the whole ruckus; eyes wide, but never moving a muscle, like he trusted his people to take care of the danger.

Rue rushed over to Dacre, her fear momentarily replaced by concern. "You're hurt."

"It's fine," he said through gritted teeth, but he winced as she helped him to his feet and guided him to the couch.

"Stay still," she ordered, rushing to grab the first aid kit from the bathroom. "I've never used this thing so many times as I have these past few weeks," she muttered.

When she returned, Dacre was leaning back against the couch cushions, his face pale, his shirt soaked with blood. Rue settled next to him, tearing open the kit. "This is not fine. You're bleeding everywhere."

Rue grabbed the hem of his shirt and lifted. She sucked in a breath, her gaze shifting from his fit abdomen to the cut across his ribs. She felt her face flame red. He was watching her closely.

Rue pressed a gauze to his injury and the smell hit her– rich, coppery, and oddly sweet. Her throat tightened, and an ache bloomed deep inside her center. Rue swallowed hard, her hands trembling.

"Rue?" Dacre's voice broke through her haze.

"I'm fine," she said quickly, focusing on cleaning the deep cut. But as she worked, flashes of memory surged to the surface... *teeth sinking into soft skin, a rush of warmth...*

Her breath hitched.

"What is it?" Dacre's gaze was piercing.

Rue shook her head, trying to push the memory back. "Nothing. Just hold still."

"You're shaking."

"You're shaking!" she snapped.

Dacre's expression softened, but he stayed quiet as she finished dressing the cut. When she leaned back, her face was pale, her hands clutching the bloodied cloth like a lifeline. Dacre leaned forward with a groan and tugged his shirt off.

"Rue," he said, his voice coaxing. "You remembered something?"

She nodded slowly, her voice barely a whisper. "I... I think I bit someone when I was younger." Fingertips went to her lips absently. "But I don't know why."

He looked like he was about to say something, but instead, "It was probably nothing," he said.

She was sitting close to him, their thighs pressed tightly against each other.

Rue's fingertips lingered at her lips. She was grasping for the memory but fragments that had surfaced were jagged and incomplete. She forced her focus on Dacre.

"It wasn't nothing," she murmured. "You know something about it, don't you?" Her gaze locked on his, searching for answers.

Dacre's jaw flexed, and for a moment he didn't respond. Instead, he took the bloodied gauze from her trembling hands, rolled it into his torn shirt, and leaned back against the couch with a wince. The movement drew her eyes to the defined planes of his chest, partially obscured by his bruised and bloodied torso.

"It's just a scratch," he said, catching her glance and smirking despite the obvious pain. "Barely even hurts."

"Barely?" Rue shot back, arching an eyebrow. "You're lucky you're still breathing. That thing was going to rip you apart."

"Me?" He grinned, teasing. "I had it handled. You're the one throwing textbooks at demons."

A startled laugh escaped her, cutting through the tension. "Hey, those textbooks are expensive and multi-purpose. Can't return it now though." She felt strange that she... missed the bloodied gauze... or something.

His smirk widened, the tension in his face easing for a moment. But when his eyes returned to hers, there was a seriousness that sent warmth up her spine. "You're tougher than I thought, little princess."

Rue's breath caught. The way he looked at her, like she was something fragile but strong, made her chest tighten.

She reached out without thinking, her fingers brushing against his arm. "You're stronger than you look too," she said softly.

"I don't know," he said with a teasing lilt. "I'm pretty sure I look strong."

She rolled her eyes, but her lips twitched into a smile. "You're impossible."

His grin faded, softened. Rue's heart skipped a beat. His hand reached up, tucking a stray strand of hair behind her ear.

"Not impossible," he said, his voice lower now. "Just stubborn."

The air between them shifted, thickened with tension. Rue's gaze flicked to his lips, and for a brief second she forgot how to breathe.

Before she could second-guess herself, Dacre leaned in, closing the space between them. His lips brushed hers, tentative at first, as if testing the waters. Rue froze, her mind spinning. But then his lips parted, tongue darting out and tracing her lips. The warmth of his mouth began melting away her hesitation.

He gripped her hips, effortlessly lifting and dragging her into his lap. She leaned into him, her hands finding their way to his shoulders, careful to avoid his injured ribs. The kiss deepened, a mix of urgency and tenderness. Her fingers stretched into his dark hair. He tasted like cinnamon. She stretched against his chest. He was warm and solid and she couldn't get enough.

When they finally broke apart, Rue's cheeks were flushed, her breathing uneven. Dacre rested his forehead against hers, his hand still cradling her jaw.

"That was..." Rue searched for words.

"Unexpected?" he offered, voice rough.

Rue nodded, biting her lip as she tried to hide her grin. "Yeah. But not unwelcome."

Dacre chuckled softly, wincing as the movement tugged at his wound. "Good to know."

Rue pulled back, frowning. "You're still hurt. You shouldn't–"

"I'm fine," he interrupted, looking disappointed as she slid off his lap. "It's worth the pain."

Rue shook her head; she had to look away from him since he was all half-lidded eyes and lazy smile and... shirtless. Her fingertips tingled from the feel of his naked skin. "You're ridiculous." A thought cooled her off. "I'm sorry. My parents hired you to keep me safe, not this." She was suddenly embarrassed. This was more than just a quick, sweet kiss at a costume party. She moved away from him and bristled.

"Don't," Dacre warned.

Rue gazed down at him, standing near the arm of the couch. "What?"

"Don't dismiss it like it was nothing."

Rue searched his face for clarification. "I just didn't want you to get in trouble for–"

A sharp pain reverberated in her skull. Rue hissed and gripped her temples.

Lucipurr, who had hidden when he saw them kissing, returned to mew with concern.

"Ah," Rue cried, her face twisting in pain.

TWENTY-NINE

"No!" she gasped, twisting as hard as she could. "Let me go!"

She kicked him, trying to break free but he barely flinched, his hold unyielding. The door loomed closer and dread settled in her gut. He was going to take her to the dungeon whether she wanted it or not. And then... bile rose in her throat.

Rue thrashed harder.

"Stop fighting," he said, his voice growing darker, the amusement fading. "It's over, princess. You belong to us now. Until Lucifer decides to kill you."

Rue's chest tightened with dread as the Demon walked closer to the door, her feet dangling as he held her against his chest with one strong arm across her middle.

RUE WOKE SCREAMING from her nightmare. Her eyes flashed open, heart pounding and the edges of her vision blurred. There was a shadow in the doorway. He was here, now. Ready to kill her. She screamed louder, scrambling backward against the headboard until until her vision cleared and she recognized the face staring back at her.

He was kneeling next to the bed. "It's a nightmare," he soothed.

Her breaths came in ragged gasps and her hands clutched the blanket like a lifeline. "I–I thought..." she stammered, the words choking off as tears welled up.

"It's okay," Dacre said. "You're safe." He placed a steady hand on her arm and her skin warmed.

Rue closed her eyes, willing her heartbeat to slow, the remnants of the nightmare clawing at the edges of her mind. "I can still feel it," she whispered. "They were going to kill me. I tried to fight back but I didn't stand a chance."

Dacre shifted closer. "It's not real, Rue," he said gently. "Not right now. They can't hurt you here."

Rue searched his dark eyes. "Are you sure?"

He nodded.

For a long moment, neither of them moved. The room was heavy with silence, broken only by the sound of Lucipurr's purring at the foot of the bed.

"I can't go back to sleep," she finally admitted, her voice small.

"Then don't." Dacre offered her a hand. "Come on."

Minutes later they sat side by side on the porch roof, wrapped in blankets. A thermos of coffee sat between them, steam curling up into the darkness. The city lights of nearby Baltimore twinkled faintly on the horizon, but above them, the stars spread out in an endless tapestry.

Rue cradled her mug, the warmth soothing her trembling hands. "I think the nightmares are memories," she admitted, her voice barely above a whisper.

Dacre glanced at her, his profile illuminated by the faint glow of the stars. "Why do you think that?"

"Lucifer is in them. My parents defeated him in the war."

She cleared her throat. "I think... that's what they won't tell me. I can't remember days before and during the war." She looked up and took a sip of the coffee. "What if he had me? What if he did *something* to me?"

Dacre was silent.

Rue cradled her mug, the warmth soothing her trembling hands. "I don't think I've ever been so scared," she admitted, her voice barely above a whisper.

Dacre glanced at her, his profile striking in the night lighting. "You're safe now."

"For now." She nodded in agreement. "Every time I think the paranoia is gone and I stop feeling like I'm being followed, another shadow demon pulls me back into the chaos. The headaches are getting worse. The nightmares..." She shook her head then rubbed her face.

Dacre didn't respond immediately. Instead, he reached out and adjusted the blanket draped over her shoulders. "Normal is overrated," he said with a smirk but his tone carried a note of sincerity. "It doesn't run in your family."

Rue turned to him, her eyes searching his face. "I'm sure there's plenty you'd rather be doing with your life than following me around."

He shrugged. "Not really. You're not so bad." He sipped at his mug.

They sat in silence for a while, watching the stars shift in the sky. As the horizon began to lighten, signaling the approach of dawn, Rue felt a pang of gratitude for Dacre's quiet steadiness.

"Thank you," she said suddenly, her voice cutting through the stillness.

Dacre looked at her, one brow raised in question.

"For being here," she clarified. "For... all of this."

He smiled faintly, his usual guarded expression softening. "Always, Rue."

The sunrise painted the sky in hues of gold and pink as they climbed through the hallway window to get back inside. Rue took a deep breath. "I should get ready," she said, glancing at the clock.

"Midterms?" Dacre asked knowingly.

Rue groaned. "Midterms," she confirmed.

He grinned. "You'll crush them. I won't let any more shadow demons interrupt your study sessions."

Rue disappeared into her room to prepare for her lecture and lab.

Dacre lingered in the hallway, a frown settling over his face.

She was remembering.

THIRTY

The Demon set Rue on her feet and she made another attempt to flee, rushing to the side and out of their reach.

A giant Hellion stood in the doorway and roared like a boar. "To the dungeons!" The Hellion walked toward Rue; oily skin, horns protruding from its mouth, strange hair like slithering snakes. Rue backstepped, searching for a way to escape the monster. Her mother told stories about the Hellions of Lucifer's time. They looked worse in real life. The Hellion lunged at her, grabbing her by the hair. Rue screamed. The Hellion slapped her so hard it knocked her unconscious. Rue's body slumped, nearly lifeless.

———

Rue groaned in her sleep, hands moving to the side of her head. Her eyes flicked open and she was relieved that her throat wasn't sore from screaming.

Lucipurr was licking her arm, his tiny rough tongue scraping her.

"Are you hungry, buddy?" she asked, reaching over to scratch between his ears.

The kitten stopped licking and was staring at her.

"What's wrong?"

She glanced at her arm and noticed blood smeared across her skin. She touched fingertips to her nose and felt wetness. With a quick intake of breath, Rue sat up. Her whole body was shaking, her stomach twisting.

"Dacre!" she shouted.

But then her eyes rolled into the back of her head and she collapsed on the bed, shaking.

———

SHE SHIVERED under the blanket and curled into a tighter ball. Rue's stomach growled. It made her think of the kitten and she wondered if Lucipurr was missing her. She hoped someone was feeding him. And cuddling him after the jerk who dragged her into that hole had tossed Lucipurr through the air like a stuffed animal. Rue wanted to go home. She sniffed back tears, noticed the blanket covering her smelled slightly familiar. A little bit like brimstone and pine.

The door opened; its hinges squealed and echoed against stone walls. Rue scrambled to the corner of the cot and in the light she noticed she hadn't been covered with a blanket, but a suitcoat. She rubbed a finger over the smooth fabric. Strange.

"Get up," the handsome Demon was back, dressed in black slacks and a black button down with the sleeves rolled up to just below his elbows.

Rue's eyes were wide as she stared at him. "I want to go home. Now."

The Demon chuckled. "Not today."

"My mother will come for me. She will kill you."

The Demon took a calming breath and waved toward the door. "Until she shows, we have things to do today."

Rue stared. The Demon's black hair was tousled, and his sharp features were unnervingly attractive. His dark eyes met hers with an unsettling calmness, betraying nothing of what he might be thinking. Dressed the way he was, he looked out of place in the grim dungeon, like a polished predator in a cage of filth. Rue was suddenly self-conscious.

"Get up," he urged, voice low and smooth but without warmth. "It's time to go."

"No," Rue rasped, fear lacing her voice.

"You're to be presented," Dacre replied, his gaze flicking over her with a hint of disdain. "The Black Mansion awaits."

Rue's heart sank as she scrambled to her feet. There was a sinking feeling in her gut. She didn't want to be left alone in the dungeon with the door open. She knew the creatures that had been left to rot behind these doors, she'd listened to their guttural cries for hours throughout the night.

———

"WAKE UP," a familiar voice broke through the haze. Something cold and wet pressed against her forehead.

Rue moaned, her stomach twisting into tighter knots.

"Rue." The voice again. It was familiar, grounding. Her eyes fluttered open, but the world around her was a blur. She blinked hard, trying to focus.

Dacre's face came into view, his expression taut with worry. His dark eyes scanned her face.

"Tell me what you need," he said, voice wary.

Rue moaned, unable to form words. The pressure in her head was unbearable, as though her memories were clawing their way to the surface, ripping through her with every breath.

"You're bleeding," Dacre said. He coughed, his voice muffled. "Wake up, Rue. Wake up now."

His hands gripped her shoulders, shaking her lightly. The motion sent a fresh spike of pain through her skull.

"No," she whimpered, her voice barely audible. "It hurts. It hurts so much."

———

Rue glanced out the window. The Black Mansion appeared as dark and foreboding as its name suggested.

The Demon opened her door and held out a palm to help her down.

Rue steadied her hands on the door and seat and jumped, ignoring him. She landed on two feet and then took a step away from the Demon. She smoothed dirty hands over her T-shirt and glanced at her socked feet. The driveway was crushed stone, sharp and glossy. It pressed through her socks threatening to cut her feet.

The Demon took notice and his eyebrow rose in offering to carry her across the sharp stones.

"Don't touch me," Rue warned.

The halls of the Black Mansion were cold and grand, every inch of the place dripping with malevolent elegance. It smelled like freshly cut wood and Rue noticed some rooms were being painted in black and silver. Elaborate wall paper was being hung, embellished with a matte black design. She decided the décor was actually pretty and if she were in a different predicament, she might have enjoyed it.

When they entered the main chamber, Rue's breath hitched. It was filled with Demons, all of them watching her with gleaming, predatory eyes. The room was lit by the eerie glow of fire pits casting flickering shadows on their sharp teeth, horns, and scaled skin. The Demons sat on dark elaborately carved chairs and lounges, like cruel kings.

The handsome Demon stood at her side, his presence both a shield and a threat. He led her toward the center of the room, where all eyes fell upon the small princess with eyes unlike her mother's and long dark hair.

"One moment," the Demon said as he walked out, leaving her alone.

Rue swallowed hard. She glanced around the room searching for a weapon or a way out.

"She doesn't look like much," one Demon sneered, his crimson eyes narrowing as he leaned forward. "So small and fragile."

"No wings. Too human," another added, a smirk tugging at gruesome lips.

Rue went stiff, her heart pounding in her chest. She knew they could sense her fear. They were feeding off it, saying terrible things to make her scared. Rue couldn't slow her heart beat and calm herself.

"She won't last long on the bargaining table," the first Demon laughed. "Too weak."

"Let's see what she's made of," a third Demon growled, stepping forward with a goblet in hand. The liquid inside was thick and red.

"No," Rue whispered, her stomach churning as she recoiled. She didn't drink blood; she was too young to need it.

"Drink," the Demon commanded, his voice a growl of amusement. "It'll make you stronger."

Rue backed away, but the Demon was too fast. He grabbed her arm and shoved the goblet to her lips. Rue gagged as the metallic taste filled her mouth, the blood spilling down her throat. She choked and sputtered, spraying droplets of blood on the grotesque Demon's face.

The other Demons laughed, taunting. Tears blurred Rue's eyes as she tried to spit out the blood coating her mouth.

"Enough!" The handsome Demon in the suit had returned, his face darkened with fury, fists clenched at his sides. His voice cut through the laughter like a blade.

———

Rue smelled fresh coffee. Not just regular though; it was pumpkin spice and smelled divine. Rue blinked, trying to open her heavy eyelids but it was so hard. They felt glued shut. Her head ached. Something heavy was leaning against the base of her neck. She reached and felt an ice pack.

"You have a fever," Dacre said.

"I... I need to get to class," Rue muttered. "I have an exam today."

"You're not going to class," Dacre said firmly.

———

The room fell silent as all eyes turned to him. He stepped forward, cold gaze locking onto the Demon who'd forced Rue to drink the blood.

"You don't touch what belongs to me," Dacre said, his voice dangerously low.

The offending demon raised an eyebrow, unfazed. "Your little pet?" he mocked. "She's not going to last long anyway. What does it matter?"

Dacre's anger flared, but before he could speak, another Demon chuckled from the corner of the room. "He always did have a soft spot for the fragile ones," he said slyly. "Maybe she reminds him of-"

"Shut your mouth," Dacre growled, stepping toward the one in the corner, hands curling into fists.

The Demon's smirk widened. "I wonder if she knows your name yet," he taunted, glancing at Rue. "Has he told you, little lost princess? Does she know who you really are?"

Rue's head spun as the Demon's words set in. His name. Dacre hadn't wanted her to know. She didn't recognize him or his name.

Dacre's eyes burned with fury, his jaw clenched. He took one menacing step toward the Demon, and for a moment, it looked like he would strike. The Demon's eyes went wide and its goblet fell to the floor, staining the tile in thick red blood.

Dacre turned sharply on his heel, and grabbed Rue's arm. "Come on," he hissed through clenched teeth.

Rue stumbled after Dacre as he dragged her from the room, her mind reeling. What had that Demon seen on Dacre's face? It was enough to scare him straight. Rue couldn't see a thing with Dacre's back to her. Her short legs were running to keep up with him. Socked feet slid on the smooth, tiled floor.

They went up the stairs to a corridor that was decorated in peach and muted purples. The décor was a stark contrast to downstairs. Dacre's grip on her arm tightened.

When they reached a closed door at the end of the hall, Dacre released her roughly, his back to her as he stood with his hands braced against the wall. His shoulders heaved with barely contained rage.

"You're burning up." Dacre cradled her head, his free hand brushing across her damp forehead.

She barely heard him. Her vision blurred, shapes and shadows swirled. "I can't..." she gasped, clutching at his arm. "Make it stop. Please, make it stop."

"I don't know how," Dacre said, his voice cracking. He

leaned closer, lowering his head to meet her eyes. "I'll figure this out, Rue. Just—stay with me."

———

RUE CLENCHED HER FISTS, anger simmering beneath fear. "What are you going to do to me?"

For a moment, the Demon was silent. Then, without looking at her, he replied, "I'll keep you alive." He knocked on the closed door.

The words weren't a comfort, not from him.

A female Demon opened the door and smiled at Dacre.

"Look what the cat dragged in," the Demon woman crooned. She reached out and drew across the handsome Demon's chest with a red lacquered nail.

He grabbed the woman's hand to stop her. "Not now." He motioned to the girl.

"Lucifer's balls," the Demon woman muttered. "What is that? A child? A human child?" The woman's eyes settled on the blood staining Rue's lips.

"Barely..." He released the woman's hand. "She needs some... assistance." He leaned closer to the beautiful Demon female and whispered something in her ear. The woman nodded, glancing at Rue a few times before she finally said, "I understand." They spoke in hushed Hellspeak for a moment.

Rue leaned closer, trying to eavesdrop. She knew little Hellspeak, only what the Hellions had taught her—she wasn't fluent. Her mother feared that if she learned the language she might be tempted to run away when she got older and be lost to the realm of Hell. Or at least that's what she'd told Rue over the years.

He stepped away and motioned for Rue to follow the woman. His eyes fell on her lips.

Rue licked them, tasted crusted blood. Her hands touched her face and scraped at the dried blood dripping down her chin.

———

RUE'S EYES FLUTTERED OPEN, her body feeling heavy and foreign. Every nerve was on fire, her blood felt like it was boiling beneath her skin. She was burning from the inside out. She moaned, her throat too dry to form words.

The faint, muffled sound of Dacre's voice drew her attention. He was standing in the corner of the room, his voice low and urgent.

She turned her head slowly.

Dacre had his back to her, his shoulders tense, one hand gripping his phone tightly while the other raked through his dark hair in frustration.

"She's getting worse," he said, his voice raw and pleading. "I don't know how much longer she can take this. Please, we need help."

There was a pause, then the faint murmur of someone responding on the other end. Dacre shook his head violently.

"No, that's not good enough!" he snapped "She's not going to last another day if this keeps up. I need you to come now. Please."

The last word came out cracked, almost broken, and Rue's heart twisted at the sound.

She wanted to reach out, to call to him, but her voice wouldn't come. He paced the room like a caged animal, his bare feet silent on the wooden floor.

"She's burning up. She can't keep anything down. And the memories... They're breaking her."

A low, pained sound escaped him and Rue realized it was a stifled sob. Dacre was always so controlled, so infuriatingly calm, yet was coming apart at the seams.

"I don't care what it takes," he continued after a beat, his voice quieter now. "Just get here. If you can't help her, I'll... I'll..."

The call ended abruptly and Dacre stood there for a moment, head bowed, phone clutched tightly in his hand.

"Stay," she whispered, barely audible.

"I'm not going anywhere," he promised, voice steady despite the storm in his eyes and the shadows dancing across his face.

———

THEY REACHED the stairs and began descending. The scent of cleaning supplies burned Rue's nose.

As she stepped off the last stair, Dacre's arm was forcing her toward the door and obstructing her view of the mansion.

"Only look at the door or close your eyes." Dacre was too close. The words brushed against her ear.

Rue turned her head to look down the hall. A hand slapped over her eyes. "I said no."

Rue froze. Before her vision went dark, she'd seen the blood splattered on the walls, floor, and ceiling. Dacre's arm snaked around her middle and lifted Rue off her feet. He carried her out the door like an insolent toddler. "You'll need to learn how to listen." He muttered in her ear before setting her on the stone driveway.

"I'm not a baby," Rue said as she turned to glare at him. "My mother was the Queen of Hell. I've seen things."

Dacre's eyes turned dark. "Do as you're told if you care to live." He brushed past her...

———

RUE DRIFTED in and out of consciousness, between vivid memories and reality. Her body ached, the fever twisting her thoughts into fragmented images.

The room was dim, lit only by the faint glow of the

bedside lamp. Dacre was sitting beside her, his large frame hunched in a chair pulled close to the bed. His hair was disheveled, his eyes shadowed with exhaustion.

"Dacre..." she rasped, her voice barely audible.

His hand brushed damp hair away from her face. "I'm here," he said softly.

The sound of voices drew her attention, faint and muffled from the living room.

"She's burning up again," Dacre called over his shoulder. "You have to do something, Jed."

Rue blinked slowly, her vision blurring as she caught movement near the doorway. Jed's tall, lean figure came into focus. Shay stood behind him, her arms crossed, concern written all over her face.

"I told you,'" Jed said, his voice low but firm. "You have to let the rewiring of her memories run its course," Jed said. "I can do nothing for her. If I try to stop it now, it could cause permanent damage."

"You think this isn't permanent?" Dacre shot back, gesturing toward Rue. "She's burning alive from the inside. She can't eat, can't drink, and when she sleeps the nightmares leave her screaming."

Rue stirred weakly, her head lolling to the side. "It's okay," she mumbled, her words slurred.

"No, it's not," Dacre said, his voice softening as he crouched beside her again.

"Jed," Shay said gently. "Look at her. She's a shadow of herself."

Jed sighed as he crossed his arms. "I didn't expect the memories to come back so violently," he admitted. "Her mind is fighting to process everything at once."

Dacre let out a harsh breath, free hand raking through his hair. "And what am I supposed to do? Just sit here and watch her suffer?"

"You know what to do," Jed said, face set.

"I don't." Dacre clapped his hands together in frustration.

Jed bent, hands on his knees so he was eye to eye with Dacre. "You. Know. It's the only thing."

"No." Dacre shook his head. "I... I can't."

Rue's eyelids fluttered, her gaze shifting between the two men. "You're arguing..." she whispered, a weak smile tugging at her lips.

Jed stepped closer, sharp eyes studying Rue. "Keep her hydrated, cool her down when the fever spikes. There's nothing else I can do. There's only what you can do."

Shay placed a comforting hand on Dacre's arm, giving him a meaningful look. "She's stronger than she looks. You both are."

Rue's lips moved but words never came out. Her eyelids drooped as sleep pulled her under again, the voices around her fading into the background.

––––––––

Someone was close, the soft click of the seatbelt releasing woke her fully. She felt an arm stretched across her lap and opened her eyes to the side of the Demon's face. He smelled good, like soap and apple scented shampoo. He went still, realizing she was awake, but that didn't stop Rue from inspecting him closely. There were no scales, no rough skin on his face or hairline.

"It's rude to stare." The Demon pulled away and held the door.

"It's rude to kidnap people," Rue replied.

"Touché." He motioned for her to get out.

"I don't want to go to the dungeon." Rue hugged the pajamas.

"Too bad."

Rue slid out of the seat. She tugged at the jeans that were a size too big for her. She glanced at the forest, didn't notice any of the dead lingering. Hellions caught her eye though. They were watching her. One sniffed the air and took a step forward like a bear ready to pounce.

———

RUE WAS VOMITING BLOOD. It bubbled up in her mouth like she was drowning.

Dacre turned her onto her side. He reached for a discarded towel on the chair nearby and pressed it to her mouth, wiping away the streaks.

Lucipurr hissed suddenly, his ears flattening as he arched his back. The small cat glared at the far corner of the room as his fur bristled.

Dacre's head snapped toward the corner, his instincts flaring to life. The shadows there seemed darker than they should've been, almost shifting, but when he blinked it was gone.

"Not now," he muttered through clenched teeth, his grip tightening on Rue's shoulder. "You're not taking her. Not tonight."

Rue's trembling eased and her body went limp. For a terrifying moment, Dacre thought she'd stopped breathing, but then her chest rose faintly and a quiet sigh escaped her lips.

Her face softened, the pain etched into her features fading slightly as her body relaxed.

"Thank the gods," Dacre whispered, his forehead falling briefly against her shoulder. He stayed like that for a moment, letting the tension drain from his body. He lifted her carefully and settled her back against the pillows, then adjusted the blankets around her.

Lucipurr curled up beside Rue, watching Dacre with wide eyes.

"I'm not leaving her," Dacre said quietly, answering the cat's unspoken concern. He dragged a chair closer to the bed and sat down, elbows resting on his knees. His eyes never left Rue's face.

He was sure the memories were tearing her apart from the inside. And he wasn't sure she'd allow him to stay. It might be the last time.

———

"MY MOTHER WILL KILL YOU," Rue muttered as she walked past the Demon and into the castle. The slippers on her feet made a scuffling sound as she walked.

He muttered something in Hellspeak that sounded like, "Then I can finally rest." Rue wasn't sure if she had the translation correct but the way he sighed made her think it was.

Rue's chest tightened with fear as they moved toward the stairs that spiraled down in to darkness.

As they descended into the dungeon's shadowy depths, Rue's last hope of escaping today slipped away, and the cold, suffocating reality of her capture settled in. She rubbed the runes on her chest. Jed had tried to increase her strength, but she was no match against these monsters. She blinked back tears and wondered if this was how her mother had felt her first time in Hell.

She kept her chin up as she followed him past oily dripping walls and thundering fists pounding on chained doors. He held the dungeon door open, looking away as she walked inside, then he slammed the door closed and locked it.

Rue paced her dungeon cell and sat against the wall; she wrapped her arms around herself, rocking against the stone wall until she drifted off to fitful sleep.

. . .

SOMETHING STRANGE WAS HAPPENING—A dream within a dream. But this one wasn't terrifying. No, this one felt like... it felt like home to Rue.

EVERYTHING MOVED like she was underwater, slow, and fluid. Rue was walking down a cobblestone street, autumn leaves of burnt orange and yellow crunched under her feet. Then she was sitting in a class with an animated professor lecturing on stones in the desert. Then ordering coffee from a cart near the library. She was moving through time in flashes. There was steam in the air and she stepped out of the shower to see a message on a phone but she couldn't make out the text. Anxiety twisted in her stomach. Something smelled like pumpkin coffee. Rue turned and then she was dressed in a costume, her periphery disrupted by the edges of a mask. She searched the cramped room, accepted a cup of beer only to set it down on a nearby table. Young people were surrounding her, dancing. Music boomed from another room. She was having fun, free and smiling behind her mask. She took a small bottle of cinnamon whisky from her pocket and drank that because it was safe. She danced, felt the beat of the music deep in her chest. Someone touched her shoulder and Rue turned to find a man in a silver mask staring down at her.

SHE WAS CALLING FOR HIM, crying.

Lucipurr's small meow mixed with Rue's cries as the cat pawed at her shoulder. The tiny creature licked her tear-streaked face, desperate to soothe her.

Her eyes were half-open.

"Dacre! Dacre," she was weeping.

He shut the water off in one motion, yanking a towel

around his waist. But when her cries grew more frantic, he didn't bother drying himself. He shoved on a pair of boxers and bolted toward her room, heart pounding in his chest.

Dacre reached the doorway and froze for half a heartbeat, terror gripping him.

Rue was thrashing on the bed, the sheets tangled around her legs. Her eyes were half-open but unfocused, and tears streamed down her pale cheeks.

"Dacre," she choked out again, her voice raw, each syllable punctuated by a sob.

Blood glistened at the edges of her ears, stark against her ivory skin. It dripped down her neck, staining the collar of her shirt.

Dacre crossed the room, his feet slapping against the hardwood floor. He knelt beside her, gripping her shoulders. "I'm here. Rue, wake up!"

Her head jerked back and she whimpered, her arms flailing. Dacre caught her wrists, careful not to restrain her too tightly.

"It's me," he said, voice steady but tight.

Her lips moved, forming his name again, but no sound came out this time.

"Damn it," he muttered, glancing at the blood. His hands hovered near her ears, unsure whether touching her would make it worse. "What the hell is happening to you?"

Lucipurr pressed his small body against Rue's side, letting out a low, mournful meow. Dacre's jaw clenched as he looked at the cat, then back at Rue.

"Stay with me," he murmured, brushing a strand of sweat-drenched hair from her face. He pressed the back of his hand to her forehead: she was burning up.

Rue's thrashing slowed slightly, her body trembling violently beneath his touch. Her breaths were shallow and uneven, her chest rising and falling like she was struggling to pull air into her lungs.

———

"I think she's dying," Dacre said, his voice hushed. "There is something not right."

Rue tried rolling over but it was too hard.

"I can't," he argued. "I can't do that. She'll never forgive me. She won't eat or drink."

He was watching her.

"If I do this, I'll have to leave," he said. "I won't be able to see her until after it passes. I don't know. I've never done this before. I swore I wouldn't do this."

He paced near the window.

"I understand. Someone will have to take my place. I'm not sure. Maybe a week. Maybe two to be safe. I DON'T KNOW!" he suddenly shouted. "I have no one to ask. There is no one left, only me. I only have family debts and those don't speak to me!"

The phone crashed against the wall.

Footsteps echoed.

He was near her again.

"You're stronger than this," he whispered, his voice barely audible as he watched her features relax, her body trembling. "I know you are."

———

A deep roar woke Rue. She sat up, realizing she was in the cot and not on the floor.

Something shifted in the shadows in the corner of the room. Rue hoped it wasn't a snake or bugs. She shivered before squinting her eyes and focusing.

"You shouldn't sleep on the stone floor," a familiar voice said from the shadows.

"Why should you care?" Rue pulled the blanket around her, rubbed her lips against its softness before remembering it was Demon's suit jacket. She released the jacket and let it fall to her shoulders.

He stepped out of the shadows. "You sleep with your eyes open."

"No I don't." Rue blinked.

"You do." He was dressed in a suit again. All black.

"No. I don't." Rue snapped. "And why are you watching me sleep like some creepy old man?"

He chuckled darkly. "Get up. It's time to go." He checked his watch. "You've slept too long."

Rue shifted, moving to the edge of the cot, and setting her slippered feet on the damp floor.

From beyond her dungeon cell there was a howling scream. Rue covered her ears and shrank back.

He grabbed her arm and pulled, unwilling to wait for her to get up. "Let's go. The longer you wait the more you'll hear. We need to leave."

Rue tugged her arm back and kicked.

"Stop," he warned, shielding his thigh.

"It doesn't matter, I'm going to die here anyway. Just end it already." Rue punched him in the ribs then kicked his knee with all her might.

He was spitting profanities in Hellspeak and hopping on one foot when a Hellion glanced into the dungeon and laughed.

"Get the fuck out of here," he shouted to the Hellion. He turned to face Rue.

Rue's heart raced; she was breathing in sharp, quick bursts as she backed away from him. The dim light of the dungeon flickered, casting ominous shadows on the stone walls. He stood only a few paces away, his dark eyes fixed on her, unblinking and cold.

"What are you doing?" He asked, his voice smooth, carrying a slight gentle tone, though the threat beneath was clear. The handsome Demon had a gift of threading fine words with threat. He took a step forward, hands raised in a mockery of peace. "Don't even try to fight me. It won't do you any good. You cannot escape this place. You cannot escape me."

Something had shifted in Rue during the night. That dream gave her some kind of home for the future which meant she did not stay here. "I'm not going to sit here and wait to be slaughtered by Lucifer. I won't be used by you in the skin trades." Rue shook her head. "That's not happening." Rue's hands trembled but clenched into fists, a fierce determination burned in her center. She had to get out. She had to escape. She had to leave. Now.

He smirked, his head tilting slightly and amusement dancing in his dark eyes. "Slaughtered? Is that what you think Lucifer will do to you? That's what he does to the Demons he rules over, makes us suffer. But you, he'll probably end quickly."

Rue didn't reply. Her eyes darted around, searching for anything she could use as a weapon. But there was nothing. Just him and the walls that felt as though they were closing in.

He lunged.

Rue barely had time to react, diving to the side as his hand reached out to grab her. She stumbled, nearly losing her footing, but she caught herself and whirled around, her pulse pounding in her ears. He was fast.

"I don't want to hurt you," he growled, his earlier calm gone.

Rue's lip curled into a snarl, defiance surging through her. "I'm gonna hurt you."

Without thinking, she charged at him, fists swinging wildly. She knew she was outmatched. He had the strength of a Demon, the speed and the power. But she wasn't going to go down without a fight. She'd fight him every day. Every step of the way.

Her first strike hit his chest, but it felt like hitting stone. A sharp ache spread up her arm. He barely flinched, grabbing her wrist with inhuman speed and twisting it just enough to force a cry of pain from her throat.

"Stop," he ordered, his voice dark and edged with frustration.

Rue twisted in his grip, swinging her other hand up to strike his face. Her knuckles grazed his jaw and to her surprise he stumbled back, releasing her arm. For a brief moment Rue felt the rush of victory, her heart soaring with hope.

But then he came at her again, faster, angrier. "If you are going to act like a child, I will treat you like one." He grabbed her by the shoulders, slamming her back against the stone wall. The impact knocked the air from her lungs and black spots danced in her vision. His face was inches from hers, his eyes burning with a dangerous mixture of anger and something else she couldn't place.

"You're wasting your energy," he snarled, his breath hot against her skin. "You won't get away."

Rue gasped, struggling in his grip. The stone at her back was cold, pressing into her spine as she fought to free herself, but he was unyielding. His fingers dug into her shoulders, pinning her in place. Desperation flared in her chest as she kicked at him but it only made his hands press her harder against the stone. "You're in a time out." There was a lilt of humor in his tone.

"Let me go!" she screamed, twisting her body.

He didn't move. A dark smile spread across his lips as if he enjoyed the struggle. "I could keep you here forever if I wanted. Do you understand that? You'd never see the light of day. Only darkness. Only the darkest version of the skin trades. I didn't want that for you."

Memories of yesterday flashed through her mind. He had

taken her away from the damp dungeon for the day. The threat stung but fueled new anger. Rue's pulse quickened and before she could think it through, she lunged forward, sinking her teeth into the side of his neck with all the strength she had left.

He froze.

For a moment, the taste of blood filled her mouth, metallic and bitter and... sweet. She bit harder, her jaw clenched, and his hands tightened on her shoulders. A guttural growl emanated from his throat, a sound equal parts pain and rage. His body tensed, his grip went so tight she was afraid he'd break her bones.

He shoved Rue away. Hard. Her head smacked against the stone wall and tiny lights danced in her vision. Rue licked her lips, noticing his blood tasted a lot different than what the Demon at the Black Mansion had forced down her throat. Her legs felt weak, her entire body was trembling. Rue wiped her mouth, glaring at him, breathing heavily. She glanced down at the smear of blood across the back of her hand and licked it away slowly.

His hand was pressed to the side of his neck, his eyes wide with shock and fury. Watching her mouth, he moved his hand from his neck and stared at his palm. Blood dripped. Rue focused on the small bite mark from her teeth. They weren't sharp and the bite was nothing more than blunt marks that had drawn blood.

"You have no fucking idea what you've done. You're going to regret that," he hissed, his voice a low growl.

He stormed out of the dungeon, slamming the door. A heavy lock slid into place.

"Don't let her out," he instructed the Hellion. "Ever."

Rue slid down the wall, her body sore and head aching. She had hurt him, maybe only a little but it was something. Rue touched her lips, watched the blood drip down her fingertips. She licked her lips, then her fingers. She swallowed down every drop of his blood and wished she had more. What was wrong with her? Her mother and the Hellions drank blood. Plenty of Demons did too. Children didn't. Rue knew why children didn't drink blood. Because it stopped their aging. A million thoughts clouded her mind but she couldn't focus on one of them. She was suddenly very thirsty.

The prisoners in the dungeon started going wild, banging on doors and walls, slamming furniture against the walls, howling and screeching like excited zoo animals.

———

THE ROOM WAS DIM, the only light coming from the pale moon streaming through the window. Dacre had opened it so she could see the stars if she was strong enough to keep her eyes open.

"Lay here with me?" Rue asked, voice hushed.

"I don't think that's a good idea." Dacre stood frozen at the bedside, his body tense, his hands clenched into fists at his sides. It looked like he'd seen a ghost.

"Please, I think I'm dying and it's all I want." She reached out to him, fingers brushing the edge of his shirt.

Her hand fell to the mattress, weak and trembling. "Please," she begged, voice breaking.

Dacre's resolve shattered. With a heavy sigh, he knelt beside her, arms slipping under her fragile frame to lift her gently. She felt too light, and since the fever passed, too cold. He gathered her in his arms and pulled her against his chest, head tucked under his chin.

Her breathing was shallow, her face pressed to the warmth of his skin "Dacre?" she murmured.

"Yes, little princess?" He pressed his lips to the top of her head.

"When I die, tell my mother it wasn't your fault." Her

voice was faltering and tears dripped down her cheeks. "I don't want her to hurt you."

Dacre's arms tightened around her as he fought the lump in his throat. "You're not dying," he repeated firmly.

Rue's hands fisted the fabric of his shirt. "You don't know that."

"Yes, I do." He pulled back enough to tilt her face toward his, forcing her to meet his dark eyes. "Because I won't let you die. Do you hear me? You're not going anywhere. You haven't read all the books in the library."

Her lips quivered, but she nodded weakly, tears streaming down her cheeks. "Every memory... it's tearing me apart. My head hurts so bad."

Dacre cupped her face with one hand, his thumb brushing away her tears. "You're stronger than this." His voice was desperate.

She stared at him for a long moment, her eyes searching his, before finally letting out a soft, broken sob. The pain was starting again, piercing through her skull. She buried her face in his chest again, her body shaking as he held her close.

The room fell silent, broken only by her quiet cries and the steady beat of his heart against her ear.

"...SHE is your burden to use as you see fit for the skin trades. But," Lucifer raised a long finger. *"She will stay here in the dungeons when you are not using her. And then, when I am ready, I will kill her. I will kill them all,"* Lucifer promised *before disappearing from the room.*

His burden.

His burden.

His burden.

———

Dacre was curled around her protectively because that was what she'd asked him to do. Rue's small fingers were threaded through his.

She moved. "Dacre?"

"Yea?"

"Did we meet a long time ago?" she asked.

"Once, when you first moved in. I passed you in the driveway and said hello, but you were unpacking your car."

"No," Rue's voice cracked. "Before that. Years before that."

Dacre's body went stiff. "Go back to sleep, princess."

THIRTY-ONE

SOMETHING DARK TWISTED IN DACRE'S GUT. SHE was remembering too much too fast. He was rethinking what Meg had told him: *Give her your blood. It's the only thing that will help her.*

Dacre pressed his eyes closed and hugged her small body closer. He'd have to leave her, like last time. He'd have to go away until he could control himself again. She was too fragile to survive him. Too small. Too innocent.

He propped himself up on one elbow and watched her sleep. Her shallow breaths concerned him. She was already small but these few days without food or drink, she'd lost weight. He touched her dark hair, then her jaw, his finger trailing over her slender neck, across her collarbone. He wanted this to be different. But, he'd known his whole life that he was destined for disaster and pain. He blinked, committing her image to memory. This might be the last time he saw her. He knew once he did this, the urge to be skin to skin would be unbearable. It was the last time he'd watch her like this. She couldn't survive him in this condition.

Dacre rolled Rue onto her back, his thumb brushed over

her lips before pulling down on her jaw and parting them. Then, he bit his wrist until the blood flowed, and pressed it to her mouth.

It hurt, letting her go. Just like all those years ago when he'd stole her out of that dungeon and brought her back to her parents.

He was a monster. He couldn't keep her. A pretty little thing like Rue deserved better than him. He'd had nothing his whole life and letting her go again was no different. He would go back to paying off his family debts as that seemed to be his only destiny.

Thirty-Two

The morning sunlight streamed through Rue's bedroom window. She stretched, surprised at the lightness in her limbs. For the first time in days her head felt mostly clear.

She got out of bed and shuffled to the bathroom, catching a glimpse of herself in the mirror. She no longer felt like she was dying and she only thought she looked a little pale. There were only faint dark circles under her eyes.

She showered, scrubbed her hair, and brushed her teeth. She paused for a moment, remembering blood being on her face, dripping from her nose, ears, and mouth. Someone had cleaned it.

She dressed in her favorite sweater and jeans and twisted her long hair in a loose braid. Her fingers felt sluggish and weak as they twisted her thick strands. She figured a quick breakfast would help. And a big cup of coffee.

But, as Rue stepped into the living room, she immediately felt something was off. Dacre's usual brooding presence was absent. The apartment felt too still, too empty for the first time in months. She was alone again.

"Dacre?" she called, glancing toward the kitchen. There was no response.

A knot formed in her chest. There weren't many places to check in the small apartment.

She walked into the kitchen. Nothing.

Her pulse quickened as she made her way to his room. Rue hesitated for a moment, her hand hovering over the doorknob. She'd never gone in there before. It felt intrusive. She pushed the door open and stepped inside.

The room was stark. A single mattress lay on the floor, covered with a plain gray blanket and one flat pillow. A small duffle bag sat in the corner, half unzipped with a few neatly folded clothes spilling out. There was nothing else; no photos, no decorations. He didn't even have a bedframe.

Rue's stomach twisted. *He's been living like this?*

She sank onto the edge of the mattress, running her hand over the worn fabric. It smelled like him. A mix of emotions bubbled to the surface. She stood quickly, strode to the kitchen counter, and grabbed her phone. She fired off a message to her mother.

Rue: My bodyguard is gone.

Meg: He had to run an errand.

Lucipurr brushed against her leg, meowing softly. Rue bent to scratch his ears. "Where is our bodyguard, huh? Did he say anything to you?"

The cat meowed and it sounded like "no."

Meg: Chel will be there soon.

Rue: Mother! Chel! Please, don't send him. I'll be fine. I don't need anyone.

Meg: I don't think that's true.

Rue: Chel is obnoxious.

Meg: He's highly trained.

Rue: Everyone is going to stare at him. He's a monster.

Meg: It's gonna be just fine. Let's meet for coffee tomorrow.

Rue: Fine.

Meg: Fine.

RUE HAD a nagging feeling that something was wrong.

———

RUE STOOD IN THE KITCHEN, waiting for the coffee maker to sputter its last few drips into her mug. Her nerves were frayed. Midterms weren't going to wait for her emotional state to stabilize. She'd lost too much time being ill. She'd have to cram all night.

Just as she brought the steaming mug to her lips, the stark sound of knuckles rapping on the front door made her jump, sloshing the coffee on the counter.

"Great," she grabbed a paper towel and cleaned it up.

The knocking came again, louder this time. Rue stomped to the door and yanked it open. She barely had time to process the massive figure looming in the doorway before a booming voice filled the apartment.

"Rue!"

Chel ducked his head under the doorframe, his head just barely clearing the wood. He grinned down at her, his sharp teeth gleaming, and spread his arms wide. He looked every bit the Hellion warrior—seven feet tall and broad as a mountain.

"Chel?" Rue blinked, startled.

"Your mother sent me!" Chel stepped inside without waiting for an invitation, the floor creaking ominously under his weight. He knocked over the lamp on the side table and it clattered to the floor with a loud crash.

"Oops," He scooped it up with a sheepish grin and set it back, albeit crookedly.

Rue pinched the bridge of her nose. "She told me."

"Since Dacre is indisposed, I've been assigned to guard you." Chel puffed out his chest proudly, which only made him seem larger and more out of place in her tiny apartment.

"Chel, I don't need—"

"Nonsense! Of course you do." He strode into the kitchen, his arm swinging and knocking into a chair, sending it skidding across the floor. Rue winced. Chel noticed the coffee cup in her hand and tilted his head. "Coffee? That's all you're having? You're not going to eat?"

Rue set the mug down. "I don't have time to make breakfast. I have to get to class."

Chel frowned, his brow furrowing in exaggerated concern. "You can't learn on an empty stomach, little princess. Want me to whip you up some eggs? I make a mean scramble."

"No!" Rue said a little too quickly. "Listen, Chel, I appreciate the offer but this isn't—"

Chel's other arm hit the fridge, causing a magnet to fall and scatter papers across the floor. He bent to pick them up, but his head scraped against the cabinet, leaving a noticeable dent in the wood.

"Chel!" Rue snapped.

He straightened, his eyes wide and apologetic. "Sorry. It's small in here..." He waved his hands and dented another cabinet door with his elbow as he said, "I'm used to much bigger spaces."

Rue groaned, pressing her fingers to her temples. "Look, I know you're trying to help, but I can't–" She paused, trying to phrase it delicately.

Chel's face fell, his broad shoulders slumping. "You don't want me here. I thought we'd have fun, you know, like old times."

"It's not that, Chel. I just..." She gestured around the small apartment.

"Okay, fine," he raised his hands in surrender. "I'll just act like a shadow."

Rue crossed the room to collect her bag. "I have to go to class and then the library." She stared at him. "What happened to Dacre?"

Chel shook his head. "No clue."

"Are you lying to me?" Rue glared upwards at Chel. He was a giant.

Chel pressed a hand to his chest with an exaggerated huff. "I would never lie to a princess."

Rue narrowed her eyes. He'd been using that exact phrase throughout her life and always when he'd lied. When he'd lied about drinking all the chocolate milk, or eating all the freezer waffles, or stepping on the daisies. She'd heard it before.

THIRTY-THREE

Meg set her phone down and looked at Dacre. "What were you saying again?"

"Rue's memories are coming back," Dacre sounded worried.

She studied him for a moment. "That's the point. She needs to remember." Meg motioned for Dacre to follow her.

"She's going to hate me," he growled.

"Don't take that tone with me." Meg's blue eyes flashed wide.

"My apologies." Dacre dipped his head, fists clenching.

"Bring her blood."

"She has always refused."

"Maybe this time she'll give in," Meg walked to the black fridge and pulled out three bags. She set them in a cooler and glanced up at Dacre, brow up. "You'll need more?"

Dacre nodded. "I gave her my blood like you suggested. That's why she's better. For now. That's why I had to leave. I don't trust myself."

Meg exhaled before grabbing five more bags and packing them.

"If my daughter is anything like me she'll be mad, but she'll come around. Maybe slip a few drops in her coffee."

Dacre shook his head. "I can't go back there until *it* passes." He was strung like a spring, wanting to go to Rue and take her away to a cave in Hell and never let her leave.

"Ah, the bloodlust is strong with this one," Meg smirked knowingly.

Dacre held back a snarl.

"Be prepared to grovel. The whole family will have to." Meg slammed the lid to the cooler closed. "We've been trying to protect her from the truth of what happened all these years and I fear we just fucked everything up." She passed him the cooler. "Is this enough?"

"For a few days. I want to go to her." His voice edged on agony.

"You can't." Meg sighed. "I didn't realize you were this bad off. Take a few days. Chel is with her. Do whatever your kind does with free time."

Dacre's brow lifted. "I don't think that's a good idea. I want to see her. I'm not sure I can control it."

"Maybe see Remington instead?" Meg shrugged. "Go spend a few days on the Hellion training grounds. You're looking soft."

Dacre blinked. Maybe he had spent too many days lounging around the apartment, drinking coffee and eating freezer pizza. The last fight he'd had with a shadow demon resulted in injury. *But that was because I can't shift in front of her*, Dacre reminded himself. Well, he could shift but that would bring a lot of questions and most likely scare the ever-loving crap out of her.

"For the last of your kind, you need to keep yourself in tip-top shape." She looked him over. "Especially if you're going to have a relationship with my daughter. She needs protection."

"Yes." Dacre shifted on his feet. "I was focused on her

getting better. Perhaps, I will go to the training grounds for the week."

Thirty-Four

The lecture hall buzzed with conversation as students trickled in, some bleary-eyed and clutching coffee, others furiously flipping through notes. Rue slid into her usual seat near the middle of the room, grateful for the routine. Evelyn was already there, doodling in the margins of her notebook.

"Hey, stranger." Evelyn grinned, tapping Rue's arm. "You've been MIA. Studying for midterms?"

"Something like that." Rue gave a half-smile as she pulled out her laptop.

Evelyn's eyes narrowed slightly, studying Rue's face. "You look... different. Less pale. You okay? Last time I saw you it wasn't looking good..."

Rue hesitated, not wanting to dive into the chaos of what had happened. "I'm fine, really. Just a stomach bug."

Evelyn arched an eyebrow. "Uh-huh. And where's hot-bodyguard? Haven't seen him lurking around lately. Did you kick him to the curb?"

Rue winced at the mention of Dacre. She busied herself with her laptop, trying to ignore Evelyn's probing look.

"Oh no," Evelyn gasped dramatically, leaning closer. "You didn't break his heart, did you? He was so smitten. Probably cried himself to sleep in that leather jacket of his."

Rue snorted despite herself. "He wasn't smitten. He was doing what my parents paid him to do."

"Uh hum." Evelyn side-eyed her friend.

"He's... out of town."

"Out of town?" Evelyn tilted her head. "Poor hot-body-guard has something better to do than follow you around?"

"Something like that," Rue muttered.

Before Evelyn could press further, the door to the lecture hall creaked open and Rue stiffened. Chel's enormous frame filled the doorway, and he ducked inside. He was trying to move discreetly, but his size and bright crimson skin made him impossible to miss. Students turned to gawk, whispering.

Evelyn's eyes widened. "What the hell is that?"

"That's Chel," Rue muttered, sinking lower in her seat.

"Chel?" Evelyn repeated, her voice incredulous. "He looks like he stepped out of a heavy metal album cover. Why is he here?"

"He's... filling in for Dacre," Rue admitted reluctantly.

Evelyn's eyes flicked back to Chel, who had squeezed himself into the back row, his broad shoulders making the desk look comically small. "He's terrifying."

"He's not that bad," Rue said, though she couldn't deny that Chel's imposing presence was a far cry from Dacre's quiet, watchful demeanor.

Chel caught her eye and gave a toothy grin, lifting a massive hand in a wave. Rue cringed, pretending not to notice. Evelyn let out a nervous laugh.

"He waved. Does that mean he likes me or he's planning to eat me?"

Rue rolled her eyes. "Chel doesn't eat people. He's just... enthusiastic."

"Yeah, enthusiastically scary," Evelyn muttered, turning back to her notebook. "Seriously, though. I miss hot-bodyguard. At least he didn't look like he'd break the furniture just by sitting on it."

Rue bit back a smile, but her thoughts lingered on Dacre. She was remembering the past few days with the headaches and nosebleeds and fevers; writhing in bed and thinking she was going to die. Her face flamed as she recalled the things she'd said to Dacre, the way she begged for him. It was pathetic. She probably scared the shit out of him and he ran away, not wanting to deal with her craziness. It was long overdue. Rue sighed as she adjusted the strap of her bag and leaned against the desk. Evelyn leaned closer, a mischievous grin plastered on her face.

"So, if you kicked hot-bodyguard to the curb, can I call him?" Evelyn asked, waggling her eyebrows.

"Won't pyramid head be sad?" Rue asked.

Evelyn gasped dramatically, clutching her chest as though Rue had just wounded her. "First of all, Pyramid Head is fictional. Secondly, no man—fictional or otherwise—compares to Dacre's brooding, dark-and-dangerous charm. Seriously, he lives in the apartment below you. How do you even function?"

Rue still hadn't told Evelyn that he'd moved in to better protect her.

"I have a great deal of patience," Rue deadpanned, dropping her bag onto the desk and searching for a pencil. "And I saw Pyramid Head with my own eyes, how is he fictional?"

"It was the idea of him being hot and bothered for me that was fictional. Turns out he's simply unbothered. Must be the engineering major in him." Evelyn sighed. "Also, patience my ass," Evelyn muttered, crossing her arms. "I think you like him."

Rue froze, mid-motion, her head snapping up.

Evelyn's grin widened like a cat who'd cornered its prey. "You heard me. I saw that kiss at the costume party. And you're always talking about how annoying he is following you around, but, babe, you don't fool me. The chemistry is epic."

Rue's cheeks were flaming. "He's my bodyguard, Ev. That's literally all he is."

"Sure, sure," Evelyn's voice was dripping sarcasm. "That's why you're always staring at him like he's a particularly juicy steak, right? You should just ask him out already."

Rue scoffed, opening her notebook to avoid Evelyn's knowing gaze. "You're impossible. And wrong."

"Am I, though?" Evelyn tilted her head, her grin softening into something more sincere. "Come on, Tink. He obviously cares about you. He brings you coffee in the library. It's adorable. And I mean, if you're not into him, that's cool. Just let me know so I can shoot my shot."

Rue groaned and covered her face with her hands. "Stop. Please stop."

"Fine," Evelyn relented, though the sparkle in her eye betrayed her amusement. "But seriously, Tink. Life's short. If there's something there, maybe you should–"

Professor Camden walked in, cutting Evelyn off mid-sentence. Rue sighed in relief and turned in her seat, hoping Evelyn wouldn't bring this up again.

THIRTY-FIVE

The fluorescent lights of the campus library flickered overhead as Rue hunched over her textbook and notes. She shook a cramp out of her hand. She had a midterm in the morning for Calculus 3 and refused to leave until she felt prepared.

Chel stood awkwardly near the doors to the room Rue was studying in, clearly not built for library life. His massive frame drew stares from the handful of students pulling all-nighters.

"Do you think they keep snacks here?" Chel whispered, or what passed as a whisper in his deep, booming voice.

"No, Chel. Libraries don't keep snacks. They keep books. And quiet."

He frowned, as if the concept of a snackless and silent building were personally offensive.

A few minutes passed before his giant hand accidentally knocked over a display of books near the door. The loud thud made Rue's pen skid across her notebook.

"Chel!" she hissed, finally turning to glare at him. Several other students joined in, their annoyed expressions saying what Rue didn't have the energy to.

"Sorry," he mumbled, his voice barely lower than before. He stood stock-still for about thirty seconds before pacing like a restless tiger.

Rue pinched the bridge of her nose. This was why she didn't want her mother sending Chel. "I can't focus with you hovering like that. Just... wait outside, okay? I'll be fine for a few hours."

His expression darkened, brows furrowing. "I can't just–"

"Please." She put her pen down and met his eyes. "One hour of silence is all I need. Go pace the hallway or something. You're distracting me."

He hesitated, clearly torn. "Fine. But I'm not going far. I'll be just past the next set of doors."

As soon as he put more distance between them Rue let out a long sigh, trying to reclaim her focus. She flipped through her notes, murmuring equations under her breath and committing them to memory.

She rubbed her temples absently; fog was starting to set in.

Recognition twisted in her stomach. The library disappeared, replaced by a flash of memory.

A DARK, stone room. Chains. Shadows creeping closer. There was water trickling across the floor. She watched it morph from a gentle stream to a river to a gushing force that started flooding the room. Someone grabbed her around the neck.

SHE JOLTED back to the present with a gasp, gripping the edge of the table so tightly that her knuckles turned white.

Her breaths came in shallow pants. She pressed the heel of her hand to her forehead, trying to ground herself. "Focus,

Rue. Focus," she whispered to herself while watching her fingers tremble.

She reached for her pen, determined to continue studying, when a familiar prickling sensation crawled up her spine. Her head snapped up, scanning the rows of bookshelves. Nobody was there.

Her eyes darted to the glass doors at the entrance. She could see Chel pacing just outside, whistling. Christ he was going to get kicked out.

CHEL SHIFTED his weight from one foot to the other, his boots thudding softly against the linoleum floor of the library hallway. He hated this. Libraries were too quiet, too dim, and filled with too many humans who glared at him like he was the problem.

He muttered under his breath, crossing his arms. "I'd rather face a pack of Hellhounds."

"Excuse me," a chirpy voice interrupted. Chel turned his head sharply. A petite human stood before him, clutching a water bottle and looking up at him with wide eyes.

"What?" he asked gruffly.

"Okay, this might sound weird, but..." She hesitated, fidgeting with her bottle. "Are you like, a bodybuilder or something? You're *huge*. Like, I didn't even think it was possible for someone to have muscles like that."

Chel blinked, momentarily thrown off. "No."

"Oh. Well, do you work out a lot? Like, how many reps do you do? Is it heavy lifting or..."

Chel sighed, glancing over his shoulder toward the library doors. "I'm busy."

"I just–I mean, you're kinda inspiring! My boyfriend's been trying to bulk up, but, like, maybe he should talk to you." She pulled a phone out of her pocket. "I'm going to tell him to come over here. He's not far away, just at the dining hall."

"I'm busy," Chel said, his patience fraying.

The girl didn't take the hint. She took a step closer, eyes wide with admiration. "You could totally be a fitness influencer. Have you ever thought about that? You'd probably make, like, a ton of money."

Chel gritted his teeth. "No. I haven't. Now if you'll excuse me–"

As he turned back toward the library doors, he caught a flicker of movement. His instincts alerted, but the girl tugged on his jacket sleeve, forcing his attention.

"Wait! What's your bench press max? Like, 400 pounds? 500?" Her phone chimed and she glanced at him. "He's coming, he said five minutes."

Chel growled under his breath, trying to shake her off without causing a scene. Rue would kill him if he caused any more of a scene.

He turned toward the room where Rue was studying. The hallway felt wrong. Too quiet, too still.

His hand went to the hidden blade at his waist as his eyes scanned the shadows.

"I have to go," Chel told the girl.

"No, he's just a minute away." She tugged at his sleeve.

Chel shook his arm to get her to go away. "Stop. I'm busy."

"You're kind of a jerk," the girl pouted.

Chel walked away.

"Rue?" he called, voice low and wary.

There was no response.

His chest tightened as he realized the girl's questions might have been more than a coincidence.

"Rue!"

He ran to the desk where Rue had been studying. Her books were there, her pencil resting on the notebook but there was a swipe of black, like someone had hit her arm while she was writing and the pencil arced over the page.

Chel scanned the workspace and saw her chair tipped over, her bag underneath, her phone was on the ground, screen cracked.

"No!" He frantically started searching the library. He searched between bookshelves. He shouted her name until the librarian came marching toward him, heels clicking on the hard floor. Chel lifted the chair, grabbed Rue's bag, and began packing up her belongings.

The scent of brimstone wafted by. He turned, followed it to a dark corner where old bookshelves met the wall and the lighting didn't illuminate, where the shadows were still spiraling like something had just crossed the barrier between realms.

Thirty-Six

Rue rubbed her temples, still haunted by the strange memory flash from earlier. She needed to sleep; her midterm was at eleven in the morning.

She glanced at the doors expecting to see Chel's hulking figure, but he wasn't there. She heard a woman's voice and shifted in her seat to see him in the corridor being hit on. She smiled and made a mental note to tease him later.

A flicker of movement from the corner caught her eye. A familiar tingle rippled up the back of her neck.

"Chel?" she called softly, glancing over her shoulder.

A book fell. There was a deep growl coming from the shadows in the corner which seemed to pool unnaturally. Red eyes flashed.

Her pulse drummed in her ears. A footstep.

Rue stood, knocking over her chair.

Then came the whisper; a soft, hissing sound that sent her heart into her throat.

"Little princess…"

Rue froze. Her legs felt heavy as lead. The air around her thickened. She whipped around, eyes wide.

A shape emerged from the shadows, dark and writhing. A cold, clawed hand clamped over her mouth before she could scream.

"No!" she tried to shout, but the sound was muffled. Shadows curled around her arms and legs, dragging her back into the dark corner of the library.

Rue kicked and thrashed as the world dissolved into a suffocating void. A memory of being dragged through dirt flashed through her mind.

Movement stopped. The air was cold and damp, and her senses blurred. She was being pulled through the void, a sickening sensation that made her stomach flip-flop.

She hit the ground, the impact knocking air from her lungs. She groaned, her hands scrambling against cold, hard stone as her eyes adjusted to the dim light around her.

Black marble floors stretched out beneath her. Tall columns reached toward a vaulted ceiling, draped with gold and black linens. The air smelled of brimstone and pine and... blood. Screams echoed from somewhere deep within the mansion.

Rue's heart stopped as she looked up.

There was the demon from her nightmares, the one who poured blood down her throat and laughed at her for being weak. Tall and grotesque, his leathery skin shimmered faintly in the dim light. His face twisted into a sneer as fiery eyes landed on her.

"Welcome back, little princess," he drawled. "It's been far too long."

Shivers of terror tore through Rue. Her breaths came in short, panicked gasps as memories fought to surface.

"No," she whispered, shaking her head as she climbed to her feet and backed away. "This isn't real."

"Oh, it's very real," the demon replied, taking a step closer. He looked her up and down as though she was a trophy. "The years have been kind to you… but they'll be kinder to me when the bidding begins. You look exactly the same. Just as I had anticipated when I poured that blood down your throat so many years ago."

Rue's blood turned to ice as she put the pieces of this puzzle together. The skin trades. Willing women. Using her as a pawn to recruit.

"No." Rue was shaking her head. She turned to run but hands caught her and dragged her away.

She kicked and screamed, but the demons dragged her out of the large room and down the hallway toward a door under the stairs.

The demon dragging her opened the door, revealing a steep staircase that plunged into darkness. Rue's heart hammered as she was dragged down. Down, down, down; she stumbled, scraping her legs as she was dragged, struggling to try and escape but the demon's grip was like iron. He dragged her across a dirt floor and threw her like she was trash into a barred cell. The impact sent pain shooting through her side. She scratched her face against sharp rocks embedded in the dirt. He slammed the door and locked it. Rue scrambled to her feet, gripping the bars and shaking the door. The walls were rough stone and chains hung from the ceiling, clinking faintly.

Above her, the demon loomed, his grin widening. "You won't escape, little princess," his voice a sickening purr. "We'll make sure of it."

Rue tried to speak but fear was choking her. Chains rattled as the demon swung a hand at them.

"You're not that important," he said. "There's someone more powerful that we want."

The sound of the demon's laughter echoed as his footsteps retreated up the stairs. The faint light above disappeared as the door above was slammed shut. Rue was left in silence, the only sound her own ragged breathing and the faint drip of water somewhere nearby.

Her fingers clawed at the damp floor, tears streaming down her face. *Think, Rue. Don't panic.*

Somewhere above, the faint strains of music began to play, twisted and haunting. Rue leaned against the bars, clutching her knees and whispered, "Dacre..."

THIRTY-SEVEN

THE FIRST THING DACRE NOTICED WHEN CHEL stepped onto the Hellion training grounds was that he carried Rue's backpack. And there was no Rue. His chest stilled as he scanned the yard behind Chel, dread creeping up his spine.

Chel noticed Dacre and jogged over.

"Where is she?" Dacre's voice was low and sharp.

Chel's brow furrowed, his eyes darting to the castle in the distance. "I was standing right there. Barely a hundred feet away." He held up her bag. "Something took her." He shoved the bag toward Dacre. "Smell. The scent is still there, lingering."

Dacre was growling low in his throat, like a lion ready to attack.

"I didn't see!" Chel snapped, his usual bravado crumbling. "Some human kid was asking me–"

"You left her alone?" Dacre interrupted.

Chel fell silent. "She was studying in the library. I only looked away for an instant."

Dacre didn't waste another moment. He knelt with Rue's bag, rifling through it for any clue. A faint scent lingered—a sickly, sulfurous tang that made his jaw tighten. He knew that smell. "Shadow demons from the pine forests." Dacre zipped Rue's bag and motioned for Chel to follow him.

"Where are you going?" Chel asked, hurrying to catch up with Dacre's fast pace.

"To kill some shadow demons."

———

DACRE STOOD in the dimly lit hall of the Hellion outpost, his arms crossed as he faced a wall of weapons.

Remington leaned against the wall, his sharp eyes studying Dacre with suspicion and concern.

"You sure about this?" Remington asked, his voice calm but edged with steel. "I will order the entire army of Hellions to destroy every spec of that forest. We could burn it to the ground and the only thing left will be ash."

Dacre's eyes flashed, his patience wearing thin. "No. I didn't come here to debate the ways in which they will die. I came for information."

A Hellion warrior entered the room, dragging a female along with him. Dacre recognized Kit, the contact he'd spoken to at the Christmas party. Dacre hated risking her safety like this, but there was no other option.

Dacre moved forward and took Kit from the Hellion.

Kit was a demon woman who knew enough to protect Rue after meeting her the first time as a child. She knew Rue was important to Dacre, had known the creature who played a demon long enough to know that Rue was his and anyone standing in the way would die a horrific death. Kit adjusted her dress and buttoned her jacket, before swiping manicured nails through her hair.

"I didn't need to be manhandled," she side-eyed the

Hellion who'd dragged her out of the store. "I would have come willingly."

"I appreciate that," Dacre said. "Now. Tell me everything."

Kit reached in her coat and withdrew a folded piece of parchment. "I was shopping." She tipped her head toward the Hellions. "One of them needs to go get my things because after this, I will never be able to return. My cover is blown wide open."

Dacre threw a glance to Remington. Remington nodded and said, "Done."

Kit unfolded the parchment and laid it out on the table. "The Black Mansion used to be here," she pointed to a rugged landscape in the nearby Allegheny mountains of Hell. "But after what you did last time," Kit glanced at Dacre, "they moved it."

"The whole building?" Chel asked.

"Demon magic is strong. Especially with a halfling of Lucifer at the helm. Alastor has only grown in his power and now with that little shit Asmodeus at his side, they have built the skin trades to be harder to find. They don't want Meg and Sparrow finding them." Kit took a deep breath and traced a path to the ancient pine forests in the west, close to the ocean. She tapped a finger over at tiny dot. "Here. They moved the Black Mansion here. It's mostly underground now. Hidden." She glanced at Dacre. "It's damp and wet there." She passed Dacre a knowing glance. Dampness in the dungeons brought wet lung disease. They didn't have much time.

"Thank you," Dacre said taking a mental snapshot of the map.

"Be careful," Kit said, touching his arm gently. "They are more dangerous than ever before. They have warding and scouts." She pointed to the map again. "Here, here, and here. They bring us through a checkpoint here." She pointed to a mark on the map. "We get patted down. There are wards." She looked him up and down. "But you know the wards won't work on you. They don't know how to ward against you." She glanced at his broad frame. "They have no idea."

Dacre nodded. He wasn't about to tell the whole room what she was referring to. That was a secret between him, Rue's family, and Kit. The reason why he'd protect Kit's life against anything and everything was that she knew and she never tried to exploit him for it. Kit had been born into the skin trades, she knew how to manipulate the system. She knew value when she saw it. She knew Dacre was special the moment she set eyes on him at the Black Mansion a long time ago. They were both there paying off family debts that could never be fulfilled.

Remington pushed off the wall, his expression darkening. "She's my sister. I'm coming with you."

"No," Dacre said flatly. His voice held an authority that silenced the room. "I need help getting there. That's all. Once I'm inside, I'll handle the rest." His lip curled into a faint smirk, though there was no humor in it. "I don't need an army. I've killed more for less."

Remington stared at him for a long moment, then nodded slowly. "You'd better bring her back in one piece," he said, his tone carrying the weight of a threat and a plea.

A Hellion commander stepped forward. "We'll get you close. We can portal hop from here," he pointed to the map, "to here and here. If their wards are as strong as Kit says we must be careful."

"Good," Dacre said, his voice sharp. "Let's do it."

———

THEY TRAVELED via a portal network that brought them from the valleys of the east to the plains of the Midwest, then the forests of the upper northwest. It took a full day and at the last portal, Chel stood nearby, shifting uncomfortably.

"You're seriously going in alone?" Chel asked, his tone incredulous. Dacre had received that a lot throughout his life. He looked more human than anything Hell had ever produced, so human that he needed no glamour on the Earthen plane.

Dacre didn't look at Chel as he stepped toward the portal. "You'd only slow me down," he said.

Chel bristled but before he could respond, Remington stepped forward, placing a hand on Chel's shoulder. "Let him go. If anyone can get her back, it's him."

Dacre glanced back once, his dark eyes cold and unyielding. Then he stepped through the portal, disappearing into the shimmering glow.

———

THE AIR WAS thick with acrid brimstone. The faint hum of dark magic vibrated under his feet. He could sense the wards like heat in the distance.

Dacre straightened, rolling his shoulders as he adjusted to the dark energy surrounding the mansion. Dacre's eyes narrowed as he scanned the old pine forest, noting the checkpoint in the distance. He moved with a preternatural grace, his footsteps silent as he approached the Black Mansion in the distance. It was an uphill trek over slippery pine needles and soft soil. After he got closer, he gripped the trunk of a skinny pine and crouched. The layout was just like Kit had said.

Screams ripped through the forest.

Two shadow demons guarded the main entrance, their hulking forms barely visible in the gloom of the forest canopy.

Dacre didn't hesitate. He stepped from the shadows, drawing his blade in a fluid motion.

One of the demons growled, its glowing eyes narrowing as it raised sharp claws. Dacre closed the distance in a blur of movement, his blade slicing through the first demon with precision. The creature dissolved into a pile of ash. The second demon lunged at him, but Dacre ducked under its swipe and drove his blade upward, impaling it through the chest. The creature howled, its body disintegrating as Dacre pulled his weapon free.

"Amateurs," he muttered, stepping over the remains and pushing the heavy doors open.

The interior of the mansion was just as he remembered. It appeared nothing really changed; same hallways, different décor.

Dacre moved with purpose, his senses on high alert. Whispers echoed through the halls, faint and disjointed, like fragments of a nightmare.

As he rounded a corner, a group of lesser demons blocked his path. Their malformed bodies twitched with anticipation as they grinned, revealing rows of jagged teeth.

Dacre sighed, tightening his grip on his blade. "I don't have time for this," he said, voice laced with irritation.

The demons lunged as one, but Dacre was a storm of movement. His blade arced through the air, cutting them to ash in an instant. Blood and gore coated the walls by the time he was done. It looked very much like the hallways the last time demons from the Black Mansion had touched Rue.

Dacre paused only long enough to wipe his blade clean before continuing deeper into the mansion. He was on the edge of shifting as he prowled.

Dacre's sharp senses led him to a door under the stairwell. When he opened it, there was a staircase spiraling down. Cool air greeted him along with the faint sound of feminine whispers.

"Rue," he called, his voice low.

The air grew colder and more damp with each step he took down the stairs. A faint, weak, shuddering breath echoed. He followed it, his heart pounding. He had anticipated at least a dozen more demons would greet him. This seemed too easy.

Dacre found Rue slumped in a corner of a cage, her hair matted and her face pale. Blood trickled from a cut on her forehead. She coughed and he recognized the wet sound. Dacre looked down and realized the dirt floor was soggy.

"Rue," he said again, softer this time. He dropped to one knee, his hands reaching for the cage's door. He pulled but it was locked.

Her eyes fluttered open, glassy but aware. "Dacre?" she whispered.

"I'm here," he said. "I'm getting you out."

"You shouldn't have come," Rue warned. "They weren't after me. They were after you."

Metal slammed.

Dacre's eyes swept the dark, damp dungeon as Rue's warning settled over him. Her weakened voice sent a jolt of unease through him.

A force shoved him from behind. Dacre stumbled forward into an open cell. The heavy iron gate slammed shut behind him.

Dacre froze for a fraction of a second before rising to his feet.

"Fuck," he muttered, a growl of frustration slipping into his voice.

Shadows mingled along the walls, taking humanoid shapes with jagged edges. The air grew heavy with dark energy.

A mocking voice echoed from the darkness. "Did you think you could just walk in and take her, Dacre?"

Dacre's gaze snapped to the source of the voice. A demon stepped forward, its eyes glowing with a cruel, fiery light.

"I've been waiting for you."

"You're going to regret that," Dacre said flatly.

The demon laughed, the sound grating. "Oh, no. This is your reckoning, Hellhound."

Shadows danced across Dacre's face as fury boiled through his veins. It took every effort for him not to shift forms and decimate the demon standing on the other side of the bars.

"You have family debts," the demon said. "They're due."

"They've been paid," Dacre replied, pacing the cell like a wild animal. "I've been free for years now."

The demon tilted its head, the corners of its jagged mouth twisting into a grotesque smile. Claws tapped a rhythm against the bars of the cage. He shook a finger at Dacre and clicked his tongue. "These debts are never paid." He walked closer. "And given what you are, everyone wants a piece of you. Especially those eyes." He slammed a metal blade against the bars. "I cannot wait to cut them from your skull." He leaned in, his hot breath reeking of sulfur. "Such a shame really. A Hellhound with the most extraordinary eyes. When I cut them from your skull, they'll make the finest trophy."

"I am *not* a hellhound," Dacre seethed.

The demon slammed a metal blade against the bars with a deafening clang, making Rue jump. Sparks scattered in the dim light.

"You'll fetch a high price, Hellhound," the demon mused, dragging the flat of the blade across the bars. "But that's not all. Word travels fast, and we know your secret."

Dacre growled as his hands curled into fists and he tamped down the wild energy threatening to take over his body. "Whatever you think you know, it's nothing but lies." His voice was laced with menace.

The demon chuckled a low, guttural sound. "Oh, but this isn't a lie. You can't swim, can you? I remember that from ages ago."

Dacre's expression didn't falter, but Rue saw the briefest flicker of tension in his posture.

"I can see it in your eyes," the demon said gleefully, his tongue darting out to wet cracked lips. "That little flicker of doubt. When the time comes, I'll be the one standing over your floating hide. Imagine it: you sinking down, down, down, unable to claw your way to the surface. Quite poetic end for a Hellhound, don't you think?"

The demon turned, his laughter echoing as he strode toward the stairwell. He climbed the stairs, looking back over his shoulder.

"When the moment comes, I'll make sure it's slow and satisfying. Enjoy your stay in the dark."

He climbed the rest of the stairs and slammed the door shut behind him, the sound of the heavy lock sliding into place reverberating through the dungeon.

"I am not a Hellhound!" Dacre shouted toward the door before pacing his cell while clenching his fists.

Thirty-Eight

Dacre exhaled sharply, pacing to the edge of the cage. He gripped the bars, his knuckles white. "Are you okay, Rue?"

She moved to her knees and scooted closer. "You can't swim? What does he mean?"

Dacre's eyes settled on the puddle in the corner of Rue's cell. His gaze slid up the wall to see a gentle dripping of water.

"It doesn't matter," he said. "Did they hurt you?" Dacre crouched and reached for her through the bars.

"The heckling didn't hurt." She looked up at him, her eyes watery. "It was the dreams. The nightmares. They wanted to trap you and I couldn't stop it. I just sat here waiting, knowing. It was the absolute worst feeling." Rue started coughing.

"It's not your fault, Rue." Dacre pulled his arm back and stood. "We need to get you out of here." He scanned the cells for weaknesses.

"It does matter," Rue pressed, her voice cracking. "He's planning something, Dacre."

Dacre turned to her, his expression softening for a moment as he saw the fear in her eyes. "I'll deal with it," he said firmly. "Right now, we need to focus on getting out of here."

Rue nodded, swallowing hard. Despite the terror pressing down on her, Dacre's calm determination was an anchor pulling her back from the edge of panic.

"We'll get out," he promised, his voice low but steady. "They underestimated the both of us."

———

Torchlight flickered against the damp stone walls. A mocking laugh echoed down the corridor that led to the stairwell.

"Well, well," came the gravelly voice. "Jiminy Christmas. Haven't seen one of you in a coon's age." Hands clapped together and the sound of slow footsteps reverberated like a sinister countdown.

A demon emerged from the shadows, tall and gaunt, his blackened skin shimmering with faint iridescence. His eyes gleamed with malice, and a twisted smile split his face, revealing razor sharp teeth.

"And all this time you've been rotting down here." He checked his watch as though it had been longer than half a day. "You could have escaped hours ago. Why haven't you?"

Dacre didn't answer immediately. His body was taut, his muscles coiled as if ready to strike despite the bars separating them. A guttural snarl escaped his throat, low and dangerous, a sound Rue had never heard from him before.

"Why didn't you?" Rue's voice trembled, her gaze darting to Dacre. "You let yourself get caught? Why would you do that?"

Dacre's dark eyes met hers and her mouth snapped shut.

The demon chuckled darkly, leaning casually against the frame of Dacre's cell. "Don't let me interrupt your lovers' quarrel." He lifted his arm, a heavy bracelet clinking on his wrist.

Rue's eyes were drawn to it. Set into the bracelet was a pair of luminous, glowing, green-colored stones. No, not stones. They were something different. Whatever they were, it made her stomach churn with unease.

Dacre's head snapped toward the demon and a growl ripped from him that shook the walls. "You bastard."

The demon grinned wider, tapping the bracelet. "Recognize these, boy? She begged for you, you know. Whispered your name with her last breath. Such a shame you weren't there to save her. Or any of them."

Rue recoiled, her heart hammering as realization dawned. "What are those?"

"My mother's eyes," Dacre finished, his voice a deadly whisper.

The demon feigned a dramatic sigh. "Oh, the tragedy. The guilt must eat at you, doesn't it? All that power within your skin, and you couldn't even save your precious family. And now you're the last one. The end of a bloodline."

Dacre lunged at the bars, the metal groaning under his strength, but they held firm. His fury was bubbling up on the precipice, a storm barely contained. "I will tear you apart," he promised.

The demon didn't flinch. Instead, he leaned closer, his grin never faltering. "You've always been too slow. It's why you've failed every time." He turned his attention to Rue, his gaze raking over her with predatory curiosity. "And you... What could you possibly be to him?"

Rue straightened, trying to quell the tremor in her legs. "I'm the reason he's going to kill you," she spat.

The demon laughed, a sound like nails scraping against stone. "Oh, I do love your fire. Let's see how long it lasts when the water starts rising."

With that, he stepped back into the shadows, the sound of his laughter lingering like a curse.

Rue sank to the floor, her breath coming in shallow gasps before a fit of coughing. "Dacre..." she began, but her voice broke.

"I'm going to make him pay," Dacre said, his voice steady despite the storm in his eyes. "For everything. For everyone."

Rue gripped the bars again, her hands trembling. "We have to get out of here first."

"We will," Dacre promised, "Princess. I'll find a way."

Rue's voice trembled, her gaze darting to Dacre. "You let yourself get caught? Why would you do that?"

Dacre's dark eyes met hers and for the first time she saw a flash of green. "So you couldn't leave me after you knew the truth," he said, his voice raw. "I wouldn't have survived it."

Rue's breath hitched, but her face twisted into a scowl. "That's kind of a shit sacrifice, Dacre." She began pacing her small cell, her movements frantic. She stopped suddenly, gripping the cold iron bars with both hands. "You don't get to decide that for me."

Dacre simply watched her.

It was night when icy water surged into the dungeon with a deafening roar as it gushed through cracks in the walls. Rue pressed her back against the cold bars, as though she might escape through them.

As the water climbed higher, she scrambled to her feet, trembling fingers gripping the iron as she struggled to keep her balance. It rushed to her knees, then to her waist. Rue's breaths came shallow and quick as panic clawed at her chest.

A heavy arm wrapped around her shoulders. Dacre pulled

her against him, holding her in place as the rushing current threatened to tug her down.

"We're going to die here," Rue said, her voice hollow. There was no way out. Neither of them could break the cages they were trapped in and from their discussion with the demon earlier, the goal was to drown them both.

"No, we're not going to die," Dacre said firmly, his lips close to her ear. "Just close your eyes. Pretend you're in a dream. Look up at the sky. You've always like that, watching the stars."

Rue's eyelids fluttered shut, her head leaning back against his chest. "I did," she muttered, doing as he said. Behind her eyelids there was only darkness. She looked up, trying to imagine a star-filled night. "The sky is starless. There is nothing."

"Keep your eyes closed," Dacre instructed, his voice a low rumble. "Don't open them. No matter what you hear."

The water crept higher, lapping at Rue's collarbone. She shivered violently, the cold seeping into her bones.

"Dacre?" she asked, her voice wavering.

"Yeah?" He was moving, his arm tightening around her as he shifted his weight against the rising flood.

Rue squeezed her eyes tighter. "I think... I think we've been here before." Her voice was laced with dread.

"What are you talking about?" Dacre asked as his entire body shivered hard, ready to transform.

She turned her head and Dacre saw... her eyes were half-lidded and white. He'd told her she slept with her eyes open years ago when he'd first met her in Lucifer's dungeon. She didn't believe him, even tried to fight him afterward. But he'd seen it clear as day. But... she wasn't sleeping now.

Fragments of the nightmare she'd had in the library returned. The rising water, the icy grip of fear–it was all the same.

"I don't think I'm having nightmares," Rue whispered, her voice trembling. "I think I've been having visions of the future. Maybe even the past. I'm not sure."

Dacre stilled for a moment, his sharp intake of breath echoing over the roar of the water rushing into the dungeon. "Then you already know we're not going to die here," he said, as he slowly started to lose his grip on the change.

Rue shook her head faintly. "No, I don't. All I saw was the water rising. And then–"

"And then what?" Dacre pressed, his tone urgent.

Heat was coming off him like Rue had never experienced before. She swallowed hard, her throat tight. "And then it was just black. Nothing else."

Dacre cursed under his breath. He let go of her briefly, pushing against the bars with all his strength, the muscles in his arms aching as the metal groaned but held firm. He was running out of options. He wasn't going to be able to hold back much longer.

The water surged higher, reaching Rue's chin. She tilted her head back, trying to keep her mouth and nose above the rising flood.

"Stay with me, Rue." His arm was wrapped around her shoulders again and she was thankful for the heat he was emitting. "We're getting out of here. I promise you."

Rue nodded faintly.

A switch flipped in Dacre when he realized he couldn't hold back any longer. He glanced down at her, the water rushing closer to her mouth as she was struggling to stand. This had to end now.

"Rue. Close your eyes and don't open them, no matter what you hear. Promise me." There was pain in his voice. "Please. Don't open your eyes."

Rue nodded. "Okay, Dacre. I'll keep them closed." Water rushed into her mouth and Rue coughed before stretching up on her toes to escape the surge. If he didn't do something soon, she was going to drown.

The bars at her back vibrated and the water around her turned warm. There were strange noises: stretching and snapping and popping, a low growl that sounded like a giant beast. His arm felt different against her chest as he held her in place. She heard a loud snap, and her body rushed backward, connecting with a hard chest.

"Keep them closed. You promised." Dacre was carrying her against his chest through the water.

"I promise." Rue snapped her mouth closed as water hit her lips.

Dacre held her close then used his free hand to snap two more bars off his cell. He stepped out, wading through the rising water, headed toward the stairs.

"We're going to be just fine," Dacre said, soothing. "Just keep those eyes closed."

"I will," Rue promised. "I am."

She shivered as he climbed the stairwell, taking them out of the cold water. He wrapped another arm around her and the unnatural heat from his body warmed her.

He stopped moving. "Things are about to get ugly."

"What do you want me to do?" Rue asked before she started coughing again. Water from her wet hair streamed down her back and puddled onto the floor.

"Just do what I say."

There was a loud cracking noise as Dacre broke through the locked door to the dungeon. Small pieces of wood fell onto Rue. He walked through the opening and took in his surroundings. The hallways were dark, shadows swirling in the corners.

The dark energy was strong. While the Black Mansion's magic didn't recognize him, it would recognize the destruction and movement. It would recognize Rue.

He prowled toward the front door as the creatures in the shadows watched.

What Rue didn't see was that Dacre had half-shifted into a creature long forgotten. A creature that no one had seen in ages. He was the last of his kind; a large cat-like beast with tentacles sprouting from his shoulders, on the end of the tentacles were pads he used to bend light and create illusions. Striking emerald-green eyes glowed with malevolence and those eyes were the reason for his kind's demise. They were hunted for their eyes which continued to glow after death and were traded as good luck charms.

Dacre had learned plenty watching his family slowly hunted and slaughtered. He knew to kill first and ask questions later. He knew that the demons of the Black Mansion feared him. But some also knew exactly how to kill him. It didn't matter, he was no longer holding back.

Dacre made his way toward the front door, knowing that the shadow demons in the hallway weren't brave enough to approach him like this. Only one demon was, and he wasn't here... yet.

"Keep them closed," Dacre warned Rue.

He was moving swiftly, glancing down at her face once to make sure she wasn't watching him.

A door opened. Rue was set on her feet.

"Run straight ahead. Don't look back. I'll find you. Don't stop running," Dacre urged. "Don't stop. Head East to the edge of the pine forest. I'll come for you."

"Okay," Rue's voice was thick with emotion as she nodded in agreement.

"Run, Rue. Run as fast as you can. Don't open your eyes until you're far away. And..."

"What?" she didn't like the tremor in his voice.

He wanted to say, *don't come back* but instead he said, "Nothing. I'll find you. I will always find you."

Then the door was slammed and it hit her back jolting her forward.

Rue ran as fast as she could. There were terrible noises coming from behind her. Loud thuds, cries and screams, things she shouldn't be able to hear from outside the Black Mansion. It echoed through the night and made her stomach twist. She stumbled, arms out. She tripped and fell and rolled downhill. Her body slammed into the trunk of a tree. Rue tasted blood in her mouth. She paused, catching her breath.

Running with her eyes closed the entire time would be instant death. She used the tree trunk to climb to her feet, then she opened her eyes and started running again. She never looked back.

It was downhill for a few hundred more yards. Her wet shoes slipped on the pine needles and soft ground. She noticed motion from the corner of her eye and veered left.

There were shadow demons to the right. They watched her, shivering as though they were getting ready to come after her. Instead their heads whipped back toward the Black Mansion as a loud roar sounded. They looked at each other then ran toward the commotion, abandoning their hunt.

Rue took a deep breath and continued her trek. There was a break ahead in the forest. She paused at the edge of the tree line. It was a road. She had to think quickly; she didn't trust anyone on the roads in Hell. There was no one who would help her out in these parts. She made sure there was no movement on the road, then ran across it.

Rue ran and ran and ran until her lungs burned and her legs ached. She ran until she started coughing so hard she couldn't catch her breath. Tears blurred her vision. The undergrowth clawed at her legs, and the night seemed darker than ever, the stars above hidden by thick clouds.

The sky *was* starless.

THIRTY-NINE

Dacre turned to face the demons. The air around him shimmered, and his body began to twist and change beyond what he'd already revealed. Muscle and sinew rippled, black fur sprouted across his skin as he dropped to all fours. His form elongated and six limbs stretched outward, each paw tipped with gleaming claws. A long, powerful tail flicked behind him, and two luminous, green orbs burned where his eyes had been.

The demon cocked his head, an unsettling grin spreading across his face. "Finally showing your true form? I wondered how long you'd hold back."

Dacre didn't respond with words. He launched himself forward, his massive frame moving with deadly grace. The air around him shimmered, his Displacer Beast form distorting reality as he struck.

The demon swung his blade but it passed through an afterimage, slicing only air. A snarl ripped through the room, and Dacre's claws tore into the demon's side.

"You should've drowned," the demon hissed, staggering back.

Dacre didn't relent. He lunged again, his jaws snapping shut around the demon's arm. With a sickening crunch, he tore the bracelet free, the severed limb falling to the floor.

The demon screamed, but Dacre wasn't finished. He slammed the demon against the wall, his claws raking through flesh and stone alike. The mansion shook with the force of the fight, dust and debris raining down from the ceiling and walls.

When the demon finally slumped to the ground, lifeless, Dacre stood over him, panting. He held the bloodied bracelet in his teeth, the green eyes glinting in the dim light.

———

THE MANSION WAS EERILY silent now, the air heavy with the metallic tang of blood. Bodies—some whole, others in pieces—littered the stone floor, their lifeless forms blending with the shadows. The ornate decor of the Black Mansion was splattered with gore, its sinister elegance now a grotesque canvas of death.

In the center of it all stood Dacre, his massive Displacer Beast form trembling with exhaustion. His dark fur was matted with blood—both his own and his enemies. The green orbs of his eyes flickered faintly, their light dimming. He tried to shift back to his human form but his body refused, rejecting the transformation. There was too much adrenaline mixed with an unsatiated blood lust that he had yet to deal with.

His breaths came in ragged pants, the hunger gnawing at him. It wasn't just physical exhaustion; it was something deeper, more primal. The fight had drained him of everything, leaving only the burning hunger that clawed at his insides.

He stepped over a mangled body, his six limbs moving with a predator's grace, though his steps faltered. The remains of the demon who had worn his mother's eyes as a trophy lay crumpled nearby, the bracelet now discarded on the blood-soaked floor.

He picked up the bracelet and tucked it into what was left of his jeans pocket on the lower half of his body.

Dacre's chest heaved as the hunger surged again, sharper and more insistent. His head tipped back, and a low, guttural growl rumbled from his throat. The coppery scent of blood was overwhelming, but it wasn't enough. None of it was enough.

His mind spun, fragmented thoughts latching on to the only thing that could sate him. The only person.

"Rue," he rasped, his voice distorted in his beastly form.

The hunger wasn't just physical. It was tied to her—her blood, her presence, her essence. She was the only thing that could pull him back from the abyss.

He stumbled toward the shattered doorway of the mansion, his claws scraping against the stone. Each step was a battle against the beast within, the part that wanted to lose itself in blood and violence. But he couldn't. Not now. Not when Rue was out there, alone and vulnerable.

The forest stretched before him, dark and endless. He inhaled deeply, catching the faintest trace of her scent on the wind. It was enough to give him focus and direction.

"I'm coming," he murmured, his voice low and guttural.

The hunger clawed again, threatening to rip him open from the inside. But Dacre forced it down, his need to find Rue overshadowing everything else. He disappeared into the shadows of the forest, moving with lethal grace.

The hunt wasn't over. Not yet.

FORTY

The forest was an endless maze of towering pines and twisting shadows. Moonlight barely pierced the canopy, leaving the ground shrouded in near darkness. Dacre moved silently through the underbrush, and looking like a big black cat he blended seamlessly into the gloom. His body ached, the strain of holding his monstrous shape gnawing at him.

Rue's scent led him forward like a thread of hope.

Then he heard it—a soft whimper carried on the wind. His ears perked and his green eyes flicked in the direction of the sound. The soft murmurs of distress grew louder as he closed the distance, each step driving him closer to her.

He found Rue curled beneath the gnarled roots of a massive tree, her knees tucked against her chest. She shivered uncontrollably, her face pale even in the faint moonlight. Sweat glistened on her brow, and she murmured broken fragments of words in her sleep; a nightmare, twisting her dreams into something dark and cruel. He'd seen her like this before. He couldn't leave her to suffer.

Dacre hesitated, his claws digging into the earth. He

wanted to shift and be the man she needed, but his body rebelled against the command. The beast still had its hold on him and the hunger lingered, whispering vile temptations.

He crept closer, his massive frame moving with surprising gentleness. Rue shivered again, her teeth chattering, and he knew she wouldn't last long in the cold. Especially with the cough.

Dacre closed his eyes, focusing. Illusions were part of his nature, a skill he rarely used but no creature in all the realms could do what he could do. He drew on the flickering remnants of his strength, weaving his form into something familiar and safe. Something that wouldn't scare her to death if he didn't wake in time.

When he opened his eyes, he was smaller, softer—a perfect replica of Lucipurr, Rue's beloved kitten. His paws padded silently across the chilled ground as he approached her.

Rue's breathing slowed slightly, sleepy eyes half opened as the illusion worked its way into her subconscious.

"Lucipurr," she murmured, her voice a soft croak. Her hand reached out instinctively, brushing against his fur. "You're so warm."

Dacre settled beside her, curling his body around hers to share his warmth. Her shivering began to subside as she unconsciously buried her face in his side, the nightmare loosening its grip. She sighed softly, her tension ebbing away.

In her dream, she was back home, curled up in her bed with Lucipurr purring beside her. The familiar rhythm was soothing, drawing her into a deep sleep.

Dacre stayed where he was, his body still aching and his mind battling the hunger.

The forest around them was silent except for the whisper of wind through the trees. He didn't move, didn't dare break the fragile peace. Her breathing had evened out and her face was relaxed as though the nightmares had gone.

As dawn broke, pale light filtered through the canopy, illuminating Rue's sleeping form. Her eyes fluttered open and she blinked slowly, her gaze hazy with sleep.

Moments before, Dacre padded off into the undercover to hide.

"Lucipurr?" Rue mumbled, her hand patting the space beside her. It was empty but suspiciously warm.

There was a noise in the forest; branches snapped. Someone or something was close. Rue scrambled to her feet. She gazed into the shadows of the forest and froze when a giant panther-like creature met her eyes.

Rue screamed and turned to run.

FORTY-ONE

RUE RAN, HER BREATH TEARING THROUGH HER chest as the forest closed in around her. Branches snagged at her hair and pine needles scraped against her arms. Behind her, the guttural sound of something large crashing through the underbrush sent her heart thrumming against her ribcage.

She stumbled into a clearing, gasping. Noises were surrounding her. She spun in a tight circle, pulse thundering in her ears.

The rustling grew louder. The shadows of the forest deepened.

A hulking figure broke through the shadow line of trees. A massive, shifting black beast with glowing green eyes emerged. It was the panther creature but... it had too many legs and strange tentacles on its shoulders that vibrated. One moment she saw the monster, the next she saw her kitten Lucipurr. It kept changing shapes in rapid succession. Was she dreaming still? Rue rubbed her eyes. She couldn't tell. Everything was so confusing.

Rue's scream tore through the silence as she turned and

ran across the clearing. But the tree line in the distance seemed to shift, shadows twisting unnaturally. The air grew cold.

A deep growl echoed in the clearing. Rue skidded to a halt just as a figure emerged from the shadows. A shadow demon. It's gaunt frame and elongated limbs reached for her with claws slicing at the air. She was trapped, surrounded by monsters. Rue glanced to the side. She'd never outrun either creature. She was as good as dead.

Rue stumbled back as more shadow demons appeared, their bodies shimmering like oil in the early morning sunrise.

One lunged for her. She threw her arms up as a scream caught in her throat. Before the demon could reach her, a black blur leaped over her head.

The monster.

The beast slammed into the demon midair, his massive claws tearing through the demon like it was nothing more than smoke. The beast's roar echoed through the forest, vibrating to her bones.

Rue backed up, tripped, and fell as the fight raged on in front of her. Her pupils blew wide as Demons surged forward, but the beast met them with a skill and speed she'd never witnessed before. It was faster than a Hellion and more deadly. Rue wondered if her parents knew about this creature. She figured she wouldn't get to tell them as it would turn on her next.

Shadow demons shrieked as the beast ripped through them one by one until the forest fell silent, except for the ragged sounds of the panther-like beast breathing.

The clearing was painted with ashy remains; black smears of ichor and blood stained the ground and shimmered on the beast's fur.

Rue gasped as it turned to face her.

Rue scrambled back, pressing herself against a tree. Her

voice trembled as she whispered, "Stay back," and held a hand out in defense. She coughed, moving her arm to cough more into her elbow.

As she waited for her last breath, the beast began to shiver and twist, the black tendrils and extra legs folding inward, its body shrinking and twisting until...

"Dacre!" Rue gasped, scrambling to her feet, and rushing toward him. He groaned as she jumped and threw her arms around him, burying her face against his neck. "You found me."

"I told you I'd find you," he said, his voice low and drained. His clothing was torn and hanging from his body in shredded strips.

"You're hurt," she murmured, her hands brushing over the fresh wounds as he set her on her feet.

Dacre was still as stone as if he was afraid to move. His face and chest were smeared with blood. "Rue," he said, his voice rough and cracked. "You're not afraid of me?"

He took a step back to give her space. After all, she probably wasn't in her right mind after everything that had happened.

Rue took a step forward.

Dacre's expression was cautious. "I would never hurt you," he said softly, kneeling so they were eye to eye.

Rue was deep in thought. The terror she'd just witnessed was him. Her breaths came in shallow gasps as she trembled. "I'm not afraid of you... like this." She searched his face. Her voice cracked. "What... what are you?"

Before he could answer, the rustling of leaves behind them made her flinch. Dacre's gaze snapped to the tree line. His body tensed, ready to fight.

"More are coming," he said, grimly extending a hand toward her, his fingers streaked with dark blood. "We need to move. Now. Come with me. Please."

She hesitated, glancing up at his dark eyes.

"Please," he begged.

Rue reached out and gripped his hand.

FORTY-TWO

Rue started to move but a fit of coughing came sharp and sudden, racking her chest and forcing her to stumble. Dacre froze, mid-step, his head snapping back to her.

"No," he murmured as he recalled the symptoms of wet lung disease he'd seen in other prisoners. He moved to Rue's side, arms circling her before she could fall. She tried to wave him off but another round of coughing tore through her.

"Enough," Dacre growled. Without warning, he scooped her up in his arms as if she weighed nothing. "We need to get you somewhere warm. Now."

Before Rue could protest Dacre was moving, the forest blurring past. Rue closed her eyes. The faint cries of shadow demons echoed in the distance as they found the mess in the clearing. Dacre's sharp gaze scanned the terrain. He didn't slow when he realized the shadow demons weren't following them. He needed to get her warm.

Dacre smelled the heated salt and earth, the sharp tang of minerals carried on the breeze. He veered to the right, running toward the smell. The realm of Hell was nothing more than a dark reflection of the Earthen plane. The pine forests were located in the pacific northwest, and nearby there were hot-springs and empty tourist areas. Not far was a portal that could bring them back to Rue's family. But first, he had to get her well enough to travel through the portals. The wet lung had set in and he was afraid she'd become too sick for healing.

Soon, they broke into a clearing where natural hot springs steamed, nestled among rocky terrain. The water shimmered, its surface alive with gentle ripples.

Dacre set Rue down on a smooth rock by the edge of the largest pool. "The heat and salt will help your lungs recover," he said, his voice softer but laced with tension. "Get in."

She hesitated, with a shiver. "What about–" She glanced behind them.

"We're safe here." Dacre didn't wait for her to argue, already pulling off what was left of his shirt. "And I'm not leaving you again."

Rue's eyes drifted over his skin; the muscle, slashes of gore, and claw marks. She took off her shirt and jeans then slipped into the water. The heat enveloped her immediately, soothing her aching muscles and raw throat. She leaned back against the smooth rock, closing her eyes as the steam curled around her.

Dacre slid into the water beside her, his movements quiet. For a moment, neither of them spoke–the only sounds were the gentle lapping of the water. They were both exhausted.

Rue tipped her head back, resting it on the cool rock, her mind drifted to a half-dreaming state. The last of her memories began to fill in... The dungeons, Lucifer, the Black Mansion, blood on her tongue...

I WONDER if she knows your name yet," he taunted, glancing at Rue. "Has he told you, little lost princess? Does she know who you really are, Dacre?"

. . .

RUE'S EYES snapped open and she turned to look at Dacre, her expression shadowed.

"It was you," she whispered, her voice rough. "You brought me to Lucifer all those years ago. You brought me to the Black Mansion." She searched his face.

Dacre went still, his jaw tightened. "Yes," he admitted after a long pause. "It was me."

Her heart clenched and her face fell in disappointment. She knew Dacre was better than that. She needed to understand why he'd done it.

"Why?" she wasn't mad, she just wanted answers. She was so tired of the lies and deception her family had fed her since she woke up on the battlefield filled with gore, having no memory of anything.

He didn't meet her eyes, instead slid lower until the water met his jaw. "My family owes debts to Lucifer. When he sits on the throne, I must continue to pay them off. They are forever," he said bitterly, his voice low. "Debts I cannot escape no matter how much I want to. Lucifer called upon me..." he sighed, "I had no choice. There are ages of debt from family before."

Rue's chest ached but not from coughing. "You took me from my father's home..." She moved closer to him. "But... you argued with Lucifer to keep me alive. I remember that. He could have killed you in an instant. But you convinced him not to kill me that day."

Dacre looked up at her. "I did."

"He could have killed you for that. Who in their right mind would argue with Lucifer?"

"It was the right thing to do."

"And... I think you killed those demons in the Black Mansion when they forced me to drink blood the first time."

Rue was searching his face.

Dacre nodded.

"You left me in the dungeon. You told them to never let me out." Rue moved closer again.

"You were a child–" Dacre was still.

"Not for much longer," Rue interrupted. "I grew up in Hell. I was not as innocent as some might think. Girls on the Earthen plane younger than me have gotten married off. I was not much of a child any longer. I had seen and done plenty." She lowered her voice. "I was *barely* a child."

"But then you bit me," his voice was heavy with regret. "You created a bond that none of us understood at the time. I didn't understand it. I was going crazy."

"My parents have a blood bond. Others do and will." Rue was staring into his eyes. "It's not as taboo as some might think. Not for royal families."

Dacre's lips pressed into a thin line. "I do not have a royal bloodline. I come from monsters. I am a monster under this skin."

Rue's hand moved under the water and settled on his shoulder.

"Don't," Dacre warned.

His confession was heavy between them but there was more. Steam danced with their breath as they watched each other. Rue's mind raced through the tangled web of past and present. Dacre had saved her. Over and over again. She could never ignore that fact. When she was unsafe, he was there. She guessed there was more he'd done that she had no memories of; a perception that only one person would know, things he'd done to help her when she wasn't aware.

She would never know that he snuck into the castle in the burning caves to get her out of the dungeon as Lucifer battled her parents. Dacre saved her from death, escaping the castle not long before it collapsed. He'd brought her straight to her parents after they'd defeated Lucifer. Rue only woke up in that battlefield because Dacre had brought her there. If he hadn't risked his life to do that, she'd have been crushed and buried.

Rue exhaled shakily. "You might be a monster underneath this skin." Her fingers moved across his thickly muscled shoulders, her voice was soft. "But I think... I think you're *my* monster."

A faint smile tugged at his lips before vanishing. "If you left after knowing the truth, I wouldn't have survived it, Rue," he admitted. "If you'd hated me after all this..."

Her chest tightened and something stirred deep within her, something she'd kept tampered down for years and years. "I don't hate you," she said, her voice almost a whisper. "And I'm not leaving." Then Rue said something she'd heard her grandmother say a long time ago, "Every treasure has a dragon."

"I'm not a dragon," Dacre frowned.

"No. I think you're something better." She licked her lips.

The distance between them vanished as Rue moved closer, her fingers sliding up his neck and thumbs brushing his jaw. His skin was warm–it was always warm–his dark eyes burned with an intensity that made her heart stutter.

With a low growl he reached out, wrapped an arm around her waist, and dragged her against him. He kissed her and it wasn't soft or hesitant. It was raw, it was fire; filled with all the things he'd held inside for years, all the things he couldn't say. She melted into him, her hands tangling in his damp hair as the heat and steam of the hot springs wrapped around them.

Rue kissed him harder, wrapping her legs around his waist and sliding both of her hands up and down his neck. Soon she was moving against him, feeling his body against hers. Large hands wrapped around her hips to hold her still.

"Rue," he whispered her name with a groan that sounded

like he was in pain.

She rested her forehead against his, her breathing uneven. "Don't stop." She tried moving again. "Please."

Dacre chuckled, the sound low and rough. "Yes, princess." His hands moved down her body and slid into her underwear, pulling them away. "Lean back," he instructed her.

Rue smiled, her body tingling with anticipation as she leaned her back against the edge of the pool and braced her arms on each side.

Dacre moved back, hands gripping her hips and pulling her up.

"I thought you couldn't swim," she joked.

"This is shallow," he growled as his tongue swept up her thigh towards her center. Dark eyes locked on hers.

Rue sucked in a breath, watching him taste her. She closed her eyes, tipped her head back, and embraced everything he gave. His mouth and fingers moved against her center until she shivered with release.

He lowered her in the water again and dragged her close. She moved against him, wanting more, wanting everything. Hips rocking against his, she sighed at the press of his hardness against her, hated that he was still wearing boxers. She reached for the waistband, but he grabbed her wrists and stopped her.

"Not here, princess," he warned.

"Why?" she dragged her tongue up his neck, controlling the urge to bite. She felt wild and free and out of control. She wanted to feel nothing more than his naked skin against hers, the pressure of him inside her.

"It's too dangerous out in the open," he warned. He simply held her, his lips pressed to her temple until her body went languid with disappointment.

"The cough seems better," Dacre said.

Rue nodded. "My lungs feel clear now." She realized she hadn't felt the urge to cough since they'd gotten in the hot springs.

"Good."

They lingered a while longer in the water, the tension between them easing into something softer.

Eventually, Dacre said, "We need to go." He hauled himself out of the spring, dripping water as he retrieved the bracelet from his discarded clothing. He crouched at the edge of the water and washed the blood and grime from the metal. The orbs of his mother's eyes gleamed in the afternoon sun, their beauty haunting.

"We need to move," he said, putting the bracelet on his wrist, wishing he had a good pair of pants with pockets. He put his damaged jeans and boots on, rolled up the shredded shirt, and tucked it in his pocket.

"There's a Hellion checkpoint cabin nearby. We can stay the night there." He looked her over. "In the morning we'll make it to the portal and get you back to your family."

Rue's face twisted. "You say that like you're not coming with me."

"I'll come with you," he said, but it sounded like he was keeping something from her.

He held out a hand and helped Rue out of the hot spring. Her body was still warm from the springs and her mind finally relaxed with truth and the release he'd given her.

She watched him move, could tell he was strung tighter than a drum, and didn't understand why he'd held back. She glanced toward the pine forest in the distance and remembered the shadow demons who'd chased them. He was probably on high alert being out in the open like this. Still, he watched her with a desire that was easy to decipher as she dressed.

———

THE HELLION CABIN appeared through the tangled vines and shadows of the pine forest and nestled in the safety of a rocky outcropping. Its silhouette was barely distinguishable against the inky sky. Constructed from dark, weathered wood and crowned with a steep roof, it was small but sturdy. Brimstone and woodsmoke mingled with the scent of the pine forest and reminded Rue of the Hellion lair she'd known as a kid.

"This is it," Dacre murmured. He placed a steadying hand in Rue's as they approached the door, sensing her weariness.

It had been a few hours' walk, and even though her cough had subsided, she was exhausted from everything that had happened.

The cabin was smaller inside than Rue expected. A stone fireplace dominated one wall, its hearth empty but ready with neatly stacked logs. A single bed covered in heavy, wool blankets sat against the opposite wall. Rue's eyes lingered on the shelves lined with preserved food, her gaze falling to the trunk and hoping for warm clothing.

Rue wandered inside. She sorted through the food and pulled down a few items. "I miss having a hot cup of coffee," she murmured.

When she turned, Dacre was crouched at the fireplace, arranging logs inside the hearth and starting a fire.

"Tell Remington he needs to stock the outposts with coffee makers." Dacre smirked. "I'm sure the Hellions would love that."

"Maybe a French press," Rue said as she opened the trunk and started going through the clothes. She found shirts and pants for both of them, and although they'd be huge on her, at least they were clean.

Dacre chuckled softly as he moved closer. "Could you imagine a Hellion trying to figure out a French press? They'd break it into a million pieces." He began rummaging through the supplies. "Let's see what they've left us." He reached up on the taller shelves and pulled out a jar of preserved strawberries, a loaf of dense, dark bread that had been wrapped in heavy paper, and a small block of hard cheese. "There is caffeine here." Dacre pulled down two cans of Coca-Cola. "They must've stocked this cabin recently."

Rue slid into a chair by the small wooden table, her body aching from the journey. The warm light from the fire bathed the room in a soft glow and for the first time in days, Rue finally felt safe.

As they ate, Rue studied Dacre. The flickering light was casting shadows across his face, accentuating his handsome features. He'd put on a clean shirt and pants. Rue toyed with the hem of the oversized shirt she was wearing and took another bite of the strange bread that was loaded with jam.

"You've been quiet," Dacre said, breaking the silence as he leaned back in his chair, watching her.

Rue hesitated. "Just... thinking."

"About?"

"Everything." She looked away. "I missed midterms for two of my classes. Those professors are going to fail me. And I've missed my independent study meeting with Professor Camden." She sighed heavily. "I was working really hard toward finishing and now everything's been delayed."

"Just tell them what happened," Dacre said with a shrug.

Rue chuckled. "Yeah, I'll tell my human professors on the Earthen plane that I was kidnapped by shadow demons and it took me a few days to escape because I was waiting for my monster boyfriend to come save me." She rolled her eyes and laughed harder. "They'll institutionalize me if I tell them all that."

Dacre leaned forward, resting his elbows on the table. "You've handled it better than most would."

Rue let out another small laugh that sounded like a sigh. "Thanks, I guess."

"Just one thing." Dacre held up his finger as he swallowed his last bite of food, making her wait a moment. "Boyfriend?" he finally asked, a playful smile tugging at his lips before he took a sip of his Coca-Cola.

Rue froze. Every bit of insecurity she had fired through her body like fireworks. She couldn't form words, only stared at him.

His chair fell as he swung around the table and was soon in front of her, gathering her into his arms and standing, lifting her like she weighed nothing at all. He crossed the room and sat on the bed, adjusting Rue so she was straddling his lap.

"Dacre?" Rue was gathering her wits but he was so handsome; there was something about the firelight that made his cheekbones sharper and his lashes darker. Tension had been building between them for hours–no weeks. Weeks and months since that first moment he'd come out of the shadows and asked her to dance at the Halloween party.

"Boyfriend?" he sighed. "You bit me so I think I'm more than that. I'm slightly offended."

Rue's jaw dropped open. "Oh. I'm sorry. I didn't mean to offend you."

Dacre was laughing and she enjoyed the deep timbre of his voice. Then for a moment, the crackle of the fire was the only sound. Rue remembered their time in the salt pool and a feeling stirred deep within her. He'd left her wanting more.

Dacre gathered her long hair and wrapped its length around his hand. His eyes held hers, steady. Before she could stop herself, Rue leaned in, her lips brushing his. It was tentative at first, but Dacre responded without hesitation, deepening the kiss. His free hand gripped her face gently as his tongue touched her lips. Rue's hands fell to his shoulders and she rocked her hips, instantly feeling that twinge in her lower abdomen. Her hands moved to his shirt and she tugged it off. Dacre released her hair and helped pull the shirt up. Then he reached for hers.

He paused while reaching for the waistband of her pants, hesitant. He met her gaze. Rue wasn't going to let him stop her this time.

"I don't want to hurt you," he whispered.

"You won't," she said as she moved off his lap. "You never have." She kicked off the pants, then her undergarments. Rue shivered, standing before him wearing nothing. Heat from the fireplace seeped into her spine and gave her a little courage. She climbed back onto Dacre's lap, her hands sliding up his muscled stomach, over his shoulders, and threading into his dark hair. She pressed her mouth to his and kissed him like she was in charge, whimpering against his lips as she felt his rough hands exploring her body. He smoothed over her thighs and across her hips, kneading and rubbing. His tongue speared into her mouth as fingers explored the vee between her thighs. Rue moaned and rocked her body against his. She reached for him, tugged at the waistband of his pants until he was freed.

Dacre sucked in a sharp breath and kissed her harder, deeper. His hands moved to her hips and guided her body to accept him. They both hissed in pleasure at the tight fit.

Rue kissed his jaw, her tongue sliding down his neck as she swore she could hear the throbbing of the thick veins there. She felt the raised scars of her teeth marks from years ago when she'd inadvertently claimed him.

Dacre tipped his head to the side. "Do it."

Rue kissed the scars. That was a conversation for another time. She'd stopped growing in certain ways when the demons gave her blood, which meant she'd never get sharp teeth. If she bit him it would hurt; being pierced open by blunt teeth was not what Rue wanted him to experience in this moment. She kissed the scars once more, rotated her hips, then took him deeper until he groaned and his eyes rolled and he tipped his head backward. She kissed his collarbone, his jaw, and forced his head forward so she could devour his mouth again.

Later, when they were done exploring each other's bodies, they settled back into the bed. Dacre dragged her close, his big body wrapped around her. He pulled the blanket over their naked skin and nuzzled her neck.

"Sorry," she murmured.

"Don't be." His voice was soft.

"I won't ever get sharp teeth," she warned him. "If I bite you for blood, it will hurt. It will always hurt." She took his hand, moved it to her mouth and pressed his finger to her teeth. "It's not normal."

"Have you ever thought that maybe I'd still like it?" he whispered in her ear. "Your kind drink blood. I've watched you avoid it long past the time in which you should have been drinking it regularly. I won't watch you suffer." He rose up on his elbow and turned her until she rolled on her back. He searched her face. "The bloodlust will come for you. And when it does I expect you to come to me, not a bag of blood."

Rue was speechless.

"Do you understand?" He rubbed his nose against hers.

"Of course." Rue nodded, the ache in her chest leaving just as quickly as it came.

"Good." He kissed her softly before settling next to her and nuzzling her ribs like a giant man-sized cat.

Rue swallowed loudly before she asked, "The bloodlust does not affect you?"

"It does."

"For how long?"

"Since the first day." His fingertips drifted across the dip of her waist.

Rue calculated the years he'd been suffering and hiding it. It had been nearly nine years.

FORTY-THREE

The nearby pine forest was unnervingly still as the morning light barely filtered through the dense canopy above. Rue followed close behind Dacre, her footsteps careful but unsteady on the soft, needle-strewn ground. She felt rested but the unease of fatigue lingered like it could assault her at any moment.

Dacre slowed until she was walking next to him. He'd done that every few steps. She couldn't help that he was so much taller than her and she couldn't keep up with his stride. His shoulders were tense and his gaze was constantly scanning the fringe of the forest. Rue could sense the beast lingering just beneath his skin.

They were nearing the portal. Rue could see the stone arch in the distance. Her nerves were on edge. Her parents would have questions. Her brother would have questions. Rue didn't want to talk to any of them about the experience.

A twig snapped in the distance. Rue froze.

Dacre turned sharply, his eyes narrowing. He held a finger to his lips, signaling her to stay silent. Her heart pounded against her ribs as she nodded.

Rustling in the underbrush echoed from their left. Rue's breath hitched and she opened her mouth to speak, but Dacre moved faster. In an instant, he was at her side, one hand clamping over her mouth, the other pulling her close to his chest.

"Quiet," he whispered, his voice barely audible. His eyes glinted green.

Rue's muffled protest died as she caught the shadowy movement beyond the trees. Something was out there, circling them like a predator stalking its prey.

Dacre slowly removed his hand from her mouth but didn't let her go. "Crouch down," he murmured, guiding her to the base of a towering pine. She obeyed, curling into the shadows as instructed, her breath nothing more than shallow gasps.

Dacre moved silently into the open. His posture was rigid, head tilted slightly as though listening to something she couldn't hear.

Then, the forest erupted.

A blur of shadow and claws shot toward him, too fast for Rue to fully register. Dacre spun, dodging the attack, and he shifted mid-movement. His human form melted away and was replaced by the sinewy, feline-like body of the beast.

The creature attacking him was unlike the shadow demons they'd faced before. Its body was twisted and wrong; a grotesque mix of bone and braided muscle with empty eyes glowing red. It let out a guttural screech as it lunged toward Dacre, striking his side.

Rue bit her lip to keep from screaming as Dacre roared in pain. His tails lashed out, striking the creature and sending it crashing into a nearby tree.

The fight was brutal and chaotic, the two creatures tearing into each other with savage ferocity. Dacre's claws raked across the monster's chest. It retaliated with razor-sharp fangs that sank into his shoulder.

Rue couldn't stay still. Her instincts screamed at her to run but she didn't want to leave him. She grabbed a jagged branch from the ground and stood.

"Dacre!" she shouted, her voice breaking. This was a death wish. She couldn't defend herself against either of them.

Her call distracted the creature. It turned toward her.

Dacre took advantage of the distraction and leapt onto the creature, pinning it to the ground. His jaws closed around its neck and with a sickening crunch, the monster went limp.

The silence that followed was deafening.

Dacre stood over the lifeless body, his sides heaving. Blood dripped from his claws and fangs, pooling onto the ground. Rue's stick slipped from her fingers as she stared at him, her heart pounding, eyes wide.

He turned to her, his form still that of the beast, his eyes glowing green and locking onto hers. For a moment, Rue thought he didn't recognize her.

But then he prowled closer, slowly shifting. By the time he reached her, his face was pale and his movements unsteady. He was covered in blood.

"Are you hurt?" he asked, his voice hoarse. He spit and wiped his face on the lower half of the shirt he'd picked up off the ground.

Rue was staring up and down at his naked body. Every muscle was contracted and tense. He was like a statue carved from marble. Rue had never seen a man so beautiful and strong. She shook her head, her throat too tight to speak. She wasn't hurt but she definitely was aching at the sight of him.

Finally she asked, "Are you hurt?"

A long moment passed before he spoke. "I'm afraid of hurting you," his voice was pained. His hands shook.

"I'm not made of glass, Dacre," she argued.

He licked his lips, body shivering from the rapid change and adrenaline of fighting. He grabbed her, lifted her like she was nothing and pressed her back against the nearby tree.

"You're not glass," Dacre whispered before kissing her roughly. He scrabbled at her clothing.

Rue didn't mind after seeing his display of power. She didn't care that he was covered in gore and sweat. She didn't care that his body pressed into hers as the rough bark from the pine scratched her back. She didn't care that his kisses were rough and hungry, that the movement of his hips was almost punishing. She wanted more. More of him. She screamed into his mouth as her core tightened around him. His body stilled.

"Did I hurt you?" he sounded worried.

"Not even close." Rue said with a sigh.

He set her on her feet. "I'm sorry. I couldn't control myself." His hands tore through his hair as he glanced at her. He worried he'd have to go away again to protect her.

"Don't be." Rue smiled as she adjusted her clothing, found her pants and tugged them on. "If I don't like something, I'll tell you, Dacre. I might even bite you to make you stop."

He smiled sheepishly. "We need to keep moving," he said, his hand brushing her arm briefly. "That wasn't the last of them."

Rue hesitated, glancing at the creature's corpse. "What was that?"

"Something sent to stop us."

Rue swallowed hard, fear clawing at her chest. "They know we're going to the portal."

"They won't touch you. Not while I'm here. I won't let them get close."

Rue's gaze dropped to the bitemark on his shoulder. It was dripping blood. She licked her lips before glancing at his pale face.

He collapsed.

Rue froze, her mind racing. There was a dozen crashes from the forest. The portal was in the distance. Rue looked down at Dacre's lifeless body. He was three times her size. She'd have to drag him.

She grabbed under his shoulders and tugged but his big, stupid body barely moved an inch. "No," Rue cried in a whisper. She tugged again and again and again. The crashing sounds were getting closer, running now.

She glanced back at the portal. "Wake up, Dacre!" she yell-whispered.

Things were running, the ground vibrating.

Rue wasn't going to leave him. She looked down at the blood leaving his shoulder in a steady stream. She licked her lips. Drinking blood gave her mother strength. Maybe she could–

A creature crashed out of the tree line and began running toward them. Rue screamed.

Just as the creature raised its claws, a bright flash of light erupted from the portal.

Through the shimmering light stepped Chel, his hulking form silhouetted against the glow. Behind him was Remington and more Hellions.

"What the hell took you two so long?" Remington shouted, his voice filled with irritation as he charged forward, slashing at the creature with deadly precision.

Chel bellowed a battle cry, barreling into the beast with enough force to send it crashing into a tree. The ground shook as Chel's fists pummeled the creature.

"It's about time you showed up!" Rue yelled, her voice trembling.

Chel spared her a quick glance. "Your bodyguard said he didn't need us." He glanced down at Dacre's body. "Guess he was wrong about that," he said sarcastically.

The shadow creature let out a dying wail as Remington delivered the finishing blow, blades slicing cleanly through its neck.

Chel turned back to Rue and Dacre, his face twisting in concern. "What happened to him?"

"He was bitten by one of those," Rue explained quickly as she brushed hair away from his clammy forehead. "There's something wrong. He's burning up."

Remington sheathed his weapons, his jaw tight as he crouched next to Dacre. "We need to get him through the portal. Now."

Chel nodded, lifting Dacre effortlessly into his arms. "He didn't need our help..." Chel muttered.

"Why is he naked?" Remington asked.

Rue's cheeks flamed red. "He shifted and killed one of those monsters." She didn't elaborate.

Remington's eyes narrowed on her as he motioned for her to go through the portal first.

FORTY-FOUR

THE PORTAL'S ENERGY FLARED AROUND RUE AS SHE stepped through, its disorienting pull wrenching her from the pine forest and depositing her onto the cool, polished stones of the castle courtyard. She stumbled forward, half-expecting to feel Remington's steadying hand, but the portal shimmered and went still behind her.

No one followed.

"Where are they?" she whispered, turning back, her voice swallowed by the silence.

A pair of Hellion guards flanked the courtyard's main doors, their expressions stoic. They offered no answers, only a nod toward the castle as if to say, *Go inside.*

Dread flooded Rue's stomach. They weren't coming. More lies. More deception. Would she ever be free from it? Rue entered the family home reluctantly, her legs heavy with exhaustion and her heart heavier than ever before. She rubbed her eyes as she walked past the Hellions, wondering if everything that had happened was just a dream. Or maybe a nightmare.

The familiar halls were once warm and inviting, but they

felt like a stone cage now. She was escorted to her room by a servant who said nothing of Dacre, Chel, or Remington.

"Where is my mother?" Rue asked. "I want to speak to her now."

The servant replied, "She's not here."

"My father? I want to talk to him."

"He's away."

"Have you seen my backpack?"

"No, princess." The servant looked away. "There is a hot bath and warm towels. I'll bring food."

Rue swallowed down the lump in her throat.

She went to the en suite bathroom and tore off the borrowed Hellion clothing. She sank into the tub and told herself she wouldn't let a tear fall. Not one. Not until she learned the truth.

The servant arrived again and took the dirty clothing. "Do you need to see the healer?" she asked.

"No," Rue said sadly. "I had a cough but it's gone."

The servant stared. "Do you need a healer for other reasons?"

"Where is Dacre?"

"You need to rest. There's food in your room. Remington ordered you to stay in your room until he comes to find you."

"My brother doesn't give me orders." Rue scowled.

"I'm afraid tonight he does. It is not safe for you to wander the castle. And, you need to rest."

Rue sank further into the water. The servant wasn't going to tell her anything.

Rue didn't sleep that night. The soreness in her body was a constant reminder of everything that had happened—the dungeons, the forest, Dacre's arms around her, his lips, his words, his absence. Her throat ached from thirst. She curled into herself on the bed, the cool silk sheets doing little to comfort her. Her heart ached in a way she couldn't quite name and all she wanted to do was go home to her apartment.

By morning, anger had replaced the hurt. No one had told her where Dacre was and it felt deliberate. Every time she asked a servant or guard, she was met with vague reassurances.

He's safe.

He's recovering.

He'll come back when he's ready.

Rue's frustration boiled over, and by midday, she was shoving her belongings into a bag wishing she had her phone so she could contact her parents. *Where the heck were they?* she wondered. Clothes, books, anything she could fit. She was never coming back. She couldn't stay here, not in this castle filled with secrets and lies. She couldn't sit still and wait for someone else to decide what she deserved to know. She left to avoid the lies years ago and it seemed nothing had changed. Her family would never treat her equally. She was nothing more than a little princess with no power or strength.

She ran her tongue over flat teeth. She'd never grow fangs. She'd always be small. She fit in much better on the Earthen plane. Here she was a misfit and a freak of nature.

She picked up the bag and stormed out of her room.

The servant was in the hall. "You can't be out here."

"I'm leaving," Rue said as she adjusted her bag over her shoulder. "I'll be out of everyone's hair in no time."

The servant ran in the opposite direction as Rue stormed to the stairwell, went down a level, and headed for the front door. She was done with Hell.

Rue stamped down the long path leading to the portal. Her boots crunched against the gravel, and her mind churned with thoughts of Dacre. Anger, hurt, and longing swirled together until she couldn't separate them anymore. Tears threatened the corners of her eyes. She wanted nothing more than a hot cup of coffee, to curl up on her couch with

Lucipurr, and text Evelyn. She wanted to watch a movie as it snowed or rained and pretend she was of the Earthen plane and not this dramatic hopeless bullshit mess.

"Running away again?" Remington's voice cut through the quiet.

The servant had tattled on her.

Rue stopped but didn't turn around. "I don't want to talk to you."

"I'm sure you don't," he said, jogging a few steps to catch up with her. "But I need to make sure you're okay before you go."

Rue turned, her chin quivering, and she slapped a hand over her face, not wanting him to see how upset she was.

"Of course I'm not okay. I was kidnapped and nearly drowned. I *remembered* the truth." She glared at her brother. "Every moment. And Dacre confessed."

"Did he hurt you?" Remington's hands were reaching toward her. "He was naked when we found you both. And you looked..." he shut his eyes for a second, "... we could smell him all over you. Did he hurt you in *other* ways?"

Rue's mouth snapped shut. Did Dacre rape her? Is that what he was concerned about?

"I've seen him shift. He's already a big dude but the beast..." he shook his head.

"No." She said quickly. "Everything was consensual. He didn't hurt me like that."

Rue turned to leave, embarrassed.

"Thank God." Remington blew out an uneasy breath and fell into step beside her, his easygoing demeanor subdued. "But you're going to listen before you leave. You're mad—at me, at him, at everyone—but you don't have all the pieces yet."

Rue clenched her jaw, her eyes fixed on the path ahead. "I'm not mad. I'm done. No one here ever tells me the truth.

It's just secrets and lies, over and over again. I am so tired of it. Nothing ever changes in this place."

"Not lies," Remington said, his voice unusually soft. "Just... things you're not ready to hear yet. Things he's not ready to say."

"That's the same thing." Her voice cracked, and she hated herself for it. "He left me here. You all did. Where is he, Remm? Why won't anyone tell me?"

Remington sighed, shoving his hands into his pockets. "Because it's not my place to tell you. You'd hate me even more if I did."

Rue stopped walking, turning to face him. "I already hate you, so what's the difference?"

Remington's face fell slightly, but he didn't rise to her bait. Instead he stepped closer, his expression serious. "I get it. You feel like you're being shut out, but Rue, Dacre isn't hiding because he doesn't care. He's hiding because he's scared and injured. He's trying to figure out how to deal with his own mess so he doesn't drop it all on you. That shoulder bite was deep, he's spent most of his time shifted and out of control. He does not want to hurt you anymore. *We* don't want him to hurt you."

She swallowed hard, her anger wavering. "How much time does he need? Forever?" Rue ran a hand through her tangled hair. "It's been..." she calculated quickly in her head, "...nearly ten years since he kidnapped me before the war. People live whole lives in that amount of time. People get married and have families."

"They graduate and become doctors," Remington chuckled.

A choked sound escaped Rue's throat at the inside joke. "I will graduate." She wiped her face as the tears took over. Wind descended from Hellsky and blew her hair around her head like a dark halo.

"I'm sorry, I couldn't help it," Remington apologized. "We are not *people*, Rue. We are something different."

"How much more time?" She held a hand over her heart. "All these years I have lived with a gaping hole here. How much more time does everyone need to just tell me the truth and let me be?"

"Enough time," Remington said, reaching out to take her hand. His touch was warm, steady. "He's a good guy, Rue. He's been through some terrible shit, and he doesn't want to hurt you with it. Just give him a chance."

Rue wanted to pull her hand away, her voice bitter. "How can I believe you? You've been lying to me for years."

"You don't have to believe me," Remington said quietly.

He dropped to his knee since he was so much taller than her and stared into her eyes. "I still remember your screams, Rue. From after the war when you weren't right." He closed his eyes and swallowed hard. "I still have nightmares of you screaming and walking the halls lifeless. Be mad, but understand that we were watching you slowly die right in front of our eyes and we all did the only thing that could help you. Putting all the pieces of this family back together won't be easy. But just know, we love you, Rue. And we only want what is best for you."

She stared at him for a long moment, her emotions warring within her. Finally, she nodded, her voice barely a whisper. "I just want the truth." She couldn't hold back any longer and threw her arms around Remm.

He stood, picking her up with his arms wrapped around her. Rue didn't mind, and she hugged him tighter.

"Just believe him. When he comes to find you—and he *will* come to find you—believe what he tells you. Not what you've built up in your head."

"I'll try. But if he doesn't come... I'm gone." She swallowed hard at the confession. She hated the idea of having a gaping hole in her chest for eternity.

Remington gave her a faint smile. "He'll come." He squeezed her one last time before setting her on her feet. "Come on, I'll walk you home."

Rue shook her head. "I'm going back to my apartment."

"I know." Remington took her hand. "I know this place hasn't been home to you for a long time. It makes me sad not having you here, little sister."

Rue nodded in understanding. Somewhere, in the back of her mind, she held on to the faintest thread of hope that Dacre would figure his shit out.

FORTY-FIVE

The room was dim and cold, carved from black volcanic stone, the air had the faint metallic tang of blood. Dacre stirred, his body feeling heavy and achy. He tried to lift himself from the cot where they'd laid him. His shoulder throbbed, the bite wound pulsating with a fiery heat that would not subside. Thick bandages covered his shoulder and were soaked through.

"Rue," he croaked, his voice raw and desperate. "Where is she?"

A shadow moved near the doorway. Remington stepped forward, his face a mask of forced calm. "She's safe."

"I need to see her. Now." Dacre's eyes burned from the smoke of a nearby fire.

"You need to heal first," Remington said, crossing his arms. "And Rue needs space."

Dacre let out a low growl, the sound rumbling deep in his chest. "Space? From what? From me?" He tried to rise, but his legs gave out, his knees slamming against the cold stone floor. "Fuck!"

Chel appeared behind Remington, ducking his head to fit

through the doorway. "You're lucky we didn't just drag you into the nearest pit and leave you there," Chel said, his tone sharp. "You were a damn mess when we found you."

"I didn't hurt her," Dacre snapped, looking up to glare at them.

"She was terrified and you were naked, covered in blood. Your smell was all over her," Chel countered, leaning against the wall. "You think we wouldn't question what happened? You think we'd risk letting you near her while you're like this? You've been shifting every hour. You're out of control."

Dacre snarled. He slumped back against the cot, panting. His claws, still half-formed, scraped against the stone floor.

"She's the only one who can help," he said through gritted teeth. "You don't understand. I *need* her. She's..." He trailed off, his head falling back as exhaustion clawed at him.

"What?" Remington asked, stepping closer. "What is she?"

"Mine," Dacre whispered. "Without her..." His gaze went glassy with pain.

Chel exchanged a glance with Remington. "You think we're gonna let you near her in this state? You're not exactly stable, mate."

Dacre clenched his fists, his claws retracting painfully. "I didn't hurt her. I'd never hurt her. I protected her. I'd die before I let anything touch her."

"Maybe," Remington said carefully, "but right now, you're dangerous. Whether you want to admit it or not."

Dacre's head dropped, his dark hair falling over his face. The need to see Rue burned in his chest. "Where is she?" he asked again, his voice steadier but still desperate.

"She's at the castle," Remington finally said reluctantly. "Resting. She doesn't need this... whatever this is on her plate."

"You think keeping us apart will make her safer?" Dacre

hissed, forcing himself upright despite the stabbing pain in his shoulder. "It'll only make things worse for both of us."

Chel stepped forward, his massive frame blocking the doorway. "You're not leaving this room until you're healed. End of discussion. You can't stop shifting. You can't see her."

Dacre's head tilted, his lips curling into a bitter smile. "You think you can keep me here?"

Chel folded his arms, unfazed. "Try me."

For a moment, the tension crackled, both men poised for a fight. But Dacre was too weak, and Chel knew it.

Remington nudged Chel, his voice low. "Let it go. He's stuck here."

Dacre slumped back against the cot, simmering with barely contained frustration. "You don't get it," he muttered. "She's the only thing keeping me from turning into... a monster." His hands tore at his hair and tugged the ends until it hurt more than his shoulder.

Remington knelt beside him. "I get it," he said quietly. "But if you care about her then you'll stay here and get better. She doesn't need another storm in her life right now. Let her rest. Let her heal, too."

Dacre closed his eyes, his chest heaving as he tried to tamp down the rage and helplessness surging through him. The pain in his shoulder was nothing compared to the ache in his chest.

"You don't know what we need," he screamed, suddenly shifting into the panther-like beast. His clothing tore, and the bandage on his shoulder became painfully tight. He rolled to the floor, tentacles raised, ends vibrating as he distorted his image to that of a small puppy.

Chel laughed loudly. "Not a chance."

The ends of the tentacles vibrated again and Dacre became a giant Basilisk, snapping its jaws.

Remington backed up. "Nice party trick, but you've shown me most of them."

Dacre's beast shivered, the vibration starting again, and he was nothing more than a man–uninjured, clean, and dressed in a suit. It was the old Dacre of Lucifer's time; handsome and deceptive and loaded with debts, his eyes were hungry and empty.

Remington clicked his tongue. "Nope."

Remington and Chel backed out the door and slammed it closed. After shoving the lock into place, they watched him shift back to his injured self.

"Do you think we should get him some of her blood?" Chel asked.

"Gross," Remington made a gagging sound.

"It worked for your mother when she was injured. It might work for them."

Remington waved the thought away.

"Maybe you should call your mother and ask her," Chel suggested.

"Fine," Remington agreed. "This is outta my wheel house. He needs a healer."

"Maybe Teari will visit," Chel smiled and winked.

"Christ, man, she's miles above you. She's an angel."

Chel shrugged before asking, "What's with his bracelet?"

Remington's back went straight. "I recognized it. A high shadow demon made the bracelet from his mother's eyes after he killed her. He killed Dacre's entire family. I'm sure dealing with that isn't helping him right now."

"Damn," Chel muttered. "That ain't right."

The two turned quickly as a roar of pain and agony echoed down the hallway.

"Maybe we could find him a tranquilizer?" Chel suggested.

"That's probably what's gonna happen." Remington pulled a phone from his pocket and began calling his mother.

Forty-Six

The apartment was quiet, the kind of stillness that pressed against Rue's ears like a hollow seashell, especially after the chaos she'd left behind. Closing the door, she let out a long breath, leaning against it as if the weight of everything would slide off her shoulders. She inhaled deeply and enjoyed the scent of home; a mix of lavender laundry detergent and a faint hint of coffee.

Her boots thudded softly against the floor as she kicked them off. She didn't bother unpacking her bag, dropping it near the door. She noticed her backpack was on the small table nearby. She dug through it and found her cell phone then moved it to the charger on the kitchen counter.

Her steps carried her to the bedroom, the blankets messily draped just as she'd left them. A small pang of comfort stirred in her chest.

"Meow," Lucipurr greeted her.

"Hey, I missed you." Rue picked up the kitten and snuggled him, rubbing her face against his soft fur. "I'm sorry I was gone so long." Rue turned and noticed an open bag of cat food and a sink full of water. At least someone had come back to feed him. Although, the kitten frequently disappeared. Rue had been told by an old Hellion that the kitten could traverse realms, so she rarely worried about him when she traveled.

Lucipurr purred loudly before wiggling to get out of her grip.

"Only one minute of cuddles?" Rue pouted. "I've been gone for days."

Lucipurr let out another meow that sounded like a scolding.

"I wasn't on vacation." Rue tugged off her clothes and swapped them for an oversized hoodie and soft leggings, the worn fabric feeling good against her skin. She stared at the bed, chewing her lip. She wanted to try and sleep, but assumed she'd toss and turn and get angry with herself.

Wandering through the apartment, she found herself standing in Dacre's room. It was sparse, just as he'd left it. His mattress on the floor was neatly made. Her gaze drifted to his neatly folded shirts on the edge of the bed.

Tentatively, Rue picked one up, pressing it to her face. The scent of him lingered; clean, earthy, and faintly smoky. A tightness in her chest twisted as memories of his touch, his voice, and his steady presence swirled in her mind. Without a second thought, she gathered two of his shirts and held them close, retreating to her room.

She tore off her hoodie and put Dacre's shirt on. Then she went to the kitchen and turned on the coffee pot. She found her laptop, set it on the couch, and plugged in the charger. Hearing the coffee maker sputter to a stop, she returned to the kitchen, made her coffee in her favorite mug, and grabbed her phone off the counter.

She returned to the couch and dragged the blanket off the back, covering her legs. She queued up Howl's Moving Castle.

Whimsical music filled the room, a gentle distraction. As the movie played, her phone buzzed with missed messages. There were a handful from Evelyn.

She messaged back.

> Rue: Hey. Back at my apartment. Feeling better. We should grab coffee soon.

THE REPLY WAS INSTANT.

> Evelyn: WHAT?! You've been MIA forever! Where the hell were you? Spill, Tink.

RUE BIT HER LIP, crafting her response carefully.

> Rue: It was barely a week. Got really sick. Family insisted I recover with them. So boring, I promise.

EVELYN'S REPLY came with a string of skeptical emojis. Rue wanted to tell her everything.

> Evelyn: Did hot-bodyguard overstep? I've never seen you sick. Do I need to gather pyramid head and beat him up?

> Rue: Ummmm… hot-bodyguard is sick himself now. No overstepping.

> Evelyn: Did you give him your sickness? Dirty girl.

> Rue: he deserved it.

> Evelyn: Mwahahaha. We'll meet up tomorrow.

> Rue: Yes.

RUE GLANCED up at the movie and Lucipurr jumped onto the couch and curled up next to her. She took a sip of her coffee and her laptop pinged. She'd missed two midterms.

Navigating to her inbox, she quickly typed up a message to her professor.

Subject: Meeting Request

Hi Professor Camden,

I hope this email finds you well. I've been terribly ill for the past week and haven't been able to keep up with my studies. I'd like to meet with you to discuss what I've missed and how I can catch up. Please let me know when you're available.

Best Regards,
Rue

. . .

HITTING SEND, Rue set the laptop aside and scooted closer to Lucipurr. The kitten purred softly. She closed her eyes, letting the familiar sounds of her favorite movie lull her in a moment of peace. For now, she was home but, without Dacre the small apartment suddenly felt so empty.

FORTY-SEVEN

The low sun was casting long shadows across the cobblestone street as Rue made her way to the Coffee Connection. The air smelled like the blooming wisteria and freshly turned soil, spring's gentle breeze brushing her cheeks. She adjusted the strap of her leather bag and inhaled deeply. The changing of the seasons always brought a sense of melancholy; she missed the changing of the leaves and pumpkin spice coffee of autumn. She missed the crisp snow and the way it drowned out noise as it fell.

Rue tugged at the sleeves of her cardigan and glanced at her phone. Her mother had texted earlier. It was characteristically vague: "Let's meet. We need to talk."

It wasn't the first time Meg had summoned her under the guise of a casual coffee date. They had been weekly before the chaos erupted in Rue's life. Her stomach churned at the thought of another blunt conversation in public where she'd have to shush her mother and smile away the strange looks.

The Coffee Connection stood on the corner, its windows fogged with the warmth of brewing espresso and the hum of quiet chatter spilling out onto the street. Rue pushed the door open and the bell above jingled softly.

"Welcome to the Coffee Connection!" the barista waved from behind the counter. He recognized Rue and pointed to the small table where her mother was sitting.

Rue gave a wave of thanks.

Meg smiled wide as Rue walked toward her. She was inspecting, watching, looking for a sign of anything being off. Meg stood and hugged Rue tightly.

"I've missed you." She kissed Rue's cheek before sitting down and sliding a to-go cup toward her.

Rue could smell the pumpkin spice and asked, "How did you get them to make this in the off season?"

Meg smiled. "You know I buy enough muffins here that they'll make whatever I ask for."

"Thank you," Rue said as she raised the cup and looked her mother over. She was sliding a leather jacket off her arms and hanging it on the back of her chair. Rue glanced to the nearby tables and noticed patrons glancing at the scars and tattoos. She sighed. This was just the way it would be. She couldn't protect her mother from the staring and realized she shouldn't. Her mother didn't seem to care and was perfectly comfortable in her skin the way it was. Rue thought of the stories she'd been told in her childhood, the struggles her mother had gone through to find out who she really was. The fights, the battles, the trauma and abuse. Rue gathered any negative thoughts she had about her life and tucked them away. Whatever she'd gone through, with the lies in lieu of protection, it wasn't nearly as bad as the physical pain her mother had endured. But still, they needed to talk about it all.

Meg reached over to rub a strand of Rue's hair between her fingers. "Your hair has gotten really long." The action was so tender it almost disarmed her. "And you look tired. Are you getting enough sleep?"

Rue's fingers curled around her cup. "I've had... a lot going on. But I'm catching up. I'm meeting with Professor Camden later." Rue glanced up at her mother. "I missed two midterms."

"I can speak to him for you if you'd like. Smooth things over." Meg smiled wickedly.

"I don't need you to fix this," Rue's said.

"I'm just trying to help." Meg shifted in her seat.

"Help?" Rue's voice dropped, and she was battling her frustration as it bubbled to the surface. "Where was your help when shadow demons kidnapped me from the library and tried to drown me? When monsters were chasing us through the pine forest?" Rue searched her mother's blue eyes.

Meg sighed, leaning back in her chair. "You're not a child. You had your bodyguard. Your brother has been keeping an eye on you."

Rue leaned forward. "Do you even know what happened?"

Meg ran a hand through her short, dark hair. "I know things happened. And I know that you're old enough to manage the problems that come your way. You don't want me and your father intervening. You've told us this. If you were in mortal danger, I would have intervened. But I knew you'd be fine."

Rue leaned forward, her eyes burning with unshed tears. "It felt like you didn't care." She paused and shut her eyes for a few breaths, gathering her thoughts.

"I know what this is about." Meg cleared her throat and when Rue looked up again, she was motioning to the barista. The barista walked around the counter and started quietly asking patrons to leave. Within two minutes the café was empty and the door was locked with the closed sign hanging. The workers disappeared to the back.

"What did you just do?" Rue asked, anxious that her

haven on the Earthen plan had just been influenced by her mother. She supposed she'd never escape situations like this. She was sitting across from the Queen of Hell and that title came with a certain power. If her mother wanted to have a private conversation, they were going to have it.

"Rue," Meg sighed, "I'm not perfect and there was a lot I didn't know back then. But what I did know was something was destroying you from the inside. Whatever happened, no one knew how to help you. I took you to many healers. Everyone was on edge while you walked the halls like a ghost and screamed all night long."

Rue was still as her mother spoke, her fingers warming around the coffee mug. She swallowed hard, her throat tightening. "I just want to understand, Mom. I can't keep living in the dark. There's been too many years of lies."

Meg reached across the table, her fingers wrapping around Rue's. "Let's talk about Dacre."

Rue's cheeks flushed.

"Did you drink his blood?" Meg asked.

"No." Rue shook her head.

Meg sighed and shifted closer to Rue. "Just. Do. It."

"Mother," Rue hissed.

"What? You're not a prude and I'm trying to give you valuable information." She studied Rue's face. "You wouldn't need so much coffee if you'd just drink his blood. It's... can you remember how you felt when you first bit him?"

"I'm not you."

"But you are *of* me, child. And *you* bit him. I mean... you were young at the time but at least you didn't bite a troll." Meg sighed with relief. "You created a bond that you must foster for both of your health. He should have been given your blood to heal."

Rue's back went straight. "Mine?"

"It works both ways. Taking blood from each other will

make you both strong. He should have fed from you after he was injured by that shadow monster. I'll make sure you're never separated in a situation like that again."

An old woman on the sidewalk tugged at the door and gave the two a bitchy glare.

"Keep your voice down, please," Rue begged, afraid the people outside could hear them. "And you knew about that? How did you find out?"

Meg smiled. "People tell me things. You know, if you would just listen to me once instead of changing the subject and running off..." Meg pulled her hands back and took a sip from her mug. "This is old shit we're talking about. You won't find this information in your Archaeology studies. There's more about him." Meg took a bite of an orange muffin. "He needs to tell you, when he's ready."

"You tell me," Rue pressed.

Meg shook her head. "It's not my place. You're an adult now."

"I'm just tired of people close to me lying."

Meg leaned closer and lowered her voice. "It's not always a lie. Sometimes it's *shame*. Sometimes it's *hurt*."

Rue nodded, tightened her grip on the to-go cup, and sipped at her coffee. She could understand that.

"Is dad ever going to come for coffee?" Rue asked.

Meg's eyes went wide. "Imagine him, here. The looks. The..."

"No one would see what he really is," Rue reminded her. "There is balance between the realms."

"That's true." Meg leaned back and broke another piece off her orange muffin. "I'll talk to him about it. I just don't want to bring chaos to your little piece of the Earthen plane that you have here. I don't want us to be the cause of you losing this if something happens."

Rue sighed and slouched in her chair. "I'd forgive you."

Meg couldn't hide her surprised expression. "Remington said you remembered what happened during your kidnapping when you were younger."

"The truth wasn't so bad," Rue said. "The problem was my mind healing and piecing it all together."

"It's not the truth we were protecting you from. It was whatever happened to your body. The change. The nightmares." Meg leaned forward. "If we had told you the truth about Dacre when you were fifteen and allowed him to live with us and you had to grow up far too early than necessary, would you have ever forgiven us? You wouldn't be here right now making your own decisions about your life, Rue. You'd be wed and bred and deeply woven into traditional royal life and all the drama that comes with it. You would have been forced upon each other. You wouldn't have been able to learn about each other in your own time." Meg sighed. "Although, I was worried you might have been blind taking six years to realize a smoking-hot-bodyguard was living in the apartment below you. I knew you were focused but jeeze, child." Meg giggled.

Rue shook her head. "No. I wouldn't have wanted that. And I wasn't looking for a relationship."

"Tell me about the dreams," Meg urged.

Rue took a deep breath. "After Uncle Jed reversed the memory spell, I realized they weren't *just* dreams." Rue looked up at her mother. "I think I was seeing the future. A long time ago when I was kidnapped, I had dreams." She blinked and swallowed hard. "But they weren't just dreams because I lived them, they were of college, and dancing with Dacre at a costume party, and meeting you for coffee *here*." She tapped her nail on the table. "I saw our last meeting here. I was seeing the future."

Meg pressed a hand over her mouth, eyes wide as she thought about what Rue had just said. "You can see the future." Her hand drifted down revealing a smile of delight. "I think we can all live with that."

Rue nodded as she sipped her coffee and glanced out the window. Shadows moved conspicuously under the budding oak trees. Someone was out there, watching.

FORTY-EIGHT

Rue tugged nervously at the strap of her backpack as she stood outside Professor Camden's office. The door was slightly ajar, revealing a sliver of the professor hunched over his desk, probably grading the midterms she'd missed. Taking a deep breath, Rue knocked lightly.

"Come in," Professor Camden's warm voice called out.

She stepped inside, clutching the strap tighter. The room smelled faintly of old books and coffee, and sunlight filtered in through the tall windows, casting a golden glow on the wooden shelves stacked high with journals and novels.

"Miss Clark," he said, glancing up from his work and giving her a brief smile. "Good to see you. Feeling better?"

Rue froze for a moment, her nerves prickling. She hadn't expected him to acknowledge her absence so easily. "Yes, much better," she said, sitting down in the chair across from his desk.

"Your mother called to let us know about your illness," Professor Camden continued, pulling a folder from his drawer. "She was quite insistent that we make accommodations for you."

Rue's stomach flipped. Of course her mother had

meddled. Still, it was a relief. "Thank you for understanding. I wasn't sure how much trouble I'd be in. I really didn't want to have to withdraw this semester."

"None at all," he reassured her. "You've been a diligent student, Rue, and your professors are willing to work with you. I'll notify the others to give you extensions on assignments and arrange for you to make up any missed tests. If you stay on track, you should have no trouble graduating at the end of the semester." He glanced at her.

The knot of tension in Rue's chest began to loosen. "I really appreciate that," she said, her voice soft.

Professor Camden leaned back in his chair, regarding her with a thoughtful expression. "You're a bright student, Rue. Just take care of yourself and let us know if you need any further support. I think you've been at this long enough. You're nearly finished. Will you be resuming the independent study we spoke about before your illness?"

"Yes." Rue leaned forward and dug in her bag, pulling out a folder. "I've started it already if you have a few extra minutes." She bit her lip and glanced at the clock. "Actually, I could leave it if you need and meet another day."

"Now is fine." Professor Camden leaned forward, folded his hands, and listened as Rue animatedly discussed her project.

"As you recall, I want to focus on Fifteenth century Nephilim in the Alleghany mountains and how they influenced modern mythology." Rue laid out the resources she'd collected from the campus library and internet sources.

Professor Camden listened carefully, nodding his head along as she detailed her thesis. Remembering how he'd choked the first time she mentioned the project, Rue noticed he refrained from drinking anything.

"I'll remind you that this is ambitious." He glanced up at her, then back at her papers. "You're clearly not afraid of the occult. I have a few colleagues who teach in Altoona and John-stown. They aren't as progressive thinkers as you... but they've discovered a lot of artifacts that could apply to this."

"I'd like that very much." Rue shifted closer. "The campus library has its limits and there are no recent discoveries reported in the books here."

Professor Camden was rubbing his chin then moved to his computer and logged in. "I'll email Dr. Malcom and see what his availability is. You could probably travel over there on a weekend. It's only a few hours' drive."

"That sounds great." Rue nodded.

Professor Camden typed on his computer for a few minutes, sending an email. After his last tap, he looked up. "It's sent. I'll forward you his information if he's up for meeting with you."

"Perfect."

"I'm interested in reading what you're going to put together with all of this."

"I won't let you down," Rue promised.

"You can do it. I have faith in you."

Rue stood and nodded, murmured another thank you, and excused herself, feeling lighter as she walked down the hallway.

"Rue!" a familiar voice called.

She turned to see Evelyn striding toward her, blonde hair catching the sunlight. "There you are. I've been looking for you."

Rue smiled. "I was meeting with Professor Camden. He's going to let me make up the missed work from last week.

"You look like you've been resurrected from the dead, so I'll buy the illness. Hot-bodyguard must be looking icky right now too."

Rue shrugged. "I haven't seen him in a few days."

Evelyn waved it off. "Who cares about boys. How about dinner? My treat. You owe me some serious catching up."

Rue hesitated, but Evelyn's wide grin made it impossible to say no. "Alright," she relented.

———

The diner Evelyn picked was a cozy place just off campus filled with students chatting over plates of pancakes and burgers. They slid into a booth by the window with red pleather seats. Rue ordered a short stack while Evelyn went for a towering stack of waffles.

"So," Evelyn said, cutting into her food. "What's the deal? You disappear for a week, look like a ghost, and now you're back. Spill."

Rue played with her fork, careful to keep her voice light. "I wasn't feeling well. It's nothing interesting."

Evelyn narrowed her eyes. "Yeah, right. You're a terrible liar, but I'll let it slide for now. Just don't go all *mysterious heroine* on me, alright? I need my best friend to be at full capacity."

Rue chuckled, grateful for the change in subject. As they ate, the tension in her shoulders eased, and for a moment, it felt like everything was normal again.

Until Evelyn's eyes flicked over Rue's shoulder.

"Holy hell," Evelyn said, leaning closer. "Is that your monstrous bodyguard again? I like hot-bodyguard better."

Rue turned just in time to spot Chel standing awkwardly by the entrance, his hulking frame completely out of place in the small diner. He was scanning the room, his expression as unreadable as ever, but when his eyes landed on Rue, he started walking toward their table.

"Oh no," Rue muttered under her breath.

Evelyn grinned and waved him over. "Hey, Chel! Join us!"

Chel lumbered toward them, pulling a chair from a nearby table and plopping it at the end of the booth, sitting down with a thud. The table shook slightly, and Rue winced.

"Hello," he said, his voice low and gravelly.

Evelyn, ever the charmer, launched into a string of questions about his size, his job, and how many squats he could do. Chel answered each one with earnest seriousness, oblivious to the teasing undertone in her voice.

Rue cut into her pancakes, wishing she could disappear. Chel's presence was like a giant flashing sign that her life was far from normal, and Evelyn's fascination wasn't helping.

"So, what brings you here?" Evelyn asked, leaning on her elbow.

"I was instructed to watch over Rue until Dacre is well," Chel said simply, his eyes darting to Rue like she was a particularly troublesome assignment.

"Well, you're doing a great job," Evelyn said, clearly enjoying the awkwardness. "What kinda disease did she give that poor boy?" Evelyn cut a bite of waffle and chewed, staring, waiting for an answer.

Rue sighed. "Chel, maybe you should wait outside."

Chel frowned, looking genuinely hurt. "But I'm supposed to protect you."

"I'll be fine for twenty minutes," Rue said, her tone sharper than she intended. "Just... go."

Chel hesitated but eventually stood, his chair scraping loudly against the floor. He gave Rue a lingering look before heading toward the door.

As soon as he was gone, Evelyn burst into laughter. "Oh my god. He's like a loyal puppy who doesn't realize how big he is."

Rue groaned, burying her face in her hands. "Don't encourage him."

"Are you kidding? He's the best thing that's happened all

week." Evelyn leaned back, still grinning. "I hope he sticks around."

Rue wasn't sure whether to laugh or cry.

"You've missed a lot of class," Evelyn said. "Dacre got ahold of me, he said you were sick. I've been emailing you all the notes." She was studying Rue. "Are you okay?"

Rue smiled and nodded. "I am."

"Wanna talk about it?"

"I don't think you'd believe me if I told you."

"There's the night before graduation," Evelyn wagged her eyebrows.

"Yes," Rue said before Evelyn had time to elaborate. "I'll go."

"Are you bringing hot-bodyguard or scary bodyguard?" She waved her knife toward the door. "That guy is going to scare the shit out of a lot of co-eds."

"I'm not sure."

"Pyramid head has a brother. We'll meet them there."

"Oh, really?" Rue forced a smile. She didn't want to see anyone but Dacre. Seemed her family had other plans though. It had been nearly a week since she'd last seen him. "Should I wear the fairy costume?"

"Nah, I have something better in mind."

Rue twisted her face in dread. "It better not be slutty. And, I'm bringing hot-bodyguard."

"Are you sure he will go?"

"Yes." Rue smiled. She knew. He'd go, or she'd escort Chel back to Hell and drag Dacre back by his hair.

FORTY-NINE

The days had stretched into weeks, and Chel had become an irritating fixture in Rue's life. His hulking presence loomed everywhere she went—at the library, classes, even when she went grocery shopping. He followed her like an overbearing shadow, quick to intercept anyone who so much as glanced her way.

At first, Rue tried to ignore him. She'd perfected the art of rolling her eyes and muttering under her breath. But it was impossible to fully block out his overbearing commentary.

"You really shouldn't walk so close to the road," Chel said one afternoon as they strolled to campus.

Rue shot him a glare. "I'm on the sidewalk."

"Still. You're small. A car might not see you."

"Chel, I am *not that* small," Rue hissed. "I am a normal-sized person with normal-sized problems, and none of them include being flattened by a car."

Chel didn't even have the decency to look chastened. He just grinned and said, "You're welcome for keeping you alive."

Rue's temper flared but she couldn't completely blame Chel, he wasn't the only thing gnawing at her. The nightmares had returned and she hadn't slept well in days. It made her temper short and her coffee intake copious.

———

THE NIGHTMARES CAME IN WAVES, night after night, leaving Rue gasping and tangled in her sheets. Shadowy figures clawed at her from the edges of her dreams, whispering her name in guttural tones. She woke up sweating, her heart pounding like it might burst from her chest. Nothing seemed like a vision of the future. She wanted to hone her skill but only chaos was invading her mind. Something wasn't right.

Her mother's blood deliveries went untouched. Rue couldn't stomach the thought of drinking it, no matter how weak and tired she felt. She knew she was running on empty, but she refused to cave. She gave them to Chel.

You'll drink my blood. Dacre's words echoed in her mind. *Not from a bag.* Kinda hard when he was MIA.

Chel watched her daily with a mix of concern and frustration, his usual sarcasm dulled.

"You're not eating enough," he said one morning, watching her poke at a dry piece of toast.

"I'm fine."

"You look like death warmed over," he said bluntly. "And I would know. I've seen that first hand."

Rue slammed her coffee mug down harder than she intended. "I don't need a babysitter, Chel. I need space. And peace and quiet."

Lucipurr looked up from his water dish with a scowl, licked his lips, and let out a concerned, "Meow."

———

THE AIR in the castle's solarium was cool and quiet, the faint scent of herbs and flowers drifting in from the open windows. Dacre stood by the tall glass panes, his shoulders hunched slightly, one hand rubbing his opposite shoulder absently. He had a sinking feeling he already knew why Meg had summoned him here.

His body still ached from the ordeal at the Black Mansion, a dull throb radiating from the wound near his shoulder. The memories clung to him like a shroud—the blood, the battle, Rue's face as he carried her to safety, and the harrowing task of burying the small box that held his mother's eyes. He could still feel the weight of the soil in his hands.

"You look like hell." Meg's voice was soft but carried an edge of concern.

Dacre turned to see her standing in the doorway, dressed in leather and a midnight blue shirt. She stepped inside, closing the door behind her.

"I feel worse," Dacre replied, his voice hoarse. He forced himself to stand straighter, pushing the pain aside. "You wanted to see me?"

Meg's sharp eyes studied him, and for a moment, neither of them spoke. She walked to the table in the center of the room, pouring a glass of water and setting it down in front of an empty chair. "Sit," she instructed.

Dacre hesitated but obeyed, lowering himself into the chair with a slight wince.

Meg sat across from him, folding her hands neatly on the table. "How's your shoulder?"

"Better," he lied.

Her brow lifted, and she leaned back slightly, her piercing gaze unwavering. "You've been through a lot, Dacre. More than most could bear. Facing the demons at the Black Mansion, confronting your past..." She paused, her tone softening. "Burying your mother's eyes." She motioned to his healing shoulder. "That bite was impressive. You'd be healed already if you'd taken her blood."

Dacre flinched, his hand tightening into a fist on the table. He didn't meet her eyes, staring instead at the grain of the wood.

"It wasn't supposed to happen like this," he said finally, his voice barely above a whisper. "I wasn't ready for Rue to see me like that—like a monster."

Meg sighed, her expression softening. "Did she tell you that you were a monster?"

Dacre closed his eyes, the weight of her words pressing down on him. "I don't know how to keep doing this," he admitted. "Every time I think I'm in control, something pulls me back into the beast. It's harder to hold onto my human form. It's harder to feel... like myself."

"That's because you've been running on empty for years," Meg said gently. "You've been fighting for so long, Dacre, you've forgotten how to rest. How to heal."

He looked up at her then, his eyes dark and haunted. "There's no time for rest. Rue needs protection—"

"She has it," Meg interrupted, her voice firm. "She has you. But she also has me, her father, her brother, and the Hellions. You've done more than enough, Dacre. It's time for you to go back."

Dacre froze, his heart pounding. "Go back? To what?"

"To her," Meg said, her tone unwavering. "You can't protect Rue if you destroy yourself here, pretending to need more time to heal."

Dacre shook his head, his jaw tightening. "I can, just not now. Not after everything. I'm not sure I can control myself."

"You will," Meg said softly. "And if you hurt her. I'll kill you." Meg narrowed her eyes at Dacre. "Is that enough to scare you straight?"

For a long moment, the room was silent except for the

distant chirping of birds outside. Dacre stared at the table, his mind a storm of emotions. He hated the idea of leaving Rue, he hated the idea of going back to her while feeling this messed up. But deep down, he knew Meg was right.

"I don't know if I can," he admitted finally, his voice breaking.

Meg reached across the table, placing a hand over his. "You can," she said firmly. "Because Rue needs you."

Dacre nodded slowly, his throat tight with emotion.

Meg left the room while Dacre sat in silence, staring into the empty glass of water. He needed to go back. For Rue. For them both. He rubbed his shoulder to soothe the ache.

Fifty

THE DREAM SHIFTED FROM THE USUAL SUFFOCATING darkness to something quieter, softer. Rue found herself standing in a field under a starless sky. The wind whispered through the grass, carrying a scent she hadn't smelled in weeks: pine and bergamot and smoke. She tasted cinnamon in her mouth. Her chest ached, and tears pricked her eyes. "Dacre?" she whispered. That empty hole in her chest she'd learned to live with was threatening to tear open and bleed her dry.

Rue woke with a start, the echoes of the dream lingering in her mind. Her heart raced—not with fear, but with urgency. She threw off her blankets, pulled on a hoodie, and padded across the apartment, her feet moving instinctively.

Chel's door was ajar, his deep snores filling the hall. Rue slipped past him unnoticed and made her way to the building's lower level.

She stopped in front of Dacre's door, her hand trembling as she reached for the handle. Locked. Without thinking, Rue drew back her foot and kicked.

The doorframe splintered, and the door swung open. She surprised herself. She'd never used force like that before.

The room was dimly lit, the faint glow of a single lamp casting shadows on the walls. And there he was sitting on the edge of his bed, his head in his hands.

"You," Rue breathed.

Dacre's head snapped up and dark eyes burned with something feral. "Rue."

She crossed the room in a heartbeat, stopping just short of touching him. "I didn't fully realize it before but when you are close, the nightmares lessen."

"Do they?" he asked.

"Did you know that?"

He shook his head. He looked exhausted, his usual calm confidence replaced with something raw and vulnerable. His shirt was rumpled, his hair wild and unkempt. But he was here, finally, and that was all that mattered to Rue.

"I wonder if they'd go away completely if we shared a bed?" Rue's voice broke. "I've been waiting for you."

Dacre's shoulders sagged. "I'm sorry."

Her gaze lingered on the scars on his shoulder. Without thinking, she reached out and touched his face, her fingers grazing the rough stubble on his jaw. He leaned into her touch, his eyes fluttering closed.

For a moment, the world outside his apartment didn't exist. It was just the two of them, tangled in a web of longing and unspoken words. That had to change.

"I've been dreaming about you," Rue admitted.

Dacre opened his eyes and a small, sad smile tugged at the corner of his lips. "Chel said the nightmares came back."

Rue's breath caught in her throat. "You've been nearby, but not close."

Dacre nodded, his voice rough. "I couldn't stay away."

Rue's hand fell away. "Why did you take so long to come back?"

"I'm having a hard time controlling it." Shadows danced

across his face. "It's on edge. I'm afraid of hurting you. Of shifting when I least expect it."

"Tell me what you are. That's all I'm asking. I want to be with you but I don't want secrets and lies. Just tell me, Dacre." Her bottom lip quivered. "I want to see you again. I'm barely holding on... just let it out."

"Promise me you won't scream?" Dacre asked.

Rue nodded.

They both heard the heavy footsteps of Chel outside the door; an insurance policy in case Dacre couldn't control himself.

He shrugged off his coat. Rue noticed he looked thinner, and there were dark crescents under his eyes.

She was the same. Staying away from each other was slowly killing them both.

But Rue couldn't live another minute in a life where those she loved kept secrets from her. He had to show her the truth of what he was.

Dacre took off his shirt.

Rue licked her lips.

"Don't," Dacre warned. "This is hard enough."

Rue took a step back and pressed her lips together.

His hair was longer, and as he moved it away from his neck she saw the four crescent shapes there. "You bit me, Rue. Remember that. I tried to keep my distance in that dungeon all those years ago, but *you* bit *me*."

"I think I want to bite you again," Rue said, examining his half naked body.

"Just so you know, I'll bite back this time."

Rue smiled as her lower abdomen did that flip flop motion.

"Where did you go?" Rue asked.

"I had to bury my mother's eyes. They were all that was left of her body." He looked away.

"I could have gone with you," she whispered. "You didn't need to do that alone. No one should do that alone."

"No," Dacre shook his head. "You don't need to see that."

"I don't think you should have decided that for me. I'm a big girl now, Dacre. I don't need you to protect me from all the little things in life. Death is natural. I would have liked to support you during that."

His body tensed then he shifted into the beast.

Rue sucked in a breath. He was magnificent.

"All this time, you could have defeated any one of those shadow demons in a heartbeat. That night you were injured, if you had just changed you wouldn't have gotten cut." Rue reminded him of the deep cut to the ribs, when she'd bandaged him and he dragged her onto his lap and kissed her senseless.

He smiled darkly as he shifted back to his human form. "But then you wouldn't have taken care of me."

"Come on."

"I didn't want to scare you. I didn't want to hurt you." His face looked pained. "I didn't want to lose control."

Rue blinked and tipped her head to the side. "And what happens when I lose control?" She smiled, flashing her teeth. "What happens when I embrace what I am and come at you with these dull-ass teeth?"

He sighed.

"We both have monsters inside us. I might be small, but I am not just a little human woman. I am bred of royal monsters. Remember that."

"I would forgive you instantly," he said.

"And I would forgive you." She stepped closer. "Now that that's out of the way. Please pick me up and kiss me and carry me to whatever bedroom has a bed in it. You have a lot of apologizing to do." She glanced at her wrist. "About two weeks' worth."

"Chel said you've been working tirelessly for weeks to catch up."

Rue's hands went to her hips. "Of course I did. Do you have something to say about that?"

"I wish you wouldn't push yourself so hard."

"I had a goal to finish this semester and that's what I'm going to do. I'm always going to push myself, Dacre. I chose a different life." She motioned to the window. "Humans push themselves to the brink day in and day out. They've got bills and families, kids and pets. They have to mow the lawn and take out the trash in the snow and rain."

He smiled.

"What?" she snapped.

"I was just thinking all of that sounded kind of nice. A simple human life. But..." Dacre's gaze darkened.

Rue's heart ached at the pain in his voice, but she wasn't ready to let him go—not again. She said fiercely, "I'll help you."

Dacre stood, towering over her but looking as uncertain as she'd ever seen him. "Rue..."

She stepped closer, her chin tilting up defiantly. "I'm not leaving."

And for the first time in weeks, Dacre smiled. It was small and fleeting, but it was real.

"Then stay," he murmured, his voice barely audible.

"Then stay," Rue repeated. She reached forward, palm stretching over warm, muscled skin. She ran her hands up his chest and around his neck, reaching up on her toes. "I've been waiting for you to kiss me for weeks." She searched his eyes.

His lips fell on hers, hungry and punishing. Strong arms lifted her and held her close.

"Dacre," she whispered. "Don't leave me again. It hurts when you're gone."

He kissed her harder and backed up until he sat on the bed

again and she was straddling his lap. He suddenly stopped touching her, slammed his eyes closed and hissed like he was in pain.

"What's wrong?" Rue asked.

Shadows danced across his face and tendrils of black began rising from his shoulders. He was starting to shift into the monster.

"What were you thinking about just now?" Rue asked softly.

Dacre's eyes opened just a slit and she could see the bright green of his monster eyes. "You. Naked. Underneath me." He hissed again and slammed his eyes closed harder.

Rue pulled her hoodie off and threw it on the floor. She took his hands and placed them on her breasts. "Stop thinking about it and just do it."

His eyes flashed open and they were his normal dark. He moved quickly and Rue was on her back, her pajama bottoms were ripped off and his hot mouth was on her, everywhere; tasting and sucking and kissing. He crawled up her body, settled between her thighs, and she felt his hardness, ached for him and wrapped her legs around his waist.

"Please," she begged.

His mouth fell on hers as a hand moved to her hips and tilted her lower body up as he pressed inside.

FIFTY-ONE

A soft golden light of late afternoon sun filtered through Rue's apartment window as she paced the small living room. Dacre sat on the edge of her couch, elbows resting on his knees. He was staring face to face with Lucipurr, who sat on the coffee table directly across from him. It seemed like they were speaking telepathically. Both turned when she sighed, watching her with a mixture of curiosity and caution.

"So," Rue began, her voice wavering just slightly, "I'm going to be out of town for a few days."

Dacre's golden eyes narrowed. "Out of town? Where are *we* going?"

She paused mid-step and turned to face him. "Outside Johnstown, Pennsylvania. There's an old archaeological site in the mountains I need to visit for my final project."

He leaned back on the couch and moved his hands behind his head. "An archaeological site?"

Rue nodded. "It's part of my independent study. Professor Camden set it up—there's a colleague of his who's been working on deciphering old runes at an old dig site. They're supposed to depict fifteenth-century giants and angels. The kind of stuff that influenced local myths."

Dacre's gaze sharpened. "Giants and angels?"

"Yes," Rue said firmly. "It's fascinating. The drawings might be linked to Nephilim lore, and I've been studying how their legends evolved into modern mythology."

"Sounds dangerous." He furrowed his brow. "Sounds like something your Uncle Jed should know about."

She rolled her eyes. "It's just a research trip, Dacre. I'm going to look at some old carvings and maybe interview a few people. That's it. I'm not involving him. He's got enough to deal with on the ranch."

Dacre was already shaking his head. "You don't go somewhere like that alone."

Rue planted her hands on her hips. "I wasn't planning to go alone. Evelyn said she'd drive me, but—" she was biting her lip, holding back a teasing smile.

"No." Dacre stood, his imposing presence filling the small room. "If you're going, I'm coming with you."

Rue stared at him, her mouth opening and closing like a fish out of water. She was suddenly reconsidering her teasing. "You at an archaeological site? You'll be bored."

He gave her a pointed look. "Do you have any idea what might actually be out there? If these drawings really are tied to Nephilim or angels, it's not just folklore. You know that, Rue."

She hesitated, the memory of the dungeons and the creatures they'd faced flashing through her mind. "It's not that kind of trip," she said weakly.

Dacre stepped closer. "I'm not letting you walk into the mountains alone with nothing but a clipboard and a few notes."

"Hey, I have Evelyn," she argued.

Dacre couldn't tell if she was serious. "You need someone who can handle... unexpected complications."

Rue crossed her arms, her resolve faltering under his intense gaze. "I didn't say you could come."

He arched a brow, his lips twitching with a hint of a smirk. "You didn't say I couldn't."

A long silence stretched between them before Rue finally sighed in defeat. "Fine. But don't hover. I'm there to work, not to babysit your paranoia."

"Deal." He clapped his hands. "But you're the paranoid one. Remember?" he laughed lightly then stopped abruptly, realizing it was probably a soft spot for her after all they'd been through.

She pointed a finger at him. "No interfering with my research. I only have the weekend. I've lost too much time already."

"Wouldn't dream of it," Dacre said, though the mischievous glint in his eyes suggested otherwise. "Single room. King bed." He picked up his phone. "I'll make reservations."

Rue shook her head, muttering under her breath as she grabbed her notebook from the coffee table. "This is going to be a disaster."

Dacre chuckled softly, his voice warm and teasing. "I'll try not to cramp your style, doctor."

Rue shot him a glare, but she couldn't quite suppress the small smile tugging at the corners of her lips.

———

THE HUM of the SUV's tires on the winding mountain road filled the silence between them. Rue sat in the passenger seat, her notebook balanced on her lap as she scribbled a few last-minute notes. Dacre was behind the wheel, focused on the road, his hands steady despite the sharp turns and steep drops. And road construction.

"Pennsylvania is always doing road construction," Rue muttered. "You could say something, you know," Rue said, glancing at him.

"I'm concentrating," Dacre replied without taking his eyes off the road.

"On what? Not driving us off the edge?"

"Exactly."

Rue rolled her eyes but smirked. "You're acting like we're headed into some kind of life-threatening situation. It's just a mountain with some caves and local lore."

"Just a cave and fairy tales," Dacre repeated, his tone laced with skepticism. "Just a cave and fairy tales. It'll be a cake walk. No dungeons or demons means we are good to go."

She sighed and looked back at her notes. "It's research, Dacre. Academic. Not everything has to end in bloodshed and chaos."

His lips twitched as if he wanted to argue but thought better of it. He didn't want them both getting heated in the SUV and needing to blow off steam. Although, he glanced at her legs and the width of the driver's seat–

"Stop thinking about it," Rue warned.

Dacre sighed and reached for the radio knob.

When they finally arrived at the cave site, a wiry man with graying hair and a rugged outdoorsman's tan waved them over. He wore hiking boots, a flannel shirt, and round glasses perched on his nose.

"Professor Camden said you'd be coming," he greeted, extending a hand to Rue. "Dr. Malcolm Royce, but you can just call me Malcolm."

Rue shook his hand. "Thanks for letting us visit. This doesn't look like much from the outside."

"That's what they want you to see," Malcolm shook his

finger at Rue, his eyes lighting up. "I've been working on documenting these carvings for years. We've barely scratched the surface, but what we've found so far is remarkable. Come on, I'll show you."

Malcolm led them up a narrow trail, the towering pine trees casting long shadows across the rocky path. Dacre stayed close to Rue, his gaze sweeping the surroundings with practiced vigilance.

The carvings were etched into the face of a jagged cliff, faint but unmistakable once you got close enough. Humanlike figures with elongated limbs and wings stretched across the stone, accompanied by strange symbols that seemed to glow faintly in the dappled sunlight.

"These figures," Malcolm said, gesturing to the largest carving, "are what initially drew us here. They're believed to depict Nephilim—half-human, half-angel hybrids. The detail is extraordinary, considering the estimated age of these carvings." His head tipped curiously. "They've changed color. Hm." He glanced at Rue. "Maybe it's the angle of the sunlight."

Rue stepped closer, her fingers itching to trace the outlines. "And the symbols? Do you know what they mean?"

Malcolm shook his head. "Not yet. Some of them resemble ancient Sumerian cuneiform, but others are completely unique. It's possible they were a local adaptation, influenced by a mixture of cultures."

Dacre stood with his legs slightly apart and his arms crossed as he scanned the cliffs and the forest beyond. "You're sure there's nothing... unusual about this place? Nothing dangerous? No bears or wolves or anything wild in these caves?"

Malcolm raised an eyebrow. "Define unusual."

"Dangerous," Dacre repeated.

Malcolm chuckled. "Just the usual hazards of working in

the wilderness. Slippery rocks, sudden weather changes, the occasional curious bear. But as long as you stick to the marked areas, you'll be fine."

"Marked areas?" Rue asked.

Malcolm pointed to a strip of bright orange tape that ran along one side of the trail and disappeared into the cave's entrance. "We've taped off the areas where the ground is unstable or where we haven't finished our surveys. Stay on the safe side, and you'll have nothing to worry about."

He checked his watch. "Speaking of which, I have to get going. I'm coaching my son's rugby team this afternoon, but feel free to explore. Just—"

"Stay behind the tape," Rue finished for him with a smile.

"Exactly," Malcolm said, tipping his hat. "Enjoy yourselves and let me know if you discover anything interesting. I'll be back in a couple of hours."

As he disappeared down the trail, Rue turned to Dacre. "See? Nothing to worry about."

Dacre didn't look convinced. "Famous last words."

She rolled her eyes and started toward the cave entrance, her excitement outweighing his cautious demeanor. "Come on, Dacre. Let's see what secrets this place is hiding."

Dacre followed. The faint glow of the carvings lingered in his peripheral vision, and a chill ran down his spine as they crossed into the shadows of the cave. Something about the air felt heavier and it set him on edge.

"Rue..." His voice echoed against the stone walls. "Don't wander too far."

She glanced back at him, her smile bright even in the dim light. "I'm not planning to. Relax."

They moved deeper in the cave, the dim light of the lantern casting flickering shadows on the cave walls, illuminating rows of intricate carvings etched into the stone. Rue crouched near one section, her notebook balanced on her knee and a pencil poised in her hand. The air was damp and heavy, filled with the scent of earth and stone, and her breath came out in soft puffs of concentration.

"Fascinating," she murmured, her fingers brushing against the cool rock as she traced the edges of a particularly detailed symbol.

Dacre stood a few feet away, his arms crossed and his gaze fixed on the cavern's entrance. "What's fascinating?"

"These carvings," Rue said, tilting her head to study them. "They're not just decorative. My Uncle Jed uses these symbols in his spells. They look like his runes."

He stepped closer, his boots crunching against the gravel.

Rue adjusted the lantern to better illuminate the carvings. "It looks like a ritual of some kind. This symbol here" —she pointed to a spiral flanked by jagged lines— "represents blood. And this one," she said, tracing a series of interlocking triangles, "is growth, or maybe transformation."

Dacre crouched beside her, his expression skeptical. "You're saying this is... what? A recipe?"

"In a way," Rue said, excitement creeping into her voice. "Look at the sequence. Blood, growth, restriction, stasis. It's like they were trying to stop something from happening."

She flipped through her notebook, comparing the carvings to her previous notes. "This entire section seems to describe a process for altering physical development. Specifically, for children."

Dacre frowned. "Children?"

Rue nodded, her brow furrowing. "The Nephilim. They weren't born as giants; they grew into them. But this—this is a ritual meant to prevent that. Blood rituals performed in childhood to stunt their growth, keep them... manageable. Less noticeable amongst humans maybe?"

Dacre's gaze flicked to the carvings. "You're saying they did this to their own kind?"

"It looks that way," Rue said softly. "Probably to fit in with humans, or maybe to avoid drawing attention. Giants don't exactly blend in." She pointed to a carving where a man towered above everyone around him.

She leaned back on her heels, her mind racing. "But it's not just physical. These runes suggest the rituals also affected their abilities—restricted them, suppressed them."

Dacre's voice was low, almost a growl. "That's barbaric."

Rue glanced at him, surprised by the edge in his tone. "It was survival. If the Nephilim grew too powerful, they'd have been hunted. Wiped out." Her brow furrowed. "This was ages ago. Something changed. My Uncle Jed, he said he's only known one other like him. The rest were hunted and killed. Some were born deformed and died. Something changed in their genealogy."

He didn't respond, his eyes fixed on the carvings.

Rue turned back to the wall, her fingers tracing the final sequence. "But what they did was not perfect," she murmured. "The suppression wasn't permanent. There's something here about... activation. Like a way to reverse the effects."

She squinted at the faint carvings, trying to make sense of the faded lines. "It's tied to blood again. Blood and..." Her voice trailed off, and she felt a chill crawl up her spine.

"What?" Dacre asked sharply.

"...and fangs," Rue said, her voice barely above a whisper. Her fingers were pressed against her front teeth.

He stiffened beside her.

She swallowed hard, her mind flashing back to her own struggles—her inability to grow fangs, her incomplete transformation with visions of the future. "This could explain why I never..." She didn't finish the sentence, her thoughts spiraling. "How would that demon in the Black Mansion have known that?"

"Some of them are ancient. Demons aren't known for sharing history." Dacre's hand came to rest on her waist, grounding her. "What does it mean for you?"

"I don't know," Rue admitted, her voice unsteady. "But if these rituals were meant to suppress Nephilim growth, then maybe... maybe it's why I've always felt stuck. Like I'm not enough of one thing or the other. It's still there, that feeling. Even after I got my memories back."

There was a long moment of silence as Rue shuffled through her notebook.

"Wait a moment..." Rue read the passage again. "I'm technically three quarters angel. But my father lost half of his angelicness. So maybe half angel?"

Dacre was watching her sort through the genealogy.

"My father is the son of an Archangel. My mother is half-darkness and half-light. Half of Lucifer's side and half Archangel." She tapped a finger against her lip.

"What does it say?" Dacre asked watching the runes glow.

"It says to drink the blood." She looked up at him wide eyed.

"Drink the blood and your fangs will come in?" he asked.

She nodded.

He smirked. "I've been telling you to just bite me for weeks." He pulled the collar of his shirt down and teased her.

"Not here." Rue closed the book.

Dacre pointed to the shrine carved into rock on the other side of a strip of orange tape. "I think there."

Fifty-Two

RUE FOCUSED PAST THE ORANGE TAPE WHERE SHE saw a tunnel opening into a wide chamber. At its center stood an altar carved from the same dark stone as the cave walls. The surface was etched with more runes.

Rue's breath caught as she ducked under the tape and stepped closer, the lantern's glow illuminating the ancient altar.

"This is incredible," she murmured, running her fingers lightly over the runes. "It's... a focal point for some kind of ritual. I think you're right."

Dacre stood behind her, his arms crossed as he watched her examine the altar. "What does it say?"

Rue adjusted the lantern, leaning in to decipher the carvings. Her voice was quiet but steady as she read aloud. "To awaken the true self, one must embrace both light and shadow. Only in unity can power flourish."

She stepped back, her expression troubled. "Light and shadow. I wonder if that means angelic and demonic. But what if..." She trailed off, her eyes darting to Dacre.

"What if what?" he prompted.

She took a shaky breath. "What if I embrace the darkness too much? What if it corrupts me, changes me? What if I hurt you?" She shivered. "What if I turn into my great-grandfather or something like him?" She cast a worried glance at him.

Dacre stepped closer, his presence steady and grounding. "You can't harm me," he said, his voice firm. "You won't turn into him."

Her eyes searched his face, doubt clouding her features. "You don't know that."

"Yes, I do," Dacre said, his tone leaving no room for argument. "Your darkness is adorable. It's like a kitten. Even if you embraced every spec of darkness you could, you'd still pale in comparison to Lucifer. I've met him multiple times."

She bit her lip, uncertainty warring with the desire to finally feel whole. "I don't know if I can control it. I told you before, I am bred of monsters."

"So am I." Dacre reached out, his hand brushing her cheek. "Don't do it alone. Let me help you."

"How?" she whispered.

A small, knowing smile touched his lips as his form shimmered and he half-shifted, his Displacer Beast powers weaving a veil of calm. His feline-like ears flicked, and the faint glow of his green eyes softened. "Like this. You don't need anyone else's blood. You'll have mine. I trust you."

Rue stared at him, her heart pounding. "You're serious."

"I'm always serious," he said with a faint smirk, his clawed hand lightly brushing her shoulder. "If we do this, it's here and now. But only if you're ready."

Rue glanced back at the altar. To accept herself fully, to be free of the chains that held her back, she had to take this step. She looked back at Dacre, his unwavering presence steadying her nerves.

She closed her eyes and swallowed hard. "Yes. I'm ready,"

she said, her voice steady despite the fear simmering beneath the surface.

Dacre stepped closer to the altar. "Then let's do this."

When Rue opened her eyes, Dacre was stretched across the roughly carved altar in just his boxers. There were candles everywhere and Rue realized he must be altering her reality with his beast powers.

Rue licked her lips. "Are you sure about this?" she asked.

Dacre stretched his hands behind his head and flexed his stomach muscles. He looked too good–exceptional really–like he was posing for a dirty magazine.

"If this is how I'm gonna die, it's a good way to go." He reached a hand out and motioned for her to come closer. "But I think this is just the beginning. Now, get over here and drink my blood."

Rue placed her hands on the cold stone, feeling the energy that pulsed through it. Dacre lay flat on his back, his warmth radiating against her as she climbed on top of him.

"You're stronger than you think," he murmured. "Focus on the balance, not the fear."

She took a deep breath as she let his words ground her. The runes on the altar began to glow faintly, a golden light mingling with a shadowy haze that rose from the carvings.

Rue's heartbeat quickened as the energy coursed through her, a tug-of-war between light and dark that threatened to overwhelm her. She felt Dacre's steadying presence as he whispered calming words.

"You're not alone," he said softly. "I've got you."

She heard a metallic click and focused on his hands. He held a small pocket knife. He cut the soft skin of his wrist. Blood flowed. Rue could smell it. She craved it. Her tongue smoothed over flat teeth, then she grabbed his arm and sealed her lips over the cut.

Dacre hissed as she sucked harder than he'd expected.

Rue ground against him as she drank. Nothing had ever tasted sweeter. Nothing had ever tasted this good. Christ why had she waited so long? Why had she denied who she was all this time? Her eyes flashed open and she focused on the scar on his neck.

His free hand tightened on her hips as the heat within her surged, something snapping into place between them, stronger than before.

She felt it and pushed his arm away. She stilled her body and licked her lips. "I feel strange," she said, moving off him.

Dacre moved off the altar and rounded the side.

Rue sat on the edge, her chest rising and falling with deep, uneven breaths. The ritual had left her trembling, her veins thrumming with a power she didn't know how to control. Her senses were sharper than ever—the faint drip of water from the cave ceiling was deafening, the scent of damp earth overwhelming. But more than that, her instincts had shifted, her hunger sharp and insistent in a way that unsettled her.

"Rue," Dacre said, his voice soft but steady, "you're shaking."

She looked up at him, her pupils dilated, her gaze almost feral. "I don't know what's happening to me." Her voice was a whisper, trembling with both awe and fear.

He crouched in front of her, his dark eyes studying her. "You've awakened everything within you that you've tried to ignore. Your body's adjusting."

"I can feel... everything," she murmured, pressing her hands to her temples. Her fingertips brushed her neck as a new, more primal craving surged. She clenched her jaw, trying to tamp it down.

Before Dacre could respond, a distant voice echoed down the cavern. "Hello? You two still in here?"

Rue froze, her pulse spiking as Malcolm's voice bounced off the walls.

Dacre's expression hardened instantly, his protective instincts kicking in. "Get up," he whispered, pulling Rue to her feet. "We need to get out of here."

She nodded, struggling to suppress the swirling sensations coursing through her. Together, they sprinted out of the taped-off area, their movements quick but careful as they approached the carvings near the entrance to the cave.

"Ah, there you are!" Malcolm's cheerful voice greeted them as he rounded the corner. His flashlight swept over them, briefly blinding Rue. "Studying the runes, huh?" he said, his tone friendly but laced with curiosity.

Dacre nodded, keeping his expression neutral. "Couldn't resist. Rue's got a knack for interpreting these." He placed a hand lightly on Rue's back, steadying her as she struggled to maintain her composure.

Malcolm beamed. "That's what Camden said. You've got an eye for this sort of thing, Rue." He gestured to the walls. "Beautiful, aren't they? It's too bad about those parts beyond the tape. Those caves aren't stable. They'll probably collapse within the next few years."

"That's awful," Rue managed, her voice strained as her jaw dropped. She'd just dipped her toes in this history.

Malcolm glanced between them, his expression thoughtful. "Well, I'll let you two get back to it. Just wanted to check in before I head out for the night. Don't want you getting lost out here. The locals say these mountains are haunted. More than bears come out at night." He shrugged. "There's lots of missing people."

Dacre seized the moment, his tone polite but firm. "Actually, we were just wrapping up. It's late, and we've got a long drive ahead."

Malcolm nodded. "Fair enough. I hope you were able to use some of this for your thesis?" he motioned for them to follow as he led them out of the caves.

"Yes thank you for helping me," Rue said. "I have a lot of good notes here. Although, I wish I'd budgeted more time."

"Maybe come back?" Malcom offered. "Have you decided where you were going to study after graduation?"

"Maybe get my doctorate," Rue said.

Malcom glanced over his shoulder with a smile. "This is a great project for that. Not well received by many, but I find it interesting." The mouth of the cave appeared. "Ah, here we are. Just in time for dinner. Well, kids. I hope to see you again soon."

"Thanks again," Rue said.

The moment Malcom was halfway to his truck, Dacre turned to Rue, his jaw tight. "Let's get out of here."

———

THE SUV WAS quiet except for the hum of the engine as they pulled out onto the dark mountain road. Rue sat stiffly in the passenger seat, her hands gripping her thighs, her mind racing. The craving she'd felt in the cave hadn't subsided—it had only intensified.

Dacre glanced at her, his concern evident. "You okay?"

"I don't know," she admitted, her voice low. "I feel... on edge. Like I'm going to snap like a twig. What's wrong with me?"

He nodded, his grip tightening on the steering wheel. "It's the bloodlust. You need time to adjust. We'll get you somewhere safe."

"Where?" she asked, her tone sharper than she intended.

Dacre hesitated. "Do you want me to take you home? Or should we find a hotel for the night? It's late, and you're..." His voice trailed off, but his meaning was clear when he swallowed hard and shifted in his seat.

Rue's breath hitched, the heat rising in her cheeks. Her

gaze flicked to his hands on the wheel, the way his muscles flexed as he steered. The craving shifted, sharpening into something more specific. She felt hot all over.

"Find a room," she said, her voice breathless.

Dacre glanced at her, his brows furrowing in surprise. "Rue—"

"Now," she interrupted, her voice tinged with desperation.

He nodded, his jaw tightening as he reached for his phone to find the reservations he'd made yesterday just in case. The tension in the car was palpable, an electric charge that neither of them acknowledged but both felt.

As they drove in silence, the air between them grew heavier, Rue's pulse thrumming with anticipation and hunger. She felt out of control.

Dacre pressed his foot down harder on the gas pedal.

———

THE TINY HOTEL room was plain but clean, its rustic charm betrayed by creaky wooden floorboards and outdated wallpaper. A single queen bed dominated the small space, leaving just enough room for a modest dresser and a chair near the window. The dim lighting cast warm, flickering shadows across the walls.

Rue stepped inside first, her shoulders rigid as her eyes darted to every corner as though searching for threats. Her blood was humming beneath her skin. The craving gnawed at her, sharp and insistent, a hunger she didn't fully understand but couldn't ignore.

Dacre followed her, closing the door softly behind them. He placed the room key on the dresser and turned to face her, his dark eyes steady.

"Rue," he said softly, his voice like a tether pulling her back from the edge.

"I'm fine," she snapped, but her tone betrayed her. She wasn't fine—she was anything but. Her hands were trembling, and she couldn't stop pacing.

"You're not," he said gently, stepping closer. "I can feel it."

She stopped abruptly, spinning to face him. "I don't know what's happening to me," she admitted, her voice cracking. "It's like... this hunger is taking over. I can't think straight. I'm scared, Dacre."

He stepped closer, his presence grounding her. "You're still you, Rue. You just need to let yourself adjust. You're fighting it too hard."

She shook her head, backing away from him until her knees hit the edge of the bed. "What if I hurt you? What if I lose control?"

Dacre knelt in front of her, resting his hands gently on her knees. "You won't hurt me," he said firmly. "I trust you."

Her breath hitched, her gaze meeting his. "You don't know that. What if I..." She trailed off, the words too terrible to finish.

"You can't break me," he said, a hint of a smile softening his handsome face.

Rue's lip quivered, but she shook her head again as tears threatened to spill. "What if I trigger your transformation? What if—" She pulled at the ends of her hair.

"Rue," he interrupted, his tone steady. "I can handle it. You've seen the worst of me, and I'm still here. Let me help you."

Her hands gripped the edge of the bed as she tried to steady herself. "I don't know how to do this."

"You'll learn," he said. "Start with me. I trust you."

The vulnerability in his voice, in his eyes, made her heart ache. She reached out, her fingers brushing against his cheek. "You're not scared?"

"Terrified," he admitted with a small laugh. "But not of you. Of losing you."

Rue let out a shaky breath. "Okay," she whispered.

Dacre moved so he was sitting beside her on the bed. He tugged off his shirt, then helped Rue out of hers. He dragged her onto his lap and tilted his head slightly to the side.

"Go slow," he said with a dark smile as his hands circled her ribs.

She hesitated, feeling sharpness graze her bottom lip. She took a deep breath then leaned in. He gripped her waist and squeezed. Her lips brushed against his neck, and she felt the steady beat of his pulse beneath her mouth. Her instincts surged but she fought to stay in control.

She pressed teeth to his neck and when her fangs broke his skin, Dacre let out a sharp breath but didn't pull away. Instead, his hand came up to rest on her lower back, grounding her as she fed, as she lapped at his neck like a kitten to a bowl of milk.

The taste was electric, a surge of energy seeming to flow straight into her veins. It was unlike anything she'd ever experienced, both intoxicating and terrifying. But as she drank, she felt something shift—a connection, deep and unbreakable, that bound them together in a way words could never describe. It had always been there, lingering. Now it was awakened and surging.

Dacre's fingers tightened briefly on her, his body tensing for a moment before relaxing completely. His beast, usually lurking just beneath the surface, remained calm like a feline high on catnip.

When Rue finally pulled back, her lips stained crimson, she looked at him with wide, tear-filled eyes. "Did I hurt you?"

He shook his head, a faint smile playing on his lips. "Not at all." Dark hair fell over his eyes.

She licked her lips, and her cheeks flushed. "My mother said that you must drink from me also."

Rue rested her forehead against his shoulder, the tension finally leaving her body.

"You want me to?" Dacre asked, licking his dry lips.

Rue nodded but refused to look at him. He tilted her chin up with a finger and gazed into her eyes. "Don't be embarrassed." He moved her off his lap and stood.

"What are you doing?" Rue asked.

"Getting us naked." He unbuttoned his jeans and Rue noticed the bulge.

She looked up at his face, surprised.

"Yes, you did that." He kicked off his boots and pants then reached for hers. "And I've heard things about sharing blood and the blood lust. And I think we should try all of them."

"What kind of things?" Rue asked as she kicked her shoes off.

"Not princess type things."

Rue pouted. "But I've embraced my dark side."

"Good. Because I'm going to bite you and be inside you at the same time."

Rue shivered and felt her core clench. "Christ," she muttered.

He shoved her back, gripped her waistband, and tugged her jeans and underwear down her legs in one move. He kissed her thigh. "I might bite you here." He nipped at the soft skin of her inner leg before crawling up and nipping her hipbone. "I might do it here." He licked her stomach. "Maybe here." He unclipped her bra and tossed it aside. His mouth settled over her breast and sucked before he whispered, "Here looks good too." And then his face was in front of hers.

"Be gentle," she said as she reached between their bodies and gripped his length, lining him up to enter her core.

He licked her neck. "Here looks good for a first time." He

sucked on her skin and Rue writhed against him as he surged forward. "I already have sharp teeth. Lucky me."

Rue felt his teeth against her neck and the fullness of his thrust between her thighs at the same time. She moaned in pleasure and scratched her nails across his back.

They fell together in a steady motion of bodies and bites, of blood and lust, of everything they had denied themselves for years.

Later, they were satiated and wrapped around each other, blankets hanging from the bed and pillows askew. Rue's head was tucked against his shoulder, her small palm rested on his chest and she whispered, "Thank you." And kissed his ribs.

Dacre spread his hand across her lower back and pulled her close. "Always."

Fifty-Three

The hallway leading to Professor Camden's office was quiet, save for the faint hum of fluorescent lights overhead. Rue clutched her notebook tightly against her chest, her steps measured. She had rehearsed this conversation a dozen times in her head but still felt the nervous flutter of butterflies in her stomach.

When she reached the office door, slightly ajar, she knocked gently.

"Come in!" Professor Camden's voice carried from inside.

Rue pushed the door open, stepping into the familiar space filled with towering bookshelves, piles of papers, and the faint scent of coffee and old books. Professor Camden sat behind his desk, glasses perched on the edge of his nose as he reviewed a stack of student essays.

"Ah, Rue," he said, setting the papers aside and gesturing for her to sit. "Right on time. How's the final project coming along?"

Rue slid into the chair across from him, placing her notebook and a few printed documents on the desk between them.

"It's coming together, but I wanted to go over a few things with you before I finalize my thesis."

Professor Camden leaned back in his chair, giving her his full attention. "Of course. Let's hear it."

She opened her notebook, flipping to a page filled with bullet points and hastily sketched diagrams. "So, the focus is on how Nephilim myths influenced modern Appalachian folklore, specifically in the Allegheny region. I've been tracing the connection between fifteenth-century European lore about giants and angels and how those stories evolved when settlers brought them here."

He nodded thoughtfully, tapping a pen against his chin. "Interesting angle. And the archaeological site you visited— did it provide any insights?"

Rue hesitated, choosing her words carefully. "It did. There were carvings in the caves that seemed to support the idea that these myths weren't just imported but might have had local adaptations or even roots. Some of the rune-like symbols suggested rituals and... well, transformations."

Professor Camden raised an eyebrow. "Transformations?"

She smiled nervously, realizing she might have said too much. "You know, the way myths evolve to fit cultural contexts. For example, the Nephilim in Europe were often described as giants, but in the Appalachians, they became more... humanized in the stories. Less about literal giants, more about individuals with extraordinary abilities."

"Ah, I see," Professor Camden said, nodding again. "And what's your working thesis?"

Rue took a deep breath. "I'm arguing that these stories were a way for settlers to explain the unknown, blending their existing beliefs with what they encountered here. But I also think there's a possibility that the myths weren't entirely fictional—that they were based on actual events or phenomena, misinterpreted over time."

Professor Camden tilted his head, intrigued. "That's a bold claim. What kind of evidence are you using to support it?"

She motioned to the papers she'd brought. "I've compiled a lot of primary sources—oral histories, old texts, and some of the findings from the caves. There's enough there to suggest a pattern, even if it's not definitive proof."

He picked up one of the documents and scanned it quickly. "Is this what you emailed me?"

Rue nodded and sat silently across from him as he read.

After ten minutes, he finally set the papers down. "This is wild stuff," he said tapping the report. "I don't think we can submit this anywhere. No one will print it."

"You think it's worthless." Something sank inside Rue but she understood this was *her* heritage and far removed from the human world she was hiding in.

"That's not what I said," Professor Camden replied. "It's worth much. It's fantastic, really, just... some people don't think like this. But some do. You're going to have to find the right minds to work with if you want to take this further."

"Does this mean I won't have enough credits to graduate?"

"You'll have plenty. I'm giving you an A in the independent study." He reached forward. "Congratulations, Rue. See you at graduation next week."

Rue smiled wide as she took Professor Camden's hand and shook it. Relief flooded through her. "Thank you, Professor."

He smiled warmly. "Good. And remember, it's not just about what you find but how you tell the story. Your perspective matters just as much as the evidence."

Rue nodded, standing to gather her things. As she slung her bag over her shoulder, Professor Camden added, "Oh, and

Rue—if you ever want to apply for your doctorate, let me know. I think this could go far."

She froze, surprised. "Really?" She was going to rub that in Remington's face the first chance she got.

"Really," he said. "Now go get ready for graduation. I'm looking forward to meeting your mother."

Rue's eyes widened just a tiny bit as she replayed what he'd just said in her head. Meet her mother... No. That could not happen. Her mother would eat the kind professor alive. Literally.

Rue left the office feeling lighter than she had in days. For the first time, she felt like she was truly on the path to something meaningful, not just in her research but in her life. Everything had become clearer. The lies and the fog that had haunted her life had cleared.

Fifty-Four

Rue sat on the edge of her bed, staring at the garment bag Evelyn had unzipped. Inside was a sleek black catsuit with strategic cutouts along the sides paired with a pair of black stilettos, cat ears, and a tail that clipped onto the back. It screamed scandalous, and Rue immediately regretted letting Evelyn take control of her costume choice.

"I can't wear that," Rue said flatly.

"Oh, come on, Rue! It's hot, it's fun, and you'll look amazing. Trust me."

Rue shook her head. "I'm going to look like I wandered out of some... adult-themed comic book."

Evelyn plopped onto the bed beside her, giving her a mischievous grin. "And? Graduation is the last time you'll have an excuse to dress up and let loose before diving into the black hole of adulthood. Might as well go out with a bang."

Lucipurr meowed softly in agreement.

Rue groaned, eyeing the outfit again. "I thought this was supposed to be a costume party, not a... lingerie show."

Evelyn rolled her eyes dramatically. "Rue, half the people there are going to be dressed as sexy pirates or witches. You'll blend right in. Besides, I'm pretty sure a certain someone will be there, and he might appreciate the view."

Rue felt her cheeks heat up. "What are you talking about?"

Evelyn gave her a pointed look. "Oh, please. Don't play dumb. Your hot-bodyguard has been glued to your side lately. Maybe this is your chance to show him what he's been missing while he's busy brooding in the shadows."

Rue opened her mouth to protest but couldn't think of a convincing retort. Instead, she sighed and reached for the costume. "Fine. But if anyone laughs, I'm never speaking to you again."

Evelyn clapped her hands in victory. "Deal! Now, let's get you into this thing. Hot-bodyguard is going to lose his soul tonight." Evelyn shimmied exaggeratedly. "I can just sense it."

"Oh my god," Rue scrubbed her cheeks as she took another look at the costume, grabbed it, and took it to the closet to change. After a brief wrestling match with the catsuit—during which Rue shouted and complained that it was too tight, too revealing, and completely impractical—she finally stood in front of the mirror. The fabric clung to her curves, and the cutouts showed just enough skin to be daring but not indecent.

"Christ almighty, Tink." She whistled. "I might lose my soul. Do you like women? I've never considered switching teams but looking at you right now makes me want to consider it."

"Meow." Rue pawed the air.

Lucipurr raised his head from the bed and narrowed his eyes at Rue.

Evelyn stepped back and grinned. "See? You look incredible. Like a sexy superhero who's about to steal hearts and maybe a few wallets," Evelyn said, handing her the cat ears and tail. "Now, let's add the finishing touches."

By the time they were done, Rue barely recognized herself. The cat ears perched perfectly atop her head, her dark hair cascading in loose waves. Evelyn had even added a swipe of eyeliner to give her the perfect feline flick.

"You're a masterpiece," Evelyn declared.

"What are you wearing?" Rue asked, suspicion creeping into her voice.

Evelyn didn't look up, a wicked grin spreading across her face. "Oh, wait until you see this." She triumphantly pulled out a vibrant red bodysuit, complete with shimmering details that caught the light. It had a plunging neckline and sculpted devil horns sewn into the collar. Evelyn held it up like a trophy. "I'm going to be a red devil. Hang on, let me put it on."

Rue blinked. "A devil? Isn't that a little... predictable?"

"Predictable? Oh, Rue, sweetheart," Evelyn said, winking. "There's nothing predictable about me."

With that, she disappeared into the bathroom, leaving Rue shaking her head. She sat on the bed and waited, her fingers drumming lightly on the bedspread.

When the bathroom door finally swung open, Evelyn stepped out, transformed. Her blonde hair was teased into a voluminous, slightly wild style that framed her face. She'd paired the fiery bodysuit with fishnet stockings and glossy black heels. To top it all off, she'd applied bright red lipstick that matched her costume to perfection. The devil horns embedded in the suit's collar gave her an impish yet glamorous air.

Rue's jaw dropped. "Evelyn, you look—" She paused, struggling for the right word.

"Hot? Stunning? Sinfully good?" Evelyn supplied, striking a dramatic pose and winking at her reflection in the mirror.

"I was going to say... like a walking fire hazard," Rue deadpanned, though her lips twitched into a reluctant smile.

Evelyn smirked, grabbing her tube of lipstick to add

another quick swipe. "Please, darling. If I'm going to burn, I'll make sure everyone enjoys the show."

Rue rolled her eyes, but she couldn't deny that Evelyn looked amazing. "You're definitely going to turn heads."

"That's the plan," Evelyn said, adjusting the devil horns and giving herself one last approving glance in the mirror. "What's the point of a costume party if you don't make an entrance?"

Rue shook her head, unable to stop smiling. "I don't know how you manage to pull this stuff off. This is so extra. Way more than what you pulled off for the Halloween party."

"It's a gift," Evelyn said, blowing Rue an exaggerated kiss. "Now, let's go dance. Last night of freedom."

Evelyn paused and glanced into the living room. "Wait... where's hot-bodyguard?"

"He's going to meet us there," Rue said checking her phone messages. "He said he's not ready yet."

Rue grabbed her coat and slung it over her shoulders as Evelyn adjusted her devil horns in the mirror by the door. The faint hum of excitement coursing through her made Rue feel a little giddy despite herself.

Evelyn turned, flashing a dazzling smile. "Ready to wreak havoc, partner?"

Rue smirked. "More like keep you from wreaking havoc. But sure."

As they stepped into the chilly evening air, Rue felt a pang of guilt. She hadn't told Dacre that they were headed to the party, and she knew he wouldn't be thrilled about her going without him. But, Rue reasoned, he'd spent the entire day downstairs in his apartment, barely speaking to her.

What was he even doing down there? Avoiding her? Brooding? Or worse—hiding something?

The thought made her clench her fists inside her coat pockets. After everything they'd been through, everything they'd shared, the idea that Dacre might be keeping something from her stung.

But tonight wasn't about him, she reminded herself. It was about her. About having fun for once and not worrying about demons, blood rituals, or whatever cryptic nonsense Dacre was dealing with.

"Let me guess," Evelyn said, interrupting her thoughts as they walked down the street. "You're thinking about hot-bodyguard, aren't you?"

Rue shot her a look. "No."

"You're such a bad liar." Evelyn grinned knowingly. "But don't worry. Tonight's about cutting loose, remember? No brooding, no shadows lurking in the corners, just music, dancing, and maybe some questionable punch."

"He'll be there." Rue reminded Evelyn and sighed, her lips twitching into a reluctant smile. "But if you get into trouble, don't expect me to bail you out."

"That's what friends are for!" Evelyn said, throwing her arm around Rue's shoulders.

As they neared the party venue, the music and laughter spilling into the street gave Rue a strange sense of relief. For once, she was going to let herself celebrate, to step away from the chaos of her life and just exist.

And if Dacre was lying about something? Well, she'd deal with that tomorrow. She'd apologize for ditching him after confronting him about lying. They'd kiss and make up. Heck, they'd *bite* and make up. A thrill zipped up her spine just thinking about it.

With a final deep breath, she stepped into the warm glow of the party, the sound of Evelyn's excited laughter echoing in her ears.

Bass thrummed through the floor, pulsing up through Rue's feet and into her chest. The room was a kaleidoscope of flashing lights and swirling costumes. She had to admit, Evelyn had been right—cutting loose was good for her.

For the first time in what felt like forever, Rue wasn't thinking about demons, ancient rituals, or the precarious balance of light and dark inside her.

Evelyn, her devil horns glowing faintly in the strobe lights, spun Rue in an exaggerated twirl. "You're getting the hang of this!" she shouted over the music.

Rue laughed, her earlier worries momentarily drowned out by the upbeat rhythm. "I'm not that bad!"

"Not bad?" Evelyn smirked. "You're killing it, kitty!"

Rue rolled her eyes but kept moving, letting the music guide her. For a while, it worked—she lost herself in the carefree atmosphere. The crowd around them was buzzing with energy; a mix of students and strangers all caught up in the revelry of the night.

But as the song changed to something slower, her focus wavered. She glanced toward the entrance for the tenth time that night. Still no sign of Dacre.

Evelyn noticed, of course. She always did. "Looking for hot-bodyguard?" she teased, her voice tinged with amusement.

"No," Rue lied, too quickly. She smoothed her hands down her costume and forced a casual shrug. "Just... yeah. He's late."

Evelyn grabbed Rue's hand. "Come on. One more song, then we'll grab drinks. Deal?"

"Deal," Rue said, but her gaze flicked to the entrance again. She wished she'd brought the cinnamon whisky from the kitchen. She didn't want to drink anything at this party.

As they danced, a creeping unease settled over her. It wasn't like Dacre to stay away for this long—not when he knew she was out, unprotected. Her earlier annoyance at his distance morphed into a gnawing worry.

What if something had happened? What if the shadow demons came back?

She shook her head, trying to dismiss the thoughts. This was Dacre. He could handle himself. He was probably downstairs in his apartment, brooding like always, deciding whether or not to crash the party.

"Hey," Evelyn said, pulling Rue's attention back. Her friend's expression softened. "You okay?"

"Yeah," Rue lied again, her voice thinner this time.

Evelyn studied her for a moment before looping her arm through Rue's. "Let's go grab those drinks. Maybe a little liquid courage will help you relax."

Rue nodded, following her off the dance floor, but the knot of worry in her chest tightened. Dacre's absence felt like a warning, like the calm before the storm.

And Rue had learned the hard way that storms always came.

"Who is that?" Evelyn asked.

Rue followed her gaze and did a double take as she recognized the green eyes watching her. "That's my brother!"

"You didn't tell me you had a hot brother! God he's not even wearing a costume."

Rue reached for her friend. "No, Evelyn. Stay away from him."

Evelyn winked and walked closer to the tall man leaning against the wall.

"No. I'm telling you. He's trouble. Worse trouble than me."

Evelyn clicked her tongue. "I like trouble. Trouble looks good." She wagged a finger at Rue. "Remember Pyramid Head? I need more trouble than that guy. He was too mid. But that..." She pointed, moving her finger up and down indicating his height. "That..." she sighed. "Hear me out. That guy looks like sin on a cracker."

Rue threw her hands in the air as Evelyn danced away from her. "It's your funeral," Rue shouted at her friend over the music.

Hands grabbed her and a familiar voice growled I her ear. "A cat?"

Rue smiled and delight surged through her body. "Do you like it? *Meow?*"

"It doesn't leave much to the imagination." Dacre was walking around her like a predator, like a... panther. He licked his lips.

"Blame Evelyn, she picked it out."

"Did she paint it on your skin?" he pinched her waist then her butt. "Jesus Christ this is so tight on you."

She turned in his arms. "I had to make you come find me."

"You could have been hurt. You didn't tell me you were leaving."

"You were being weird. You lied to me. I can tell. And this is my last night on campus before graduation. I'm not going to sit around in my apartment because you think there's some danger out here." She was jabbing her finger into his hard chest.

"I was trying to surprise you," he leaned down and hissed between gritted teeth. "I talked your brother into visiting you for graduation."

Rue stepped back, her face going slack. "Oh no. I forgot. We can't both be here." She glanced across the room to where Evelyn was dancing very dirtily with Remington. Evelyn's arms were slung around her brother's neck, their movements teetering on the edge of indecent. Rue's stomach sank. "Oh shit. We have to get him out of here."

Rue grabbed Dacre's hand and started crossing the room. Dacre's towering presence parted the crowd like a wave.

They weaved through the party and Rue became acutely aware of the shift in the air. A strange tension prickled at her senses, like static electricity. She glanced at Dacre, his sharp eyes scanning the room.

A sudden vision hit Rue…

RUE AND REMINGTON TOGETHER, both with a half a foot outside the runes of protection, lit the skies above with a silvery ethereal light like nothing ever seen before. Two rays blasted to the sky and illuminated the night clouds. Every illegal creature that didn't belong on the Earthen plane saw it.

Creatures slid between the Veils separating realms. Good and bad, dark and light, they all seeped to the Earthen plane, drawn by forbidden fruit. A tempting aura that begged for inspection, a light that hadn't been seen in years; curious creatures and those looking to consume, made their way closer–made their way into other's bodies and took over by possession.

"DACRE," Rue whispered urgently. "Something's coming."

He nodded, his posture stiffening. His hand dropped to the knife hidden at his hip.

The air thickened further as a shadow began to coalesce near the edges of the room. The music seemed to distort, the beat slowing and warping as if the party itself were falling under some spell. The energy of the crowd shifted, turning from carefree to uneasy.

Before they could react, a man stepped into their path; Justin, the party host, with an unsettling grin on his face. His slicked-back hair and tailored suit made him look out of place amidst the costumes. He stood unnaturally still, his gaze fixed on Rue like a predator sizing up its prey.

"Leaving so soon?" Justin asked smoothly. His voice had a melodic, almost hypnotic quality.

Rue tensed. "We were just—"

"You're not going anywhere," Justin interrupted, his grin widening unnaturally.

Dacre stepped in front of Rue, his voice a low growl. "Move. Now."

Justin's grin faltered slightly, but he didn't back down. "I don't think you understand the situation."

"Oh, I understand perfectly," Dacre said, his voice cold. His grip tightened on the knife hilt. "I'm going to drag you across the pavement and make you wish you never looked at her."

Justin's eyes darkened, his smile fading entirely. "You can try."

Before Dacre could act, Chel charged in the front door. With a single, fluid motion, he disarmed Justin of whatever malevolent energy had taken him over, sending him stumbling backward.

"Enough," Chel said, his voice ringing with authority. His gaze lingered on Justin for a moment before turning to Dacre and Rue. "You two need to leave. Now." He glanced at Remington and sighed in disappointment.

Rue hesitated, glancing at Evelyn, who was now staring at Chel with wide, suspicious eyes. Recognition dawned on her face as she looked between Rue, Dacre, and Chel.

"What the hell is going on?" Evelyn whispered, her voice barely audible over the distorted music.

Rue's heart sank. Evelyn was starting to piece things together, her sharp gaze darting between them and the unnatural glow of their auras.

"Evelyn, later," Rue said quickly, tugging on Dacre's arm.

Chel stepped forward, placing himself between them and Justin. "Go. I'll handle this. Once you get them back to Rue's apartment, everyone will get bored and leave."

Dacre hesitated but eventually nodded, guiding Rue toward the exit. Rue cast one last glance at Evelyn, her friend's confused and slightly terrified expression burning into her memory as she grabbed her hand and pulled her along. Then they all disappeared into the night.

Thankfully, Dacre had driven to the party because Remington hadn't wanted to walk from the portal.

They got inside and Dacre sped away. Shadows swirled around the windows to Justin's house.

"What happened to Justin?" Evelyn asked. "I've never seen him like that before."

Rue took Evelyn's hands and shooshed her. "We'll explain in a minute."

Dacre pulled into the driveway, launched himself out of the SUV and ran to Rue's door. He grabbed her and dragged her toward the stairs to her apartment. Remington and Evelyn were close behind.

Once everyone was inside, Dacre locked the door then leaned his back against it, breathing heavy. "No more costume parties."

"Yeah," Rue agreed. "Never again."

"Are you... aliens?" Evelyn asked.

"No," Remington replied with a laugh. "Not even close." He was rummaging through Rue's kitchen.

"Then what are you?" Evelyn wiped at her mascara.

Remington poured a shot of cinnamon whisky and handed it to her. "You wouldn't believe us if we told you." He poured a shot for himself. "And if we told you, we'd have to–"

"Wipe your memories," Rue interrupted.

Chel's voice came from the other side of the door and Dacre let him inside. They whispered to each other.

Evelyn bit her lip and pouted. "But I want to keep my memories of dancing with your hot brother, Rue. That's just not nice. Why do you get all the hot ones? Hot-bodyguard, hot brother." She glanced at Chel. "Whatever that thing is." She added absently with the wave of her hand.

Evelyn held out her glass for another shot.

Remington filled it, his eyes glinting with amusement as she threw it back.

"I like this one," Remington said.

"No." Rue waved her hand. "Absolutely not."

"Why?" Remington whined. "She thinks I'm hot. She's cute." Remington was staring at Evelyn so hard it was starting to get uncomfortable for those around them. "Why should you get to have all the fun on the Earthen plane?"

"Who says that? Earthen plane?" Evelyn slammed her shot glass down.

They all glanced between themselves.

"She's my friend and off limits," Rue said.

Remington moved closer to Evelyn and wrapped his arm around her waist. "I want to keep her."

"No."

"Don't be mean, Rue."

"Yeah, Tink, don't be mean. Let hot-brother have whatever he wants." Evelyn wiggled in his grip.

"I don't have time for this, children," Chel reached for the door. "I'm going home."

"Where's home?" Evelyn asked.

"Hell," Chel replied absently.

Evelyn erupted into a fit of giggles but stopped abruptly when she realized no one was laughing with her. She pointed at them.

"That's his home," Remm clarified. "We split our time between Heaven and Hell."

Evelyn blinked before looking at Dacre.

"This is my home," Rue corrected her brother. "I have been granted approval each year by the White horse."

Evelyn blinked again. "I'm too fuckin drunk for this conversation. You get approval from a *horse*?"

"In Montana," Dacre added.

"Oh, I just have to ask the White Horse if I can stay here and hang out with my new human devil woman?" Remm asked.

Rue shrugged. "You should do it before she casts you out with a bolt of lightning. You know what happened to mom."

Evelyn raised her hands. "Whoa. Whoa. Who is your mother?"

"She's the Queen of Hell," Remington said proudly.

"And your father?" Evelyn asked.

"A King of Heaven." Remington's hands circled Evelyn's waist. "That makes me a prince, she-devil."

"A good prince or a bad prince? Wait... a *dark* prince?" Evelyn wagged her eyebrows.

"Dark. One-Hundred percent dark." Remington smiled wide.

"I think I'm gonna be sick," Rue said. "I can't be around these two any longer. Thanks for stealing my only friend, Remm."

"She can still be your friend, you just have to share her." Remington was pouring another shot with one hand, gripping Evelyn's waist with the other.

"I shared a womb with you, that's enough sharing."

"Hold on a second!" Evelyn shouted, raising her hands up. "A womb? You're twins?"

"Yup. But she's older so she tries to boss me around all the time." Remington pouted his lip.

"Oh, my poor baby." Evelyn gripped his cheeks and pressed a kiss to his lips. "How dare she boss you around, you sweet, wicked thing." She pecked a dozen kisses on his lips. "She's so mean and serious all the time."

"Fuck yeah. I'm keeping you." Remington gripped her waist and threw her over his shoulder. "I'm taking her back."

"You can't," Rue said. "You can't do that. She has graduation tomorrow."

"Shit," Remington bit his lip as he thought for a moment. "Shit. I don't like waiting. I actually despise waiting. I'm an instant gratification kinda guy."

"Too bad." Rue was glaring.

"Maybe take her back to her place, then go see the White horse in the morning," Dacre suggested.

"That's a good idea." He slapped Evelyn's ass.

She howled then laughed, gripping Remington's butt with both her hands. "God you're fit too. These puppies are rock hard."

"That's not the only thing." Remington slapped her ass again.

"Harder!" Evelyn shouted, kicking her feet.

Rue pressed a hand over her mouth and made a gagging sound. "I'm gonna be sick if I have to watch any more of this."

FIFTY-FIVE

RUE ADJUSTED AT THE STRAP OF HER BAG AS SHE approached the coffee shop. The faint smell of roasted coffee beans wafted through the street. Dacre walked silently beside her, his presence steady and reassuring, though he said little. Her mother wanted to meet.

When they reached the shop Rue paused, her brow furrowing. The interior was eerily quiet, and the usual crowd of patrons was absent. Through the glass, she could see her parents seated at a corner table.

"Empty coffee shop," Rue murmured. "No way that's a coincidence."

Dacre opened the door for her, and she stepped inside, the bell above tinkling softly. Meg stood when she entered, a warm smile spreading across her face. Sparrow, on the other hand, was seated with a comically large plate of muffins in front of him, one in each hand.

"Rue," Meg greeted, pulling her into a brief but tight hug. "Thank you for coming." She reached out and gripped Dacre's arm in greeting.

Rue glanced at her father, whose grin was hidden beneath

a bite of muffin. "Sorry, I couldn't wait to eat these. They're even better before they've gone through a portal."

Sparrow swallowed his bite and chuckled, setting one of the muffins down. "Muffins are important, but not as important as this." He moved to embrace Rue.

Dacre hovered near the doorway, but Sparrow gestured toward the table. "You too, boy. Sit."

Rue stifled a groan. "Please don't scare him, Dad."

Dacre shot her a subtle smirk before taking the seat beside her. His quiet confidence made Rue's nerves settle—just a little.

Meg leaned forward, her hands folded on the table. "We wanted to talk to you about what's next, Rue. You've accomplished so much already, and we're proud of you."

"Very proud," Sparrow added, punctuating his words with another bite of muffin.

Rue blinked, taken aback by the praise. "Uh, thanks?"

Meg smiled. "But we're curious—what are your plans for the future? Do you want to stay here, or...?"

Rue hesitated, her mind racing. She hadn't expected such a direct question. She glanced at Dacre, who gave her an almost imperceptible nod of encouragement.

"I want to continue my research," she said finally. "I've been analyzing the artifacts we found at the dig site and doing a lot of reading. There are connections between our kind and the Earthen realm. There is a lot of history that has been lost over the years or misinterpreted."

Sparrow and Meg exchanged a glance, their expressions shifting from curiosity to relief. Rue knew they'd been through a lot in their lives, her mother's scars and her father's demeanor were a trophy to that.

"That's... quite the undertaking," Meg said. "But, it could make a real difference."

Sparrow leaned back in his chair, crossing his arms.

"You've always been the curious one, digging for answers. If this is what you want, we'll support you."

Rue felt a warm glow of validation, but her father's gaze soon shifted to Dacre.

"And what about you, boy?" Sparrow asked, his tone light but probing. "What do you think of all this? Living a human life, being tied to this world?"

Dacre met Sparrow's eyes without hesitation. "I love the idea of it." He paused, his voice softening as his gaze drifted to Rue. "As long as we're together."

Rue's breath caught. The vulnerability in his words, the way he looked at her—it was impossible to ignore. She kept his gaze and beamed.

Meg smiled knowingly, breaking the brief silence. "It seems like you've both thought about this a lot."

"We have," Dacre said simply, his eyes never leaving Rue.

The table grew quiet, save for Sparrow nibbling another muffin. Rue fidgeted with the hem of her shirt, debating whether to bring up the lingering subject that had gnawed at her for weeks. Finally, she couldn't hold back any longer.

"I've been meaning to talk to you," she said, looking between her parents. "About... the memories you took."

Meg's smile faltered, and Sparrow straightened in his chair.

"Rue—" Meg started, but Rue raised a hand.

"Let me finish." She took a deep breath, forcing the words out. "For a long time, I was angry. I felt like you didn't trust me enough to handle the truth. Like you kept me in the dark about who I am and where I came from. I felt very different from the rest of the family, like I didn't fit in and no one liked me."

Meg's eyes glistened, but she stayed silent.

"But now I think I understand," Rue continued, her voice softening. "You gave me a chance to have a normal childhood, to make my own choices without the weight of all of this hanging over me. Without the weight of being bonded to someone at such a young age. I didn't know what I had done but... I think I'm glad I did it. And... I'm grateful for what you did. I might not have seen it at the time, but you did what you thought was best for me."

Sparrow reached across the table, placing a large hand over hers. "We never wanted to hurt you, Rue. But we wanted you to grow into yourself on your own terms. Not because of some mistake you made in a moment of chaos and trauma."

"I know now," Rue said, her voice cracking slightly. "And I forgive you. I just... I want us to be honest with each other from now on. No more secrets."

Meg reached out and squeezed her other hand. "No more secrets."

Sparrow cleared his throat, breaking the emotional moment. "Now, you'd better take a muffin before I eat them all. And I mean *all* of them."

Rue laughed, her tension easing. She grabbed a muffin, feeling a weight lift off her shoulders.

Fifty-Six

The crisp scent of autumn leaves and the faint aroma of fresh paint filled the air as Rue folded a heap of laundry in their new living room. Golden light filtered through the windows, casting warm patterns on the hardwood floor. The house was small but charming, nestled on the edge of a quiet neighborhood with a view of the forest. It was theirs—a place to call home after all the chaos they'd endured.

From the kitchen, she could hear the soft clinking of glass jars and the low hum of Dacre's voice as he muttered about shelf space. "Do we really need this much almond milk?" he called out, his tone laced with mock exasperation.

Rue rolled her eyes, folding the last of her sweaters. "Yes, we do. I need it for my coffee."

Dacre appeared in the doorway, holding a jar of pickles in one hand and a container of salsa in the other. "Coffee and freezer pizza, huh? A gourmet diet."

She shot him a look, biting back a smile. "Some of us are busy starting a doctorate program. We don't have time for fancy dinners."

He smirked and disappeared back into the kitchen. Rue

followed the sound of his reorganizing spree, leaning against the doorway to watch him. Dacre, in his usual effortless way, moved with precision and grace as he rearranged the shelves of their refrigerator. His broad shoulders stretched against his plain gray T-shirt, and the way his dark hair fell over his brow made her heart skip a beat.

Without looking up, he said, "If you keep staring at me like that, I might start to think you like having me around."

Rue scoffed. "Don't get ahead of yourself, cat-boy."

Finally glancing up, he grinned at her, mischief dancing in his eyes. "Should I clear some space for bagged blood? You know, just in case."

Rue rolled her eyes and crossed her arms, a playful smile tugging at her lips. "Absolutely not. Only fresh in this house. Your rules."

Dacre chuckled, closing the refrigerator door with a flourish. "Yes only the best for my girl, your highness."

She shook her head, but her gaze lingered on him as he wiped his hands on a towel and started toward her. There was something mesmerizing about the way he carried himself, the way his presence seemed to fill every corner of their home.

He stopped abruptly, catching her staring, and in two strides, he was in front of her. Without hesitation, he placed his hands on her hips and lifted her effortlessly onto the counter. Rue's breath hitched as he stepped between her legs, his hands steadying her.

"You keep looking at me like that," he murmured, his voice low and teasing, "and I might have to kiss you. Or bite you. I haven't decided yet."

"Dacre," she started, her voice soft but firm as she placed a hand on his chest. "You've been acting strange all day. What's going on? You know I don't like lies or secrets."

His expression flickered with surprise, then something

warmer—a spark of affection. "Hang on." He held up a finger and stepped back, disappearing down the hallway.

Rue frowned, her curiosity piqued. Moments later, he returned, a small, brown paper-wrapped package in his hands. He held it out to her, his lips twitching into a sheepish smile.

"Open it," he urged.

Rue tore at the paper, revealing a white ceramic mug with a familiar snowy owl design. Her heart clenched as she recognized it immediately–she'd broken the original one months ago during a nightmare.

"You found a replacement Hedwig mug?"

Dacre rubbed the back of his neck, looking uncharacteristically shy. "I know how much you liked the old one. I searched everywhere to find it."

For a moment, Rue could only stare at the mug, overwhelmed by the simple yet thoughtful gesture. Then she looked up at him, her heart full.

"You still can't drink out of it," Rue teased.

"I'll steal sips when you're not looking."

"You're ridiculous," she said, her voice thick with emotion.

He tilted his head, a soft grin tugging at his lips. "Ridiculously good-looking, maybe."

Rue laughed, setting the mug down carefully before pulling him closer by the collar of his shirt. "That too," she whispered, brushing her lips against his.

Dacre deepened the kiss, his hands sliding her closer and anchoring her firmly as the world melted away around them. For the first time in what felt like forever, everything was exactly as it should be.

As they broke apart, Rue rested her forehead against his, a small smile curving her lips. "I think we're going to be okay."

Dacre's arms tightened around her, his voice steady and sure. "Better than okay."

"I'm sorry I bit you when I was fifteen after you trapped me in a dungeon."

"I'm not." Dacre tipped her head up and gazed into her eyes. "The moment you bit me was the happiest moment of my life up until that point."

He'd told her about his life at the Black Mansion, and how his involvement in the skin trades was at the lowest level. He was traded. He'd told her about watching his entire family be slowly killed off. She was glad that he'd escaped that life. No one deserved that. Tears spilled down Rue's cheeks as he kissed her again.

Outside, the leaves rustled in the breeze, and Lucipurr meowed from the hallway, as if agreeing. Their future stretched ahead of them, bright and full of possibility.

They were home. Together.

Preview of: The Night is Endless

*This is unedited rough draft. The Night is Endless is another standalone in the next generation Veil of Shadows world.

The Night is Endless

By M. R. Pritchard

Chapter 1

Evelyn brushed her gloved hands over the ancient stone surface, her heart racing with anticipation. The symbols carved into the rock were faint, eroded by time and weather, but unmistakable: a giant towering over an angel with outstretched wings. She leaned closer, her breath fogging the crisp mountain air as she traced the delicate lines with the

419

wooden tip of the brush she'd been using to discover the carvings.

A drop of red hit the stone.

"Shit," Evelyn pressed her sleeve to her nose. The altitude of the mountains sometimes made her nose bleed. "Goddamn it." Evelyn was searching for something to wipe the blood away with, but when she turned back to the runes, the drop of blood was gone.

Evelyn moved her sleeve away from her nose and saw a bright red dot. No, she definitely had a nosebleed. And she was sure she'd seen it drip on the stone. She blinked a few times. "That's weird."

"Find anything?" Rue's voice cut through the quiet, startling her.

Evelyn turned to see her friend approaching, her dark hair tied back and a smudge of dirt streaked across her cheek. Rue carried a tablet, its screen glowing faintly as she recorded notes.

"Oh, another nosebleed?" Rue's eyes went wide with concern.

"I'm fine. It's just a few drops. I think I found something," Evelyn said, stepping aside to let Rue inspect the discovery. "The carvings are consistent with the ones we found last week. Giants and angels. Do you think they're what we've been searching for?"

Rue crouched, her sharp eyes scanning the markings. "It's possible. These look similar to Dr. Malcom's cave outside of Johnstown, Pennsylvania."

Dr. Malcolm Royce, was working on deciphering old runes at an old mountain cave dig site. A focus on Fifteenth century Nephilim in the Alleghany mountains. They're supposed to depict fifteenth-century giants and angels. The kind of stuff that influenced local myths.

Professor Camden, Rue's Dean back at Loyola University,

had colleagues in Johnstown and Altoona who were working on unearthing sites that depicted giants.

Evelyn was nodding. "We're not that far." She gazed over the ridge and pointed. "A creature this size could make it over that ridge in a day."

Rue tracked Evelyn's gaze and nodded in agreement. "I think you're right."

Rue had been working on her doctorate project for the past year in these mountains, she'd come to know them like the back of her hand. And she'd been thrilled when her best friend Evelyn applied to join her. Although, she'd expected Evelyn to join her in the doctorate program, but she'd confided in Rue that she couldn't pay for more college.

Evelyn smiled, a flicker of pride warming her despite the chilly air. This dig side, high in the mountains, was like a dream come true. She'd spent years studying artifacts and ruins in textbooks, but now she was uncovering pieces of a forgotten history with her own hands. And her best friend.

"There's something about these symbols," Evelyn said softly, her gaze drifting back to the carving. "They feel... important. Like they're trying to tell us something."

Rue's expression grew thoughtful. "You might be right. We'll have to cross-reference with the texts back at campus. For now, let's get some photos before the light fades."

As Rue moved to set up the camera, Evelyn's attention was drawn to a faint hum in the air, so low she almost didn't notice it. Her brow furrowed, and she glanced around, the hairs on the back of her neck standing on end.

"Do you hear that?" she asked.

Rue looked up from her camera, frowning. "I was hoping you couldn't."

Evelyn hesitated. The sound was gone. Shaking her head, she forced a smile. "Probably just the wind."

A memory of Rue's first visit to Malcom's cave discoveries came to the forefront of her mind:

"These figures," Malcolm said, gesturing to the largest carving, "are what initially drew us here. They're believed to depict Nephilim—half-human, half-angel hybrids. The detail is extraordinary, considering the estimated age of these carvings." His head tipped curiously. "They've changed color. Hm." He glanced at Rue. "Maybe it's the angle of the sunlight."

Rue stepped closer, her fingers itching to trace the outlines. "And the symbols? Do you know what they mean?"

Malcolm shook his head. "Not yet. Some of them resemble ancient Sumerian cuneiform, but others are completely unique. It's possible they were a local adaptation, influenced by a mixture of cultures."

Rue had seen the rune's glow at Malcom's cave, but she hadn't heard anything like the faint hum Evelyn had noticed.

Rue pressed fingers to her mouth, remembering the blood ritual she'd come across at Malcom's cave. Dacre, her bodyguard and fiancé, had encouraged her to perform the ritual and it had brought out her fangs and had helped her complete the half-formed blood bond she'd created between her and Dacre.

"Are you okay?" Evelyn asked. "You look pale."

Rue nodded. "I'm fine."

"Is hot-bodyguard still out of town?" Evelyn looked Rue up and down. "I've noticed you get that way when you're apart for more than a few days.

"He comes home tonight." Rue smiled and wiped at a smudge of dirt on her face. She was hungry.

Evelyn knew about Rue's heritage since that night before graduation when they were at a costume party and her twin brother Remington had shown up to surprise Rue. The real surprise was the demons that infiltrated the party, drawn by auras of Rue and Remington being on the Earthen plane together. They'd barely escaped without a fight, but Evelyn was there and saw everything. She knew Rue and Remington were twins and that their parents were a King of Heaven and the Queen of Hell–a secret war waged between bloodlines in their veins. Rue drank blood and could see the future. A gift she'd only recently discovered and was still learning to control.

And Evelyn was one of the few humans who knew about everything. Most days, she tried not to think about what that meant. Probably not much because Rue had chased Remington away and forbid them from seeing each other again. So it didn't seem like it would mean much. She tried not to think about Remington's sharp eyes, same proud tilt of the chin as his sister, all swagger and cryptic smiles.

Rue straightened, her brow furrowed in concern. "Okay, it's back." The faint hum had returned. She set the camera down and scanned the surroundings, her hand instinctively moving to the small dagger strapped to her belt.

The air around them thickened, the temperature dropping noticeably. Evelyn shivered, clutching her jacket tightly as the humming grew louder, resonating in her chest like the deep toll of a bell.

A sudden gust of wind whipped through the clearing, scattering loose papers and sending a chill down Evelyn's spine. Then, just as abruptly as it had started, the sound stopped.

Rue exchanged a worried glance with Evelyn. "We should head out. Now."

Evelyn nodded, her heart pounding. As they packed up their gear, she couldn't shake the feeling that they'd just stumbled onto something far bigger–and far more dangerous than they'd anticipated.

Chapter 2

When Remington's parents returned to their summer home and left him in charge of Hell during their vacation, they never mentioned he'd be thrust into the middle of a disagreement between the demon families of the Adirondack mountains and their distaste for the Basilisk breeding program his mother had started.

"The Black River is teeming with beasts!" A man with horns curled at his temples shouted. "We can't even bathe! My goats were eaten yesterday afternoon. All fifteen of them."

"Fifteen?" Remington raised his eyebrows. "That seems like a lot." He glanced to the Hellions flanking him.

Hellions were giant creatures of the Royal Guard. With black leathery wings and massive size, any creature of Hell would .... Add more.

"Why does the Queen of Hell desire so many Basilisk?" the demon asked.

Remington searched his brain for a logical answer. "Darkness is never far. The war with Lucifer was not that long ago, and I'll remind you my mother's Basilisk played a key role in defeating his army. Lucifer killed the rest. They were extinct."

"Lucifer is dead." The Demon argued. "I was there."

"And whose side did you fight for?" Remington challenged.

"You know, prince, that we did not have a choice. When Lucifer rules things like free will are gone."

Remington lowered his gaze. "Then I will remind you that my mother's is very invested in the protection of Hell and its people. The Basilisk are a key element."

"Could they be moved to a different river?" the demon asked, sounding defeated.

Remington sighed. "I will replace your goats. Stay away from the Black River."

The demon opened his mouth but a Hellion grumbled.

The demon swallowed his arguments and bowed. "Thank you for your generosity, Prince."

Remington waited for the demon to walk away then said, "Lock the doors. I can't handle another moment of this."

The Hellion's obeyed.

Remington paced to a nearby window and gazed out, suddenly missing his childhood of obscurity. He was the Shadow Heir, an unexpected twin who was hidden from the public until the age of fifteen, when his real heritage became known just before the war. He missed those days of freedom, of running around unknown, creating chaos with his cousin Thrush while his sister took the brunt of the attention. But, her being known as a princess didn't help her, his thoughts drifted to her kidnapping at the same age. She was okay, rescued and finding her own path on the Earthen plane. His mother had warned him, he'd be dead if anyone figured out who he was before he was old enough to defend himself. He gripped the blade at his belt. He could definitely defend himself these days. Standing taller than his father at six foot ten, Remington was an intimidating height, the only thing he lacked these days was the wings. Everyone told him that they'd appear when he earned them and to have faith. He itched the runes tattooed on his shoulder, waiting was for the birds.

"Remm," a familiar voice called.

He turned as Chel walked into the room. Chel was mysterious, quiet, and when he walked toward Remington, it looked like he only moved in the shadows; a skip and a ripple of movement. Remington had known the Hellion his whole life and behind the scenes the guy was goofy, but he put on a good show when he was working.

"What's up?" Remington asked.

Chel thumbed toward the door. "I heard about the goat guy."

Remington shrugged. "Yea–"

"Did you promise him fifteen goats?" Chel's eyes were wide like he couldn't believe it.

"I thought it was necessary, the basilisk ate the rest of them." Remington walked toward a ledger on the table and wrote down the transaction.

"Are you sure the basilisk ate them?" Chel pressed. "Some of these demons are very good liars. Don't forget you are in Hell right now. Your father's side of the family can't like but these demons thrive on it. Lying is a way of life."

"He seemed sincere." Remington wrote in the ledger.

"What would your mother have done?"

Remington stood up straight. Shit. She'd have flashed her teeth and demanded a carcass or a picture. When he looked up again, Chel was waiting.

"I didn't ask for this," Remington said. "I wanted a summer of fun."

"You wanted to run off to the Earthen plane and smash." Chel crossed his arms, a smirk spreading across his lips.

Remington shrugged. "You're not wrong."

Chel slammed his hands down on the table. "Your sister forbids it. Get your head straight, man."

His sister Rue's words echoed in his mind for the thousandth time: *Stay away from her, Remington. Evelyn's not part of our world.* Yet no matter how hard he tried, Evelyn was always there, lingering in his thoughts like a forbidden melody.

She wasn't just any human. Evelyn was Rue's classmate from college, the one who had smiled at him like she wasn't terrified of the shadows clinging to his presence. They'd graduated over a year ago but the memory of their meeting at that costume party still burned bright in his mind. He'd been brooding in a dark corner, uncomfortable and out of place among the humans, until Evelyn waltzed into his orbit, her infectious laugh cutting through the haze of alcohol and chatter.

She'd been dressed as a red devil, complete with little horns on a headband holding back her long, golden hair. He'd pretended to be unimpressed, but her confidence and easy grace had disarmed him. They'd danced–or rather, she'd dragged him onto the dance floor–and he could still feel the warmth of her body pressed against his as she moved to the music, her laughter bubbling in his ear. For the first time in hears, he'd felt freedom.

A sharp snort from Chel brought him back.

"What?" Remington threw up his hands.

"Stop thinking about her, she's human," Chel growled, his voice gravelly but tinged with exasperation.

Remington frowned, turning his gaze to the window where the ochre sky of Hell stretched endlessly. *Human.* The word felt like a curse, but Evelyn was so much more than that. Everything about her was etched into his mind like a brand. He could almost feel her small hands on his shoulders as they danced, her breath against his ear as she whispered to him.

Chel smacked him on the shoulder. "Pull yourself out of it, Princeling. You've got goats to deliver."

Remington scowled but couldn't help a faint smirk. Chel had a talent for snapping him out of his brooding.

He pushed off the edge of the desk, adjusting his jacket. "Fine. Goats it is." A long drive to the mountains sounded perfect. Maybe he'd stop by the Black River and see if the demon had been lying.

Chel chuckled as he made his way to the door. "A nice long drive to the mountains will do you some good. Clear your head. Maybe even knock some sense into it."

Remington ignored the jab and glanced out the window

again, his mind shifting to the Black river. Anything to distract him from the persistent ache of wanting someone he couldn't never have.

But as he stepped outside and the scent of brimstone and pine hit his lungs, one thought lingered stubbornly: *What if I saw her again?*

AUTHOR NOTE

Dear Reader,

I have been writing in the Veil of Shadows world for so long that I'm finding it hard to leave. Thus, I have at least 4 more books planned for 2025 from the Veil of Shadows world. These will be next generation, focusing on Meg and Sparrow's children and side characters that we have loved throughout the years.

Thank you for diving headfirst into this world of angels, demons, vampires, zombies, Heaven and Hell. It's been a wild ride. Buckle up, there's plenty more on the way!

A special *Thank You* to my lovely daughter Marrissa, who, when I told her I needed a powerful creature who was the last of its kind and deadly, she drew upon her D&D knowledge and told me about a few creatures, but the one that fit the bill was the Displacer Beast. Thank you, child, for the inspiration.

Another *Thank you* to my husband who has listened to me type away for all of these years and also tapes up all of the book boxes for me.

Another *Thank You* to my editor, Kristy. Look at all these books we've worked on! Here's to many more!

Another *Thank You* to my readers, I can't do this without your support and enthusiasm

A final *Thank you* to Booktok! I have met so many wonderful reader and gained new fans. Long-live BookTok!

About the Author

M. R. Pritchard delves into the profound clash between good and evil, the mystical realms of gods and monsters, and the intricate transformations of ordinary people into beings of immense power. Her gripping narratives often unfold within the haunting backdrop of apocalyptic or post-apocalyptic landscapes, offering a unique blend of suspense and wonder.

M. R. Pritchard is a two-time Kindle Scout winning author, her short story "Glitch" has been featured in the 2017 winter edition of THE FIRST LINE literary journal. Her short story "Moon Lord" has been featured in Chronicle Worlds: Half Way Home (Part of the Future Chronicles) and will be time capsuled on the moon on the Lunar Codex in 2024.

Visit her website MRPritchard.com and Subscribe. You'll get subscriber only content, deleted scenes, updates, special previews of new projects, and book deals.

ALSO BY M. R. PRITCHARD

Other Books by M. R. Pritchard

Science Fiction/post-apocalyptic:

The Phoenix Project

The Reformation

Revelation

Inception

Origins

Resurrection

The Phoenix Project Compendium Edition

The Safest City on Earth

The Man Who Fell to Earth

Heartbeat

Asteroid Riders Series

Moon Lord

Collector of Space Junk and Rebellious Dreams

Steampunk:

Tick of a Clockwork Heart

Dark Fantasy:

Veil of Shadows Series:

Sparrow Man

Nightingale Girl

Scarecrow

Raven King

Nightjar

Night Owl

Etched in Darkness

Embrace the Night

Shadows of Destiny

Midnight Serenade

Echoes of Treachery

Temptations of Fate

Omens of Darkness

Temptations of Fate

Veil of Shadows Omnibus 1

Veil of Shadows Omnibus 2

Veil of Shadows Omnibus 3

Veil of Shadows Omnibus 4

The Sky is Starless

The Night is Endless (2025)

<u>Standalone Fantasy</u>

Thread the Bone

Fantasy/Fairy Tale Love Story/Romance:

Muse

Forgotten Princess Duology

Midsummer Night's Dream: A Game of Thrones

Poetry/Short Stories

Consequence of Gravity